WILD CARD CHARLIE

THE DRAGON MAGE 11

SCOTT BARON

Print Edition ISBN 978-1-945996-48-1

Cover by MiblArt

"Who overcomes by force, hath overcome but half his foe."

– John Milton

CHAPTER ONE

Explosions pummeled Kip, the near misses rocking the poor AI ship like a tiny boat in a vast, tumultuous sea. Fortunately, his digital reflexes were up to the task and he avoided any direct hits, but not for the Urvalin's lack of trying.

What was more concerning was that these attacks were more than just conventional in their nature. Yes, technological weaponry was targeting Kip as he engaged in a frantic dogfight, but also magical attacks of blistering intensity.

But Charlie and his friends had known what they signed up for when they picked this fight.

"Ara, a little help, please," Dukaan requested as calmly as he could given the circumstances. "We seem to be a bit outnumbered."

The Chithiid pilot had all four arms moving in a blur of activity as his hands flew across consoles, assisting the AI ship in flight while also targeting the enemy with pulse cannon and railgun rounds. Fortunately, they were not alone in this battle.

They were part of a small attack group, fighting alongside their new ally's rebel fleet, this particular wing of which was currently led by Charlie and Ara, as the ships engaged the

Urvalin battle cruiser and its complement of smaller fighter craft.

Nakk had an additional contingent of heavily armed ships staged nearby as a backup force, not to mention the multiple squadrons concurrently engaged with the Urvalin ships orbiting the planet as well as its two moons. It was a battle on four fronts —three massive battles in space and one stealth mission on the ground—and the advantage was shifting constantly.

The Urvalin, overconfident as they sensed a possible victory, hadn't even noticed Nakk's casters were actively blocking them from jumping away. As for using their warp instead, the rebels would target the drive systems of anyone who attempted to power them up. It was imperfect, but hopefully enough for what they needed.

"Bank hard left," Charlie transmitted over his direct line to Kip and Dukaan.

The pair didn't hesitate, breaking left immediately. The Urvalin ship on their tail followed right behind them, locked onto the ship's energy signature as best it could. It was a different sort of power, though, and one that they found vexing at times. That was the only reason Kip had been able to break free repeatedly. But their luck could only last so long.

If all went according to plan, it woulds be the Urvalin's luck that was about to run out first.

Ara let loose a stream of magical fire just as Kip flashed past. The Urvalin simply didn't have time to shift course, and moments later the craft was engulfed in flame, reducing it to a lump of drifting slag despite its Allpower defenses. The Zomoki's other galaxy magic was not only incredibly powerful, but it also reacted oddly with their own Allpower, and the Urvalin had not yet come up with an answer for her attacks.

Kip leveled off and ceased his evasive maneuvers. "Thanks. That was getting close."

"They are proving to be more difficult to handle than we had originally anticipated," Ara replied.

"Yeah, I know. Stay sharp," Charlie said. "We've still got a ways to go."

"Copy that," Kip replied, then banked hard and headed back into the fight, weapons blazing.

He was a robust and well-armed ship, one equipped with not only warp tech but also a powerful konus fused to his airframe. Back home that combination made him somewhat special, not to mention a difficult target to say the least.

Here in this new galaxy, however, that was nothing unique. Nakk's people as well as the Urvalin used Allpower and tech together as if it were the most normal thing in the world. And they were damn good at it.

"*We've got to keep their attention up here,*" Charlie silently told Ara. "*The Urvalin have to believe they have the upper hand for as long as we're able to mislead them.*"

"*Obviously,*" she agreed. "*Fortunately, it would appear they are singularly focused on the three-pronged attack underway in space.*"

"*Yeah, we definitely got their attention, as we hoped.*"

"*Yes. But should they decide to turn their gaze groundward, things might get difficult.*"

It was the weakest part of the plan, and the one they had little control over. The secret ground assault.

In space at least there was the ability to unleash a sudden wave of sheer firepower to try to overwhelm the enemy and keep them focused on the battle. But on the ground? And during a stealth operation? No such overt actions were acceptable. At least, not until it was too late for the enemy to do anything about it.

Bawb and Hunze were on the planet's surface stalking through a wooded area outside of a mid-sized city. While the others were locked in battle above, they were leading a small team of surprisingly talented fighters in an infiltration and capture operation on one of the Urvalin outposts below.

Intelligence gleaned from Nakk's contacts told them that not only was the facility relatively undefended—for an Urvalin base of operations, that is—but it was also reported to be housing a large cache of rather powerful Allpower-storing bandas as well as other Urvalin tech weapons.

With a nascent rebel fleet itching to get into the fight, Charlie and Nakk had both agreed it would be well worth the risk if the intelligence proved true. They'd been picking off smaller targets for a few weeks now, but something substantial was needed if they wanted to truly turn the tables. And this might very well be what they were seeking.

While the Ghalian and his mate took the front position, Skohla provided a rear guard, ready and very able to take out any Urvalin who might stumble upon them before they reached their objective. She'd proven her skills to Bawb and gained his trust already during Hunze's rescue, and the scary Ghalian's approval was good enough for the others.

With their magic working for the most part, Bawb and Hunze were once again an exceptionally deadly pair to deal with. But the Allpower here also seemed to interact with their spells from the other galaxy oddly at times, though no one knew how or when such a misfire might occur.

Fortunately, Skohla and her team were adept at casting with Allpower, and while their spells were somewhat different, they did often achieve a close enough result. And working in threes allowed them to bolster their spells by overlapping their power, just as the Urvalin did. It also made average-strength casters far more difficult to deal with than if they were operating alone.

Bawb stopped in place, the team behind him freezing immediately. He gestured for the others to drop low, crouching to a knee himself. While his shimmer cloak was functional once more, it was not exactly reliable in this galaxy. When this degree of stealth was needed, he simply couldn't risk it.

The bloodshed would have to come *after* they had reached their objective. Anything sooner and the Urvalin would send reinforcements from above, stymieing their efforts.

"Bob, how's it going down there?" Charlie asked.

The Ghalian reached for their silent link, courtesy of Ara, not about to risk a verbal reply. "*We have arrived at the perimeter of the target area. A patrol is nearby, however. We are awaiting their departure.*"

"*Gotcha. Do what you do, and we'll have your back. Everything's going as planned up here.*"

"*Charlie, what is it you always say about tempting that Murphy fellow?*"

"*Well, yeah. But we've got our power back—*"

"*And it doesn't always work.*"

"*And we have functional tech as well. We've got this, Bob. We just need to drag the diversion out long enough for you to get inside that facility.*"

"*Soon, my friend,*" Bawb replied, then released their connection.

"Looks like we need to stall these guys a bit longer," Charlie transmitted to the fleet. "Watch each other's backs. Once they've made it in, we gang up on—"

A dozen Urvalin ships abruptly flashed into the area, exiting their jumps and warps. They didn't come in with their weapons hot, though. It looked like they were simply arriving at this system to regroup. Unfortunately for Charlie and his friends, that meant that Mr. Murphy had indeed just paid them a visit.

"Shit. We've got incoming!" Charlie warned the others. "Dammit, fall back and regroup. Hit 'em hard! Keep their eyes on us."

Ara spun away from an incoming barrage. Charlie shifted a bit uncomfortably in the new makeshift harness instead of Ara's original one, that piece of tech lost when they were thrown into this strange galaxy.

"Whose brilliant idea was this ambush?" he grumbled.

"*Yours*, Charlie," Ara replied, unleashing a stream of magical fire at their enemy.

"What was I thinking?"

"That we need resources. Weapons and ships."

"Yeah. And who better to take them from than the Urvalin? I *do* so enjoy taking the Urvalin's stuff," Charlie admitted as he cast what should have been a disabling spell.

The magic flew true, but the result was less than what he'd intended. The Urvalin ship wobbled a bit, and it definitely took a beating from the misfired spell, but it was still flying.

"This is getting out of hand," he grumbled as he let loose with a wide range of spells, opting for the shotgun approach rather than the pinpoint accuracy of a highly specific spell.

"Which is why I suggested we start smaller," Ara said.

Charlie cast again, then let off a few rounds from the pulse weapon he'd mounted to Ara's new harness. The combination of magic and tech caused the Urvalin shielding to buckle, finally doing the trick. The craft fell silent, drifting without power, magical or otherwise.

"Got it!" Charlie exclaimed. "We don't have time to start small. Go big, go home, or die trying, as they say."

"Except we cannot go home," Ara noted. "And in case you had not noticed, the last part is a very real possibility."

CHAPTER TWO

The give-and-take of the battle in space had abruptly shifted to more of a frantic struggle against a suddenly numerically superior opponent, and Charlie's friends were on the receiving end. *This* was not in the plan.

"There are too many of them!" Kip called out. "We've gotta change tactics. Call in the reserve ships!"

Much as Charlie wanted nothing more, they simply couldn't play that card prematurely. They would only have one shot once the main body of Nakk's fleet jumped in, and this was not the time.

"Not yet, Kip. Roll in with the others and cover each other's six," Charlie replied. "Bob's almost in. Just hang in there."

"We're doing the best we can," the AI replied. "But, Charlie, we're taking a hell of a pounding."

"Shields holding?"

"Yeah, but me and Dookie are working as fast as we can to shift the tech phasing while re-casting the magical defenses. It's brutal; these guys never let up."

"They're working in threes, overlapping spells," Charlie

replied. "Hang on, I just had an idea." Charlie shifted his focus to his Zomoki friend. "*Hey, Ara. Do you think you can focus in on the particular smell of just one person's unique magic signature?*"

"*I think I should be able to. What are you thinking?*"

"*If we can stun just one of their casters—*"

"*Then there would be a pause in their spells. A good idea. Let's see if we can make it work.*"

"Kip, we're gonna try something. Be ready to fight back."

"What do you mean, be ready? We *are* fighting back."

"You'll see."

Ara shifted course, focusing her attention on the Urvalin ships hectoring their friend.

"*All three casters are on one ship, as expected,*" she noted. "*I think I sense their different Allpower signatures.*"

"*Can you target one of them?*"

"*Already done,*" she replied. "*I am dialing it in now.*"

"*Then key me in and we'll cast together. If we're lucky—*"

"*Now, Charlie!*"

Charlie didn't hesitate, layering his magic with Ara's, focusing all of their potential on just one caster. They felt the magic reach its mark a moment later, latching onto the lone signature.

The Urvalin caster's power was not so impressive on its own, they found, and they overpowered that person's individual defensive spell in short order. From there it was child's play to blast them to unconsciousness with the vicious stun spell.

"What did you do?" Kip asked. "There's a pause in their attack, and a gap just flickered in their shielding."

"Took one of them out of the equation," Charlie replied. "With only two they can't maintain it all non-stop. Next time it shifts, take them down."

"Will do," Kip said. "Get ready, Dookie. It's payback time."

"*Ara, do you have the energy to spare for us to help a few more of our friends?*" Charlie asked, well aware she drained of magic faster in this system than back home.

"*I am feeling the drain from the sustained effort, but yes, I can safely engage more of them.*"

"*Then let's do it. This'll buy Bob the time he needs. No way the Urvalin will shift focus to the surface while their people are under fire like this. Not if their ships start going dark.*"

"*Agreed. Let us hope Bawb is quick with his mission. I do not know how long my power will hold.*"

Bawb was definitely being quick. In fact, with the aid of Skohla and her band of fighters, he and Hunze had managed to penetrate the innermost defenses of their target structure without a single alarm being sounded. Meanwhile, Skohla's people raced through the perimeter chambers silencing any who might happen upon them in the midst of their operation.

It was, putting it simply, as smooth an operation as Bawb could have hoped for given his handicap and the use of unfamiliar assisting forces.

They had also been quite fortunate that the Urvalin storage facility happened to be on the outskirts of the populated area. A full incursion into a major city would have required far more resources and time than they had. For once, fate was smiling upon them, and when Bawb deactivated the booby trap spells and opened the final chamber's door, it became clear to what extent.

"There is so much here," Hunze gasped, scanning the stacked contents of the chamber. "Bandas, rifles, even some weapons the likes of which I am unfamiliar with."

"We will claim it all," Bawb said with a grin. "Nakk can instruct us in their use later, after we've cleaned out this facility." He did a quick calculation. This was a substantial haul, but it should all fit in one ship. "Skohla, we have secured the cache. Do we have a clear path to the rear of the structure?"

"Our people have taken control of the rest of the facility. The route is clear," she replied.

"Fantastic work. Send more hands to help relocate the weapons to the outside of the building. I shall contact the fleet for extrication."

"Three of our people are on their way."

Bawb nodded to Hunze, who was already moving to the doorway to direct Skohla's people inside. "Charlie, the objective has been achieved. Send two ships, as planned."

"Great news, man. Kip, you hear that?"

"We're on the way," the AI replied.

"You hear that, Bob? Kip and the other ship are heading down to you. He'll hover as support while you load, then he'll drop down and pick you guys up. His active camouflage *should* keep him out of sight to watch your back until he lands."

"Excellent. We shall be ready upon their arrival."

A pulse cannon blast shook Charlie and Ara's shields, then another, sending them tumbling before she could regain level flight. Two large Urvalin ships were pursuing them, firing with all they had. Realizing the Zomoki was unharmed, one abruptly changed course and attempted to jump away, but the Allpower blocking spells did their trick.

"*Looks like Nakk's spells worked,*" Charlie said with relief. "*But someone took note of us.*"

"*Yes,*" Ara agreed. "*And unfortunately, they are now heading away from the battle and jump-damping spells, making for open space. They appear to be powering up their warp drive system.*"

They both knew what this meant. If word of their attack got out before they'd loaded the stolen gear all of the effort and progress they'd made could very well be for naught.

"*We have to stop them,*" Charlie said, trying to get a target lock with the pulse cannon they'd managed to mount to Ara's harness. "*They're too far. Can you catch up to them?*"

"*I will try,*" Ara replied, expending a bit more energy than she wanted in the pursuit.

"*They're powering up. We're not going to—*"

The ship abruptly burst into pieces.

"*Uh, Ara?*"

"*It was not me.*"

Nakk's command ship flashed into sight, shifting location from the darkness and letting the sun's rays illuminate its outline as it made a tight circle of the remains of the Urvalin ship. The rest of the motley fleet not already engaged around the planet and moons appeared right behind him moments later.

Tamara and Shelley's repainted Urvalin warship took the lead and was buzzing through the wreckage, looking for any lingering threats. From what Charlie could see, there was nothing left.

"I'm sorry I had to waste a perfectly good ship," Nakk transmitted, "but it looked like it was about to make a run for it."

"And tell him about the other two," Tamara added.

"Oh, two additional craft were spotted on the outskirts. Tamara and Shelley made quick work of them."

"Yeah," Tamara said, "but we were able to leave one of 'em mostly intact. Figured we could likely salvage it if we've got enough spare parts."

"Nice work," Charlie replied. "The ground team was successful and are ready to load. We just need to buy them a little more time. And with you here, that means we change strategy and take those ships."

"As many as we can," Nakk agreed. "My people are shifting their engagement spells to maximum stun and targeting the casters only."

It was audacious. Cocky. Impossible. A group of rebels engaging the Urvalin and actually *stealing* their ships? No one had ever dreamt of such a thing. But then, maybe that was why it had worked so far. They'd already added several craft to their nascent armada, and Charlie, as unlikely as it was, had become the defacto admiral.

Of course, he *had* been a king already, so transitioning from one form of leadership to another wasn't too much of a stretch, even if it was in another galaxy. And with Bawb at his side, he felt surprisingly confident, despite their predicament.

As for Nakk's forces, they all followed their leader's example and fell in under Charlie's command. Nakk was still the one they were loyal to, but they'd never have escaped the prison planet if not for the newcomer and his friends. He was an ally, and one they would follow without complaint.

Additionally, Bawb and Hunze had been working with Skohla and her elite combat troops, giving them that extra edge that only the Ghalian could provide. While not all of their spells and tricks were compatible with this galaxy's Allpower, they found the parts that were, weaving them into the training regimen, and all without accidentally killing themselves in the process.

That was an issue in and of itself. Hunze's magic came from her Ootaki hair, and powerful as it was, her golden locks seemed to have a somewhat volatile nature in this place. Unpredictable. As a result, they had to be very, *very* careful traversing the minefield of her novel magic, and all while keeping the secret of the source of their power hidden.

No one here knew what an Ootaki was, and as a result, Hunze was actually safe from those wishing to harvest her hair. For once, no one was after her power.

It was the only thing she was protected from.

A blast of magic slammed into her as she exited the Urvalin facility, knocking her back into the building.

"Hunze!" Bawb shouted, a relatively new feeling for the assassin flooding his body. *Concern*.

She scrambled to her feet. "I am all right." She rested a hand on her belly a moment. "The baby is fine."

Bawb let out a visible sigh of relief. "You are both unharmed?"

"Yes. The spell was negated easier than anticipated," she said, a slight crackling rippling through her hair.

"An unexpected benefit of the situation," he mused. "But we seem to have company. Skohla, what happened?"

"Additional Urvalin came upon us from the ground. They must have been away from the facility but on the surface. Our perimeter team is pinned down."

"Ah, Murphy," Bawb said.

"Who?"

"Charlie will explain later," the Ghalian replied. "Can you reach your people?"

"Negative. We are blocked by a group of strong casters."

Bawb and Hunze shared a look then drew their vespus blades in unison. They knew what had to be done, and talented as their students had proven so far, this was no time to rely on the inexperienced. The blue swords glowed with renewed power, their magic the one kind remaining strong and steady in this galaxy where every other bit of their power seemed to have issues.

"We are coming," Bawb said, taking off at a run.

Hunze followed a few paces behind him then peeled off down a different corridor. They'd mapped the layout of the building when they entered and had pinpointed the egress points early on.

Bawb passed Skohla on his way out the door, his defensive magic locked in place strong while he simultaneously cast a diversionary spell. He couldn't take down the casters from here, not without a direct line of attack, but he could make them falter.

Stinging pain like a swarm of bees unexpectedly assailed the

Urvalin forces, the utterly novel spell slipping through their defenses simply because it was not a powerful offensive spell and was too small to trigger any counterspells. It wouldn't kill. It wouldn't even cause real harm. But it would distract them.

Bawb was charging ahead as the casters' magic wavered. It wasn't a big opening, but for the master assassin it was enough.

As soon as the enemy came into sight, daggers flew from his free hand in rapid succession while his vespus blade powered through their defenses. The troops guarding the casters swarmed to action, ten to one. Bawb liked those odds.

A whirling blur of metal and death ripped through their ranks, severing limbs and taking lives. A secondary contingent shifted their focus on this new attacker and moved to flank him while he engaged their comrades.

Hunze tore into them without mercy, seemingly out of nowhere, her golden hair bright in the sun as sprays of blood filled the air. She and Bawb quickly spun nearer to each other as they fought, the two instinctively working close, their bond unbreakable.

In less than two minutes the fight was over.

Skohla peered out from cover and couldn't believe what she saw. She had witnessed his skill, yes, but never against so many heavily armed opponents like this.

"You killed them all," she marveled, walking closer, stepping over the limbs and bodies littering the ground.

"Not all of them," Bawb replied, nodding toward an unconscious caster with a growing knot on his head and a low-ranking grunt writhing on the ground minus an arm. "These two will live, though I suggest binding the caster's mouth so he cannot end himself."

Skohla's people moved in quickly, stripping the dead of weapons and securing the survivors.

A breeze drew their attention. Moments later Kip dropped in

low, followed by one of their fleet's smaller ships. "Holy shit, guys, what a mess."

"We faced unexpected resistance," Bawb replied. "Have the craft set down here. We shall load it as quickly as possible."

"Great," Kip said. "Then we get out of here."

"Yes," Bawb replied. "Then we return to the battle."

CHAPTER THREE

Charlie's fleet had flipped the tables on their Urvalin counterparts in a decisive manner. The Urvalin were very skilled and wily opponents, wielding Allpower and technology seamlessly, and the three orbital battlefields around the planet and its two moons were closely matched engagements. But when Nakk's reserve fleet jumped into the fray, the Urvalin found themselves suddenly minus their numerical advantage.

Even so, the Urvalin were still dangerous combatants, and the battle could have easily swung either way. There were simply too many of them for Charlie's fleet to overwhelm as they had done with their earlier raiding missions.

They fought back hard, but there was one wildcard this particular batch of Urvalin ships had no answer for. The one variable that ultimately turned the tide.

Ara.

The Borzalik were their own galaxy's equivalent of Zomoki, but they'd been driven to extinction some time ago, leaving generations of fighters oblivious to the tactics one would need to combat one. But now Ara was engaged and in the mix, and she was no mere Borzalik. She was an ancient and powerful Zomoki, and her magic tore into the Urvalin fleet like a hot knife through butter.

Tactics are tactics regardless of whatever galaxy one might be in, but when something as unexpected as a full-powered Zomoki suddenly came into play, those carefully laid plans tended to go out the window.

The Urvalin captains responded as best they could, engaging the massive beast briefly before separating and attempting to combine forces to better defend against the terrifying creature. But with Ara and Charlie casting in unison, their other-galaxy magic was penetrating the Allpower shields and immobilizing casters left and right, leaving those weakened crews ripe for the picking by their allies.

Their fleet of stolen ships would grow on this day. By how many they would only learn when the battle was over. Given the way things were going, that looked to be sooner than later.

Ara and Charlie had finally found a groove in this strange galaxy, blending their power as they cast in unison. Or so they had thought.

"Oops," Charlie said as a lesser-powered Urvalin ship tore to pieces under the weight of their magic.

"*Oops*?" Nakk transmitted. "What happened? That vessel was ready for boarding."

"Yeah, sorry about that," Charlie apologized. "We just had a little, uh, *issue* with our casting. Won't happen again." He really hoped he was right about that.

It seemed that their magic was still somewhat unpredictable at times, as had just been made very apparent. Where it had been silenced in the convergence of black holes, here in the full flow of this galaxy's Allpower they had to be careful when they cast. Not every spell worked quite like it did back home. And where some were weaker than normal, others were far more powerful, as they'd just quite unintentionally demonstrated.

"*Charlie, this could become a real problem,*" Ara silently said.

"We must use extreme caution until we fully understand how the Allpower of this place affects our magic."

"Yeah, that's for sure," he agreed. *"We'll do what we can. But hey, it's battle. Shit happens."*

Of that they were both well aware. A point driven home when a trio of Urvalin ships suddenly pulled together, their casters falling into unison, and came at them, blasting out a continuous stream of powerful spells.

One of Nakk's ships was caught up in the barrage and broke into pieces, its casters nowhere near powerful enough to combat the onslaught. Even Charlie and Ara were abruptly put on their heels.

"Whoa, these ones are tough," Charlie said, pulling deep and shifting his magic to compensate while simultaneously switching their tech shield phasing, anticipating a follow-up attack.

He was correct in that assumption. A flurry of pulse blasts rained down upon them moments later, but the casting did not ease one bit. The Urvalin had mastered the skill of triumvirate casting, and the lack of any gap in the magic made them an annoyingly difficult enemy to deal with.

"Ara, what do you say we tap into the banda we took?"

"While I would have preferred to disable this craft, I feel that perhaps a more assertive approach is required in this instance," she agreed.

"Yeah, and you're just as curious as I am to see what it'll do," Charlie added.

"Admittedly, yes, I am."

Charlie opened the small storage container he'd mounted to Ara's makeshift harness and removed the magical belt. It was an interesting device, mixing a bit of technology with Allpower storage in a way a konus never could. But then, in this galaxy the combination of the two was completely normal, both systems having developed in unison.

The banda was obviously far too small for Ara to wear in any manner, but they'd decided that, with the way they were bonded, the most likely way to make it function for them both would simply be for Charlie to put it on.

He'd actually tried a few small spells with it on his own a few days prior, and had found it worked very much like a konus in its Allpower storing abilities. But to be drawn upon in combat, and by a Zomoki and her linked human? Anything could happen.

"Hey, Nakk," Charlie transmitted. "We're going to try something here. Keep your people a little bit back."

"The command has been sent," he replied a moment later.

"Great. Wish us luck."

With that, Charlie began pulling Allpower from the device. At first the sensation was all kinds of wrong. This sort of magic simply didn't blend well with his and Ara's. It was like mixing oil and water, forcing it into an emulsion, but with magic. The only big difference was that with Allpower and magic being blended, the end results could be far more catastrophic, to say the least.

"*Ready?*" Charlie asked.

"*Ready.*"

The spell they cast was a basic stun spell, designed to incapacitate but no more. They figured that with their magic acting in strange ways, the worst that might happen would perhaps be their intended targets took a longer nap than normal.

The Banda fed its power into Charlie and Ara, bolstering their spell but also adding a somewhat violent twist. Yes, it would render its target unconscious, but it would do so in a very painful manner. Given the circumstances, Charlie was willing to let that little detail slide. This time, anyway.

The Urvalin ship abruptly stopped casting, at least two of its casters incapacitated by the spell. But despite the magic being drawn from the banda, both Charlie and Ara felt drained.

“Didn’t expect that,” he said, shaking the fog from his head.

“Nor I,” Ara agreed. “Our power seems to deplete more rapidly than normal in this place, especially when blended with Allpower. Fortunately, the end result was satisfactory.”

“That it was,” Charlie said. “Now, let’s see what exactly we’ve captured.”

CHAPTER FOUR

Mopping up the last of the Urvalin was still underway when Charlie and the main captains of the fleet's forces landed on the planet's surface for a post-battle meeting. While they'd not have dared just a few hours earlier, once Bawb's team had taken their objective there was no longer a concern about alerting ground forces who might apply additional security measures.

Instead, once the aerial engagement was under control, troop ships peeled off from the fight to lead raids on the remaining Urvalin facilities, taking what they could, destroying the rest. And most importantly, blocking any craft they might have missed from taking off. If they did this right, by the time the Urvalin leadership found out what had happened they would be long gone and far away.

"So, I'd call that a success," Charlie said with a pleased grin. "Two moons and a planet? Not bad, my friends. Not bad at all."

"To be fair," Nakk said, "the orbiting moon stations were lesser outposts and relatively easy to take. As for the planet—"

"Yeah, not so much."

"It took much more work than anticipated for us to secure the surface."

Charlie nodded his agreement. "True, but that doesn't change the fact that our people did a good job."

Skohla nodded her agreement. "No, it doesn't. Our people fought well. And now we control all of the Urvalin strongholds in this system, and most of their ships are now ours."

"*Most*?" Charlie asked, a worried arch to his brow.

"Yes. Unfortunately, a few of the Urvalin managed to slip away, though we did capture most of them."

"But if any of them ran for help—"

"Relax, Charlie," Nakk said. "Tamara took a few fast raiders with her and went after them. They should reconnect with us soon after they make a quick reconnaissance run. There are a few systems our people think might contain hidden Urvalin supply depots."

"Great, recon is vital. But the ships that ran? That's a risk. There's no guarantee they'll be able to catch them," Charlie grumbled.

"No, there isn't. But we have all of our ships on high alert, each of them ready to jump away if the Urvalin return with reinforcements before we have departed. And all of the weapons have already been loaded."

"Which is great, but we need to gather any other supplies we can dig up too. An army fights on its stomach, and ours has been growing. Our forces, I mean, not our stomachs."

"Clearly," Nakk replied with a grin. "Many ships have already loaded up with the spoils of our conflict, and others are in need of some repairs. I will have them all jump ahead to the next system while the remainder collect whatever supplies we can find."

"Not from the civilians, though," Bawb interjected. "We must always be perceived as on the side of the non-combatants. Word will spread no matter what our actions are. We will take care to ensure the *right* stories are passed along."

"Of course," Nakk agreed.

"Two hours, Nakk. No more, okay?" Charlie said.

"I will have them begin loading at once."

The commander then hurried off to relay the information to the captains awaiting orders. The fleet had really come together in the short time they'd been in operation, a testament to Nakk's skill and the loyalty of his people. But as they grew, bringing in new stolen Urvalin craft as well as fresh volunteers sick to death of their rule, Charlie and Bawb reiterated some of the key points gleaned from his time as king. Most importantly, do not harm innocents.

"Do you think we shall have enough supplies for the new mouths to feed?" Bawb asked as he and Charlie walked toward the emptied Urvalin weapons depot.

"Ya know? I really do. Now we just need to take what we can and get the hell out of here. Our time's limited."

"I agree. The enemy will undoubtedly receive word of our victory soon enough, and when they do, they will retaliate with disproportionate force if given the opportunity."

"My thoughts exactly. We need to be long gone before they arrive."

Bawb watched Nakk's people hurrying through the storage buildings surrounding the depot. "They are motivated. I think we will be fine."

Nakk proved true to his word, and barely two hours after the conflict had ended their fleet was loaded up with the spoils of war. Fresh produce, equipment, and even some additional weapons missed in the first go-around were procured in the process. But there was a lot they simply lacked the time and manpower to take with them.

"We can't let them have all of this stuff," Charlie said. "And this facility? I think we need to blast it from orbit. It's the only way to be sure."

Bawb's lips split into a cheerful grin. "I have a better idea."

"Oh?"

"I have been looking forward to seeing exactly how my wand will function in this galaxy. Our other forms of magic are affected, but few are so powerful."

Charlie only pondered it for a second. "Hell, why not? We've tried out the rest of our toys. Let's see what it can do." Charlie keyed his comms. "Hey, Nakk, just wanted to confirm, are all of your people clear of the depot buildings?"

"Yes, they are aboard their ships and preparing to depart. Why?"

"Oh, Bob just wants to test out his wand. It's a little finicky at times even back home, and in this galaxy, well, it's only gotten worse. Didn't want any casualties from friendly fire."

"That will not be an issue. You are clear to begin."

"Cool. Thanks." Charlie turned to his friend. "Well, you heard the man. Blast away."

Bawb unfastened the carrying case strapped to his leg and carefully withdrew his wand. Its energy was palpable, an amalgam of Hunze's hair, Balamar water, and a fair bit of Earth's sun. It was powerful back home, and more than a little dangerous. But here? Here, there was no telling what it might do.

"I am glad for an unfettered opportunity to try this," Bawb said, calling up a basic fire spell. "I believe I shall start with flames, burning part of the structure."

"Your call, dude. Have at it."

Bawb pointed his wand and cast the spell, only giving it a fraction of the power he usually would. The spell, however, flew strong and wild, spraying incinerating flame across the entire structure. In mere seconds the whole thing was ablaze.

"Uh, I thought you were just going to test it out. You know, go easy to start."

"That *was* easy, Charlie."

"Well, damn. That's kinda nuts. Did it drain your wand more than usual?"

Bawb reached out to his wand, sensing its power. "Actually, no," he replied, a little surprised. "It seems to have barely tapped into its potential." A curious look flashed across the pale man's face as he slowly raised the wand. "Hmm. I wonder..."

A flash of power crackled free of the wood leaving an ozone smell in the air. That was not normal. Not one bit. Even less was the way the entire structure imploded upon itself, the outbuildings collapsing inward from the violence of the force.

Charlie, for once, was at a loss for words. At least, for a few moments. Bawb sniffed the wand, examining it for any sign of burns or damage. It was pristine.

"Most unusual," he said, carefully re-sheathing the length of magical wood. "Most unusual, indeed."

"What happened?" Nakk's voice crackled over their comms. "My scans showed the depot imploded. My people are laying waste to the other Urvalin facilities here and orbiting the moons, but nothing like this."

Charlie finally found his tongue again, though not without effort. "Uh, it was just us, Nakk. Nothing to worry about. All good here."

Nakk would undoubtedly want a more thorough report on this later, but for now it would suffice. "Very well. We should depart."

"Yeah, I'm with you on that. It's definitely time to go."

Charlie and Bawb headed to where Ara and Kip were waiting for them, each quickly mounting their rides, then lifting off into the sky, streaking toward space.

As soon as the area was clear of the victorious rebels, a lone Urvalin soldier crawled out from cover. He'd been fortunate enough to have selected a hiding place close enough to hear bits of the enemy's conversation. He had also seen the destructive power they had at their fingertips. It was terrifying. Terrifying, and something he would report to his superiors at once.

Precisely as Bawb and Charlie intended.

The Ghalian had noted the man's presence the moment they arrived, but sometimes the enemy's own people could be used as an unwitting tool. And, hopefully, the Urvalin would be frightened enough of this new power to think twice about attacking them upon their next encounter.

Or not. Only time would tell.

Streaking up into orbit Charlie opened his comms line with his friends.

"Okay, y'all. We jump out of here in a minute."

"We made good progress today," Hunze noted. "This was a victory for our forces. One that will bolster their spirits, undoubtedly."

"Yeah, but we're still stuck in this damn galaxy," Charlie replied with a sigh.

"We *will* make it home, Charlie."

"You're damn right we will. I've got a kid on the way, and I'm gonna sure as hell be there for it."

"*It*?" Dukaan chimed in. "But, Charlie, gender is automatically determined with even the most preliminary prenatal health scans."

"We wanted it to be a surprise."

Bawb's low chuckle filled the airwaves. "If I recall, not long ago you said you'd had enough surprises to last you a lifetime."

"That's different."

"I know. Do not worry, my friend. We will get you home, whatever it takes."

CHAPTER FIVE

"Take that, scum!" Marban bellowed as an enemy craft took the full brunt of his conjoined magical and pulse cannon barrage. "*This* is what happens when you attack my friends."

High above the central plains of the continent, the *Coratta* was flying fast under its pirate captain's command, weaving around the alien invaders as Marban deftly guided it through the clouds. No one had ever heard of the Urvalin and their tech-magic ways, but the numerous modifications and upgrades Cal had provided him not so long ago were all proving very handy against them right about now.

Sometimes, Murphy was meddling in *someone else's* affairs, and this was one of those days, it seemed.

One of the enemy ships spun abruptly to the side, falling victim to Earth's gravity as its casters tried desperately to keep it aloft. Judging by the speed it was plummeting, as well as the gut-wrenching spin it had begun, Marban had little doubt they would fail in their attempts. Today was not the day for capture and pillage. This was war.

"That's right, you bastards. Who else wants some?"

Rika's voice crackled to life over his comms. "Careful. Don't fly too high. You're getting close to the hard ceiling."

"Yes, I know. I'm in battle. Stop nagging, woman!"

An uncomfortable silence hung over the comms link. Long enough to let him ponder just how badly he'd screwed up.

"Did you just call me a nag?" Rika asked, cool as can be. A little *too* cool, in fact.

"Uh, no. I'd never—"

"Because I can go help out somewhere else and let them beat up that pretty ship you love so much. We've got plenty of other engagements underway, you know. I'm sure *those* pilots would be grateful for the assistance."

If Marban had learned one thing from Charlie over the course of their friendship it was to suck it up and apologize, even if he personally didn't think whatever he'd done wrong was that big of a deal. Rika did, however, and that was all that he had to be concerned about.

"I'm sorry," he said. "I was caught up in the moment and misspoke. I did not mean to offend you, and I greatly appreciate all you do for me."

Another long pause.

"Forgiven," Rika finally replied. "Now, if you don't mind blasting more of those bastards out of the sky, we've still got a lot of work to do, and our friends aren't nearly well enough equipped to handle them."

"On it," Marban said, spinning off into the fray, guns a-blazing.

It was an issue the non-magic-using Earth ships were having trouble with. The attacking alien craft seemed to have entered the atmosphere using some variant of a magic drive system but then switched interchangeably between conventional and magical apparatus. It was dizzying trying to adjust weapons and shielding to deal with the shifting parameters of the encounter, and a good many craft had already been lost as a result.

Marban's ship, however, was sporting a similar mix of magic and tech, and with his many years of pirating under his belt, the *Coratta* was flying circles around the invaders, oftentimes quite literally. And his weapons crews were exceptional, having decades upon decades of experience between them. What they shot at, they hit more often than not, and the aliens were paying the price.

"Captain, the thrust-blocking spell took out their magic-based drive system, but they've switched to some form of tech-based propulsion," Marban's tracking specialist called out. "I've got three others using the same type of system from what my scan spells are able to discern."

"This is not good."

"No, it is not, Captain."

"Rika, are you seeing this?"

Her mech soared past in a flash, all of its systems firing on all cylinders, a crackling buzz of magic adding to its power. She'd retrieved the mech from its desert hangar when the *Fujin* had come tumbling to Earth, swapping her now-inert flying machine for a more viscerally engaging type of craft. A massive digging mech now outfitted for flight and combat.

Rika unleashed her own power, stunning the casters on another ship, sending it into a wobbly dive. Unfortunately, a moment later it recovered, its systems switching to machinery-based drive apparatus. It was looking like every time they knocked out a caster, the enemy would just shift tactics.

Marban ran a hand across his stubbled chin. "All gunners, keep up the magical attacks. Knock out their casters."

"But they're adapting."

"I realize that," Marban replied. "Just keep casting."

"Aye, Captain."

The *Coratta* continued to pummel the enemy ships with punishing magical attacks while Rika did the same as her mech even went so far as to physically engage with their ships, punching them with its metal fists the few times she managed to get close enough. The very idea of a huge mechanoid negating their magical shielding and beating on their craft was enough to make the enemy think long and hard about altering their tactics even more.

Ship after ship had its drive system knocked out, forcing them to switch to tech propulsion. It was beginning to look like the tide was finally turning. Or so it seemed.

Abruptly, all of the alien ships pulled back, switched from magical to tech-based drive systems, and then re-entered the engagement, their conventional pulse cannons firing a punishing barrage. Their targets, it appeared, were two very specific enemy craft. Namely, the ones that had been proving so difficult in battle.

"They're only coming after the *Coratta* and the mech," Marban transmitted. "All other ships, pull clear."

"But we can help," a smaller Earth vessel replied.

"Negative. We can draw them away while you regroup."

"There are over a dozen of them."

"I know. Now get clear!"

Marban didn't wait for a response, instead spinning away, firing off all of his weapons in a deadly blossom of firepower as he did, then streaking downward. The surprise maneuver failed to stop the enemy attack, but it did manage to slow them, at least for a moment. Rika followed suit, unloading on the alien ships then diving toward the surface right behind him.

"They're on our tail," she transmitted. "Looks like we've got a lot of company."

"Yes, I see them," Marban replied. "Fourteen, to be precise. And all running on their tech systems from what I can tell."

"Affirmative, I've got the same readings."

The *Coratta* shook as its shields absorbed blast after blast from the enemy's pulse cannons. Rika's mech was smaller, but even so, it wasn't faring much better. The attackers were simply too focused in their engagement. By ignoring the non-magical ships they had effectively multiplied their force capabilities, layering them upon one another in the pursuit of just two ships. And those two ships were very much on the run.

"Dive faster!" Rika shouted.

"I'm going as fast as I can, woman!"

"It's not good enough. Move it!"

The enemy was close on their tails as they blasted toward the ground, streaking from tens of thousands of feet over Missouri down to the city of Saint Louis. The historic six-hundred-foot arch still stood tall, a massive monument that had survived the Great War and everything since. And it was that they were heading right toward.

At the last moment Marban and Rika pulled up, leveling off their dives and flying straight through the arch, all of their magic working at its maximum. Behind them the tech-driven assailants followed, gaining on them by the second. It would not be long now before they caught up to them. And when they did, these two troublesome ships would be no more.

Or would they?

The fourteen craft flew through the Saint Louis Arch at high speed, and it was at that speed that they spun out of control and slammed into the ground, exploding into thousands of pieces one after another.

"Ha! Suckers!" Rika chuckled with malicious glee as she circled back to survey the carnage. Not a single ship had survived. "Bet you didn't see that coming!"

"Clearly not," Marban noted. "And it seems the plan worked."

It had been more of a backup plan, all told, but that didn't make it any less effective. A huge EMP apparatus had been installed into the arch itself, and anything that flew through it would face catastrophic loss of power.

For magically driven craft that would pose no problems, but

for those relying on tech? Well, the results were clear. There was simply no time to switch back to magical drive systems at that speed and that low to the ground. In one fell swoop they'd taken out an entire wing of enemy ships.

An AI-driven swarm of bots and drones swooped in as soon as the craft had been destroyed, working with the speed and efficiency only machines could achieve as they stripped the remains of the ships, moving the smaller pieces for study and hiding the larger ones they wouldn't have time to break down. If their friends came looking, they'd not find a trace of the downed craft.

As for survivors, the few life signs they did come across showed that at least a handful of the aliens had managed to cast their own self-preservation spells, but that was the extent of it. They would be in custody in minutes, stripped of their gear and secreted away to underground internment facilities in the remains of an underground shopping mall.

Marban grinned wide as he circled the crash site.

"A great success!" he called out. "By my count, that's fourteen ships down."

Rika, however, was a bit more restrained. "Yeah," she said. "Fourteen down. Only like a bazillion more to go."

CHAPTER SIX

While Rika and Marban helped lead Earth's aerial defenses against the invaders, the reality of the fight on the surface was a far different sort of thing. For one, no one had expected any sort of invasion—not that those sort of things were typically telegraphed, but at least one normally had at least little bit of warning.

These aliens, however, had come out of the blue, and as of yet, they had made no demands. They merely attacked without mercy. And any of them who happened to be taken prisoner seemed to wind up dead, though precisely how was as of yet unclear.

At first, everyone was confused as they engaged with the hostile force. These people used tech and magic interchangeably, and it was not the sort of thing they'd ever planned or prepared for. After all, only a handful of parties from either galaxy could utilize both power sources with any degree of skill.

These newcomers, however, *all* appeared to do so, and it seemingly came as naturally for them as breathing.

It had been a rough few weeks, to say the least, and several of Earth's terrestrial defenses had fallen in that time. But, as the Great War had shown, the denizens of this world were not ones to roll over for anyone, and as they learned more about their enemy's strengths and weaknesses, the planet's inhabitants began adapting. Adapting, and fighting back. And much of that was with guerrilla warfare.

Small raiding parties sprang up across the globe, secretly organized by the surviving AIs and their networks of fighters. Denizens who would not take this invasion lying down.

One such group was led by a most unusual woman. One with a nanite arm and a bone to pick, accompanied by a massive alien, a pair of four-legged killing machines, and a very, *very* pregnant woman who possessed the power to stop them all, if only she could control it.

"There do not appear to be any survivors," Grundsch transmitted to the air as he walked between the bodies of the fallen alien troops strewn around the waste-processing plant. "Nicely done."

"Check around behind the northern outbuilding. There's an old storage facility there. We wouldn't want to let our guard down if any of them are still lurking back there," Sarah said over their comms.

"I have already dispatched Baloo and Bahnjoh for the task," the Ra'az replied. "They should return shortly."

"Copy that. I'll do a final perimeter sweep then join you at the pagoda."

"I will meet you there."

Sarah slowly crawled back from her slightly elevated position in the brush of the hills bordering the waste treatment plant. The barrel of her heavy rifle was still warm from the rapid succession of shots she had fired while Grundsch and their canid companions distracted the troops.

Fifteen shots. Fifteen bodies.

In the short time she had been leading this unlikely group through the dangerous streets and hills of the city, Sarah's skills had returned with a vengeance. Nothing, not even motherhood and domestic bliss, could wipe away that neuro-stim implanted training. Add to that her own real-time practice and you had one bad hombre ready to do harm. And that she did, repeatedly, and all over the region.

Charlie and his friends may have had all of their magical toys, but Sarah had gone full bush sniper, and she had a freaking arsenal at her disposal.

"The Ghost" she had heard herself referred to on more than one occasion. A wonderfully grim nickname considering the violent invaders who had saddled her with it, and one she'd embraced, raining death from the shadows upon those who dared invade her home.

She showed more restraint than usual, though. Leila was under her protection—as well as Grundsch and the boys—so she couldn't just go blasting bad guys willy-nilly. Leila could waddle in her present condition, but there was no way she could run.

"Stay here," Sarah said as she broke down and stowed her long gun in its tactical backpack. "I'll be as quick as possible." She handed a pistol and a small hand communicator to Leila. "If you see anything, call me."

"I will," Leila said from her shady spot under a large tree.

Sarah wasn't terribly worried about her friend, truth be told. She had seen firsthand what her Magus stone would do to anyone who tried to harm a hair on her head, and it was not a pretty sight. She was ready to pop, and it seemed the faint menace of the pendant around her neck had slowly grown in time with her belly.

To attack Leila was pretty much certain death.

Sarah slung her pack onto her back and took off at a fast jog toward the waste treatment facility. It was a lush Japanese garden disguising the location's true purpose. Fresh, repurposed water nourished the vegetation, and the flowing water—while a part of the plant's normal operations—served as a tranquil decorative feature, feeding a trio of small lagoons and the streams that connected them.

But for all of its lack of tactical value, this facility had something else to it. Something that was of great interest to Sarah and her friends. As it was tied into the area's infrastructure, this location had been outfitted with one very useful addition.

A secret hardline to Cal's tertiary backup communications network.

It was one of only a handful that existed throughout the region and the only one readily accessible by foot. And so it was Sarah had slowly led her team there over the past week, hiding out and letting Leila rest along the way.

Sarah hurried along and reached the subterranean accessway a few minutes later. Grundsch was waiting, as were Bahnjoh and Baloo.

"It is secure," Grundsch said.

"And the bodies?"

"Make your connection. I will dispose of them in the microbial waste-digesting pond," he said, then turned to set to his grim task.

Sarah opened the door and made her descent. It was an innocuous chamber she finally reached at the bottom. A simple monitoring station for the ponds' water and pH levels. But hidden in plain sight was an unimpressive console with an unnotable keypad. It was also her one chance to connect with Cal.

Sarah keyed in her access code and waited. Nothing happened that she could discern. No thrumming scans, no sweeping video cameras. Just her sitting quietly in the room. But

Cal would never be so overt as to announce his presence. It was how he'd survived as long as he had.

"Hello, Sarah," the AI said. ***"I am glad to see you are well. And with Grundsch and the four-legged duo as well."***

"Leila's with us too," she replied. "Hidden up in the hills."

"Ah, that is good to hear. I see you have eliminated quite a few of our unfortunate visitors."

"Yeah, they made the mistake of taking a break right where we needed to go."

"And there are now less of them for it," Cal replied.

"Cal, what's going on? We've heard bits and pieces, but nothing concrete. An invasion, clearly, but what happened? And why hasn't Zed sent down the fleet to kick their asses out of here?"

"Unfortunately, our adversary has managed to put in place a dampening field of some sort all around the planet. The moon as well. A field that drains all craft who encounter it of whatever power they have in use."

"So, those streaks from the sky..."

"Yes. Those who were unfortunate enough to have discovered this the hard way."

Sarah felt the anger build in her gut. "They've got to pay, Cal."

"And they will, in time."

She felt a knot form in her throat. "My family. Ripley, she was with Marty and Arlo. They were going to fly to Dark Side base. Did they?"

"They are fine," Cal replied. ***"They did not fly into the dampening field. In fact, they stayed much closer to the ground. I can connect you if you'd like to talk to them."***

"What? Of course I want to! How did you manage that? You're cut off from your wireless systems."

"Another hardline," he replied. ***"Running to their current location."***

"And where exactly is that?"

"NORAD."

Sarah had to admit, she had not expected that particular reply. "Hang on, that place was blown to shit, and I should know, I was there when it happened."

"Yes, but Joshua has been rebuilding a small section near the mouth of the entrance for just this sort of emergency. Finnegan, Vince, Arlo, and Ripley are all there, and quite safe. I can connect you if you have a moment."

Sarah felt an enormous weight lift from her shoulders. Her family was all right. Better than that, they were safely away from the fighting in Los Angeles.

"Hell yes, put me on," she said.

A moment later Marty answered the line.

"Yello," he said. "What's up, Cal?"

"I have Sarah on the line."

"Oh, damn, wasn't expecting that," the AI ship said. "Hi, Sarah! We were wondering how—"

"Put Ripley on," she interrupted, her emotions running high.

"Right. Okay. Hang on a sec."

"Hey, Mom," Ripley said a few moments later.

"Rip, you're okay!"

"Yeah, we're fine."

"And you're warm enough? It's a cave and they can get cold."

"We're warm. It's climate-controlled in here."

"And you've got enough to eat? And I mean real food, not freeze-dried rations."

"Yes, Mom, I'm eating fine. You know Dad would never let me starve."

Sarah chuckled. "I suppose that's true. But you're not hurt, are you?"

"Mom, I told you, we're all fine. Stop being weird."

"You're my kid, I'm allowed to worry."

"Well, we've got Uncle George with us, along with a bunch of his commando buddies, so stop worrying."

"Sergeant Franklin is with you?" she asked, her stress levels dropping by fifty percent in a flash. "If that's the case, I guess everything is better than I'd expected."

"Gee, thanks for that vote of confidence, Hon," Finn's voice joked from nearby.

"Babe, you're amazing, and you know I think the world of you. But George is a battle-hardened, elite, spec-ops combat cyborg. Nothing personal, but if anyone's protecting our baby, it's him."

Finn knew better than to argue with his wife, especially over something like their only offspring.

"Hey, Sarah," George called out. "Don't worry, I'll keep an eye on Finn too. No extra charge."

"Hey!" Finn griped. "Teaming up on me? No fair!"

"Hey, Aunt Sarah!" Arlo chimed in.

"Good to hear your voice," Vince added.

"Glad you're all okay," she replied, then took a deep breath and refocused on the task at hand. "Now, let's get down to brass tacks. I just took out a squad of aliens, so I likely don't have too much time here."

They bantered a bit for a few minutes more as they exchanged updates on what had been going on with the invaders. The bad guys had taken out a lot of infrastructure, thanks to some traitors, it seemed, but the home team was finally getting a feel for how best to fight them. Combat in the skies as well as on the ground were common these days, but the upper atmosphere was still cut off. Worse, wireless comms were limited to very short range, if at all. Long and short, it was a mess.

"Okay, you stay safe," Sarah said as they wrapped up. "No foolish risks."

"Mooom, we'll be fine," Ripley grumbled.

Arlo elbowed his cousin. “Don’t worry, Aunt Sarah. Nothing’s gonna happen to us. But I was wondering. Uncle Cal hasn’t heard anything from my mom. Have you spoken to her?”

“No, I haven’t,” Sarah replied. “But knowing your mom, I’m sure she’s fine.”

“Yeah,” Vince said. “And very likely wreaking havoc, wherever she is.”

CHAPTER SEVEN

Commander Fraxxis's shock troops were among the toughest, fittest warriors within the Urvalin forces currently at his disposal. Armed with both formidable tech and Allpower-charged bandas, they were capable in both hand-to-hand fighting as well as combat casting and were wreaking havoc in the magical galaxy where the mere mention of technology was still something most had only heard rumors of.

As a result, Fraxxis was steamrolling his way through system after system, rounding up power users who might prove useful tools one day, while eliminating those either too reluctant or too underpowered to be of service. His forces were spread out ahead of his command ship, clearing a path and leaving conquered worlds ready for him to make the Urvalin's ruling presence known.

That is, usually.

On one particular world, however, the shock troops invading the largest city built of stone and steel were currently experiencing something they were utterly unfamiliar with. Namely, lying in the street, bleeding out. Or, at least, trickling away what little was left of their Allpower-charged blood after

Daisy's living sword had drunk his fill before moving on to the next course in this all-you-can-drink buffet.

She was engaged in fierce combat, utilizing all of the weapons at her disposal, from a pulse rifle to an old-fashioned projectile pistol, to her magically charged sword, and it was throwing the Urvalin for a loop.

Stabby was thriving in combat, relishing the strange new power he was absorbing, his bloodlust singing as he deflected Allpower attacks with ease. Their novel magic was part of him now, and countering it, at least at this level of casting, was child's play.

Daisy wasn't having quite so easy a time of it as her sentient sword, but her familiarity with technology had negated the Urvalin advantage they held over natives of this place.

While magic was still a novelty to her, she had trained with enough power users to have a good understanding of its function, and Freya's neuro-stim had been drip-feeding her a steady diet of spells and counterspells while she slept for nearly a year.

She wasn't a true caster by any means, but Daisy could at least hold her own in battles that included the use of magic, and that was precisely what she was doing.

Interestingly, she noted that pretty much every single Urvalin they killed possessed their own power in addition to whatever they were drawing from the belt-like storage device they wore around their waists. From what she understood, being able to cast was normal here, but actually generating power? It should only be a select few with that ability.

Yet here was an enemy comprised almost entirely of casters. It was a boggle to say the least. And with the help of her Ghalian friends, Daisy intended to get to the bottom of it.

That was the key to this whole engagement. Daisy would provide a very distracting diversion, drawing all of the Urvalin attention her way, while the Ghalian escort quietly snatched up higher-ranking individuals in hopes of collecting intel.

"Sonofabitch!" she grumbled as a shock spell deflected off of Stabby's counterspell. "That still hurts!"

"Beats the alternative, though," Sarah silently noted. "*And, yes, it did hurt.*"

It was one of the interesting quirks of having her dead-not-dead sister riding along in her head. Daisy ran this show, but Sarah could still feel a lot of what Daisy did. And in this instance, it was not pleasant.

"Farmatta and her gang need to hurry it up out there. I'm getting tired of this cat-and-mouse bullshit, and Stabby's starting to enjoy this a bit too much."

"*Yeah, I noticed he's feeling really aggro. You think it's this new kind of magic?*"

"Wouldn't surprise me. But I've gotta let him drink his fill for now. We're burning through a lot of power defending against these assholes, and Stabby's gotta stay on his A-game."

The sword abruptly lashed out, pulling her arm as it impaled a particularly powerful Urvalin who had managed to sneak up on Daisy's flank. The man cried out once, then deflated to a husk as Stabby drained him dry.

"*I don't think that's going to be an issue, Daze. The problem's gonna be getting him to stop.*"

She knew Sarah was right. This Urvalin blood had a strange effect on Stabby, almost like how certain types of alcohol would turn a jovial lush into an angry drunk. She just hoped the Ghalian would have what they needed soon and they could break off from this engagement before her sword went *truly* aggro. Given the power he'd absorbed, there was no telling what might happen if that occurred.

"*The Urvalin seem to be getting a second wind, here,*" Sarah noted. "*We're going to need to hurry this up before it gets really ugly.*"

A pulse blast slammed into the wall beside Daisy, showering her with sharp bits of debris.

"Oh, it is *so* about to get ugly. But not for us." She looked out at the battlefield and saw at least a dozen more Urvalin heading her way, peppering the area with spells and pulse fire as they advanced. "Enough of this shit. We're capturing *all* of them."

"*What are you gonna do, Daze?*"

"Me? Nothing. *Freya*, on the other hand… Hey, Kiddo, it's time to put an end to this nonsense. You ready?"

"Ready," Freya chirped over her comms.

"Great." Daisy popped her head out and shouted to the Urvalin, using the translation Freya had compiled. "Stop your fighting. Surrender and you will live."

The Urvalin troops didn't even hesitate, their fire increasing its intensity.

"All right, then. Freya, if you'd please."

The stealth ship abruptly decloaked her active camouflage, the hovering form of the deadly craft suddenly becoming entirely visible to the startled troops. She was no more than five meters from the ground, and she was armed to the teeth.

"Okay, you idiots," Freya said over her external comm system. "You have an easy choice here. You can either give up, or you—"

An immediate barrage of pulse fire and spells assaulted her shields. The pulse blasts were easy to deflect—she was a massively powerful ship, after all—and her nanite-skin had long been generating, manipulating, and using what this galaxy called magic. The result was a novel shielding that blocked the Urvalin Allpower spells, though their strange version of magic did very nearly sneak through before she managed to adjust her defensive casting.

"Okay," Freya said. "You clearly opt for Plan B. *Death*."

Daisy shouted out from behind cover. "We're happy to oblige if that's what you want, but you don't have to—"

The weapons fire only increased its intensity.

"*They would rather die than be captured,*" Sarah marveled.

"Yeah, it's nuts," Daisy replied. "They make the Council fighters look like freakin' pacifists by comparison. Well, I hope Farmatta got what she needed, 'cause I'm through with this shit. Freya, shall we?"

By way of response, the ship simply opened fire, but utilizing a lower-powered stun spell she had been refining. The Urvalin commandos dropped to their knees from the blast but struggled back to their feet, advancing with grim determination.

"Oh, for fuck's sake," Daisy grumbled. Then she charged them, Stabby positively humming with anticipation.

By the time the Ghalian returned it was over.

Master Farmatta and Master Zilara walked the street, stepping over the pools of blood and severed limbs. The two killers looked at one another and shared a little grin. It was certainly a bit of overkill, the carnage Daisy and her sword had wrought, but they had to admit, for a non-Ghalian she was quite efficient.

"Hey, did you guys notice the weird power in them?" Daisy asked as she jogged over to the two women. "I mean, again with this weird-ass magic. And every single time we fight them. They all have it."

Farmatta nodded. "Yes, it is very strange, indeed. Something about this adversary is clearly unconventional. And their power, it is *odd* for lack of a better word. Unlike any we have encountered before."

"Stabby felt it too," Daisy noted. "It was weird at first, but then he got used to it, and he's definitely stronger for taking it in. But he also feels a little *off* now. Almost like it was a meal that didn't quite agree with him."

"Which, one might note, is actually the case," Zilara pointed out.

"Well, yeah. But did you all feel that when you drank from them?"

"Not to that extent, no. But it does sit differently than what we are used to. But this area is not safe. We can delve into this issue once we are clear. Come, we must get clear of this world."

"And your prisoners?"

"Only one survived. For how much longer, however, I cannot say."

CHAPTER EIGHT

The tavern was a cozy establishment nestled in a quaint little hamlet on a quiet little planet. The sun was only modestly powerful, and as a result the system was not really a destination spot for those who were sensitive to such things.

Or anyone, for that matter.

That made it perfect for the Ghalian's needs.

The owner was not part of the Ghalian network, nor was he privy to the nature of dealings and discussions going on under his nose. Frankly, he did not care. He was doing good business, especially for this solar system, and that was all that mattered to him.

What he was unaware of was that at any given time the majority of his customers were in one way or another affiliated with Master Farmatta and her ilk. To his benefit, the Ghalian were not stingy when it came to establishing a safe base of operations. The coin continued to flow steadily, along with the food and drink, and the locals were none the wiser.

The small private booth tucked away from the main body of the tavern was still within earshot of several other tables, but whenever a meeting of any importance was taking place, every one of them was populated with the Ghalian's people, chatting and laughing, seeming like ordinary patrons. No outsiders would be able to overhear the discussions taking place. Even the somewhat heated ones involving worked-up visitors from another galaxy.

"The way the Urvalin focused their power? It's not normal," Daisy said. "I mean, magic in and of itself isn't exactly a thing where I come from anyway, but the Urvalin seem to have been able to connect across both galaxies without using any kind of probe or satellite. Even we can't do that."

Master Farmatta and Master Zilara reclined in their seats, casual and relaxed to any who might be observing. But Daisy knew these two unassuming women were far more than they appeared. Great tactical minds were hard at work as the seemingly sweet women sipped their beverages.

"You know," Zilara said, "as we are well aware, the Bakana rods possess the strength to connect across galaxies so long as a portal exists. It is not impossible that the Urvalin possess a similarly powered item."

"Hang on, the what does what, now?"

"We do not know what manner of item the Urvalin use, but it must be similar to the Bakana rods we used to negate Malalia Maktan's power."

"But those were a weapon."

"Yes, it is true that working in unison they can allow casters to join their power for offensive spells. But they do more. In Malalia's case, they were used not to share power but to take it from someone. A shame we lost the fifth rod during the rescue of Hunze. But thus is the unpredictable nature of battle."

In that instance, they had used the rod to temporarily drain Hunze, stopping Visla Dominus from using the captured Ootaki to power the secondary portal being used to invade Earth's galaxy. But while it had done its job, not only freeing Hunze but also knocking Visla Dominus for a loop, that rod was lost in the mayhem that followed. But the four that still remained were more than powerful enough for what the Ghalian had in mind.

"It's still not quite making sense to me," Daisy said. "I mean, yes, it makes sense, but it also doesn't. My people can't send any signals through the portal. The only way to communicate is with messenger probes or having someone cross over. But sending power and coordinating? You're talking billions of light years of space between our galaxies."

Farmatta nodded. "Just as our ways are strange to you, so too is your technology to us. But as you well know, while technology does one thing, magic is a different matter entirely, which is why we need to get the rods into Charlie and Rika's hands."

"Which we failed to do," Daisy added.

Zilara shrugged. "Yes, it was most unfortunate. But we will learn more about our enemy and their plans in due time."

"*Sounds like the Ghalian have something in the works, Daze.*"

Yeah, it does, Daisy agreed. "One question. These guys are new to your stomping ground, from what you've said. Mine too, for that matter. No one's seen them before, so how can you hope to infiltrate them? They're busy taking down vislas and emmiks left and right, and we don't know how to stop them."

Farmatta took a casual look around the tavern, clocking every face near them just to be sure.

"Yes, the Urvalin are a disturbing new variable, and it is true, we do not have the benefit of years of subterfuge with which to have placed our spies within their leadership networks. However, your point about their taking of power users is a valid one. And something we are in the process of taking full advantage of."

Daisy's curiosity was piqued. "Oh?"

The Ghalian allowed herself a little grin. "Yes, indeed," she said with a wink, slipping perfectly into her sweet older woman persona. "You see, dear, while we do not have our people positioned within the Urvalin ranks, we *do* have agents installed in the highest levels within the Council of Twenty's staff. It has taken a lot of effort to place them there, years in some cases. And *those* agents are standing by, ready to loyally follow their employers wherever they may go. Even if that means into the service of the Urvalin."

It was a clever plan, Daisy had to admit. The leaders of the Council of Twenty were not part of the Ghalian network, clearly. Good as they were at their job, even the master assassins could not plant one of their own in that particular role.

But the support staff for power users of that caliber tended to be enormous, and to become a faithful and trusted aide was the perfect way to hear pretty much everything that transpired behind closed doors. And serving staff, even those a visla might be fond of, were still ignored when it came to sensitive discussions. A great many secrets had been revealed not by breaking into someone's offices or file systems, but by simply standing in the right place at the right time, ignored by the so-called elite.

"It's a good idea," Daisy said, "but what do we do in the meantime?"

"Do? We *do* nothing, dear. We must have faith in our brothers and sisters and give them the time to complete their task. Difficult as it may be at times, we must wait."

"Wait?"

"In the most general sense of the word, yes. We will wait, but we will also be quite active as we do, never fear. It was merely a figure of speech," Zilara said with a smile, casually tossing an enchanted blade from hand to hand. A knife Daisy hadn't even seen her draw.

"But the Urvalin? We don't engage them anymore? We just wait?" Daisy griped. "It's been weeks, and we've taken a lot of them out."

"Yet we have not been able to extract much information of any value from the survivors."

"Their killing themselves every time kinda puts a damper on that," Daisy noted.

"A fair point. But there are other things we can do besides engaging in active battle. Trust me, Daisy, it may be waiting, but it shall be productive waiting," Zilara replied. "And we will be quietly making plans as the pieces fall into place."

Daisy rose from her seat. "Freya, warm up the warp drive, I'm coming to you. We're going for a little ride."

The two assassins looked at her with curious expressions but made no move to stop her.

"Where are you going, Daisy?" Farmatta asked. "Our plans are already underway."

"I don't just wait," she replied. "There are still things I can do even in this galaxy. And by the looks of it, we'll need every bit of help we can get. Lucky me, I know just the guy."

CHAPTER NINE

Visla Skirbal had his heavily warded wooden chest of riches laying open beside him out in the courtyard in front of his primary offices. Normally, the box would have been tucked away deep in his vaults, protected by wards and booby traps galore, for Skirbal was a cautious man, and one who aspired to ascend to a seat on the Council of Twenty in the turmoil following the defeat of Visla Dominus.

He ruled over his world and the surrounding system with a strong hand, steering policy and bending others to his will. In this place, he was the undisputed ruler, and what Visla Skirbal decreed was law. And given his power, only a fool would dream of challenging him.

Apparently, the Urvalin were fools. Or so he had thought at first.

He had since come to a very rude awakening.

"Another!" the visla bellowed to what was left of his staff, his deep green skin paling from the strain of the magic he was wielding.

Rovalla, his most trusted aide, rushed to his side and dug deep into the open chest, pushing aside coin and jewels with little care for them. In this moment, all of the riches in the world mattered less than the other contents of the container. What the visla needed were his magical implements, and fast.

The burgundy ropes of her knotted hair swung side to side as she moved, punctuating just how frantic the moment was.

"Dammit, where is the next one?" the visla shouted.

"You only have one left!" she replied, pulling the last konus from beneath a spilled sack of coin.

Rovalla rushed to his other side, slipping the magical device onto his wrist just as he released his hold on the one riding on his other arm. To wield two konuses at once could be done in a pinch, but even for a powerful visla such as he, it could be perilous. And in his weakened state it could even lead to death.

Rovalla pulled the expended band from his other wrist and tossed it aside, the metal still hot from the unexpected drain the visla had been putting on it. The new one, however, was still fresh. It would not begin to truly heat for at least a minute or two. That is, if he could sustain his casting that long.

The assault had been utterly unexpected. No one ever dared confront Visla Skirbal. In fact, after the brutal trouncing he'd given the last man foolish enough to even try, he had been left quite alone, his power unchallenged for ages.

But the trio of casters who now stood before him had put his skill and power to the test. And much as he loathed admitting it, he was losing. The casters were using a very strange form of magic against him.

At the beginning, his confidence was high, and his forces had believed they would easily trounce this mystery fleet that had foolishly invaded their territory. But the tide of battle quickly shifted, and his troops fell in droves.

It was baffling. These casters individually did not appear to be terribly powerful, but the manner in which they linked power and cast continuously meant that even a visla of Skirbal's power would eventually sustain damage. He was but one person, after all, and to cast he had to utter the desired spells, and that meant breathing. And breathing required taking a breath.

It was during those brief pauses that the attackers peppered him with increasing frequency. He was tiring, and his own internal power was failing him. Normally, a konus's stored magic would afford him the respite to allow his own power to recharge, but not under these circumstances.

Even so, Visla Skirbal was making quite a show of it, his defensive spells and offensive retaliations clearly the work of a master of his craft. But his forces were shattered and the residents long gone, having fled the fighting early on.

Abruptly, the engagement stopped, and the three alien attackers simply walked away, boarding their ship and lifting off.

"What happened?" a servant named Margitt asked as he and the other staff huddled behind their visla.

"I don't know," Rovalla replied. "They just stopped. It makes no sense."

"Quiet, all of you," Visla Skirbal said. "We must take this opportunity to regroup. Rovalla, I want you to contact Captain Quintz. Tell him I—"

A low rumble filled the air as a new ship arrived, dropping straight for the surface like a stone. It stopped abruptly, a cushion of magic halting its descent just above the ground. This craft was different. More ornate. More robustly armed. This was something new.

The forward hatch slid open, and a tall pale-green woman stepped forth.

She was wearing the garb of a leader, that much was clear. And not just a military unit. This one was more than that. The faintly glowing stone set in some sort of mechanical bezel swung gently from around her neck. The woman walked calmly toward the visla, utterly unafraid.

Skirbal recognized that look. It was one he'd worn on his

own face on more than one occasion. This enemy had used her underlings to soften up the visla's defenses. To drain their power. And all of that was to ease the *true* invader's arrival.

Skirbal had to admit, it was a sound plan. But what this newcomer didn't realize was that *this* particular visla was very quick to recharge, and he felt his power rebuilding already. All he needed was a moment longer and the smallest of opportunities.

"I am Commander Prin," the invader said. "And you will bow down to your new—"

A blast of furious magic blasted out as Visla Skirbal cast a killing spell. The konus he wore drained almost entirely from the effort, but the one called Prin merely batted the spell aside. Skirbal paled as he realized just how powerful this person was. Just before wave after wave of magical bombardment began pummeling his shielding spells.

Skirbal braced himself, casting defenses, waiting for a gap in the lone attacker's spells for him to launch his counterattack. But no pause presented itself. Impossibly, this woman's magic did not cease.

What the visla couldn't know was that Prin, while not as powerfully linked with Torgus and Fraxxis as she would have been on her casting podium, was still intertwining her power with theirs across three galaxies, the pendant around her neck allowing all three to cast as one regardless of the distance separating them.

And as their power was now operating in these three galaxies, it was even more powerful than ever. The stories about the intertwined worlds enhancing their abilities, it seemed, were true.

Rovalla and Margitt rushed to their visla's assistance, bracing him as best they could, keeping him on his feet despite the traces of magic striking them where his shielding spells were failing.

A surge of magic slammed them all to the ground, sending the other staff flying as it did. Rovalla and Margitt's bodies were the only things cushioning the visla's fall.

Prin surveyed the scene and eased up, her casting fading as she confirmed the threat was neutralized. She then walked to the fallen man, looking down on him with calm eyes.

"I do wish you hadn't done that," she said. "But I also admire your dedication to the fight. And for that reason I will offer you a choice."

Visla Skirbal slowly sat up, his konus no more than a useless chunk of hot metal on his wrist, his own power drained further than he'd ever felt it go. He looked up at Prin, stubbornly proud, but knowing he'd met his match.

"What is your offer?" he asked.

Prin smiled. "A simple one. Surrender and join us, or die."

It was horribly cliché, but, then, he had made the same offer to others in his time, and Skirbal didn't need to be convinced this one meant what she said. Slowly, he climbed to his feet. Rovalla and Margitt, likewise, stood up, dusting off their visla then standing silently behind him.

Visla Skirbal, defeated as he was, held the green woman's gaze a long moment before speaking.

"Very well," Visla Skirbal finally said. "I submit."

Prin's smile broadened. "A wise choice. You fought well, Skirbal. You have significant power. I believe you will fit in well with the Urvalin collective."

Skirbal wondered exactly what that might entail, but for the time being he would simply go along. He'd survived, and that was more than he'd expected upon his defeat.

"Now what?" he asked.

"Now you will board my ship. My crew have already prepared a comfortable suite for you."

"And my people?"

Prin glanced at the dozen men and women who had stayed

with their leader through it all. Loyalty was hard to come by, but it could be a double-edged sword where conquest was concerned.

"You are a leader. As such, you may bring a few aides with you. But choose wisely. Any misbehavior by your underlings will be treated as though it was your own."

Visla Skirbal nodded. It was as fair a deal as he would get. He turned to his staff. All were dedicated. Loyal. And all had been with him for years. But right now, with only a moment to choose, he gestured to Rovalla and Margitt. The two who had been at his side, quite literally, through the worst of it.

"You will accompany me," he said.

The two simply nodded and stood silently, awaiting their next order.

Prin let out a killing spell, all but one of the remaining staff dropping dead in an instant. Skirbal felt his rage bubble up but knew better than to challenge his new leader. She walked to the lone survivor, a trembling woman named Jinzzus, and rested her hand on her shoulder.

"You will tell the others what happened here. That Commander Prin of the Urvalin defeated the mighty Visla Skirbal with ease." She leaned in closer and gestured to the fallen all around them. "And tell them that all who would dare stand against me will meet the same fate as your friends. Do you understand?"

The woman nodded, tears welling up in her eyes.

"Good," Prin said. She turned to her new captives. "Now, my men will escort you and your aides to your chambers. Clean yourself. I will summon you shortly."

With that she strode off to survey her newly conquered realm while Skirbal, Rovalla, and Margitt followed.

It was a crushing defeat.

Visla Skirbal, once so close to becoming the next member of the Council of Twenty, was now no more than a servant. A slave to a conquering force the likes of which none of them had ever seen. It was a terrible fall from power and an omen of the worst kind. An enemy this powerful? How could they possibly be defeated? It seemed impossible.

But what none of them knew was that fortune had just smiled on those who were resisting the Urvalin threat, for Rovalla, the ever-faithful servant of Visla Skirbal, was actually a spy named Soria. A master spy at that, and a Wampeh Ghalian.

CHAPTER TEN

Rovalla and Margitt had carefully undressed their visla, bathing him gently in the large tub provided in his surprisingly comfortable quarters before dressing his wounds. They then clothed him in the fresh attire provided by the Urvalin.

It was a loose-fitting set of trousers and a modestly ornate tunic, along with a slender belt made of some sort of woven metal. Clearly the clothing of a high-ranking individual, but, nevertheless, one in the service of the Urvalin, not an independent visla ruling an entire system.

Once that had been accomplished, the pair left him to his thoughts and stepped into the side chamber that would be their home for the foreseeable future, where they performed the same acts for themselves.

With their bodies finally washed from the sweat and grime of the day's toil, they then dressed in what the Urvalin had left for them.

The attire was similar to that of their liege in coloring and cut, but plain and coarse. Clearly that of the servant class. They were just grateful it was clean, because if the labors of the day hadn't ruined their regular uniforms, the blood and soot of battle certainly had.

After several hours left to sit and ponder his fate, an Urvalin guard finally came to Visla Skirbal's suite to fetch him.

"Commander Prin requires your presence," the man said.

Not *wishes to see you*. Not *requests*.

Demands.

Visla Skirbal calmly rose to his feet, his face neutral despite being ordered about. His power had actually restored considerably in his short time aboard the Urvalin ship, but it was nowhere near what it usually was. That fact, and given that he had no konus to boost his abilities meant that escape wasn't an option, so he resigned himself to going along with things. For now, anyway.

The sad reality was that even if his power was fully restored, the odds of overpowering a ship full of guards and either taking it over entirely, or making an escape while in flight, were slim to none. And for all he knew they could currently be in the depths of space where the slightest mishap could blow a hole in the ship's hull and spell the end of them all.

No, he would play the obedient captive for now.

"Follow," he said to his aides, then turned to the lone guard. "I am ready. Lead the way."

The guard was armed with a technological weapon, he noted. But he also had an aura of magic about him. Clearly a user of both systems. It made the visla wonder if perhaps these Urvalin were allied with the pesky forces from the other galaxy that had made things so difficult for the former Visla Dominus.

If so, he might almost thank them for clearing the way for him to ascend within the Council of Twenty. But now, as a captive, those plans had been stymied. At least, for the time being. But this Commander Prin struck him as an interesting character. A woman of great power, that was clear, but she had also said something that piqued his interest.

She'd said he would fit in well within the Urvalin collective. The way she'd phrased it sounded more like a position of some status rather than just a worthless cog in their machine. His Council plans were on hold, but perhaps there was more for him in this new situation after all.

The long walk down the silent corridor took him past several windows.

Ah, space, he noted. Indeed, they were no longer planet-bound. Any use of power would have to be very measured.

The path wound toward the central parts of the craft, then curved a few times before arriving at what appeared to be a barracks or troop staging area of sorts. Not exactly where he had thought the commander would wish to see him. A private command center, perhaps. Or even her own receiving chambers. But here? It didn't seem appropriate for a prisoner of his status and was more than a little confusing to say the least.

A dozen of what had to be the commander's elite guards stood flanking them on either side as they walked in. Their expressions were blank, but their posturing, motionless as it was, nevertheless radiated a readiness to leap into action. These were not men and women to be trifled with.

Their leader was seated at the far end of the chamber. Commander Prin was clothed in a more leisure-suit styled outfit than earlier, but she still wore the glowing pendant around her neck. Skirbal was sure it contained power in some manner, though he was not foolish enough to try to find out at the moment. This was the time to play along and survive.

Prin gestured him closer, rising to her feet as he did. Rovalla and Margitt moved to follow but were directed to stand against the wall. They obediently shifted to the periphery, remaining silent as servants were meant to be. Unheard and barely even seen, which was perfect for Rovalla's purposes.

The visla stopped before the commander and gave a little bow, dipping his head but not deigning to offer up a full submission. Prin didn't seem to mind, but then she said just one word.

"Kneel."

Visla Skirbal felt his power flare within his body. Commander Prin, however, seemed much more amused than worried, her pendant brightening slightly, confirming Skirbal's guess that it somehow increased her power. More than that, at this proximity, he could feel the true scope of the magic channeled through it.

In a word, it was shocking in scale, and he realized at once there had been absolutely no way he could have bested her in combat, even if he had been at full strength.

Reluctantly, Skirbal slowly dropped down to his knees. If she had wanted him dead he already would be. This was simply another layer to his defeat. The kissing of the proverbial ring, it seemed.

"I am at your service, Commander Prin," he said just as the warm metal of a control collar slid around his neck, locking in place with a powerful spell.

"What is the meaning of—" he started to say, his magic getting the better of him in his moment of angry surprise.

The collar quickly put an end to that, shocking him to submission before he could so much as summon the most basic of spells. Margitt moved as if to help his visla, but Rovalla subtly shook her head. This was not the time for heroics. Theirs was to stand quietly by, no more.

Margitt pulled himself together and pushed his back against the wall, watching as the visla slowly rose back to his knees.

"Stand," Prin said.

With the help of a guard, Skirbal rose to his feet as the shock of the collar wore off. It had been a handy bit of local Allpower the Urvalin had discovered. Collars that made their work so much easier that they incorporated the local device into their own repertoire. And as the visla had just demonstrated, even the most powerful could be brought under control with the deceptively simple-looking bands, if they were imbued with the proper spells.

Commander Prin smiled at her captive and rested her hand on his shoulder, staring silently into his eyes. What she expected of him was abundantly clear.

"You have my obedient service, Commander," he said.

Prin nodded, satisfied. "Good."

"If I may ask, what comes next?"

"Next? Why, next is something you are quite familiar with, dear Skirbal. Next is *conquest*."

"Conquest?"

"Oh, yes indeed. You see, your power is considerable, and I believe you will be a valued piece of the Urvalin plan."

"How will I be of service, then?"

"You shall still wield power against others, and without restriction. The collar is only to keep you in line where the Urvalin are concerned. You will wield your power not for your beloved Council of Twenty—which we have dismantled, by the way—but rather for the Urvalin collective."

He nodded, unsure how to process what he'd just heard. The Council of Twenty was no more? The Urvalin were even more powerful than he'd thought. Commander Prin watched the realization dawn on her new pawn.

"Yes, I see you understand. But I promise you this, Skirbal. If you serve me well you will be part of something greater than you ever dreamed of with the Council of Twenty. You will be part of the Collective that will control so much more than just one galaxy."

"Two?" he said. "You mean to conquer the other galaxy? They are difficult foes, Commander. A lesson Visla Dominus learned the hard way."

"Yes, she did. And they removed that troublesome woman from the equation for us. And with her exceptional power gone, they've unwittingly helped make our victory all but assured." Her smile grew wider and filled with glee. "And I'll let you in on a little secret," she added. "We will not conquer two galaxies."

"But I thought—"

"We will be conquering *three*."

CHAPTER ELEVEN

Sitting quietly on their respective seats nestled in the center of each command ship's casting podium, the three Urvalin leaders silently connected via their pendants, the glowing stone blending their power across the vast distance between galaxies.

The tech bezel in which they were mounted helped focus the Allpower, refining it for more efficient use, but it was the rare stones themselves that allowed such contact to take place. And over the centuries that the stones had been handed down through the ranks of Urvalin leaders, more and more nuances of their use became known, allowing the technological side of their culture to have a hand in directing the Allpower's use.

In conjunction, the podiums and pendants allowed a far greater sharing of Allpower between the three commanders during battle, permitting the seamless swapping and overlapping of spells. It was part of the reason the Urvalin had successfully expanded their reach across their home galaxy until it finally fell under their rule.

But at the moment they were using their casting podium's massive power to ease the strain of their communications connection, allowing them to expend far less Allpower than would otherwise be required. The combined strength of both the pendant and the casting podium driven by their ships' massive reserves meant their connection would be robust and clear.

"Your results have been most satisfactory, Prin," Commander Torgus said. "Well done."

Torgus was the trio's clear leader, the most powerful of the three as well as the architect of many of their more ambitious plans, the most audacious of which was currently underway across three galaxies. The one with years of work behind it. The one that required quietly amassing forces in not one but three galaxies, all of them ready to move when the signal was sent.

So far, it was all going according to plan.

"Thank you, Torgus," she replied. "The last visla I encountered was a very strong man. So much so, in fact, that I wonder if I would have been able to defeat him without our Allpower connection."

"A good thing the link is strengthening by the day," Torgus said. "It would seem the legends were true. Utilizing Allpower across these three galaxies now that they are connected only amplifies our strength, and soon our power will be absolute."

Prin thought about the other part of the legends. The one that would make them even more powerful than any could imagine. And if true, their enemies would be removed in the process.

"The taking of Allpower from each and every power-carrying life-form," she mused aloud. "To be able to access not only our interlinked Allpower, but also a limitless, regenerating, uncontestable power source such as that? We will never face opposition again."

They all longed for such a day, and they seemed well on their way to success. But Fraxxis had some less than ideal news.

"About that," he said. "There is now incontrovertible proof that Charlie and his Zomoki are apparently still alive."

"So, the rumors are true. How is this possible?" Torgus demanded. "You said our forces reported the wreckage of their ship and the corpse of their winged friend."

"Apparently, a second ship crossed over with them, as did a beast from the other galaxy. It was *those* two who did not survive their arrival through the portal. Charlie and the others were apparently far more resourceful than we had given them credit for."

Torgus was not happy with this bit of information. Not one bit. Too much was at stake for the troublesome human and his Zomoki partner to make an unexpected return.

"Is the portal secure?" he asked. "Have they made an attempt to cross over?"

"No," Fraxxis replied. "Fortunately, it seems that positioned as it is among the black holes, even if Charlie and Ara were fully powered, the drain would be so intense as they approached it that they would not be able to retain enough power to cross over by the time they arrived. So, while they are free of our trap, they are still unable to return to their home galaxy."

"Good."

"Yes and no," he continued. "It seems they did, however, manage to escape the planet."

"What? How?"

"From what the few survivors of the conflict said, it seems Ara somehow tapped into some form of Allpower that still functioned in that place."

"Impossible!"

"I thought so myself. We all did. But it seems we were mistaken. And not only did she get clear of the planet, she also managed to take down our dampening array in the course of their escape. It took our forces some time to repair the damage and replace the destroyed units."

"How annoyingly troublesome," Torgus grumbled.

"More than we originally realized," Prin agreed. "In their

escape they also restored power to a large portion of the enemy ships we had stranded on the surface."

"You mean—"

"Yes. The castaways have been busy, it seems. The ships were apparently maintained in spaceworthy condition despite the lack of power, and once the dampening array was down they launched, fleeing into space with Charlie and his team."

"So, we now know what happened to our outpost," Torgus mused. "And this would explain the reports of an unusually aggressive band of craft attacking our ships and stealing resources."

Prin agreed with her fellow commander. "Precisely. And while the fleet itself is operating with functional weaponry, we now know that the frighteningly powerful weapon they have been deploying is not from any ship at all but rather the beast known as Ara. She and Charlie are casters of devastating strength, though they are also quite erratic in their abilities."

Torgus took in the information, seeing the chessboard spanning three galaxies before him in his mind's eye. "Excellent," he finally said.

"Excellent?" Prin wondered. "How is this excellent?"

"Oh, come now, Prin. You know how much more satisfying a victory is when there is at least a little bit of a challenge."

"And the weapons they have commandeered?" she asked.

"While we did not know the full nature of the parties responsible, nevertheless all is going according to plan."

Prin, while an integral part of the linked trio, knew better than to question Torgus's multi-layered machinations. The man was a genius at this sort of game, and if he said the pieces were falling into place, then they surely were. There was a different question, however.

"And the other galaxy?" Prin asked. "The Earth people and their allies are a more difficult lot than originally anticipated.

How goes it there, Torgus? Fraxxis and I have sensed some difficulty in your engagements."

"Yes," he agreed. "It has been more of a challenge than we had anticipated. The one with that damnable mixture of Allpower known as Rika was not pulled through with Charlie as we had thought and has been proving to be a rather troublesome pest."

Prin had heard as much. "We know she did not cross over. A rather vexing failure, it has been. That one, operating within Earth's atmosphere, is disrupting our operations. And she has a dragon working with her."

"But no such problems at Taangaar, correct?" Fraxxis asked. "We have successfully subjugated the majority on that world if I am not mistaken."

"Yes, brother, we have," Torgus replied. "Though there are still pockets of resistance, but that is to be expected in any conflict. Earth, on the other hand, is proving far more difficult to bring under the yoke. Despite our agents' best efforts, the planet still possesses powerful guardians in both Rika as well as its advanced computing network."

"So, we did not destroy them all as we'd hoped," Prin said.

"It would appear not. In fact, from what we have seen, it would appear there are still several of them operating secretly from deep hiding."

Prin's mind raced through possible options. "What do we do about them?" she asked.

Torgus chuckled. "Rika? We are working on a plan for her and her dragon friend. The latter? We unleash hell across their world and neutralize their power sources and backups."

"We destroy their grid?" she asked. "Cut off the electricity?"

"Yes," Torgus replied. "We starve them."

CHAPTER TWELVE

"This is a lot more than I expected," Nakk said as he surveyed the latest additions to their captured weapons spread out on the ground between his parked command ship and Kip's much smaller vessel.

"Pretty good haul," the AI said. "What do you think, Dookie?"

Dukaan was perusing the seized goods, all separated into piles based on fabrication, value, and use.

"Almost good enough for us to take up a new profession in piracy, I'd wager," he said with a wry grin. "If we'd known we'd be able to get this much out of raiding Urvalin facilities and ships, we would probably have shifted tactics on day one."

Nakk agreed. "Yes, perhaps we would have. We did know there would be some plunder in this most recent engagement, but I did not imagine it would be anything of remotely this scale. I do not think anyone did."

"It is an impressive selection," Skohla agreed. "And some of these are particularly powerful. I, for one, am surprised we were able to take them intact. As we all know, the Urvalin are notorious for destroying their equipment and even taking their own lives rather than fall into the enemy's hands."

Charlie and Bawb had likewise been surprised at the quality of deadly tech and Allpower implements they'd managed to capture from their most recent engagements. The magical items were fairly substantial in power, consisting of not only bandas, but also some rifle-like devices that fired magical rounds rather than pulse, plasma, or bullets.

It was all protected by what amounted to firewall spells, but Nakk and his people seemed to have devised workarounds for most of them and were hard at work getting the remaining ones functional.

The conventional weaponry, however, was another story.

Skohla picked up one of the pulse rifles and clicked the trigger to no avail.

"Useless," she said, tossing it back on the pile. "We have been able to overcome their Allpower locks on the other weapons, but these are no better than scrap metal."

Hunze moved from the Allpower devices she'd been inspecting and picked up the discarded rifle. Her magic flared slightly, feeding into the weapon itself. She carefully took aim and pulled the trigger.

Nothing.

"Hmm. I fear Skohla is correct about this portion of our haul," she said. "Nothing I cast into it seems to release whatever is binding it from functioning."

"It is common for the Urvalin," Nakk said. "They often key weapons to an individual user or small group, requiring a specific access code to activate. It's impossible to crack. We've captured them for years and have not once prevailed in unlocking a single one."

"Oh?" Charlie said, a cocky grin spreading across his lips. "Let me take a look. Maybe I can get it to work."

Hunze shrugged and handed him the rifle. "Good luck, Charlie. But I believe that if Nakk's people have been unable to crack the Urvalin technology, someone from a different galaxy will likely have an even harder time."

Charlie laughed. "You do know how I got started in this whole business, right? I mean, you know I was a spaceship engineer before my life took a very abrupt shift in direction."

"And? That was another time, and another world."

"And? And maybe I can crack this thing," he said, his fingers already at work looking for seams and access points for breakdown and cleaning. Once he accessed the inner workings of the gun he would understand how the thing functioned and, hopefully, devise a solution to their problem.

Nakk moved close and peered over his shoulder as he removed a small dust cover to access what looked like a charging port of some kind.

"You know, Charlie, *our* spaceship engineers also attempted to disable the Urvalin locking devices and failed."

"Sure, but I've got a fresh pair of eyes. From another galaxy, no less. Maybe I'll see something your people missed."

"I can assure you, my techs are among the best," Nakk said.

"I'm sure they are. But like I said, I'm not from round these parts, and that might be a benefit rather than a handicap. Besides, if no one else has been able to make any progress, what have we got to lose? Sometimes you need to ignore what's possible and what's not and just try something new."

Nakk mulled over Charlie's words. "Well, there is an old saying among some of the older generation. 'The impossible is achieved by those who are too foolish to know it cannot be done.' Perhaps it applies to this situation."

"Exactly! Wait. Are you calling me a fool?"

Bawb and Hunze shared the briefest of looks then both burst out laughing. "Oh, my friend," Bawb said. "You have likely been called worse on occasion. In fact, I am certain of it. Why, do you recall that time when—"

"Hey, no fair ganging up on me!" Charlie griped. In his distracted state, he absent-mindedly pulled on a seemingly solid portion of the weapon in his hands. Surprisingly, a hidden seam revealed itself and slid open, exposing some rather complex internal componentry. "Ooh, now that's what I'm talking about!" Charlie exclaimed. "Bob, you see this?"

"Yes, Charlie. A jumble of parts that still do not have much meaning for me."

"Well, tech isn't your strong suit. Probably the only thing that isn't, actually."

Charlie pulled a small tool kit from his pocket and began probing around the inner workings of the device.

"Do not harm yourself," Nakk warned.

"Nah, I'll be fine," he replied. "See this? It's a mini voltage meter."

"And?"

"And it's telling me where the power flows in this thing, along with which pieces are holding a charge and which ones aren't. It looks like this thing is actually kind of similar to Earth tech in a way. I mean, once you get past all of that alien hardware part of it."

Charlie's hands were busy, effortlessly lost in the familiar meditation of tech work, probing every aspect of the weapon, checking for power and noting which direction it flowed. He hadn't really spent much time working with his hands like this in quite a while but muscle memory kicked in and his fingers just seemed to know where to probe next.

The componentry appeared to be fairly straightforward in design, and, so far as he could tell, it *should* have been working. But something was keeping it from functioning, so he just kept tinkering.

"You know, I was thinking," he said. "With all of the weapons we've managed to take so far, even if some don't work, I think we could probably split off a couple of smaller raiding parties from our main fleet. With the extra firepower they'd be able to hold their own even without additional backup."

Sparks suddenly leapt from the weapon's open panel.

"Careful, Charlie," Dukaan chided.

"I *am* being careful," he said, blowing away the trace of smoke. "Science is a trial-and-error process sometimes."

"Better we avoid error where guns are involved," the Chithiid said.

"Yeah, yeah. But seriously, what we've got already could make a difference. And if I get these bigger guns working? We're talking a full-on game-changer."

Nakk stroked his chin and turned to his right-hand. "I would tend to agree with you, Charlie. Skohla, what do you think?"

"It is a reasonable assumption," she said. "And, tactically, if we were to operate in multiple theaters we could confuse the Urvalin's response to our forces. Bawb? This is also your area of expertise. Do you agree with my assessment?"

The master assassin had already been considering how they might utilize the additional weapons as a force multiplier. They had more ships than troops to properly crew them, though people were slowly joining their cause. But if they could essentially *over*arm both the individuals as well as the craft they were flying in, then a lesser force could have the same potency as a larger one.

If they were proficient in the use of their armaments, that is. Fortunately, all of Nakk's followers were well versed in the art of combat, and providing them with bonus guns and bandas was like giving a kid a shiny new toy in one hand and a fistful of caffeinated sweets in the other. In short, they were itching for a fight.

"The tactical assumptions are sound," Bawb said.

A gust of wind informed those not magically connected with Ara of the Zomoki's return. She had been hunting on this quiet world, filling her belly and replenishing her strength. Her deep-red form grew large in the sky above them before she touched down and settled into a comfortable crouch.

"Good hunting?" Nakk asked his marvelous new ally.

"Indeed. Thank you again for selecting this world on which to plan our next steps. The game is plentiful and the waters clear and refreshing."

"I am glad to hear it is to your liking," he replied. "Not a terribly exciting world for travelers, but perfect for our current needs."

Ara nodded her massive head. "And the moons provide convenient cover for the craft that did not descend to the surface."

"Another benefit of—"

A pulse blast ripped out of the weapon in Charlie's hands, missing both ships and Ara but igniting a nearby tree.

"Shit. Sorry," he said sheepishly.

"You see? I told you to be careful," Dukaan said.

"I *was* careful," Charlie shot back as he jogged over to the damaged tree. "But would ya look at this? Damn, this thing has some kick to it."

The others had indeed noted the damage the pulse weapon had caused, and not without a little concern. Nakk, however, had other things on his mind.

"Charlie," he said. "Can you replicate this? Can you unlock the other weapons in this manner?"

Charlie studied the modification his fingers had made almost on their own as he fiddled with the device. "Yeah, I think so," he replied.

Nakk smiled wide. "Good. *Very* good," he said. "I do believe this has made up my mind."

"Oh?"

"Yes. If you can get the rest of these weapons functional, I would say I am confident that dividing our forces is the right move at this point in our engagement."

Now it was Charlie's turn to grin. "I'll get right on it."

CHAPTER THIRTEEN

Charlie had spent the better part of the prior afternoon and evening working on the rather impressive collection of commandeered weapons. The variety was wide, but there seemed to be a common thread between them; an electronic lock that prevented the weapons from being fired without the release key.

But now that he had stumbled upon it and quite accidentally discovered the deactivation key, it was looking like these formerly inert hunks of metal could actually be made to function once more. It was something of a coup, given the needs of the growing rebel forces. If they could truly get these guns working, then splitting off into smaller groups to stretch the Urvalin defenses thinner would be a totally feasible plan.

"I think I have the hang of this," Dukaan said, testing the power cell of yet another re-activated pulse rifle before adding it to the pile of salvaged gear. "We are lucky Charlie found a workaround."

Bawb closed the hidden compartment on the weapon in his hands and repeated the same power cycle test that the Chithiid pilot had just done. "Yes," he said. "Lucky."

"What is it, Bob? Afraid to just take the win?" Charlie asked.

"It was you who introduced me to your friend Murphy," Bawb replied. "I cannot help but wonder how he will rear his head in this instance."

Charlie tossed a stolen pistol into the pile. "Leila's about to pop out our first kid, and I'm stuck in another galaxy. I'd say Murphy's already made his appearance."

"True, and I am sorry for your circumstance. But I was referring to the weapons."

Charlie pushed the thoughts of Leila from his mind as best he could and forced his head back into the game at hand. "Let's not tempt fate, okay? The important thing is we have enough of these now to equip several raiding parties. A more efficient use of resources than sending the whole fleet out each time we take an Urvalin flight group."

"And about those," Bawb said. "Wasn't Skohla's team scheduled to return by now?"

Charlie didn't need to look at his chrono to know Bawb was correct. She was late, and that was very unlike her.

"She'll be fine," he said in a not terribly convincing tone. "She's armed to the teeth. With all of that new firepower, even a full-on Urvalin battle group couldn't stop her. Why, I bet she's just taking extra time to strip the carcasses of her target clean."

Several systems away, a desperate, losing battle was raging. Skohla had led her raiding party to the reported location of a juicy prize; a fleet of supply ships with only a modest guard detail because only a lunatic would dream of attacking the Urvalin.

Skohla and her team were, however, just those sorts of lunatics. And more than that, they'd already been proving themselves quite adept at taking down their targets, as the growing number of captured ships and equipment in their rebel fleet would attest.

Unfortunately for them, this particular convoy was not what they'd been led to believe. In fact, it was something far larger and *far* deadlier than they would have ever dreamed of attacking in their right minds. But once engaged, they were in it for the fight.

"Their shields?" Commander Fraxxis asked.

"Still holding, surprisingly," his first officer replied.

"Fascinating. Have the flanking ships continue to hit them with pulse weapons, but also incorporate staggered waves of Allpower fire. Break them down, bit by bit."

"It will be done, sir."

Commander Fraxxis leaned back in his seat atop his casting podium and watched the battle unfold. The enemy had elected to utilize both warp tech and jump Allpower when arriving into this airspace—a clever tactical maneuver that provided an overlapping variation of shielding that had likely saved their lives. Annoying as it was, he had to give credit to the flight group's commander. But now it was time to put an end to them.

Fraxxis's battle group had been waiting for them, expecting a warp arrival as the rebel Charlie's fleet was reported to rely heavily on tech rather than Allpower. It made sense in a way, as they'd lost all use of it while trapped on that wretched, powerless world. But this lot was something of a surprise, mixing the two forms of travel and shielding. More than just that, they had also unleashed a blistering attack from weapons several orders of magnitude greater than what a group their size should possess.

But the misinformation had been delivered and acted upon, and now the trap was sprung. Commander Fraxxis's main battle group was more than capable of taking down this group of upstarts.

The command ship rumbled as a series of powerful blasts

hit their shielding. Fraxxis was not concerned, however. His own Allpower was linked with the other two commanders and was more than enough to protect his ship. More than that, his team of casters working beneath him were casting in unison to apply pressure to the enemy craft.

More pulse fire rocked the Urvalin fleet. Fraxxis couldn't help but laugh.

"Sir, our smaller decoy fighter craft are having a difficult time handling this barrage," his second-in-command reported.

"Very well," Fraxxis replied. "I was hoping to draw them in a bit closer, but I suppose this will have to suffice. Key the *real* attack ships. In a moment they will be ours."

"Yes, sir."

Fraxxis watched as the squadrons of his finest pilots took to the battle, racing toward a seemingly superior force without fear. But their confidence was not unfounded. Fraxxis keyed in a single command on the console mounted on the armrest of his seat atop the casting podium. A simple transmission emitted from his ship in a flash.

The rebel forces' guns fell silent for the most part. The weapons originally outfitted on their craft were still functional, though, but most of the captured ships as well as their own craft that were now sporting additional armaments found themselves fighting at a handicap.

"Now watch as our fleet picks them apart and tears this upstart fleet to bits," Fraxxis said.

The tide of the battle shifted abruptly, the rebel forces suddenly on their heels as they found themselves in a gunfight with no more than sticks and stones. This wasn't a fight anymore, it was a rout.

Two of Skohla's fighters lost shielding as well as weapons without warning and were sent spinning out of control by a series of carefully placed shots before being finished off by the enemy's forces. More found themselves on the receiving end of this suddenly uneven fight, shifting all of their efforts to defense as their offensive capabilities were clearly compromised.

"What the hell just happened?" Skohla asked just as her people engaged the enemy. "Where are our big guns? The extra firepower?"

"I don't know," her tech officer said, her fingers flying over her controls. "Oh no."

"How bad?"

"Bad. Nearly all of the captured Urvalin weapons have been deactivated."

Skohla felt like she'd been punched in the gut as the reality of their overwhelmingly successful raids sank in.

Their own weapons as well as those they'd captured from the Urvalin early on were still working, but the ones taken later in their unexpected windfall had failed all at once. They weren't a valuable prize captured in battle, they were a Trojan Horse left for the rebels to give them false confidence and lure them into flying into an unwinnable situation.

And they'd just taken the bait.

"Everyone, get out of here. Meet at emergency rendezvous point six!" Skohla sent to every ship in her fleet.

"Commander, what's happening?" one of her captains replied.

"No time to explain. Go now!"

A brutal flurry of weapons fire and Allpower smashed into the shields of the ships that were closest to the Urvalin forces, overwhelming several and breaking the damaged craft to pieces. The others, however, had managed to react a hair faster than their attackers and broke free of the engagement, warping and jumping away as quickly as they were able.

Fraxxis watched the rebels' escape from the comfort of his seat, the pendant around his neck glowing bright as he remained linked with the other commanders.

"Several fell, but we failed to take out Charlie," he told the others. "And there was no sign of their winged beast."

"It is of little concern," Torgus said.

"Though we had intended to cause a bit more damage to their upstart fleet," Prin added.

"Yes," Torgus agreed. "We had hoped to lure in their key players and cut the head off of their little insurgency. But we have dealt them a serious blow all the same. Now they will be forced to rethink their attacks. They will begin to doubt their own intelligence. And hesitation will be their downfall."

CHAPTER FOURTEEN

Skohla's battered raiding fleet had taken care to visit multiple layover waypoints before returning to their main hiding place. It was still up in the air exactly what had happened to them in their engagement with the Urvalin, but one thing was clear. *Something* was wrong.

The enemy had not only known they were coming, but had somehow negated their firepower advantage as well. To call it disconcerting would be an understatement. Even calling it disastrous felt rather short of the mark.

They had survived, though, and after making damn sure no one was sniffing around on their trail, they'd made their way back to Charlie and the main body of the fleet. As soon as Charlie and Nakk heard what had happened, they ordered all affected weapons to be gathered in a clearing not far from their main base camp. Even the captured Urvalin ships whose cannons had fallen silent were brought to the surface for inspection.

What Charlie found was unsettling.

"A deadman switch?" Nakk asked. "You mean the Urvalin weapons are all equipped with a means to deactivate them from afar? This is terrible news. Much of our growing fleet and gear has been taken from the Urvalin."

Charlie dug deeper into the inner workings of the pulse cannon mounted to the underside of one of their ships, comparing the hidden mechanism with that he had found within the pulse rifle now resting at his feet. The similarity was clear now that he knew what he was looking for.

"Yeah, I see what they did here," he said. "It was a clever trick. Honestly, I don't think there was any way to see it ahead of time. I mean, we had no idea how these things worked, only what was keeping them from functioning. But it seems they'd made deactivating the locking system intentionally simple."

"What are you saying, Charlie? It was a trap? They intended for us to figure it out?"

"Pretty much," he replied. Charlie turned to Skohla. "You said they had a full battle fleet waiting for you, right?"

"Yes."

"So, not that convoy of cargo ships we'd heard about by a long shot."

"Most definitely not."

"Well then, yeah, that's a trap if ever I've heard of one. But we extracted that information from a very unwilling Urvalin, and that tells us one interesting thing."

"What is that?" Nakk asked.

Bawb shook his head. "What Charlie is saying is that the Urvalin have spread false information within their own fleet, relying on the possibility that we would capture them and act on this intelligence."

"But there are so many Urvalin out there," Skohla said.

"Yes, and we now know they value their lives quite little if they were willing to go to such lengths to stop us." Bawb's fingers slowly caressed the metal case on his hip. The one containing his dangerously unpredictable wand. "This adversary is willing to sacrifice a sizable number of loyal men and women to put an end to our raids. And they went to great lengths to lure us into this trap."

"They don't want their power contested," Nakk said.

"That, yes," Bawb agreed. "But also this tells us that we are making them worry. One would not go to such extremes for a mere inconvenience. No, we are harming their plans. And to that end, we must find a way to continue."

The others nodded their agreement. Ara sniffed at the pile of deactivated weapons.

"There is the faintest trace of their Allpower magic on these," she said.

"Yeah, I noticed that," Charlie replied. "They seem to have zero issue switching between magic and tech. But the kill switch was purely electronic. Hell, if we'd scrambled the signal, I bet we could have stopped it from affecting most of them."

"But we didn't," Dukaan noted. "And we had no idea what frequency it would have been sent on even if we did hope to block it."

"Yeah, Dookie's right," Kip agreed. "It looks like our guys were gonna be screwed no matter what we did."

"Well, yeah, I get that. But here's a fun fact. Did you know that all of these weapons, from the cannons on the ships to the smallest pistols, all still have a charge in their power cells?"

Nakk and Skohla shrugged. "And?" Nakk said. "How does this help us? Do you want us to drain them to power other equipment?"

"No, that's not what I'm saying at all. The thing is, these are still operational. All we need is to overcome their kill switch."

Skohla picked up an inert rifle, pointed it to the sky, and pulled the trigger repeatedly. Nothing happened.

"The very nature of a kill switch would imply we cannot overcome it," she said. "It is now just a useless piece of metal."

"Ah, but is it?" Charlie asked as he pulled from his magic, sending a trickle into the gun.

It was an unusual bit of casting, and something utterly foreign to Nakk's people. But to Charlie's engineer mind, this magic/tech workaround made perfect sense. A magical bridge to bypass the kill switch and allow the weapon to discharge as it was designed to do.

"What are you doing, Charlie?" Ara asked. "That spell feels strange."

"Magic works weird here," he replied. "But I think I've got enough of the hang of it for this to work. At least, I hope so." He focused on the rifle and completed the last bit of his casting. "Okay, now try it."

"I don't see how—" Skohla said as she pulled the trigger.

A pulse blast ripped out of the weapon, sending a chunk of soil flying.

"Point it somewhere safe!" Charlie quickly added.

Skohla looked at the weapon in her hands. Nothing seemed to have changed so far as she could tell. It shouldn't have fired, but somehow it was now functional. She aimed high and fired off another shot.

"Amazing. How did you manage this?"

"Thinking outside the proverbial box."

"Remarkable." She pulled the trigger again, then several more times, but the rifle remained inert.

Bawb raised an eyebrow. "Charlie?"

"Hang on, lemme think."

"This does not bode well."

"I know, man. I said, gimme a second."

Charlie took the weapon from Skohla and probed its inner workings, taking readings as he pushed his unusual spell onto the weapon. He'd managed to find a magical way to overcome their technological kill switch, but, for whatever reason, it seemed that his little trick would only unlock it for a few shots.

"Dammit," Charlie grumbled. He picked up a pistol and tried the same spell, unlocking the gun. He aimed to the sky and fired. This time five shots rang out before the pistol seized up. "Interesting," he said, reaching for another pistol. He fired off a single shot. "Okay, I think I've got a grip on this."

"A grip on what?" Nakk asked.

"What we're dealing with. I don't think the Urvalin ever expected magic from someone like me or Ara to come into play once they triggered their kiddie locks."

Skohla cocked her head. "Their *what*? My translation comm patch must be malfunctioning."

"No, you heard right. A kiddie lock is from my world. Something that keeps children from getting into things they aren't supposed to. Only, in this case, they're locking up weapons that fall into enemy hands, making sure they can't be used against them."

"But you just made them work."

"Yep. But it looks like that's only a temporary fix. After a few shots, there's no telling when the damn things will conk out on us."

"But you *can* make them functional for at least a short period," Nakk said.

"Yeah, but there's that whole no-longer-functional-in-the-middle-of-a-battle part."

"Yes, but they would be able to fire off enough rounds to give the *appearance* that we have far more firepower, and *that* can be used to our advantage."

Bawb and Hunze were nodding their agreement, and Charlie could feel Ara was of the same opinion. Maybe this could give them an edge, even if only a brief one.

"I'll get to work unlocking the rest of these, then," he said. "And who knows? If I'm lucky, maybe I'll be able to find a way to keep them from freezing up again despite the Urvalin's tricks."

Bawb grinned wide. "If you can achieve that, my friend, we may yet provide our enemy with a most unexpected surprise.

And perhaps then we will have the odds in our favor to find the power needed to cross the portal and return home."

"Funny you should say that," Nakk interjected.

"Oh?" the assassin said.

"My people have been pursuing a lead. It was the longest of long shots, but it seems we may have stumbled upon something quite interesting. Interesting, and with great potential. Prepare yourselves, my friends. Once confirmed, we will need to move quickly and decisively."

Charlie began casting, not wanting to go anywhere until he'd unlocked all of the weapons they had. No sense leaving their allies at a disadvantage if it could possibly be avoided.

"We'll be ready," he said.

"Good. But I warn you, it will not be easy."

Charlie and Bawb chuckled.

"It never is," Charlie said with a little grin. "But if there's really something that can get us home, we'll do whatever it takes. Now, what exactly are we getting ourselves into?"

CHAPTER FIFTEEN

Charlie's forces had very carefully made their way to a heavily traveled Urvalin-controlled planet in a blue sun-powered solar system. They'd approached with the utmost stealth, utilizing disguised ships masquerading as mere trading craft to evade suspicion. Based on what Nakk had told them about their destination, there was no other logical course of action.

The burning orb at the center of the system emitted a significant amount of Allpower, making this particular cluster of worlds a valuable position to control. And Lord Florin, with all of his amassed wealth and influence, had chosen to make this his home.

The Sovereign ruled a great many other systems as well, though he did so with the clever use of puppet monarchs and bought-and-paid-for ruling coalitions. He preferred to work behind the scenes, his coffers growing exponentially as all of his underlings continuously streamed tribute to their patron and liege.

The Urvalin had never tried to seize Florin's wealth. While they could have done so if they wanted, the man's network of influence was extensive, and he was more than happy to be an integral part of Urvalin rule while remaining independent.

Or, at least he told himself he was, though had he tried to end his arrangement with the Urvalin he would likely have discovered just how strong he was on his own after all.

It was a ballsy move, making waves in Florin's realm, but Nakk had procured valuable intel that this unusual man, financier and backer of the Urvalin's most nefarious ventures, could hold the key to crossing back through the portal, and in the most unusual way.

The intelligence Nakk had come to possess had been extracted from a captured command-level caster they had taken during one of their early conflicts. The battles *before* the Urvalin had set their Trojan Horse plan into motion. It had taken weeks to break the man down, but he had been stripped of his suicide spells and hidden poison teeth. It was a bloody process, but he'd been rendered unable to end his questioning with an easy death.

In this case, that questioning involved a fair bit of torture.

Charlie had a serious aversion to such things, and even Bawb was not inclined to opt for the more primitive forms of coercion. But, given the nature of what they were up against, they had been more inclined to let Nakk's people try their hand at getting some tactical details from the man, within reason. He was command tier, after all, and who knew what secrets he might hold?

But after the Urvalin had set that most cunning trap for them, they had decided to look the other way as Nakk's people did their best. And by best, they meant worst.

The man finally broke under the greatly enhanced torture, spilling what proved to be the most unexpected of information.

The Urvalin, it seemed, had been searching for power in more ways than just connecting the three galaxies. They had also been on a quest for items of particular Allpower potency.

One in particular was of great interest. A relic that was rumored to be so powerful it could overcome even the strength of the black holes and allow one to cross over the portal hidden between them.

The Vortaxis.

There was just one problem. Like most things relegated to fairy tales and legends, no one actually knew what exactly the legendary item looked like, or where to find it for that matter.

"You're sure this guy's not just yapping to save his skin?" Charlie had asked as he and the others licked their wounds after their defeat at the hands of the Urvalin.

"Quite certain," Nakk replied. "He does not fear death, and thus, we have not bothered threatening him with it. But pain can break a man down when applied correctly. And given enough time, and enough creativity, even the strongest will eventually crack."

Bawb nodded his agreement. He was one of the best at extracting information in a variety of ways, just as Hozark, his mentor and friend, had taught him in his youth. And from what he had seen of Nakk's people's work, they had inflicted great pain but minimal damage. A process that could be extended almost indefinitely.

It was just a matter of time before the man finally spilled whatever it was he knew. But what he ultimately revealed was far more than any had expected, and the revelation would set them on a most dangerous path.

"Well, then," Charlie said. "I guess we're paying a visit to this Lord Florin."

Barely a day later the disguised ships arrived at the landing fields dotting the area within and around Lord Florin's capital city. From all they had been able to glean from their captive, this was legit intel and not another trap.

It made sense. The Vortaxis was no more than a myth. A legend. And even the Urvalin didn't know where it was. There were plenty of stories across hundreds of systems about the power it contained and the destruction it had wrought. A power so great no one should be allowed to wield it.

It was for that precise reason the Vortaxis had supposedly been boxed up within a magically reinforced container and sent far away where no one could find it. A few tiny fragments of an ancient journal had allegedly hinted at its original hiding place, but those were also lost to time.

Or so it was thought.

Apparently, the Urvalin had discovered that some brokers of power had traded in these scraps of knowledge over the centuries, and one such purveyor of knowledge was their very own Lord Florin.

"Holy crap, will ya look at that?" Charlie marveled as his small team moved toward the man's gaudy estate.

"He is not tight with coin, that much is clear," Bawb noted. "Such extravagance is the hallmark of a lesser man."

Hunze agreed. "Likely making up for one shortcoming or another," she added with a raised brow.

"Nakk's people reported that he is not a particularly powerful caster in his own right," Bawb said. "But if the intelligence is correct, he more than makes up for it in both influence as well as the two extremely strong casters he has on his payroll to act as the other part of his Allpower triumvirate."

"Those who can, do," Charlie said. "Those who can't, hire those who can." He subtly nodded to the scores of troops milling around the grounds as well as posted up in the parapet walls and towers around the building. "This guy's living in a fortress."

Bawb grinned. "Ah, but that is his weakness."

"Another Ghalian parable about strength is weakness and weakness is strength?"

"No. Just an observation after many years of dealing with

this sort of person. Namely, those who bolster their surroundings with this much brute strength, while frightened at first, eventually become overconfident in their lackeys and the fear of all those around them."

"That's a good point, actually," Charlie agreed. "I mean, you'd have to be kinda nuts to go barging into that place."

"Precisely. And neither Florin, his guards, nor even the denizens of the city around him would ever expect anyone to be so foolish as to make an attempt on him in this, his most reinforced of locations."

"Too bad your shimmer cloak is still spotty," Charlie grumbled. "And it sucks your disguise magic won't stick on a human in this place. It would make things far less uncomfortable."

He was griping because the lack of properly functioning Ghalian shifting magic had meant they had all been forced to resort to more practical forms of disguise, though Bawb and Hunze's outfits were still largely enhanced by their power. Additions were made, but Charlie's getup was entirely practical in nature. And that wasn't fun.

While the makeup and prosthetics were certainly good, they were also far less pleasant to operate in than a simple spell altering their appearance.

Because Charlie and his friends were all of races not known in this galaxy, they had to put in a little extra work to make sure no one paused to look too closely at their disguises. And that meant more than a little disgusting olfactory dissuasion added to the mix. It was enough to make Charlie gag a little, and that was the whole point.

"We've got to find a clear path in and get this done," he said. "I don't know how much longer I can stand wearing this stinky shit you smeared my coat with. What is it, anyway?"

"You had it correct," Bawb replied.

"What do you mean I had it corr—aww, man! You mean that's *actual* shit? Not cool!"

"Yet quite effective," the assassin added. "There really is nothing like it to motivate people to keep their distance. Now quiet down. We have work to do. Nakk will be expecting us to complete our reconnaissance of the perimeter while he and his people acquire one of Florin's casters. With them in hand we will know how best to obtain access to the stronghold."

CHAPTER SIXTEEN

As Charlie's reconnaissance team moved through the streets and walkways surrounding Florin's residence, Nakk's people were operating across the city, spreading out in small groups, ready to unleash diversions if need be to help the actual incursion groups achieve their objective.

The goal, of course, was to avoid raising any such fuss altogether, but sometimes the best laid plans went awry. Something Charlie was very well aware of.

Nakk and Skohla were casually stopping into taverns and shops, posing as well-off tourists visiting this lovely system. Naturally, the locals were more than happy to help relieve them of their coin, overcharging for food and trinkets, all with smiles on their faces.

Just as planned.

It really didn't matter about the coin. They'd stolen it from the Urvalin in the first place and had plenty more where that came from. What did matter was that the promise of milking these naive tourists dry was plenty to motivate the proprietors and service staff to be loose with their lips.

Details about the planet, its system, the city, and the

fascinating man who ran it all, were forthcoming without the need for more than an expression of interest.

Talking would keep them spending, and that was all the unscrupulous wanted, not realizing that the scammers were actually the scammees.

After hours upon hours traversing the city, visiting places their advance scouts had identified as likely locations in which to come across one of Lord Florin's casters, they finally tracked one of his lackeys down in a rather high-end tea shop. It wasn't the sort of place one could simply approach a stranger and strike up a conversation, so Nakk and Skohla took a nearby table, ordered a modest tea service, despite being full from their many previous meals, and observed the woman.

She was quite young for her position, but it was clear she had a strong grasp of the Allpower flowing through her. Some people were like that, with an almost tangible confidence in their power. It was no wonder why Florin had taken her into his organization.

She was young, though, and for that reason she would not have access to the innermost workings of the stronghold. Not yet, anyway. But she was nevertheless of the leadership caste, and whatever she would be able to tell them about the fortress would be enough. It had to be.

"Four," Skohla said. "Two at either end of the room, two more across the street at opposite ends."

"A security team," Nakk mused. "Not overt, but definitely watching over her despite her seemingly lower rank. Yes, I believe this one will do just fine."

Nakk flagged down the wait staff and paid the bill. The two of them then took their time sipping their tea and finishing their snacks before finally rising and taking their leave of the establishment. It was all so casual, so utterly unrushed and normal, that the odds of drawing attention to themselves was almost nil.

Once they stepped out of the establishment, however, it quickly became apparent there were more of Lord Florin's henchmen lurking around. It seemed that in addition to his usual retinue of guards, there was a loose network of eyes, ears, and muscle keeping tabs on his more prized employees.

"This complicates things," Nakk murmured.

"We should notify our friends," Skohla replied. "Their skills would be most welcome given this new wrinkle in our plan."

"Agreed. Continue ahead and contact them with our location. I will step into a shop that has the tea room in view with the pretense of purchasing you a gift."

A short while later Hunze stepped forward and greeted Skohla with a warm hug and chatty pleasantries. The Ootaki didn't show it on the outside, but Skohla had felt Hunze's pulse when they hugged. She may not have run, but her detour across town to meet her and Nakk had required a rapid pace.

"Bawb?" Skohla asked.

"Already near Nakk's location, blending in and keeping an eye, ready to step in as needed."

"And Charlie?"

"Pulled back and acting as a backup in case things should go awry and require it. But I think you and I are best suited for acquiring this caster, wouldn't you agree?"

Skohla, in fact, did. It was a way of life on this world that sometimes women were treated as less worthy of being taken seriously than men. It was not that way everywhere, and, in fact, very few systems still followed this outdated mode of thinking. But here it still existed, though for how much longer no one could say.

More importantly, it explained why a caster of her power would be shadowed by men of far less power than she possessed.

"Working in tandem I believe we can divert her to a lesser used street with a bit of subterfuge," Hunze mused. "I think that would be best. Create a conflict and let her believe we are concerned for a fellow woman's safety as well as our own. Her guard will almost certainly treat the situation seriously and change course."

"Even if she is more than capable of handling the threat herself."

"Exactly. More likely than not, she will move impatiently when ushered along by her guards. She will be annoyed, and annoyed is distracted. *That* will be our opportunity."

"But first we need to successfully redirect her," Skohla noted.

"Yes. So we will wait. When she exits, you will move ahead while I will approach her guards in distress and ask if I can walk with them to avoid the ruffians who attempted to accost me. With the caster under their guard they will likely move from the route I mention to avoid any conflict so long as she is there."

"To the side street. And all of their guards will fall in, leaving no surprises."

"Precisely. I will go with them, staying toward the rear. Once we have moved from general view, you will rush toward them from the front, again with a tale of bandits ahead. If I am not mistaken, they will shift their caster to the rear for protection and form a small circle around her while the rest move to the front. I will be at her side. As soon as the first of the guards falls, I will stun her."

"Am I to take down the guards, then?" Skohla asked, a little concerned.

"Eventually, we all will. But Bawb and Nakk will provide a suitable distraction for the process to begin."

It was ballsy, but they had to move quickly, and Hunze didn't think they'd have a better opportunity than this. With Nakk and Bawb teamed up, and with Charlie running as their backstop preventing any surprise guests, as well as keeping their target from fleeing, the odds were in their favor. The plan *should* work, but the toughest part would fall to the women.

Hunze and Skohla were as ready as could be.

"You must help me!" Hunze cried out a short while later as she rushed toward the imposing men escorting the caster.

"Stay back," the lead guard said calmly, conveniently identifying himself as the one in charge in the process. Now they knew whom to take out first.

"There are two horrible men assaulting a woman just up ahead. Please, let me walk with you until we've passed."

The man looked at the other guards. They could certainly handle two men. Likely drunks by the sound of it. But they were on protection detail, and if anything was to happen to one of Lord Florin's casters on their watch there would be hell to pay.

"Very well," the man said, nodding to the other guards who had been casually blending in behind them as well as ahead.

The others shifted position, moving closer as the group redirected down a side street.

"Why are we going this way?" the caster asked.

"A safer route," the guard replied.

"We can handle a little squabble."

"Yes, but this is the wisest course of action."

She looked as though she was about to protest further, but it was clear she'd had this conversation before and knew the eventual outcome.

"Fine," she huffed, allowing the guards to form up around her. "But we take her with us."

"Oh, thank you! Thank you so much!" Hunze gushed, going so far as to hug the woman. Of course, she was checking her for hidden weapons in the process, but the display of gratitude also helped lower the woman's defenses, at least as far as this damsel in distress was concerned.

They made relatively quick time down the smaller street, the annoyed caster pushing the pace. At least, she was until another woman came rushing ahead. Her clothing, Hunze noted approvingly, was disheveled, and an angry red mark radiated from her cheek. From what she could tell, Skohla had not only roughed herself up, but she had even slapped herself to add to the disguise.

And judging by the guards' looks, it worked.

"Oh, thank God," she said. "A man accosted me. I barely escaped!"

The lead guard drew a pulse pistol, not a blade, Hunze noted.

"What sort of man? And where did this happen?" he asked.

"Just up ahead. They were so aggressive, I didn't know what to do. Someone stepped in to help and the two began to brawl."

On cue Bawb and Nakk spilled into the small street from an adjoining alleyway, throwing punches and grappling as they did.

Hunze immediately cast her strongest stun spell, unsure how well her magic would work in this galaxy and not wanting to take any chances the caster would remain a variable in the fight. She needn't have worried, the woman dropped like a rag doll.

Hunze then spun into the two guards behind her and dropped them before they could shout out a warning to those whose eyes were all fixed on the men up ahead.

Skohla was in the middle, surrounded by guards on all sides, but not seen as a threat. At least, not until she began tearing through them with brutal fists and elbows. Hunze possessed significant power, but Skohla needed to engage with other tools in her arsenal.

"What are you—" a guard blurted just as Hunze cracked him in the jaw with a kick.

Skohla moved toward her immediately, the two women fighting in close quarters with a particular ferocity. They dodged and parried while landing blow after blow. The guards hesitated drawing weapons, the combatants were in their midst and a misplaced shot could take out one of their own. This gave them the window of opportunity they needed.

Startled men fell in quick succession to either impact or magic, or sometimes a combination of the two, in the duo's fantastic display of ass-kickery. Bawb and Nakk had ceased their faux combat and taken out the pistol-wielding guard, but were now standing back, admiring the women at work.

"Impressive," Nakk said.

"Yes, they are," Bawb replied as the last man fell. He quickly moved to the fallen caster. "Well done," he said as he lifted her up.

"Thank you," Hunze replied with a warm smile.

"You two should work together more often," Nakk added. "This was a most impressive display."

"Take their weapons, apply sleep spells, and load them onto this," Bawb said, gesturing to a cart he and Nakk had procured somewhere. "Then follow me. I have sourced a locked storage facility around the corner. It will be secure for our purposes."

"But it's locked," Skohla said.

Bawb cracked a little grin. "Not for long."

CHAPTER SEVENTEEN

The room was clean, thick-walled, and relatively well lit. In the middle sat a lone woman, tied to a chair. Her breathing was slow and steady, as it had been since Hunze had stunned her. But now it was time to have a little chat.

Hunze intoned the counterspell, and moments later the woman's breathing changed, speeding up as the magic released her. She moved in her seat, and the air in the room shifted, a tug of Allpower now lingering.

"Good, you are awake," Hunze said as their captive's eyes fluttered open.

The caster immediately tried to fire off a spell as soon as her eyes focused. To her dismay, she was unable to cast, and only a tiny bit of her Allpower could be felt, though not connected with.

"What did you do to me?" she asked, looking around the room for any signs as to her location.

"Nothing you will not recover from," Hunze replied calmly. "That is, if you tell us what it is we wish to know."

The woman's gaze turned frostier than it already had been. It was one thing to be treated as less than she was by Florin's guards, but it was an entirely different thing to have some petty thieves dare talk to her in this manner.

"Do you have any idea who I am?"

"Actually, no, we do not. Only that you are one of Lord Florin's lackeys."

The woman's ire flared. "I am not a lackey. I am Sithrakka, caster of Lord Florin's household, and you have made a very grave mistake. One for which you will pay dearly."

Hunze chuckled, though more for effect than actual amusement. "That's nice, dear," she said, shaking her head. "Did you hear? She says we will pay dearly for this."

Bawb strode from across the room, very intentionally lifting his feet high as he stepped over the unconscious bodies of her guards. Sithrakka had somehow overlooked the sprawled-out men in her initial rage. But now, seeing them all like this, helpless and unable to provide her the aid they were intended to, the caster began to realize just what sort of a predicament she was actually in.

"You know, we can make this all quite brief and entirely painless if you would just help us with the most simple of things," he said.

Sithrakka sized him up as he moved closer. "Somehow I don't think whatever it is you want will be so easy as you make it out to be."

"All we want is the layout of Lord Florin's compound," he said.

"Oh, is that all?" she asked with a laugh. "Would you like me to have him give you a massage while we're at it? Or perhaps you would like the hand of his firstborn?"

Bawb had to admire the woman's spunk, but time was of the essence, so he had to keep the play to a minimum.

"You should take the request seriously," he said. "Provide what we ask and no harm shall come to you. You have my word."

Sithrakka shifted in her seat, pulling at her restraints, but there was no slack. No escape. At least, not yet.

"You won't harm *me*? Oh, when my Allpower restores, this will be a very different conversation, I assure you," she hissed.

Bawb stared at her in that disconcerting way he had mastered over the years, then shrugged and stepped back. Hunze, however, began pacing in front of her, casually tossing a small blade from hand to hand.

"A mere blade? You think that will scare me into talking?"

"No," she replied, not slowing her pace. "I do not. But let me tell you a little story."

"Now you intend to bore the information out of me?"

"I think you will find this quite interesting. And pertinent."

Sithrakka shrugged and sighed, resolved to listen to whatever tale her captor felt like telling. She was bound, after all, but she had no intention of helping no matter what the woman might say.

"In a faraway land, there exists a race of men and women with a rather *special* set of skills," Hunze said. "Those select few trained from youth in the deadliest of arts."

"Yes, yes," Sithrakka interrupted. "We have assassins and mercenaries too, you know."

"Of that I have no doubt, but these assassins are different from any you've come across. Masters of not only weapons, but also magic, or what you call Allpower."

"Again, this is not something new. Do you really think you'll impress me with this tale of—"

"These assassins can easily do more than just kill," Hunze interrupted. "In fact, they are legendary for it. You see, they have one innate ability only a fraction of a fraction of their race possess."

"The ability to talk incessantly?"

Hunze grinned. It was not a friendly expression.

"No, Sithrakka. They have the ability to take your Allpower

from you, drinking it from your blood like others might imbibe wine. To leave you utterly powerless. An ordinary woman with no abilities whatsoever."

"Nonsense," Sithrakka said. "There is no such being. What you describe does not exist."

"Not here, perhaps. Not in *your* galaxy. But in *our* galaxy, well, that is quite a different matter."

Sithrakka continued with her bluster, but beneath it was a tiny hint of fear. Her own power had been reduced, that was for certain, and there was no telling what had been done to her while she slept. But this being capable of taking her power? It seemed impossible.

Still, the mere possibility of losing her Allpower, however unlikely it might be, was horrifying. Of course, Hunze had failed to mention that those drained by a Ghalian would eventually regain their power on their own, but what Sithrakka didn't know would be to their advantage.

"You're lying."

"So you keep trying to convince yourself," Hunze said. "But I see doubt in your eyes."

It was clear that this woman, accustomed to wielding her Allpower for the most powerful man in several systems, was starting to feel powerless. For someone like her it was terrifying. Bawb watched with pride as Hunze manipulated the woman. She had indeed learned well. But now it was time for Bawb to deliver the coup de grace.

"So, are you feeling more cooperative?" he asked, his voice smooth and low, tinted with just enough subtle magic to make even the most hardened mercenary uneasy.

"It's all just a bluff. A charade. And besides, if I were to tell you anything, you know Lord Florin would have my head. So my answer is no."

The smug grin on her face might have fooled most, but the master assassin had broken far more difficult people than her.

And rather than violence, all it usually took was just a little push in the right direction. He had just the thing.

Bawb leaned in close, smiling wide as his gleaming fangs slowly slid into place. He heard Sithrakka's breath catch in her throat and knew she was his.

"The choice is yours," he said with an amused tone. "And come to think of it, I *am* feeling a little peckish."

Sithrakka's resolve melted like an ice cream cone on a sunny day as she paled in the face of the Wampeh Ghalian. A rapid calculus flashed through her mind, weighing her options in an instant. In this scenario it was clear that her own survival left her only one choice.

"Perhaps I was a little hasty when I spoke. What exactly do you want to know?"

CHAPTER EIGHTEEN

The intelligence Sithrakka had provided was far more detailed than they'd expected of a lower-tier caster, even one of her power. But apparently Lord Florin had taken a liking to this minion, and as a result she had seen more of the compound than would normally be accessible to one of her standing.

The plethora of information was something of a boon for Charlie and his gang. It also made something else very clear. They would need a very small team to penetrate the innermost elements of the stronghold if they hoped to be successful. Anything more and they'd certainly be noticed.

Bawb was still unable to rely on his shimmer cloak, and for an incursion of this nature there was no way he would even attempt to make do with that particular bit of magic if it wasn't functioning at the highest level. Most of their spells worked in this galaxy, but they were still figuring out which ones lacked the same power as back home, as well as which ones might backfire horrifically.

"No more than five," he said. "Any more and we run too much of a risk of discovery before we corner Lord Florin."

"Makes sense," Charlie agreed. "Sorry, Ara," he transmitted

to the Zomoki hiding out on a nearby moon with a few of their ships, "but I think you're a little too big for a stealth mission."

"That is quite all right," she replied over comms. "I am looking forward to working with Kip and the others to provide a diversion for you. This system's sun has proven most restorative."

"Yeah, I can feel it too," Charlie said. "Nice to be firing on all cylinders again, right?"

"Cylinders?"

"It's an Earth thing. Cars and whatnot."

"You and your obscure slang. I thought your people ceased using that mode of transit centuries ago."

"Well, we did, but I'm technically *from* centuries ago, so old habits and all that jazz."

"A fair point. We are all a bit out of our original time. In any case, I will be ready and close should you need me if things do not go as planned."

"When do they ever?"

"A fair point. But let us hope that on this occasion your friend Murphy does not pay a visit. I believe we have experienced enough of his shenanigans to last quite some time."

Charlie chuckled. "You can say that again." He turned to the core of their team. "Well, it looks like it's going to be us again."

Bawb and Hunze were two of the obvious selections for the mission, and, as Rika and Leila were in another galaxy, filling out the ranks would fall to the most talented of their new allies.

"Skohla and I are prepared," Nakk said. "But from what the caster has told us, the initial entry will not be the greatest obstacle to overcome."

"Yes," Bawb said. "Tell us about the Drizzax she mentioned."

Nakk and Skohla shared a look. Both were seasoned fighters yet they were uneasy. Clearly the Drizzax was not something to be trifled with.

"They are large beasts, their shoulders coming as high as

your head," Nakk said. "Their hides are knobbed with thick growths akin to the material of nails or claws."

"Like a full body covered with bits of rhino horn," Charlie said. "Lovely."

"And they are known to be voracious animals, devouring their prey in but a few bites."

Hunze perked up at that. "They are motivated by food, you say?"

"I couldn't say. But from all accounts, their appetite is a defining trait."

"Interesting," she mused. "Bawb, do you think a Festarim spell might work in this situation?"

"A *what* spell?" Nakk asked.

"Festarim," Bawb replied. "A specialized bit of magic from our galaxy used to stretch one's food when times are lean. Essentially, it makes a small meal feel like a much larger one. Commonplace among the poor, but I believe Hunze has come up with a rather novel application for one. The question is, can it be enhanced enough to satiate these creatures?"

"If not, we will have to find a way to slay them," Skohla said. "It will not be easy."

"And it will make our presence known within the compound," Hunze added. "And these are merely animals doing what is natural to them. I would not harm them if it can be avoided."

"Agreed," Charlie said. "But what do you even feed a Drizzax?"

"Whatever you can," Nakk replied. "They are known for eating just about anything. But not Lord Florin's people, who are certainly protected with a specific bit of Allpower deterrent."

"Which we do not possess," Bawb noted. "So, food it is."

He drew his wand from its sheath and carefully felt its power. It was clearly too strong and uncontrolled to cast the spell they needed, so he slid it back into its protective case. This would have to be done with konuses, it appeared, though perhaps the bandas of this galaxy might be able to cast it as well. There was only one way to find out.

The infiltration past the first layer of guards proved to not be terribly difficult. As Sithrakka had informed them, the troops outside were for show, but the master of the estate did not want his valued guests to ever feel put-out by his security forces. As such, it was the inner guards who handled actual verification of identity and permission to pass, but only after visitors had been shown to a comfortable waiting area.

It was from there the teams would each deploy after providing false identification chits to the guards. The terrified caster had given them clear instructions on what they would need, and she had even provided them with one she happened to have on her person. Nakk was confident his people could duplicate them in no time.

If the visitor pass failed, however, then weapons it would be, and a hurried rush to find Lord Florin before he had a chance to either counter attack or run for backup.

"Ready," Kip transmitted as the five regally clothed travelers walked toward the front entrance to Lord Florin's fortress.

"As am I," Ara added.

"We'll be going inside in one minute," Charlie quietly transmitted back. "Wish us luck."

It would take luck, yes, but it was far more about skill than anything else at this point. Especially Bawb's skill at disguising Charlie as one of the races that more closely resembled humans, though a rather obese one. He and Hunze had managed to make their magical disguises stick better, though practical applications had been put in place as well, but poor Charlie was forced to yet again wear an uncomfortable disguise.

At least they hadn't smeared him with shit this time, so there was that to be grateful for.

"None may enter," the heavily armored guard at the gate boomed out, just as Sithrakka had said he would.

"We are here for an audience with Lord Florin. He is expecting us," Nakk said, taking the lead, as his appearance was unaltered and his speech lacking the slight accent the visitors had when repeating Kip's translations.

The five visitors handed over their entrance chits and waited, looking for all intents and purposes as though they didn't have a care in the world. The guards weren't concerned either, because once through the entry, true Florin visitors would be protected from the Drizzax while any who dared intrude would quickly become their lunch.

The guard checked the tokens and determined them to be legit, a testament to the skill of Nakk's forger, then ushered the group into a waiting area.

"Lord Florin is rather busy today, but you will be summoned when he is ready to see you."

"Thank you so very much," Nakk said as the man left.

No sooner had the door closed than the team hurried across the room and into the corridor leading into the inner sections of the compound.

"You hear that?" Skohla asked as a whuffing sound reached their ears.

"Yep," Charlie replied. "Better get the food ready."

He proceeded to undo his clothing, withdrawing the large hunks of meat they had wrapped, sealed, and hidden on his body.

"That was seriously gross, by the way," he said.

"And utterly necessary to get this past the guards," Bawb replied.

"Tell me again why you guys couldn't carry some?"

"Because our disguises are largely magical. We couldn't risk the shifting load causing them to fail. Now hurry up and unwrap the bundles; we will need them straightaway."

They continued forward until the corridor opened into a larger chamber. There, two massive animals guarded the door to the inner sanctum. Charlie gulped. Yes, he rode atop a fire-breathing dragon, but these things were primal. Vicious. And, from the way their noses twitched the moment they entered the chamber, *hungry*.

"Now, Charlie," Hunze instructed. "One for each."

"I know how to feed a dog, Hunze."

"These are not dogs."

"Jeez, it's a figure of—oh, nevermind."

He heaved the hunks of meat to each of the Drizzax. The two of them snatched up the food, chewing it greedily.

"Is it working?" he asked.

"Shh. Give it a moment," Bawb replied.

The Drizzax seemed to be enjoying their food at least, but there was no telling if the spells layered upon it were having any effect. In no time they had devoured every last morsel and were licking their lips.

"Throw the next bit," Hunze said.

Charlie tossed them each another piece.

"I hope it's working, because that's the last of it."

"I think it may be," Nakk said. "Look."

The Drizzax, notorious for their appetites, were only licking the meat on the ground before them. Then, amazingly, one lay down and rested its head on its front paws, its enormous lower teeth jutting up outside of its lips in what would have been a comical underbite under any other circumstances.

A moment later the other followed suit, curling up and actually falling asleep, its ravenous hunger sated for quite possibly the first time ever. A sense of genuinely serene tranquility fell upon the room, replacing the crackling feeling of tension and pent-up rage.

"I think this is our cue," Charlie said. "Come on!"

The group hurried past the two beasts and through the door they had been guarding. Once through, all five breathed a sigh of relief. The second-hardest part was over. All that remained was Lord Florin. And that was where things would get interesting.

CHAPTER NINETEEN

The team split up immediately once they had passed into the inner workings of Lord Florin's compound. They had ground to cover, and a lot of it at that, and all without raising an alarm.

Charlie went up to the upper level of the compound and headed to the right of the central courtyard while Bawb moved left. Hunze and Skohla fanned out as they took the lower level, splitting directions as well. There was no telling who would make first contact, but whoever it was, tact would be essential.

Hunze was the first, as it turned out, when she came across a small group of Urvalin pacing the corridor. She stayed cool and did her best to seem as though she belonged there, walking past them as aloof and entitled as possible, hoping they'd not dare offend one of Florin's guests with an impromptu search.

A simple nod of respect sent her way was all she received as the Urvalin headed down the hallway. With a silent sigh of relief she continued on her way.

Up on the top floor Charlie had a similar situation, but in his case, it was not just Urvalin or random guards. It was a more elite group, judging by their weapons and attention to the area around them. The question was, were they simply more prominent members of Lord Florin's team, or were they something more?

"Guys, I think I may have found something," he transmitted. "I'll let you know what I find out."

If this truly was Lord Florin's personal guard, their employer had to be nearby. But in an estate as expansive as this, that could be just about anywhere on this level. He would have to move carefully, to say the least. And there was no guarantee these guards were actually protecting Florin. It could just as easily be another of his elite teams patrolling but not guarding the man himself.

Charlie was still far down the hallway, but heads had turned in his direction. To divert now would draw even more attention, and not the good kind. He would just have to see what happened when he drew closer.

Charlie reached for his magic and felt it strong as ever, though still rather unpredictable. This was going to be interesting.

Meanwhile, Nakk quietly made his way into the spacious and lush central garden courtyard, also hoping to come across Lord Florin.

He had no such luck, however, as Florin was nowhere to be seen. His guards, though, were on hand, along with a middle-aged man in a leisure outfit sitting comfortably among them. The guards that were seated beside him jumped to their feet as the others stepped toward the intruder. Apparently, having anyone in the innermost gardens was a big no-no.

"You, there! What are you doing here?" the closest guard asked, his hand instinctively resting on his pistol's grip.

"I'm lost, I'm afraid," Nakk replied, keying his bone conduction comms so the others knew what was about to transpire and hopefully move even faster. "I must have taken a wrong turn."

"No one is allowed in the gardens without Lord Florin's express permission. Let me see your pass."

"Oh, of course. I have it right here," Nakk said, reaching into his pocket.

What he withdrew was far pointier than the guard expected. The knife, plain in design and clearly not meant for battle, was innocuous enough that it had passed the security screening with no alarm. The blade was not particularly sharp, and it possessed no enchantment whatsoever.

As most people on this world carried at least some sort of cutting implement on them, it had been allowed. And no one would be foolish enough to make an attempt on Lord Florin with so inferior of a blade.

It was, however, heavy and with a strong enough point to make for a very deadly weapon in the right hands.

Nakk was already running forward as the knife flew true, embedding itself in the guard's chest. He dropped to his knees in shock, not even able to fire his weapon before he drew his last breath. Nakk snatched the gun from his hand and targeted the other guards, letting off a series of shots as fast as he was able as he dove for cover.

The pistol was fully functional, and two of the guards fell in an instant. The others, however, fanned out in formation. Clearly, they were well trained. Worse than that, it was more than just normal weapons fire that blasted back in Nakk's direction.

Allpower was suddenly in use, and a considerable amount of it.

"I believe I have stumbled upon a member of Lord Florin's casting triumvirate," Nakk transmitted. "I'm afraid I am quite pinned down, here."

As soon as the fighting broke out in the gardens within the courtyard, the guards on the top floor leapt to their feet. They were clearly tied in to the others, and if that was one of the triumvirate of casters that included Lord Florin, that meant they were guarding one of the two remaining of the group. The question was, which one was it?

Florin was not terribly powerful on his own, but linked with the other two, he would be a force to be reckoned with, and that made him extremely dangerous. But first Charlie would have to deal with the guards. Pistol fire flew his way. No one even bothered to ask who he was. Intruders were in the compound, and any unfamiliar face was a threat.

Charlie dove aside, quickly taking cover in a doorway.

"Sonofa—hey, guys, I'm taking fire too."

"I am close," Bawb replied. "I can get to you in under a minute."

"Be careful, these guys are good, and they've got all directions covered. No sign of either the caster or Florin yet."

"Then we still have an advantage. I will be there soon," the Ghalian replied.

As Nakk fought off the caster in the courtyard and Charlie dealt with the guards on his level, Hunze and Skohla moved quickly through the lower level until they met up once again.

"Did you see anything?" Skohla asked.

"No. I fear he is not down here. The others are engaged, however."

"We should help Nakk. He is in a more dire situation."

"Agreed. There was an access point to the courtyard just—look out!" Hunze blurted, pulling Skohla aside.

Strong Allpower flashed past them, slamming into the wall and cracking the stone.

"Get them, fools!" a voice shouted.

The tone was unmistakable. Entitled, aloof, and utterly unafraid.

Skohla peeked around the corner. "It is Lord Florin."

"I gathered as much," Hunze replied as pulse weapon fire peppered the wall.

"His personal guards have entered the fray as well."

"I can handle his guards," the Ootaki said. "It is Florin himself who will prove difficult. His Allpower is incredibly strong."

"The triumvirate. They are feeding their Allpower into him. And *they* are strong."

The wall shook from the Allpower and pulse fire chipping away at it. Apparently, Florin was enraged that someone had dared violate his personal space and was willing to do extensive damage in the pursuit of them. An example would be made, even if repairs were later required.

"We have found Florin," Hunze transmitted. "He is too powerful. We cannot engage him."

Bawb and Charlie were now in the thick of battle upstairs, the caster having stepped from his chambers and joined the fight. He was a very strong caster, that much was clear, but a significant amount was being redirected to his employer. If not for that, even fleeing would have no longer been an option.

"Bob, we have to retreat," Charlie called out in English. "They're layering spells, and there's no way to get close. We need to join up and take them out together."

"Agreed." He shifted his thoughts to his mate. "Hunze, get clear. We shall make our way to you and regroup. Nakk, hold on, we will get to your location as soon as we are able."

"Don't divert for me," he replied. "Florin is all that matters. You must take him."

Bawb and Charlie hated to admit it, but he was right. There was much more at stake, and if they didn't capture the man this would all be for naught. Bawb's fingers ran along his wand's case but didn't open it. Frustratingly, it was a weapon of last resort in this galaxy.

Hunze and Skohla moved to flee the corridor, but pulse fire flew at them from the other direction.

"We are pinned down," she transmitted.

"I will be to you shortly," Bawb said.

"There is no time. I will have to make an attempt at Florin."

"But he is too strong."

"I will find a way."

Hunze keyed off her comms and sized up the situation as Bawb felt a flush of concern rush through his body.

"Charlie, we must sever the link. She cannot handle the attack with Florin at full power."

Charlie had been listening and agreed. There was only one thing to do, but it would hurt.

"You're right. Ara, I'm going to pull hard," he warned his bonded friend. "Be ready, and let me know if it's too much."

She too had been following the goings-on, standing by to create a diversion if need be. But it seemed that was pointless now. The fight inside would rage no matter what she and Kip did. But she could, at least, offer some of her strength. It wouldn't be quite like the triumvirate casters did with their Allpower, but it would have to suffice.

"Do what you must," she said. "I am safe and prepared. Kip, Dukaan, be ready to fly in if evacuation is needed. I may not have the strength."

"Ready and standing by," Dukaan replied.

Charlie didn't hesitate, drawing as much killing power as he could muster. There was no need to stun and capture anyone on this floor. All he had to do was get a clear shot as the caster's defenses were stressed. At least, he hoped so.

"Bob, I need a massive diversion, then make sure you're well out of the way."

"Done," the assassin replied, leaping out into the open and loosing multiple brutal spells from his end of the hall.

The caster and his guards shifted the bulk of their defenses to block the attack coming from his direction. They were still defending the opposite end, but the reduction in power directed that way could possibly be enough for the plan to succeed. Possibly.

"Hope this works," Charlie muttered as he stepped out into the open and unleashed all of the magic he had built up.

A devastating wave of power flashed down the corridor, shattering the lesser defenses of the guards and dropping them to the ground. Charlie felt weak in the knees but stayed upright, leaning against the wall as his power flowed like a raging river. More guards fell, some dead, some badly injured. The caster, however, remained unharmed.

He pivoted, locking eyes with Charlie.

"Oh, shit."

The caster briefly pulled his power back from the others in his triumvirate and directed it at Charlie. The spells were fast and furious, and his defenses were barely holding.

"Bob, do something!" he called out.

A single pulse blast rang out and the onslaught abruptly stopped. Charlie's watering eyes focused down the hall. Bawb had moved in a flash, rushing the caster rather than attempting a magical or technological attack, favoring the one thing he wasn't casting defenses for.

Being grabbed and bitten.

The assassin had pulled enough power from the man for his defenses to falter, then put a pulse blast through his back, ending the engagement once and for all. He let the body drop to the floor.

He and Charlie shared a nod then took off running. "Hunze, we are coming," he transmitted.

Hunze and Skohla, however, were quite busy on their own defending against multiple pulse weapon attackers while Lord Florin ranted and hurled spells at them, toying with the lesser-powered intruders.

That is, until his own power taken from his linked casters abruptly diminished.

Hunze felt the shift in the air.

"Cover me," she said, casting as fast as she could while she raced toward the startled man.

His guards fell quickly as their master's power was no longer bolstering their own defensive spells. Hunze kicked one of their pistols back toward Skohla as she ran, not breaking stride.

Skohla snatched it up and opened fire on the other set of guards that had been pinning them down. "You're clear!" she called out.

Hunze charged right at Lord Florin. He stared at her with shock and disbelief. No one had dared stand up to him in longer than he could remember. And a woman? It seemed impossible. A fury rose up in him, causing his Allpower to flare. He cast hard, hard enough to have likely killed an unpowered being. But Hunze was Ootaki, and she was in full control of her power.

Her magic clashed with his Allpower as the two forms of power grappled for dominance. Hunze didn't stop running, closing the gap until she was right in front of him.

"How dare—" Lord Florin managed to blurt before his spell abruptly ended, courtesy of a brutal flying knee from the golden-haired woman.

As soon as he fell the last caster standing realized his peril and disengaged from Nakk. He was more powerful by far, yes, but the writing was on the wall. This fight was over, and his was not the winning side.

"The courtyard is clear," Nakk told the others.

"And we have Florin," Hunze added.

It was what they'd been waiting for. And now that the master of the house was not defending it, the remaining forces within and without would rally to his defense. Unless something distracted them, that is.

"Teams, go!" Nakk commanded.

All around the fortress, firefights broke out as small groups of guerilla commandos from Nakk's most skilled forces engaged

Lord Florin's troops. It took them entirely off-guard. It also forced them to focus their attention on the pressing matter before them rather than the fortress itself.

"Kip, we need you in the courtyard, ASAFP!" Charlie called out over their comms. "Come in hot, and be ready for immediate dust-off."

"On my way," the little ship replied. "Let's go, Dookie!"

With Lord Florin trussed up and gagged, Hunze and Skohla hurried to meet the others. Charlie and Bawb arrived moments later just as Kip flashed down from the atmosphere and dropped into the courtyard. In less than a minute they were aboard and aloft, their prize captured and not a single member of their team lost.

"Disengage and retreat to the rally point," Nakk transmitted to his people then sat back in his seat and took a deep breath as the adrenaline diminished. "Let's hope he was worth it," he said.

Charlie looked at the unconscious man unceremoniously dumped at their feet. "He's still out," he said, a little confused. "What spell did you use, Hunze?"

"I did not use a spell," she replied. "I hit him."

"Seriously? And he's still out?" Charlie said with an amused chuckle. "Not bad for a pregnant woman. Not bad at all. Exactly how hard did you hit him?"

Bawb crouched over the inert man and examined him, then flashed an amused look at his mate. He turned to Charlie, chuckling. "Get comfortable. I believe he may be out a while."

CHAPTER TWENTY

In a galaxy run by magic, a collection of some the most powerful vislas in all of the systems sat quietly within the belly of a small flotilla of secure Urvalin prison ships, always on the move and never staying in the same system for long.

These invaders had planned long and hard and were leaving nothing to chance, especially where their prized captives were concerned. They knew full well that, as unlikely as it was, a rescue would be disastrous. As a result, they were constantly changing location to avoid that possibility. No one would know where they were, and no escape would be possible.

As for containing such a massively powerful group of individuals, Commander Prin had really taken to using the control collars employed in this galaxy.

The devices had been modified with Urvalin tech, but at their core they were still powered by what these people called magic. At least, most of the time. Allpower was, on occasion, similar enough to magic to suffice for the bonding spells in the case of lesser casters being restrained.

For the truly powerful, however, a native touch was required.

Fortunately for the command triumvirate, with the Council

of Twenty being picked off one by one, Visla Skirbal had been swayed to join the Urvalin cause and was more than glad to lend that much-needed helping hand. With the help of his treachery, countless power users had now been bound in this manner. If Commander Prin had her way that number would only continue to grow.

At Skirbal's side at all times were his two aides, ever-ready to carry out his requests. But the Ghalian spy he had come to know as Rovalla was anything but passively going along with this plan. It was risky, and she had to time her relays carefully, but she had been supplying the Ghalian network with whatever intel she could manage.

What she reported was quite worrisome, even to the hardened assassins.

It seemed that the novel combination of tech and magic in the modified control collars was controlling the captives in three ways—one a shocking magical pulse, another a power-muting spell, and, in case the magic should somehow fail, a good old-fashioned explosive restraint as a final fail-safe.

The Urvalin always worked in threes, and their use of these collars was no different. What's more, they were even more effective tools because of it.

If the captives deactivated one layer of spells, two remained, and all were intertwined. Additionally, the prisoners had been divided into threes, their collars linked together. It was just one more layer of their three-part system. If one captive did something wrong, all three would face the consequences.

It was an interesting variant of the prisoner's paradox, only the stakes were higher, and with their lives on the line the captives were given little choice but to cooperate with one another to survive.

Interestingly enough, that meant that some captives were forced to overcome their differences with one another—sometimes feuds with a long and bloody history—to survive.

Visla Nikora Palmarian was one such example. Incredibly powerful, yet fiercely opposed to the machinations of the Council of Twenty, having sided with the other-galaxy coalition to overcome Visla Dominus and her Council goons, he was no friend to the Council.

Unfortunately, he had found himself tied to a pair of unsavory types. One was Visla Samanna, formerly of the Council of Twenty. A man Visla Palmarian had actually banned from his system after helping drive his forces from power.

The other was a somewhat diminutive woman with wild hair and wilder eyes. Sparkling eyes that seemed to contain galaxies within. She was a disconcerting sort and possessed a fiery spirit that could easily get all three of them in trouble.

She wasn't a visla, that much he was certain of, but she possessed power. What kind Visla Palmarian couldn't be sure of, but for her to be bound to him and Visla Samanna, her magic must be potent indeed.

Suffice to say, the woman he had learned was named Nipsenni was something of an enigma, to say the least.

"You keep staring at me," she said.

"I'm sorry, are you speaking to me?" Visla Palmarian asked.

"Does it look like I'm talking to anyone else?"

"We are all locked in here together. I was merely asking for clarity."

Nipsenni crinkled her nose with a little snort. "Oh, please. You were totally being a creeper."

"A *what*?"

"You heard me."

"You have a rather unusual manner of speaking, and your eyes are unlike any I've seen before. Might I ask where you are from?"

She laughed loud enough for other prisoners to turn their heads. "Oh, you can ask all you like, buddy. Doesn't mean I'm gonna tell you anything."

Nikora Palmarian wasn't used to being spoken to like this. Not only because he was the ruler of an entire planet, but also people simply got nervous around a man as powerful as he was.

Nipsenni, however, was not impressed.

"She was raised by pirates," Visla Samanna said. "Not just any pirates. The *Coalition* are her people."

"The *Coalition?*" Palmarian asked, not sure whether to be impressed or disgusted.

They were notorious. The most prolific group of pirates and smugglers in the galaxy, and they had friends in high places. If criminals had anything like an organizing body, the Coalition would be it.

"Yes," Samanna said, catching Palmarian's look of surprise. "A feral young woman from a most wretched band of scum, this one is."

Even with their control collars on, the magical energy brimming beneath the surface was palpable. Samanna expected her to react and was primed to defend himself as best he could. But the strange young woman just grinned at him in a most disconcerting way. Visla Palmarian couldn't help but be intrigued as well as a little amused.

"Pirates, eh?" he said. "And the Coalition, no less? I would not have guessed it."

"Why? Because I'm so lady-like and proper?" she joked.

Palmarian chuckled. "A charmer, you most certainly are. But more than that, I simply have a very hard time reading you."

Her eyes sparkled brighter for a moment. "You're a *reader*?"

"No, not really. But I do have a sensitivity, one could say. You, however, are unusual. I am unable to get a fix on your nature."

Nipsenni's mischievous gleam intensified, if that was possible, and a moment later a flash of *something* assailed Visla Palmarian's senses. Then, as quickly as it had appeared, it was gone.

"What was *that*?" he blurted.

"What was what?" she asked innocently.

"Such an unusual magic. Powerful. Almost like a Zomoki," he marveled. "What *are* you?"

"I'm *me*. And it's *who* am I, not *what*, thank you very much."

"My apologies. I meant no disrespect."

"Sure you didn't."

Samanna chuckled. "This one is a handful, that much is for certain."

Nipsenni flashed a wry grin. "If you think *I'm* a lot to handle, you should hear the stories about my great-great-great-great grandmother. Now *she* was a force to be reckoned with."

The two men looked at one another. Though enemies any other day, Visla Samanna and Visla Palmarian had come to an understanding quite early on in their imprisonment. Namely, for the moment, the enemy of their enemy, while not a friend, was at least a temporary ally. It was something the majority of those now locked under the yoke of a control collar on this ship had realized as well.

Their quarrels, some far bloodier than others, would be resolved later. For now, at least, they were on the same side.

"Your great-great-great-great grandmother?" Samanna asked. "Ah, of course. The eyes. I should have known."

"What of her eyes?" Palmarian asked.

"I knew it struck a chord for some reason," he replied. "A pirate of old. Something of a legend, really. A small and exceedingly violent woman possessing the most particular set of eyes. The last of a rare race with spectacular abilities, they say."

"Such as?"

"She was supposedly a reader, for one. And a woman possessing the magic to jump vast distances, like the Zomoki of old."

"A *person* jumping?"

"I know. It is pure folly and obviously just a tall tale. No one could live up to the stories."

The young woman leapt to her feet. "Don't you say that about Grandma Henni!" Nipsenni growled. "She *was* real."

The two men would have been amused if not for the surge of power that leaked out from her carefully composed muting wall. She was strong. *Very* strong. And if she truly was a descendant of a pirate of legend, there was no telling what she might be able to do.

Visla Palmarian sized up the young woman and felt a flicker of hope. Maybe, just maybe, she could be of use in breaking them free. He had family in harm's way and desperately wanted to get back home.

But Kara was almost certainly with her uncle Korbin, and he was a very talented caster. She would be as safe as was possible given the circumstances, and that would have to suffice.

CHAPTER TWENTY-ONE

Out in the depths of space, the Urvalin transport ship looked normal from a distance. Up close, however, it was clear something was wrong. Very wrong.

For one, a small section of it was open to space where a concentrated grouping of pulse blasts had torn through its hull. For another, a mid-sized, heavily armed craft was latched onto its hull.

This ship was being boarded.

"On your left, Kara!" Amazara shouted over the din of combat.

Karasalia Palmarian, her hair tied back and her violet skin flushed with the heat of battle, spun and ducked aside, avoiding the heavy stun spell her Urvalin attacker had launched at her. The man didn't stop there, however, following up with a series of pulse blasts from his pistol. Nothing strong enough to pierce the hull, but more than enough to drop an adversary.

The mixture of fighting styles was novel here and had given the Urvalin quite an advantage in this galaxy, leaving nearly all of their opponents at a loss for how to deal with such an unusual mélange of attacks.

Kara was not one of those people.

She fluidly shifted her defenses, broadening them to blunt the tech attack while sending one of her own daggers hurling toward the Urvalin, pushed hard by her rapidly increasing magic. The blade flew true, but this opponent was also well versed in adjusting for multiple types of attacks and reacted accordingly.

The blade abruptly deflected aside, falling to the ground harmlessly. The Urvalin didn't hesitate to gloat—a sure sign of an amateur if ever there was one—but rather pressed on, casting and firing on the young woman in unison.

Kara did not flee, nor did she give any ground, but, rather, she charged ahead toward the man, ready to do her worst. The Allpower the Urvalin was casting was strong, drawn from the banda worn around his waist. Kara, however, was easily his match and then some in terms of raw strength. But tactics and experience often overcome a stronger opponent, and it was looking as if this wily commando just might get the better of her.

A small peppering of spells, so innocuous and weak compared to the flurry of magic and Allpower in the air, wrapped the man's ankles, making him stumble. He didn't fall, he was far too calm and collected for that, but when he glanced at the golden-haired girl casting at him awkwardly, he saw something else. Something that actually did have him concerned when he registered what it was.

The unexpected spear put that thought out of his mind as it pierced his skull, dropping him to the ground in a heap. Korbin dashed in and snatched up the weapon, looking all around the girls as he ensured their safety.

"Are you two okay?"

Kara glanced at Vee and nodded. "We're fine, Uncle Korbin."

"Well done. Solid tactics. Now, stay behind me. Watch the flanks. Amazara will cover the rear. There are still a few more of them out there," he said, then without hesitation led them back into the fray.

They had managed to bribe a cargo loadmaster handling the Urvalin supply craft on a commerce world for a general idea of where and when the larger ships such as the one they were currently boarding were heading next, all under the pretense of wanting to set up ahead of time for some lucrative trade.

The reality, of course, was something far different. They were going to find Kara's father and break him free. At least, that was the intention.

"Korb, there are more cells down the left-hand corridor," Amazara called ahead.

Korbin's focus was locked in, but not in a tunnel-vision sort of way. This was battle, and something he was quite familiar with. As such, his magic was primed and ready to fly, and his senses were heightened, aware of all that was happening around him. Korbin diverted immediately, following the path Amazara had laid out.

"There will likely be resistance," he told the girls. "Kara, Vee, I need you to pay close attention to your casting and weapons use. We do not want to harm the prisoners."

"Got it," Kara replied. "We're ready."

"Good, because I'm pretty sure that door is the one we're looking for."

He didn't wait any longer. The time for pep talks and last-minute instructions was long gone. These girls were as ready as they'd ever be, and there was simply no time to waste. Pulse pistol in one hand and a konus on the wrist of his spear hand, Korbin burst through the door.

Pulse fire peppered him as soon as he cleared the doorway, but his shielding spells reduced the charges to no more than a bunch of minor pinches. He followed the shots, tracking them back to their source, and opened up with a volley of his own, layering devastating spells on top of them.

An Urvalin cried out then fell silent, dead or dazed, he couldn't say. It didn't matter as Korbin was moving quickly through the compartment, casting minor protective spells around the clusters of captives as he moved, hoping to spare them any wayward shots by their captors.

But more fire did not come.

"Korb, this space is clear," Amazara called out. "And I sense a group of panicked Urvalin getting farther away."

"Farther? What could they be—" It suddenly hit him. "An escape ship!"

Korbin rushed from the chamber, heading straight for command. The door was sealed shut when he arrived.

"We have to get inside," he growled, straining against the sealed doorway. "Kara, Vee, I need your assistance."

"What can we do?"

"You know the pushing spell? The one you use to guide your thrown blades?"

"Yeah."

"Cast it against this door. Right here at this spot," he instructed, pointing out what he sensed was the weakest point in the sealing spell.

"Shouldn't we free the—"

"No time to waste. Cast now!"

Kara and Vee didn't hesitate. It was rare to see her uncle in this state of concern and urgency, and they knew far better than to question it. Both girls cast at once, Kara's magic flowing much stronger than Vee's, but both putting all they could into the spells. Korbin joined them, carefully layering his magic with theirs so as to not cause hull damage when they finally broke through.

The door stayed shut, but the locking spell was beginning to splinter.

"Careful," Amazara said. "I feel it weakening."

"I know. I'm pulling ba—" Korbin began to say when the spell abruptly broke apart.

The door flew open, bent out of shape from the force of the magic. Korbin rushed into the command chamber, not concerned about Urvalin waiting to ambush them. He had something far more worrisome on his mind.

"Dammit. I was afraid of this," he said as he crouched beside the command chair.

Amazara was by his side in a flash. "Booby traps?"

"Worse. A proximity destruct sequence. When their escape ship is clear this vessel will break apart."

Kara and Vee paled. "Can you stop it?" Kara asked.

"No," he replied, leaping back to his feet. "We have to go. Now!"

"But the prisoners? My father?"

"We get as many to my ship as possible. Zara, run ahead to the ship and start casting umbilical spells."

"Inside the ship?" she asked.

"Yes. They're not meant for it, but if we are too late it may provide enough of a stable path to make it to the ship."

"What are you going to do?"

He looked at her with resolve. "I'm going to save as many as I can."

With that he was off and running.

"Uncle Korbin!"

"Let him go," Amazara said. "Come on, we have work to do."

The girls followed her back to the hull breach they'd used to board the ship and began casting a long umbilical spell as best they could. It was not only much, much longer than designed for, but was also weaving through the corridors of the ship as close to the cell block as possible.

Three by three clusters of men and women of varied races rushed toward them a minute later.

"In here! Hurry!" Amazara directed them.

There was no need to tell them twice. Their survival instinct was overriding pretty much anything remotely resembling clear thought. Escape was all that mattered right now.

The ship began to shudder and rumble.

"Girls, get aboard," Amazara ordered.

"But my uncle—"

"Will be here. Now go! We'll be right behind you."

Kara hesitated a long moment, then turned and boarded the ship.

"Come on, Korb. Hurry up," Amazara muttered anxiously.

A violent bucking threatened to throw her off her feet, but she somehow stayed upright. Escaping prisoners rushed past her as best they could, but a sucking wind appeared out of nowhere, pulling those running beside rather than inside the umbilical out into the void of space.

"Where are you?" Amazara braced herself as the ship around them sped its demise.

In the distance at the end of the corridor, a figure was running at full speed toward her, using all of his power to seal the umbilical behind him as he did. It was the only thing keeping them from losing their oxygen and being sucked into space. Korbin was casting fast and furious, but he could only go so long before he would need to pause to take a breath. And when he did, all would be lost. The spell would fail. Amazara focused hard to keep the umbilical intact, but it was clear he would not make it.

A blast of magic pinched the umbilical shut just as Korbin stopped casting and sucked in a deep breath, casting full-force again an instant later. Amazara turned and looked to find Kara and Vee standing behind her, casting way out of their league, doing all they could to keep their atmosphere intact.

Korbin gestured for them to get aboard as he raced toward

them. A moment later he dove into the ship, sealing the boarding hatch and drawing in ragged breaths.

"You shouldn't cut it so close," Amazara said, hugging him tight, not daring admit just how close to death he had been.

Korbin turned to his niece. "That was some pretty impressive casting. Both of you. Well done."

"My father?" Kara asked.

Korbin's face darkened. "Not on this ship. I'm so sorry, Kara. This transport was not carrying anyone of significant power. Just people whose local knowledge and connections might prove useful to the Urvalin."

Kara's magic began crackling around her with frustration.

"Kara, breathe," Amazara said. "Control your power."

Kara hadn't realized what she was doing at first, but Amazara's calm voice keyed her in. Blushing, she did her best to calm herself, and a few moments later the dangerous spillover subsided.

"What do we do?" she asked. "How do we find him?"

"We will need more intelligence," Korbin said. "We knew this was not a sure thing, but our Ghalian friends are working on digging up other information from their sources."

"And how do we even find them?"

"We do not," he replied. "We will go to my retreat estate and wait for them to contact us. It's only a matter of time before they reach out."

"Will it be safe there?"

"Only a few there know I possess any power at all, and none are aware to what degree. Yes, some word got out during the battles with Visla Dominus, but that was almost entirely in the other galaxy. Here in this one? I believe I have been successful in misdirecting people into believing it was others who were responsible for the actions that would have been attributed to me."

Amazara rested her head on his shoulder. "You do love your anonymity," she said.

"And it looks like today that works to our advantage. Now, let's see about releasing these captives somewhere neutral then getting somewhere safe. I think we will all feel more secure once we're in familiar and defensible territory."

CHAPTER TWENTY-TWO

Korbin's ship swung into a low orbit above the tranquil world that he called his second home, gently entering the atmosphere without any hint of urgency.

The people they had rescued from the Urvalin had been dropped off on a small, neutral planet from which they could reach out to their respective clans, families, and employers from a safe location. There were simply too many for Korbin to ferry home himself no matter how much he wished to help.

They cleared the exosphere and began the slow descent toward the region where Korbin had built his retreat. He lived just outside a small hamlet when on this world, but he was also a short hop from the planet's main city should he wish to frequent a more populated and bustling area.

He almost never did.

The sky was a clear blue, its wispy clouds pulling apart in the thermocline. Down below, forests, rivers, and fields stretched out in all directions, the looming mass of the main city of Nootsa rising above it all, a testament to magical building prowess besting even nature itself.

But something was wrong.

"Hey, what's that?" Amazara asked, pointing to wisps of smoke rising from the outskirts of the city. "That doesn't look industrial in origin."

Korbin zoomed in his ship's optics spells. "No, it doesn't. In fact, I'd argue it looks a bit too familiar. Like destruction on a battlefield."

Amazara realized he was right. It was just so unexpected on this world of all places. A world with no real power users of note —at least, not that the locals knew about. Yet conflict had found its way even here.

"There!" Vee said, pointing out a landing site with what appeared to be corpses scattered around a smoldering ship.

Korbin weighed the options and chose the one he liked the least, yet was also the most needed.

"I'm taking us in," he said. "We have to know what happened here. That's an Urvalin ship, and those are Urvalin dead. *Someone* has declared war on the Urvalin, and on a world I am rather fond of."

He swung the ship low and dropped into a hover, scanning the area from the ground to space with both his magical as well as tech-powered devices. Not a single threat registered. He set down close to the dead and stepped outside. Amazara and the girls followed close behind.

"It appears to have been a scouting party," Amazara said. "Look. Their attire, their weapons. These people were almost certainly a tiny appendage of a much larger beast."

"Agreed. But what happened here?" Korbin wondered. "The people of this world are peaceful, not warriors. Who could have done this?"

"Uh, guys?" a voice said out of the ether. "Yeah, sorry for the mess. That was kinda me."

The group spun, eyes searching for the source of the words. That became abundantly clear a moment later when Freya uncloaked in all of her stealth and magic-producing nanite glory. The hatch opened and Daisy walked out, her disquieting blood-and-magic-drinking bone sword in her hand.

"Hi, everyone!" Freya said. "Great seeing you!"

"Yeah, what she said," Daisy said with a wry grin.

Korbin scanned the carnage around them. "Daisy, did you do this?"

"Well, yes and no. I mean, when I came across these guys they decided to get all pushy and tried to take Stabby from me."

"They attempted to take your sword?" Kara gasped. "Oh, that was dumb."

"She's right about that," Sarah noted silently.

"You said it, kid," Daisy agreed. "Stabby didn't take too kindly to that, and, well, things led to things, and long and short of it, he drained them all dry. He's kind of developed a bit of a taste for this Allpower stuff."

"And I took down their ship," Freya added. "It got messy, but they were powering up weapons."

"You did good, kiddo," Daisy said with a proud smile.

Amazara cocked her head. She was the reader of the group, sensitive to others' power, but when it came to the living sword, all of them could feel the weapon positively thrumming with stolen, violent energy. Allpower sat oddly within him, and he had drunk his fill.

"There is a disquiet within your sword," Amazara said. "An aggression that was not previously there, even when he would drink from a power user."

"Yeah, tell me about it," Daisy agreed. "I think I might need to avoid letting him soak up too much of this Allpower stuff. I mean, he's more antsy than ever, and I really don't want him going and turning into some kind of evil, cursed blade or something."

Amazara reached out, refining her read on the weapon. "I would not worry about that, Daisy," she finally said. "He is much more closely tied to you than to any magic or Allpower he may absorb. It might take more effort than you are used to back in your own galaxy, but ultimately, it is you who controls him."

"So when he goes ham on someone, that's my fault? Freaking excellent."

"A little violent? Kinda moody? Takes after his mom a bit, I'd say," Sarah joked in her head.

Hey, it's not my fault he's super kickass, she shot back.

Korbin was moving through the wreckage, pulling free anything that might be of use to them. The strange belts the fallen wore seemed to still have Allpower in them, so he stripped them from the dead. Kara and Vee gathered up the weapons and tucked them in a sack to be cleaned of blood and sorted at a later time.

"Someone's going to miss these guys eventually," Daisy said. "Anyone have any suggestions?"

"Actually, I think we should just hide the wreckage and the bodies," Vee replied.

All eyes turned to the young Ootaki.

"You want to what, now?" Daisy asked.

"I mean, these Urvalin were clearly not part of a strike team, right? So I'd guess they've been world-hopping, moving around a lot."

"And that means if they go missing, no one will know exactly where from," Korbin mused. "At least, not for a little while."

"Pretty smart," Daisy agreed. "As long as they don't check in with freakish regularity, their bosses won't know where to look for them. At least, not precisely."

This reminded Korbin of one thing that had been bugging him. "Daisy, how exactly did *you* find us? No one knew we were coming here."

"Oh, Freya's got star maps to pretty much everyone's hidey holes."

"Yep," the ship added. "I've been saving everyone's info since we first crossed over here."

"So we knew where your place was," Daisy continued. "We actually stopped there first but didn't see you. That's when we decided to swing by town to see if anyone knew where you'd gone off to. You're one of the strongest casters we know, so we figured we'd better link up, what with all this madness with the Urvalin."

"You were at my retreat?"

"Yeah."

"And there were no Urvalin there?"

"Nope. There were a bunch of dead ones over in the city near Amazara's place, though. That place was a mess. Your doing?"

Korbin nodded.

"Figured. we went there first since it was closer to our location at the time," Daisy said. "Anyway, after we found the dead Urvalin, we thought it would be best to come here to track you all down."

"And you were successful," Korbin noted.

"Yeah. If you didn't swing by here, we were going to try your primary residence as the next spot on the list. You're kinda easy to find since you only have just a few locations you frequent, unlike most people."

"He can be a bit of a hermit at times," Amazara said.

"I know. I figured if you weren't home there either then the Palmarian estate would be our next stop."

The team's demeanor shifted.

"What? Was it something I said?"

"Visla Palmarian has been taken," Korbin replied. "The Urvalin are in control of the entire planet."

"Oh, Kara, I'm so sorry."

"We *will* find him," the teen replied. "We might have been unsuccessful so far, but he's out there, and someone will talk."

Freya ran through her mental list of power users they had confidence would join their cause. It was shrinking rapidly.

"Daisy, this is worse than we thought. If they were able to take him, that means our pool of potential allies is getting smaller."

"I know, which is why we need your help, Korbin. The Urvalin are making moves."

"We know. They're capturing power users all across the galaxy."

"Not just that," Daisy said. "They've taken over the portal somehow and dropped it into the sun. I can't get home."

Amazara's gift touched the woman's energy, and she sensed just how upset Daisy was at being cut off from her family. "With the solar plasma coming through the portal, no ship would survive an attempt. I'm sorry."

"Yeah, well, thanks."

A realization flashed through Kara's head. "Hang on. If they dropped the portal into the sun, then that means they're active on *your* side of the portal too."

"Obviously."

Kara's cheeks flushed. "Is Arlo okay?"

"I honestly don't know," Daisy replied. "But I'll tell you this. If they so much as touch a hair on my kid's head, I'll let Stabby do his worst with my blessing. And right about now, I think that would be pretty damn bad for anyone on the receiving end."

Korbin paced anxiously, running this new information through his head. All it did was reinforce his opinion they needed more help. Some *specialized* help.

"We need to talk to the Ghalian," he said. "And sooner than I had expected. We cannot wait for them to contact us."

"Oh, I agree."

"But they are impossible to track down under the best of circumstances. And these?"

Daisy grinned. "Don't worry about that. We're good. Me and Freya? We have friends in high places. And by high places I also mean low places. Or hidden places, to be more precise."

"You can reach the Ghalian?"

"Oh yeah. And it looks like that's just become a priority. Grab your stuff and come with us; we'll head out at once."

Korbin did a quick calculation, assessing their numbers and resources.

"Zara, please gather what you need from our gear. We will go with Daisy to meet the Ghalian, then stop at my home to retrieve additional weapons. Then we will come back here." Korbin turned to the girls. "Kara, I want you and Vee to take my ship back to my property. It is already set to autopilot to that location. You should be safe there, and from what Daisy said there are no Urvalin in the area. At least not yet."

"But what if some arrive?"

"My estate here is heavily warded, but the spells will recognize you and Visanya. You both can pass safely. But if anyone else should attempt to enter, they will have a *very* unpleasant surprise."

CHAPTER TWENTY-THREE

Earth was a hot mess.

Once the Urvalin had realized they had quite likely failed to take out many of the planet's most powerful AIs they were forced to shift their tactics to adjust for this new paradigm.

Power grids were targeted. Cities went dark as battles raged across the planet as Earth's defenders managed to inflict significant losses to the Urvalin invaders despite operating at a severe handicap.

This was their home, and as invading forces had learned throughout history, an occupied people would often fight with the ferocity of a group many times greater than their actual numbers.

On top of that, these combatants were not mere citizens. All had survived the Great War, or were descendants of those who had, and *all* of them had at least basic training in weapons and tactics. After nearly being wiped out of existence by an alien invasion, it was only logical.

When the forces on the ground and in the air displayed an organization beyond what would be expected of disparate resistance groups, the Urvalin shifted their attacks again, targeting more than just normal power generation facilities.

Fusion reactors were sabotaged by their insiders, and solar arrays were shattered from above by attack ships. It burned those resources they were hoping to keep secret, but the time to use their ace in the hole was here.

But the AIs appeared to still be avoiding termination. Tenacity, it seemed, was something they possessed in abundance. As did those flying under their command.

"Darby, you've got a pair on your three," Rika called out to the modified space fighter flying at her side. "Break right. I'll cover your six."

"Roger that," the pilot replied.

Rika's ship, the *Fujin*, was still inoperable, but Rika had more than just tech on her side. She had magic. And powerful magic at that.

Her mech, taken from its storage hangar and thrust into battle, soared through the air. It was currently powered by its normal drive systems, but her magical energy was also flowing through it, bolstering its offensive as well as defensive capabilities. It was quite a thing to witness, a giant mechanoid flying, of all things, and for many Urvalin, it would be the last thing they would see.

The Urvalin had been attempting to block the use of this galaxy's magic through the clever use of their own Allpower, but Rika's disruptive mix of Earth and the other galaxy's magic had been stymieing them repeatedly. Something about that mix was anathema to the powers from not one but two other galaxies, it seemed, and she was leveraging it to its fullest.

"We need reinforcements!" the pilot called out as he engaged the two ships in a heated dogfight.

"We've only got what we've got," she replied. "Nothing in or out of the atmosphere, you know that."

"We're taking a beating, Rika."

"No shit. Now focus!"

Whether it was her anger flaring up or just a fortuitous alignment of an Urvalin ship and her weapons systems, Rika fired off a magically enhanced burst of railgun sabots, the hypersonic projectiles ripping through the Urvalin shielding and punching right through the ship. It wobbled erratically a moment, then began a tumbling fall toward the surface.

There was just one problem.

"Shit! It's heading for the city," Rika called out over her comms link. "Get down there. You need to stop it before it hits."

"How am I supposed to do that?" the pilot asked.

A massive shadow flashed by them, streaking towards the ground.

Rika felt a tiny flash of relief as it passed by. "I wasn't talking to you."

Orgalius had taken to aerial combat quite naturally since their return to Earth. And now, with a customized harness containing not only comms and shielding apparatus, but also weapons, he was a stealthy, deadly part of her team.

Winged death from above, and unseen more often than not.

Working in tandem, he and Rika had been more than just a thorn in the Urvalin's side. With their magical prowess, they were the main disruption to their plans for conquest. As a result the Urvalin had been unable to advance on other objectives as planned. In fact, the duo had even prevented the Urvalin tech-dampening array from being lowered to extend its reach closer to the surface.

That particular headache was still operational and in full force, but it remained limited to the layer of microsats hovering in orbit. Constrained as they were to atmospheric operations, Rika and her dragon partner had flown the globe, teaming up with resistance forces in their fight against the invaders.

"I've got it!" Orgalius exclaimed as his claws pierced the inert ship's hull. "It's a bit heavy. I'm going to drop it on the—"

A heavy barrage of weapons fire blasted his shielding, sending him off course, but his grip on the craft held fast.

"I'm taking heavy fire," he called out. "Rika, there are more substantial forces on the surface than our intelligence reported."

Another salvo flew skyward, this time mixing Allpower along with pulse cannon fire. Rika felt the intensity of it and gauged the strength of the enemy below. It would be a tough one, but she and Orgalius *should* be able to handle them.

She hoped.

"I'm coming down," she replied. "Darby, you got this?"

"Just one up here right now," the pilot replied. "Yeah, you go."

Rika didn't wait to be told twice.

The mech shifted course and dove fast, straight down, her weapons firing at every Allpower signature she could sense. At first, when they didn't know who they were up against, it would have been unthinkable to fire at a populated area like this, but now that she knew the enemy and what their power and tactics were, she felt confident any bystanders had either fled or been captured by this point.

Both options pissed her off to no end.

A squat building collapsed under the impact of her pulse blasts, crushing whoever was firing up at her and Orgalius from the relative cover of its front windows. Several other targets shifted and avoided her fire, responding with shots of their own.

Rika spun her mech, twisting in midair and dropping down to the street with a pavement-shattering impact. She had the mech up and running in an instant, her magic providing ample shielding from the Allpower flying at her hard and fast. The pulse cannons, however, were more difficult to deal with.

"They're pivoting," she transmitted. "Trying to flank me."

A stream of magical dragonfire erupted from above, blocking the Urvalin's line of sight temporarily. It was all Rika needed to adjust on the fly. She moved the mech as if it were her own body at this point, years of piloting making it as natural as breathing. When her magic was incorporated into its systems, for all intents and purposes, it really was a part of her.

The mech hadn't merely been in storage at the AI skunkworks lab, it had been receiving gradual upgrades at Rika's request. Yes, it was an antiquated device, but she was very attached to it. More than that, she proved extremely capable at utilizing it to devastating effect against just about every enemy she'd encountered with it.

"Bite me, you bastard!" she shouted as a caster rushed from cover, letting loose a massive Allpower attack.

Rika swung the mech's leg hard, planning to kick the man into another time zone if possible, but it moved slowly, as if stuck in molasses. His counterspells were blended with another's, she realized. It was that damn trick the Urvalin used, casting in threes.

She thumbed free the railgun safety and let loose with a few blasts. It would have been a waste of armament designed to take out spaceships and heavily armored vehicles in any other situation, but in this case, she was more than willing to make an exception.

The sabot wasn't one of the rounds impregnated with her own unique blend of magic, but the supersonic velocity was all she needed. No matter how powerful this man's shielding was, the disruption of the airspace around him at that speed would likely be enough to implode his organs, if not worse.

"Gah!" Orgalius cried out just as the caster in the street fell in a heap.

"Orgalius!"

"I am all right. A hidden caster's burning spell took me by surprise, but its intensity abruptly dropped significantly."

"Yeah, I just took out one of their other casters."

"Ah," he said with relish, "then the tide has turned. They are diminished."

Rika knew what that meant. Orgalius was a kind and thoughtful creature, but he was also a dragon. And dragons had to eat.

He spun toward the ground, ripping the façade off the building from which the attack had originated. The cowering wizard inside didn't stand a chance.

"Satisfied?" she asked as his feet disappeared down the dragon's throat.

"Not remotely," Orgalius replied. "Be wary, there are still conventional weapons at play." With that, he was moving in a flash.

Rika realized that while Orgalius had the advantage due to his kind's raw speed, her mech could only move so fast on the ground. In an urban setting like this, where her enemy could be hiding anywhere yet she was not free to destroy everything around her, a different strategy was needed.

"Going in on foot," she transmitted. "Activating my locator. I'd appreciate if you didn't eat me."

"Noted," the dragon replied with an amused chuckle.

Rika raced to a space between buildings that was just the right size to nestle her mech, then crouched the machine down, hopping out as the unit folded itself into its reinforced transit configuration. In that shape it was almost impervious to most attacks, and with the additional wards she placed on it, only a freakishly lucky shot or incredibly powerful caster could damage it.

The former she had no control over. The latter did not appear to be present on this battlefield. That meant she was free to hunt.

Pulse pistol in one hand and a wicked long dagger in the other, she raced off into the dust-swirling streets, her magic-channeling tattoos crackling with power, ready to strike down anyone in her path.

The first three Urvalin she came upon were simply foot

soldiers and fell quickly to her spells. There was no need to fire her pistol or dampen her blade with their blood. The next combatant, however, required far more effort.

She was the third caster, it seemed, and a reasonably powerful one at that.

Rika took the brunt of the wave of Allpower thrust at her, batting aside the vast majority of it even as she began casting her violent response. The two power users exchanged spells and weapons fire across the roadway, dodging and weaving, each showing considerable prowess in combat.

A pulse blast narrowly missed Rika but slammed into the wall beside her, sending shards of stone into her arm and side.

"Sonofa—" she growled, her power flashing out violently.

The Urvalin caster countered the spell, but only just. Rika kept right on casting, pushing harder and harder. It looked as though it was a stalemate when Rika abruptly shifted her spell's direction, pushing it downward. The caster realized what she was doing, but it was too late. The ground beneath her shattered, and without the extra bandwidth to protect herself from the onslaught while also stopping her fall, she tumbled into the chasm.

Her Allpower spells cut off abruptly.

Rika walked to the hole in the road and peered over the edge. Satisfied with what she saw, she turned and returned to the fight at hand. With their casters gone, the end was inevitable. She would join Orgalius in tracking down the rest of the Urvalin forces. And once they were done with them, the dragon would feast.

CHAPTER TWENTY-FOUR

In the weeks since the Urvalin first made their presence known, Orgalius and his closest friends had reached out to as many other dragons as they could find. Unfortunately, while they were plentiful compared to Ara's lonely status as the last of her kind in her own galaxy, this realm's dragons were nevertheless spread out. Reaching one another was not exactly a simple thing.

Even so, several had been contacted and brought into the fold. Their home galaxy was under attack, and eventually nowhere would be safe. One and all volunteered to fight, and a fight they would have.

Some flew straight to Taangaar to help in the battle, teaming up with the joint fleet's ships that were still far away and had thus managed to avoid the power-sucking traps in Earth's solar system, though where else the Urvalin had deployed them was anyone's guess.

Others set off to search for hidden Urvalin staging areas, torching them when they came upon them if possible, or at least forcing the enemy to scatter in a panic. The dragons had proven an unexpected and rather disruptive variable in the Urvalin conquest, and they were making a good showing of it. In the process, however, some were lost.

It was an inevitability in war, but these were peaceful space dragons, for the most part. None had experienced this sort of conflict in their lifetimes, nor did they expect to. But now their new friends were in a bind, and this was not something they could ignore. Eventually, the war would reach them all, and it was far better to fight early than run and suffer later.

As the conflict spread it became clear that these were exceptionally desperate times, and as a result, dangerous moves would have to be taken.

A few of those who had visited the magical galaxy happened to be near Earth at the onset of the hostilities and were helping as best they could. Those dragons were meeting up with various pockets of resistance fighters and the AIs guiding them, working as teams to fight off the Urvalin threat.

One of them was Nixxus, the dragon with a splash of violet across her back and a green underbelly. She had been given a tour of that realm along with her friend Gazz by none other than Ara herself.

It was she who would first heed the call to take the ultimate risk.

"I'm going to fly through the portal," she said in the security of the seemingly abandoned hangar her flight team was staging out of.

"You cannot," Cal said, his connection to the facility from his network of diversionary hardlines and comms hubs tenuous at best. ***"You will burn."***

"Maybe not," Nixxus replied. "We need magic to win this fight, and far more than my kind can provide."

"We have Rika on our side," a Chithiid pilot named Morka pointed out.

"Yes, we do," Nixxus said. "But as effective as her magic is against the Urvalin, she is just one person. And her power is not limitless. We need numbers if we ever hope to overcome them."

"Your point is valid," Cal agreed, ***"but that does not negate the fact that the portal now rests within the sun's plasma. To attempt to reach it is to burn, both on this side and the other."***

"Again, maybe," Nixxus said. "But maybe not. The magic this sun gives off is strong. *Extremely* strong, in fact. It powers more than it detracts."

"A net gain."

"Exactly. And if Ara can do it—"

"But you are not Ara, Nixxus," Cal interrupted. ***"You are from* this *galaxy. She is so strongly affected by our sun because its power is not of her world. It's novel to her. But you? You can't possibly know if you will react the same as she does. And if you don't—"***

"There is no other choice. We *must* reach them, and if at all possible, we must find a way to bring their casters back to this galaxy to help deal with the Urvalin's magical threat. We've been cut off, and magic is what will even the playing field. I don't see any other option."

"I have to think you'd be facing an enemy you can't defend against," Morka interjected. "Yes, your magic is strong, and you are very capable in combat, but this enemy also wields technology in their arsenal. Even if you should make it to the sun, you would still have to get past their forces."

It was something Nixxus had thought about herself, but she had planned on simply bum-rushing the portal and utilizing speed and surprise to make it through. But Morka was right, the odds were that she would face at least some weapons fire from the Urvalin, and not of the magical variety. Her own spells likely wouldn't be enough to shield her from them.

"I have to try," she said after a long pause. "Even if I am wounded in the process. There is too much at stake. Someone has to get across to contact the others. We need to find a way."

The AI was silent a long while, which for a mind that processed as fast as he did was quite unusual.

"Very well," Cal finally said. ***"If you are set on this attempt, the least I can do is provide you as good a support system as I can. I need you to fly to one of my peripheral fabrication facilities. I've tasked one of the AIs who avoided deactivation with adjusting a new harness we were testing out. It was originally meant for Orgalius, but you are similar in size."***

"What will a harness do for me?" the dragon asked.

"Think of it as a technological upgrade for a biological system," Cal replied. ***"Phase shielding, integrated weapons systems, and, of course, a full scanning and comms array. It is state of the art. I just hope he's had the time to finish it."***

"Who?"

"The one overseeing the project. An odd fellow, to be sure, but his attention to detail is exceptional, and I can think of no one better suited to make any alterations for it to fit you better should they be required."

"Is this the odd AI you are talking about?" Morka asked. "The one who will not cease talking about clothing?"

"Yes," Cal said. ***"Habby is a bit single-minded in that regard, but for this task I trust him implicitly."***

"Well," Nixxus said. "I suppose I should get to him as soon as possible. Where exactly am I going?"

One benefit of being an AI was the lack of requirement for a physical body beyond the processing core. Other than that, the electronic minds could move about freely—at least, before the Urvalin invasion—and take up residence in any number of locations.

After the attack, however, such freedom of movement was greatly restricted. Cal and the other major AIs across the globe had their secret networks of processors that backed up their minds, as well as multiple hardlined redundancy systems. The problem was they had to be incredibly selective with who would be allowed to utilize them. It was a harsh fact of war, but the closely guarded fail-safe system would no longer be secret if too many AIs suddenly ported into it.

Some would die, or at the very least be trapped in their own minds, unable to reach out as traitors cut their external lines, but others would live, free to operate in the shadows, directing Earth's resistance.

Habby, odd as he was, happened to have transitioned from a quirky haberdashery shop AI into a still quirky but impressively thorough city AI. His upgraded processors had been a thank you from Cal after his help during the Great War, and, once dialed in, he had adapted to the expanded intellect with great aplomb.

It was that unusual perspective on things that had helped him make the very short list of who Cal would include in the secret evacuation of their minds. And that was in part due to his processors not being housed at his normal location of operations. He actually resided in a hardened bunker, far from the city he oversaw. Like Cal, he had avoided termination because when the Urvalin struck, he wasn't actually there.

"Oh, this is just dreary. Dreary, I tell you," he said as his cybernetic workforce cleared up the fabrication lab hidden in plain sight in what appeared to be a defunct home furnishings warehouse. "Not acceptable. Clean this up. We must be presentable for our guests."

It was the perfect place to have set it up. After all, in case of hostilities, no one in their right mind would prioritize furniture over food, weapons, and power. So it was the Urvalin had ignored it completely.

"We have company coming, and I will not have them see our new home like this. Now, chop-chop! There's work to be done."

By the time Nixxus arrived, Habby's loyal cyborg minions had whipped the place into shape, transforming the exceptionally well-equipped, yet messy, facility into a gleaming showroom of high technology. And its centerpiece was a brand-new harness with all of the bleeding-edge bells and whistles and then some.

"No, not that harness," Habby said to the dragon as his workers confirmed the measurements he had collected at a glance from his myriad scanners and cameras. "Yes, it's an impressive unit, the best, actually, but the cut simply won't work for your build."

"It should work, I would think," she said.

"Oh, never! Orgalius is much broader at the pinch points. No, I'm afraid we'll have to whip you up a new one. But don't think of it as a problem, think of it as a fun adventure in haberdashery!"

Nixxus wasn't sure about this unusual AI. He was quirky, as Cal had warned, but maybe a bit too much for so important a task. Or, at least, so she thought. Cal had all the confidence in the world in him, however, so she would go along with what he proposed.

"Gustav, Anastasia, heat up fabricator number three. Maxine, I'm going to need one of the new railguns, if you'd be a dear and fetch it. And the smaller sabots. You know, the ones with the modified tips."

The cyborgs, smartly dressed to a one, immediately rushed off to work. While their duties had changed with their boss's new position, his requirement that they all be impeccably dressed had not.

"I need to go, and soon," Nixxus said. "How long will this take?"

"Oh, a day at the most."

The dragon rose to her feet. "I do not have time for this."

"Wait, wait!" Habby blurted. "I'm supposed to fit you with a new—"

"I told you, I don't have the time."

Habby paused. "Well, there *is* that prototype framework unit. If you give me an hour I can have it outfitted with a solid defensive system, comms, and a really nice weapons upgrade. Please? Cal said it was important you have a quality harness."

Nixxus thought on it a long moment. "An hour?"

"Yes, only an hour."

"Very well. But after that, whether it is complete or not, I fly."

CHAPTER TWENTY-FIVE

The tech harness Habby had made for Nixxus was surprisingly comfortable, she found. Her limbs were utterly unencumbered, and her wings had not only full range of motion, but the more vulnerable spots on her underside at the joints were now partially shielded by an ingenious folding of the ceramisteel material, layering it like her own scales allowing for range of motion as well as protection. Habby was right, this fit much more comfortably than the unit designed for Orgalius. And the toys were top-notch.

Utilizing the comms systems had proven quite simple, and the shielding array operated via a minor AI, automatically activating it and adjusting as might be required in combat. The computer wasn't a true, self-aware entity, but it did enough thinking for itself to be almost a co-pilot where the tech was concerned.

For the magical dragon, that was a good thing, as she'd never owned a pulse cannon or railgun before, let alone operated one. With the firepower now strapped to her body, it was her opinion that some things were best *not* to learn on the fly, especially where things that went boom were concerned.

"You will need to avoid the dead spots if your systems are activated," Cal informed her. ***"Your harness guidance system is admittedly somewhat bare-bones, but it also possesses a particularly clever incorporation of guidance tech into the harness design with a minor AI assist."***

"And it's working without a hitch," the haberdasher said.

"Well done, Habby. With that in place, Nixxus, it should help you navigate the invisible power-dampening mine fields that are floating around out there."

"Yes. Yes, indeed," Habby chirped, thrilled an AI as important as Cal appreciated his work. "And the weapons are tied in as well, keyed by the comms interface. Tell it what to do and you will be able to multi-task without a second thought."

"But I must reiterate, it is crucial you avoid the dead spots," Cal added. ***"You are a living being, and magical at that, so you will be unaffected by them. But if you should fly through one without shutting your systems down first, your entire harness will deactivate and go cold, and that would rather defeat the purpose, not to mention cutting off any communications you may be able to send. Of course, the Urvalin have been blocking comms already, but we hope to have a workaround for that reasonably soon."***

Nixxus flapped her wings and quietly spoke to her AI assistant. "Target where I blow flame."

She let out a tiny puff of magical fire across the workspace. The pulse cannon and railgun both swung around and let off simultaneous shots, blowing a hole in the far wall.

"Oh. I'm sorry," she said. "I didn't mean to do that."

Habby's crew was already racing into action, clearing up the mess and patching the hole before the dust had settled.

"That's on me," the AI said. "I should have warned you about that."

"The way it just shoots holes in things?"

"Oh, heavens no. But if you don't specify which weapon you wish to use, it will default to both. Given the nature of our

Urvalin enemy, I thought it would make the most logical base setting seeing as you would be accessing it in a high-stress situation. More firepower and all that. And I must say, the streamlining of those two systems really is flattering to your physique. I can't wait to see what we can do for you when we aren't so rushed."

Nixxus found she couldn't help but like Habby. He was weird, yes, but he was a good flavor of weird so far as she was concerned. She deactivated the system all the way to a full shutoff as Habby had instructed her so the apparatus might survive the dampening field blocking Earth's atmosphere and her path to space. She'd find out soon enough.

"Well, then. It's time. Thank you for your help, both of you. Wish me luck."

"Have fun storming the portal," Habby called out as the dragon leapt into the sky, heading straight up.

She was gone in a flash.

"Do you think she'll make it?" Habby asked.

"It would take a miracle."

Nixxus activated the clever computer operating her harness as soon as she was safely out of the danger zone surrounding the globe. At first, there was no response, leaving her wondering if all of that effort had been for naught. She was sure she'd flown beyond the dampening field's reach, but now she was having doubts.

A low hum ran through the harness, tickling her body before it settled down. A few moments later the core began powering up as the AI woke from its full deactivation and slowly brought the systems back online, one by one. In less than thirty seconds her harness was fully operational.

Here we go, she thought as she raced through the space between worlds in a circuitous route to the sun. The Urvalin had laid a complex network of invisible traps, but enough poor souls had been observed falling to them that a relatively comprehensive map now existed.

Cal had compiled one on Earth, thanks to the terrestrial telescopes monitoring the skies, and Sid had done the same from the moon, though neither was able to communicate with the other.

Nixxus flew quickly, feeling the power of the sun's rays increasing as she drew closer to the submerged portal. Urvalin resistance, to her relief, had thus far been nonexistent, but for how much longer that would remain the case she had no idea.

They were sneaky bastards, and there was no guarantee they wouldn't appear out of nowhere and open fire. Though she hadn't seen it herself, it had been reported that they apparently had some sort of cloaking ability akin to a shimmer. That could prove incredibly problematic in her solo attempt.

Closer and closer to the sun she flew when a large Urvalin craft jumped in front of her, opening fire with its pulse cannons.

Nixxus spun aside, but there was no way she could avoid the blasts entirely. It was what the Urvalin counted on. A magical being was no match for their tech weaponry. But her AI was, and, without her having to do a thing, it registered the attack, fired up her shields, and modified their phase to almost totally negate the pulse fire.

The Urvalin would adapt quickly, no doubt, and Nixxus only had the briefest of windows to act before they shifted to a more difficult assault. They had already launched smaller attack craft, which were moving into position, flanking her for the kill.

The power of the sun was strong, and she felt her magic surging, but the heat was so intense as well that it was almost impossible to stand.

Die trying or die fleeing, she thought, the decision a simple one.

A moment later she jumped, arriving right at the edge of the sun's plasma, immediately diving headfirst into the molten fire. She sensed the portal's signature and pushed as hard as she could for it, using every bit of her power to keep from combusting as she did. She was draining herself faster than she ever had, but she was also drawing so much of the incredible power from the sun.

Even so, the pain increased from unbearable to even worse, but still she persevered, a flash of relief registering for a split-second as she crossed the portal before being once more engulfed in fiery death. But she did not perish. Somehow, her power had held and the heat was decreasing.

She was through, and she was going to make it.

Pulse and magical blasts flashed all around her as she burst from the plume of the sun's plasma, a waiting Urvalin contingent spinning and firing on the unexpected arrival. Nixxus was exhausted but her magic was stronger than she'd anticipated. Despite the pain and pull from her reserves, the sun had charged her as well.

She focused her magic as best she could and jumped away. To where she didn't know, but anywhere was better than here. She had to regroup. To think. To plan.

The Urvalin were on *both* sides of the portal. That meant the magic users of this galaxy already had their hands full, and then some. It was the worst kind of news she could imagine. She'd risked her life to bring help back across, and now it appeared this realm was in just as much trouble as her own.

It was time to regroup and come up with a new plan, but what that might be was anyone's guess.

CHAPTER TWENTY-SIX

The pounding in Lord Florin's head was quite possibly the worst thing he'd felt in longer than he could remember. Everything was dark around him, and he had a foul taste in his mouth. On top of that, his pulse echoed in his ears with annoying regularity.

The fog in his mind began to lift, and a realization dawned on him right about the same moment that the painful pulling of his eyelids informed him that it wasn't actually as dark as he'd believed, but his eyes were shut. *Stuck* shut, from what he now realized, and for quite some time it seemed.

He moved to rub his hands across his eyelids to loosen the crust. That was when he suddenly realized things were worse than they seemed. His hands were firmly bound and the foul taste in his mouth? A rag caked with dried blood and partly damp with saliva tied tightly in place.

Someone had captured him, he realized. Didn't they know who he was? Who his friends were? Heads would roll for this, and not quickly. Whoever had done this to him would suffer a slow and miserable demise.

And speaking of heads, only now was he realizing his was

sideways. He was apparently lying down. Florin pushed himself up onto one elbow and righted himself. A wave of fresh pain washed over him, making him reconsider if his pounding head was the worst pain he'd felt or the throbbing bruise on his jaw.

A woman, he suddenly remembered. Yes, it had been during an attack on his compound when a golden-haired woman attacked him. He had been winning easily when his triumvirate's power abruptly failed. The last thing he saw was a dervish of a woman flying at him, her knee aimed at his chin.

A splash of water hit him full-face.

"Glad to see you're finally awake," Charlie said. "You were out a long time there."

Florin rubbed the backs of his bound hands painfully across his gummy eyelids, prying them open with a sticky pop. He blinked repeatedly until his vision cleared and his eyes adjusted to the lights.

He was in a windowless room, sparsely furnished and with only one door. None of his guards were anywhere to be seen, but that made sense. This was not his estate. A ship, perhaps? He didn't know. What he was certain of was the precarious nature of his situation.

A pinkish man was staring at him. Clearly the one who had spoken. Nearby was a pale fellow with an ominous air and a few members of the rebel forces he had helped disperse on more than one occasion. There was also a golden-haired woman. The woman who had attacked him.

Lord Florin glared at her with unmasked distaste as he rubbed his aching jaw. Hunze merely stared calmly back at him. Charlie, however, couldn't help but laugh. From what they'd learned about Lord Florin prior to their mission, he was not only extremely full of himself, he also believed women to be lesser beings.

Hunze had very clearly, and rather painfully, proven him quite wrong.

"Betcha didn't know a girl could hit that hard, did ya?" Charlie asked with a mischievous grin.

Florin did not look amused.

"Be glad that's all she did. You have no idea how easy you got off."

Their prisoner mumbled something through his gag.

"What was that?" Charlie asked. "Oh, right, you're trussed up like a Thanksgiving turkey. Hang on, let me get that for ya."

He pulled the gag from the man's mouth.

"What is a turkey?" Florin spat.

"Well, it's a—"

Florin seized the opportunity, immediately attempting to cast a killing spell.

A massive slap of restraining magic hit him, knocking the wind out of him violently while dissipating the Allpower spell he had tried to cast. The man who was so used to being feared and in total control of those around him felt an unfamiliar surge of adrenaline course through his body as he reeled from the counterspell.

Charlie watched as he blinked away the tears the impact had drawn from him, waiting until he'd regained some of his composure before leaning in close.

"Yeah, you probably don't want to try that crap with us," he said. "You're all alone here, and without your other casters bolstering your Allpower, I'm afraid you're incredibly outmatched. I mean, you're really not terribly strong on your own, now, are you?"

"He is not," Nakk said. "If not for his wealth he would be selling prazzis buns in the marketplace."

Charlie thought back to the ultra-wealthy on his own world back in his own time. It seemed some things were the same no matter which galaxy he found himself in. A meritocracy was typically overruled by those with the money to impose their will on others. And people would do just about anything with the right carrot dangled in front of them.

It was a manipulation tactic they were now going to turn on its head, but it was not money they would be offering Lord Florin.

Charlie nodded to Hunze and Bawb. It was time for the duo to work the man over. Unlike mere thugs, however, it was highly unlikely they'd have to lay so much as a finger upon him.

Hunze walked to Florin and stood in front of him. Hatred blazed in his eyes, but he made no attempt to cast. She nodded, then slowly drew a dagger from her belt. With one deft movement she sliced his restraints. His hands free, the prisoner properly wiped the remaining grit from his eyes.

"You're brave with your men's Allpower protecting you," he hissed with open contempt.

"Oh, is that so?" Hunze replied, a little smile curling the corner of her lips.

She grabbed his hand, forcing it open, then startled him by slapping her dagger's handle into his open palm. His fingers instinctively closed around the weapon, but his eyes betrayed his confusion. Hunze let go and stepped back, her hands empty.

Lord Florin looked at the others in the room. All of them were much too far away to lay a hand on him before he could strike. Only the woman was close. After the humiliation he'd endured at her hands the temptation was simply too great.

He lunged forward, surprisingly quickly for a man of his age and stature, slashing out with the blade. All he connected with was air. Again he moved to strike, but again the woman was frustratingly out of reach. But Lord Florin had trained with his captain of the guard and had a few tricks up his sleeve.

He spun, feigning a high slash, but the knife was in his other hand, sneakily switched mid-turn. *That* hand stabbed lower, going for a gut shot, but rather than the satisfying hot gush of blood he expected to coat his hand, all he felt was the painful cranking of his wrist as the knife was deflected and snatched away, followed by an elbow to the formerly unbruised side of his jaw.

Lord Florin fell back into his seat, stars in his eyes from the impact. Hunze flipped the knife around, holding it by the blade, offering him the grip once more. As his vision returned to normal, Florin considered making a reach for it, but the amused calm look in the woman's eyes made him think twice. She saw his decision before he voiced it.

"You have chosen wisely," she said, then threw the dagger across the room, lodging it firmly in the slender arm of a chair.

She hadn't even turned to look at her target.

The pale man walked to her side and smiled. The prisoner was horrified to note the fangs that slid into place as he did. The once powerful Lord Florin didn't need to know what a Wampeh Ghalian was to realize he was in far more trouble than he could have possibly imagined.

Bawb reached down and effortlessly hoisted the man into the air, a terrifying blaze lighting his eyes. He didn't *actually* have flaming orbs in his face, but the spell had always been a favorite of his when he found an interrogation needed a little extra something to help move it along.

"We have questions for you, little man," he said, another spell adding a disquieting fly-like buzzing to his words. Like a demon from hell, if this man believed in such a thing. "Lie, and people will tell their children the tale of the legendary suffering of a man called Florin."

The assassin dropped the man back down into his chair, letting out a terrifying animalistic growl as he did. Charlie almost had to turn away, but he managed to keep a straight face as his friend laid it on thicker than he'd ever seen. Bawb was pulling out all the stops, but in this galaxy where their magic didn't always work exactly as intended, he might have overdone it a little.

It was at that moment an unexpected scent filled the room. Florin shifted uncomfortably. Hunze and Bawb had, quite literally, scared the shit out of him.

The release of his bowels seemed to deflate the man. He wasn't merely humiliated, all the fight within him was gone. As if a balloon had been popped. He slumped in his chair, soiled, smelly, and utterly resigned to his fate.

"What do you want to know?" he asked, his voice cracking.

Now it was Nakk's turn. The rebel commander walked to their prisoner and stared down at him, locking eyes with an unwavering conviction.

"You are in possession of knowledge," he said. "A rare item that stores Allpower far beyond measure."

Florin almost maintained a blank expression. Almost. Nakk saw the faintest realization in the man's eyes and smiled.

"Yes. You know what I am speaking of," Nakk said. "The Vortaxis. Where is it hidden? Tell us everything you know. And I do mean *everything*."

The prisoner paled. "It-it's a legend. A fairy tale," Lord Florin stammered. "And even if it did exist, it would be nearly impossible to find. Lost to the ages."

Nakk nodded slowly. "And *that* is why you are going to help us find it."

CHAPTER TWENTY-SEVEN

In his prolonged state of abject terror, Lord Florin had wound up spilling far more than just what he had filled his trousers with. In fact, once he started talking, it was as if a massive spigot had been opened, releasing a long-stagnant pool of information in a deluge.

Lord Florin had been accumulating knowledge for a very long time, hiding away his secrets, keeping them close to his chest at all times. But trusting no one was exhausting, as was always paying close attention to every word uttered so as to not inadvertently let anything slip.

He was good at it, though, as evidenced by his long rise to power. But while he wasn't aware of it at the time, all of that pressure had been weighing on him, and once he began to let his guard down and release some of that build up, he wasn't able to stop.

Nakk and Skohla recorded everything he said, parsing it out to members of their team where the intelligence could prove useful. But as for the information about the legendary Vortaxis, Florin had proven the most surprising.

He had been known to use his wealth and influence to

accumulate more power, but he had apparently also leveraged for information. And when it came to the Vortaxis, he had accumulated more knowledge than anyone, it seemed.

Unfortunately, while it was a wealth of knowledge, it was released in a firehose torrent of information, dumped upon them with no discernible structure. By the time he had told them all he knew, it was as if someone had handed them a giant bucket full of feathers and said, *Now make me a duck.*

When Nakk's people finally removed Lord Florin from the room after his exhaustive info purge, Charlie flopped into the nearest seat with an exhausted sigh. "How in the world are we supposed to find this Vortaxis thing?" he groaned.

Bawb stroked his chin in thought. "It *is* a rather daunting quantity of folklore, history, and what appears to be pure conjecture. We shall have our work cut out for us, indeed."

Hunze and Skohla were huddled off in a corner for much of Florin's interrogation, quietly going over the disparate snippets he was providing. It was a mind-bender, to say the least. Some of the clues and records were seemingly straightforward enough, but a good selection of them seemed to have been written in an ancient tongue and later translated, as many religious texts had been over the ages.

Unfortunately, there is often much lost in the translation as not all words share the same meaning as the original author's intent. With that in mind, the task of finding a common thread linking it all was almost Herculean in nature.

What was particularly fascinating was that Lord Florin, for all of his faults on so many fronts, was nevertheless a very intelligent man, possessing a surprisingly keen intellect that extended far beyond mere finance and political leveraging. In his accumulation of knowledge about the Vortaxis, it seemed he had actually *memorized* a great portion of the translated texts, much the way a schoolboy might commit sonnets to memory.

It was a boon for the rebel fleet. They would have had to visit a great many of Lord Florin's properties, overcoming guards and staff, to have retrieved them all. He may have been cooperating, but his people would have sensed the change in the man the moment they saw him.

But with his oral record, that step was thankfully avoided. Now they just had to figure out what the hell it all meant.

"It's a damn riddle, Bob," Charlie groused. "I mean, what the hell does '*the flow, the flame, sleeping secure. The Vortaxis among the source most pure,*' even mean?"

"It means the ancients were apparently none too fond of the obvious," Bawb replied.

"You're telling me. The guys love alliteration, but how is this going to help us now? We've got a whole book's worth of this stuff, and it could mean *anything*."

"*Actually,*" Skohla interjected, "there seem to be recurring themes within the passages, regardless of original language or age. It is not a concise road map by any means, but one could assume the repeated usage would signify a core importance."

Charlie rubbed his temples and closed his eyes. This was far more brain work than he'd anticipated, and his was starting to ache. Fortunately, there was someone else on their team who was more than capable of multitasking with all of this data at hand than all of them combined.

"Hey, Kip, you got your ears on?"

"Come on, Charlie. Don't I always?" the AI replied. "I mean, I *am* running everyone's real-time translations after all."

"Fine, valid point."

"Not to mention all of your neuro-stim info feeds, though if not for your translation spells starting to work a little I don't think you'd be able to understand each other at this point. I mean, it's only been a few weeks."

"Yes, Kip, we know. Just answer me this. Can you make anything out of all this rambling nonsense Florin dumped on us? Is there a pattern? Anything tying it all together?"

The AI paused a moment, but not out of hesitation or uncertainty, but because he was quintuple-checking his work before speaking.

"Yeah, there's some of it that seems to align," he said. "Mostly this spewing stuff."

"Uh, *phrasing*?"

"*Fine*. The repeated references to flows, and flames, and spew —I mean, *spraying* stuff—"

"Not much better."

"Seems to relate to natural phenomenon," Kip continued, ignoring the interruption. "So, what I make of it is a likelihood of something that incorporates all of those elements."

"Such as?" Charlie asked.

"I was thinking, it sounds rather volcanic, doesn't it?"

Charlie and the others looked at one another. Could it be something as simple as that? Using a volcano as a landmark to find the most powerful artifact in the galaxy? Or, at least, so legend had it.

For all they knew, the Vortaxis could actually just as easily be a broken toaster or a shiny rock. But that was just one more part of the mystery, though one they would need to address sooner than later.

"So, it's hidden near a volcano," Charlie said. "Do we know what this thing even looks like? I mean, is it big? Small? Can we carry it? Wear it? Finding a likely planet with volcanic activity that also correlates to the last alleged recorded sighting of it will be difficult enough, but we can't really do a planet-wide search for something we know nothing about."

"We can ask Lord Florin again," Hunze mused. "Though in his current state I do not know how much use he will be."

"Yeah, you guys did kind of break his brain with fear a little bit," Charlie agreed. "But with all the things he spilled, I doubt he'd have had the resolve to have held anything back from us."

"I agree with Charlie," Bawb said. "So, it is now incumbent

upon us to not only determine a likely resting place for the Vortaxis, but also discern what it is."

Charlie shook his head. "Needle, meet haystack."

"You know, there might be something here," Kip said. "Some of what he told us was translated from songs."

"And?"

"And oftentimes some of the more enduring tales were passed down that way. Like the Chithiid do, right Dukaan?"

The Chithiid pilot uncrossed his arms. "Kip does have a point. My people sing songs that trace their lineage for dozens of generations, if not more, with little if any change or error over the years. The act of singing, passed down within family units, ensures the song is learned correctly as opposed to a fallible written document."

"So, you're saying the bits he gave us that are taken from songs are probably our best bet?" Charlie asked.

"I think so. They would possibly be the least changed over the years."

"Okay, but how do we figure out what part of his rambling purge was a lyric and what was just some jet stream of random babbling?"

"I'm working on it," Kip replied. "It's gonna be a mix of translating multiple alien, and sometimes ancient texts, then compiling that data into various pentameters, all hopefully correlated to one another with a common thread pointing us in the right direction."

"What he means is, he needs a little time," Dukaan said. "Don't worry, we'll let you know as soon as he has something actionable."

"Do you think that will take long?" Nakk asked.

"Not too long, I'd wager," the AI replied. "I am pretty amazing, right, Dookie?"

The Chithiid pilot didn't think that warranted a reply.

Charlie gestured to the door through which their prisoner

had been whisked away. "Nakk, are we good with Florin? Don't want him throwing a wrench in our plans."

"Our people have already whisked him away to a secure location for safekeeping. Not just to prevent him from leaking our plans, but I think given his relationship with the Urvalin, he might prove to be useful leverage in the future."

"Cool," Charlie replied with a grin.

"Indeed," Bawb agreed. "A man of his considerable resources existing in fear for his life will often do anything to draw breath for one more day. That can be leveraged if the need arises."

"Yep," Charlie agreed. "For now, I guess we just wait until Kip is able to—"

"Okay, I think I've got it," Kip interrupted.

"Got what?" Nakk asked.

"A possible location," he replied.

Nakk was impressed. "Already?"

"He may talk shit, but he *is* a supercomputer," Charlie noted.

"Thank you, Charlie."

"Sure thing, Kip. Now, whatcha got?"

"Well, according to my cross-referencing with multiple star charts, a planet that seems to meet the requirements set forth by the adjectives most heavily used in the various songs is not terribly far away."

"This is wonderful news!" Skohla said. "How long will it take to get there?"

"Not long at all," the AI replied. "And I, for one, think we should leave sooner than later. You all ready to go?"

CHAPTER TWENTY-EIGHT

It had taken nearly a day of bathing in the rays of a moderately powerful sun for Nixxus to restore her power and heal her injuries. While she had made it through the portal intact, the journey had left her in a weakened state. Had she not already been brimming over with power when she began the attempt, there was now little doubt in her mind she would not have survived.

But for a dragon of her strength she had proven crossing over was a doable thing, albeit uncomfortable. And if she was able to carry an additional source of power, such as a konus, for example, she could very likely make the passage unscathed.

More than that, the proximity to the sun would allow her to supercharge her magic in the process rather than utilizing every drop she took in to keep from burning up.

With her hurt no more than a memory, she shifted her attention and began to properly take stock of the situation. She needed help, that much was clear, but from whom? The Urvalin had thrown a wrench in her plan, and she now had to adjust on the fly.

Fortunately for Nixxus, while she may not have been from

this magical galaxy, and she had not really spent a very long time exploring it in her prior visit with Ara, one thing she did have.

A very good sense of smell.

Of course, in the case of space dragons, it wasn't so much smelling magic—there is no actual scent in space, after all—as it was *sensing* it. And amidst all of the myriad remnants of magic floating in space, she picked up on the faint but recent traces of a familiar bit of Drookonus magic used to power a particular ship, and mixed with it, warp technology from Earth. Not something one would expect to find here, and that was good. *This* ship she knew.

Hmm, Korbin, if I'm not mistaken, she mused. *He's a powerful one.*

Nixxus shifted course, following the trail of the man who could hopefully help her cause, not to mention fill her in on what was going on here.

This certainly wasn't panning out as she'd intended when she had made her dash for the portal. Based on what she encountered upon her arrival, it was looking like this galaxy needed all of the casters they could muster, given the surprising presence of the Urvalin here. But if she could join up with someone as powerful and tied-in as Korbin, she might be able to at least get a better handle on just how bad the situation really was.

She feared the answer would be *very* bad. But there was only one way to find out.

Nixxus focused hard, locking in on the fine thread that would hopefully lead to some answers. A heading established, she pulled upon her power and jumped.

There was a smell in the air of the world she arrived at. A new smell, and one she had quickly grown to loathe. *Urvalin*. They were here, and recently at that. But there was something else. Another familiar aroma. That of death.

With the greatest of caution, Nixxus entered the atmosphere, slowly descending toward the surface, scanning the area from on high as she did. What she saw down below fascinated her. The Urvalin, it seemed, had met an untimely demise, and Korbin's ship had apparently been here not long ago at all.

She felt a wave of relief flow over her. He *was* the right one to help her fight against this enemy. And judging by the scent, he was still close by.

Nixxus adjusted her angle, flying wide of the city and its deceased invaders, targeting instead a quiet estate on a hillside not too far away.

There, she thought as she spied his ship parked in an open field. *He's still—* she paused. There were wards here. Strong magic. Korbin's magic. If she came too close, there was no telling what sort of defenses she might trigger. Nixxus would have to get his attention from afar if she could.

This was an interesting wrinkle to the plan. But she was a dragon, and if anything would make someone take notice, a massive flying fire-breathing creature of her size certainly would.

She blasted out a stream of flames, careful not to trigger the defenses but close enough that anyone inside would sense her presence. She then settled down in the field a safe distance from the visla's warded property and ship.

"Korbin, I would speak with you," she called out. "I am Nixxus, a friend of Ara's. Please, lower your wards."

She waited patiently but did not sense the protective spells lessening in strength. She did, however, see the door to the property open, but it was not the mighty caster who stepped forth, but rather a young woman with pale-violet skin and a close-shorn Ootaki of the same age.

"Hello?" the violet girl called out. "Did you say you're a friend of Ara?"

"Yes. I am called Nixxus. From the other galaxy. I fly with Orgalius."

"Hey, we know Orgalius!" the Ootaki said. "But what are you doing here?"

"I am looking for the visla known as Korbin. I followed the scent of his ship to this place."

"Oh, yeah, that," Kara said. "We kinda flew the ship here ourselves. I'm sorry, but my uncle isn't home at the moment."

Nixxus felt a knot of unease form in her rather large stomach. "It is imperative I speak with him. There has been an invasion on Earth and the other worlds in the alliance. A race called the Urvalin. These attackers have found a way to negate the technology of that realm. It is magic that is needed to combat them."

"We've been dealing with them here too," Kara replied. "They've been rounding up the most powerful casters in the galaxy."

"They've *what*?"

"Capturing whoever they can, killing those they can't. The Urvalin are trying to take out anyone who might be able to stand up to their magic."

Now Nixxus was *deeply* concerned. It would be a challenge in any case, but her friends on the other side of the portal appeared to be in even greater peril than was first apparent. If no casters would be forthcoming from this side, they would be woefully underpowered and on their own, and *that* was a battle she was unsure they could win.

"I need Korbin. When will he return?" the dragon asked.

"He's with Daisy, if you know her."

"Only by reputation."

"Well, they went to meet the leaders of the Wampeh Ghalian."

"The *who*?"

"Ghalian. They're basically the deadliest assassins in the galaxy. And, apparently, they might actually be on our side."

"So, there is no telling when he will return?"

"Sorry, but we don't know. All he said was after they met with whoever it is they're off to see, they'd be stopping at his home to gather some supplies and weapons before coming back here. It might be a while."

"Is it far from here? His home?"

"Not terribly, but there's no way to know how long they'll be away."

Nixxus lowered herself to the ground. "Then I will wait."

"It sounds like there's no time," Kara said. "From what you told us, it's getting worse on that side without magic to defend them. We need to cross over. I'm a caster too. I can help them."

"You're not your uncle," Vee noted. "You're strong, sure, but he's a visla."

"Someone needs to warn Cal."

"We *can't*, Kara."

"Vee, this isn't just dropping in to say hi. *Arlo and Ripley are in trouble*," she replied, her concern readily apparent. "We have to do something."

Vee knew there was no changing her friend's mind, and, truth be told, she was much of the same opinion herself. "All right, so let's say we *did* want to cross over. There's one problem. Your uncle's ship was set to fly us here and that's it. Its controls are locked down. We can't use it."

"The portal is submerged in the sun anyway," Nixxus pointed out. "Your ship would not survive."

"Wait, so how did you get here?" Kara asked.

"My magic is boosted by the sun's power. It was difficult, but I drew power from it as I crossed over."

"You flew *through* the sun?"

"More or less, though the portal was only submerged near the surface."

An idea blossomed in Kara's head. "Hang on. *You* can take us through!"

"I don't know that I can."

"Sure, why not? Ara does it all the time. Just use your magic to protect us."

Nixxus saw where she was going with this, and in her own galaxy it made fairly good sense, but here?

"There is a problem, Kara. This is not my galaxy, and my power may not function here the way it does back home."

Kara and Vee looked at one another, the same idea in both of their minds.

"How about a little test, then?" Vee asked.

"Yeah, you have a harness," Kara added. "Why not give it a try?"

Nixxus seemed uncomfortable at the thought.

"I am not sure I could keep you safe. Perhaps with an additional source of magic, but on my own, I fear—"

"Oh, we've got our own," Kara said, releasing a flash of her own potency.

Nixxus almost flinched. When the surprise wore off, however, her look of concern shifted to one of great curiosity.

"Oh, you do indeed have power of your own, little one!"

"A bit. And a boost as well, thanks to Vee's Ootaki braid," Kara replied.

"More than a little, I'd wager. And the braid you mention does indeed possess great magic, yet I can sense that it only serves to bolster your already formidable power, not replace it." Nixxus did a few calculations and came to a decision. "Very well, then. A little test. And, if a quick run into space should be successful, you should gather your things and prepare to jump. We may yet have a means to help our allies on the other side."

CHAPTER TWENTY-NINE

Freya was flying in full stealth mode as she carried her passengers back to Korbin's home property. Her nanites, while directly tied to her core command systems, still had something of a mind of their own in their particular way, and as such she was constantly interfacing with them, adjusting their actions.

They were curious by nature, designed to adapt and improve functionality. When Freya introduced them to the thing her friends from this galaxy called magic, they took to it with the enthusiasm of a toddler on a sugar high. Namely, it became the most wonderful, all-encompassing thing in their microscopic world.

With Freya's guidance, as well as her amazing mind breaking down the novel elements in play to understand their core functions, the nanites had grown quite adept at utilizing magic, acting as a full-ship konus of sorts, absorbing the energy from the galaxy itself as well as figuring out novel ways to generate it on their own.

Best of all, she didn't have to speak to cast her spells. The nanites would transmit the cosmic vibrations, or energy focus, or whatever you wanted to call it, that seemed to trigger the magic at a microscopic level. As her magical friends had said, it was just as much about the intent behind a spell as the words themselves. She simply improved upon that process.

It was all still highly experimental, however, and Daisy had instructed her that only things she had quadruple-checked for safety should be used for now. Even for a brilliant AI, magic was quite a new concept to work out.

One of those new systems was her own version of a shimmer cloak. She still had her nanites' active camouflage, capable of rendering her essentially invisible without the use of magic, but she now had that additional layer of magical obfuscation in her arsenal. That, along with bleeding-edge stealth tech to defeat any scans imaginable, had made her pretty much untrackable.

Her course, however, was laid out clearly, as flying with her was another stealthy craft. This one, shimmer cloaked but lacking her tech camouflage, belonged to Master Pimbrak, the dapper Ghalian Daisy had managed to convince to accompany them back to Korbin's home.

Originally, she had expected Master Farmatta or Master Zilara to join them on the trip, but Zilara had been off on another task, and Farmatta was busy dealing with the Urvalin threat, pulling strings via her network of spies and assassins.

Pimbrak, however, was free, and he possessed the unique gift among his kind of being able to take power from another not only by drinking their blood, but he could also do it by touch alone. Against the new threat, that could prove very handy.

"Almost there," Daisy skreed to Pimbrak's ship as they exited their warp just above the world Korbin called home.

It was still a bit odd using a magical device to speak rather than good old-fashioned comms, but while the Ghalian had used technological communications devices in prior engagements fighting alongside their new allies, it was still not a standard part of Pimbrak's ship.

"I am with you," the assassin replied. "I will see you on the ground shortly."

"Great, see ya down there," Daisy transmitted back. "Okay, Freya, you're good to go."

"Descending," the ship replied. "Hey, Daisy?"

"What's up, Kiddo?"

"I was thinking. Maybe I could reinforce a comms probe with some modified nanites. You know, teach them to cast protection spells."

"Okay, but why?"

"The portal, Daze," Sarah replied. *"She's trying to find a way to reach Joshua and the others."*

It made sense. She was a machine, yes, but a living mind who had a family of her own. It was only natural she would be concerned for their well-being. And with a mind like hers, it was also no surprise she was actively trying to find the means to connect with them.

"Sarah's right," Freya said, reading the discussion through the slender neurostim unit Daisy wore in her hair. "I'm worried about them."

"Hey, Joshua's the most badass tactical AI to ever live. And I know he won't let anything happen to Marty. Or the others, for that matter."

"I guess," the AI replied. "It's just hard being cut off from them."

Daisy felt that one in her aching heart. "Boy, don't I know it. But our people are smart. Resourceful. I'm sure they're okay. And we've gotta focus on what we *can* do, and at the moment that's figuring out all we can about these Urvalin pricks and finding how to stop them before our next run-in."

"Uh, Daisy?" Freya said. "I think we just found them."

"What?"

"Look!"

Freya flashed images of the surface.

"Oh no," Korbin said. "The Urvalin are here."

Judging by the dead aliens, the locals had put up a fight when the invaders entered the city, but the Urvalin had not given up, and it seemed they had summoned reinforcements.

"I fear we are running out of safe ground," Amazara sighed. "What do we do, Korb?"

He rose from his seat. "This is my home. The emmik here is a good man, and these are my friends. Drop me on the ground and take off. Lure their ships away. I will engage their casters and attempt to clear the town."

"No, there are too many of them. You need to get those big weapons from your property," Daisy objected. "*We'll* go to the city. You need to go home and gather what you can. We'll keep their attention on us until you get back."

"But—"

"No buts. This is just Murphy paying a visit. They don't know about you, Korbin. Your estate is untouched. But if you engage before we can be sure they won't escape, the jig is up, and I, for one, prefer to keep my surprises hidden until there's no other option."

Korbin thought about it a long moment. He hated stepping back from a fight, but she was right. They needed the weapons from his home, and they needed to be acquired as stealthily as possible. They couldn't let the Urvalin know about Korbin's power or his involvement. Not yet, at least.

"Very well," he groused.

"Great. Now sit down; this is gonna be a rough landing. Freya, drop us just outside of town then get Korbin to his home. Once he's clear, decloak and engage the Urvalin ships. Distract them and make them launch and follow. We clear?"

"Crystal," Freya replied, already dropping to the ground.

"Pimbrak, you ready for a fight?"

"Oh, Daisy," he replied. "You know I am *always* ready for a fight."

Pimbrak landed across town from where Daisy and her team were deposited, ready to cut a swathe through the Urvalin on his way to meet up with them.

Freya flashed back into the sky and bee-lined to Korbin's estate. She dropped him off as quickly as she was able, and as soon as he was clear, she took off, weapons hot, and flew right back into the thick of it.

"You good to go?" Daisy asked Amazara.

The woman raised the pulse rifle to her shoulder and nodded. It wasn't her weapon of choice, but given the circumstances she would make do.

"Okay, then. Let's do it."

Korbin felt the commotion before he heard it, the magical defenses of the Urvalin ships so suddenly under attack tickling his senses. Freya had decloaked and engaged the ships on the ground, hitting them with pulse fire.

She had been working on her magic, but Daisy's orders were no casting of things until they'd worked the bugs out. That meant sticking with tech, at least for the time being.

Daisy felt a tug at the sheath strapped firmly in place. It seemed her sentient weapon had developed even more power than she realized, and with it, the drive to move freely on its own. In this instance, that wasn't a bad thing.

"Okay, buddy, you ready for this?" Daisy asked as she carefully unsheathed her bloodthirsty sword, making sure he was paying attention to his master.

Stabby was positively humming with anticipation.

"*Controlled*," she said firmly. "Don't get sloppy."

Amazingly, the sword responded, his battle thrum lowering to a faint pulse.

"*He's listening,*" Sarah said.

"It's about freaking time."

"What was that?" Amazara asked.

"Nothing. You ready?"

"I am."

"Then let's go."

She knew Pimbrak would already be fast at work, closing the gap from the other side of town. With his speed and skill, it wouldn't take him long before the Urvalin were reduced in number, and significantly at that. As for Daisy and Amazara, they would have a bit more of a fight on their hands.

"You there!" an Urvalin shouted when he saw the armed women approaching. It was all he managed to say.

He clearly wasn't expecting a tech attack in this galaxy as the shot Amazara let off took his head clean off. Daisy looked at her, impressed.

"He was casting defenses for magic," Amazara said. "I felt it. But that advantage won't last. We should move quickly."

Stabby abruptly moved on his own, blocking an incoming killing spell with ease. Daisy turned and saw the squad of Urvalin troops rushing their way, another joining them from an adjacent street.

"Well, I guess we don't have to go find them," she said, then rushed into the fight.

Stabby swung with a mix of Daisy's direction as well as his own will. Mostly he went where she wanted, but sometimes he would react before she could, slashing and slicing, bathing in Urvalin blood even as he countered their spells.

Amazara peppered them with rifle fire, forcing the advancing enemy to shift course to address the combination of magical, bladed, and pulse attacks. A shot landed square in the chest of one of the Urvalin, but he only fell to the ground, bruised and charred, but not dead.

"They're adapting their shielding," Amazara called out.

"I can see that," Daisy replied. "We may have to cut this little engagement short until Korb's back."

Daisy spun, the force of her sword's motion pivoting her feet for her. Stabby sliced clean through the war club being swung at her then halved the pulse rifle that the startled Urvalin tried to unsling and take aim with before planting himself deep in the man's chest.

He sucked deep, draining him of blood and power in a flash. The bone sword was in his element now, the glory of battle, and it was all Daisy could do to keep him from rushing headlong into a suicide attack.

"No, Stabby!" she growled just as a familiar shape streaked through the sky.

Freya had managed to lure all of the Urvalin ships from the ground, forcing the troops still aboard to remain out of the fight. But there were a lot of them, and even with the AI engaging them, the Urvalin still managed to open fire on the ground. They didn't land direct hits, but Daisy and Amazara found themselves pinned down.

"Pimbrak, where are you?" she skreed to the Ghalian.

"Heading your way," he replied in a hushed voice. "There are far more than we anticipated."

"No shit. We're pinned down here."

"I am trying to reach your position, but you will need to hold on a little longer. The fire from above is blocking my path."

At that moment Freya managed to land a direct hit on one of their ships, a nanite-coated sabot from her railgun piercing their magical and technological defenses. But there were still so many more.

"Good shot, Freya."

"Thanks. I'm trying to keep them away from you, but they're swarming me."

"Keep it up, we'll be okay." Daisy turned to Amazara, frustrated. "We should be wiping the ground with these assholes. How long will it take for Korbin to get here if Freya can't pick him up?"

Amazara thought a moment. "His home is at least ten minutes from here by regular conveyance."

"We don't have that long."

Blasts rained down from above, the Urvalin fleet letting loose without restraint as they hoped for a lucky shot.

"*They're moving closer under that covering fire,*" Sarah said.

"We need some help here!" Daisy transmitted.

"I'm trying!" Freya replied as she dealt with multiple opponents at once.

A flash registered at the edge of the atmosphere. Daisy and Amazara scanned the sky above.

"What the hell was that?" Daisy blurted.

"Another arrival," Freya replied.

"Shit, they must've called reinforcements. We need to come up with a way out of here, and quick!"

"I'm trying!" Freya said, a faint desperation in her voice. "Daisy, I'm going to try a spell."

"We don't know what'll happen."

"I know, but do you have a better idea?"

Daisy thought hard. They were screwed, no two ways about it.

"No. No, I don't," she said. "Okay, Kiddo. Give it a go. And, Freya, good luck."

CHAPTER THIRTY

"Hurry up, Freya," Daisy said as she watched the aerial combatants swarming her AI child. "Whatever it is you're gonna do, you'd better do it fast."

"I'm trying, but it's all new, so I need to—"

A pulse cannon blast rocked Freya, causing no damage but throwing her off course a moment before she spun out of the tumble and shifted direction out of their line of fire.

"Activate your shimmer!" Daisy cried out.

"I can't. Not when I'm about to cast a new spell. The nanites don't have any muscle memory for this one yet."

"Multitask, Freya. Active camouflage."

"I'm trying."

It was quickly becoming clear that as much as the new nanite magic was a useful tool, it could also pose a problem in ways they hadn't thought of yet. And this was rapidly becoming a trial by fire.

"*She's fighting with her hands tied, Daze. We have to do something.*"

Sarah was right and Daisy knew it. "Screw this. Peel off, Freya. Get clear."

"I won't leave you here."

"I'm not asking you to leave. I'm asking you to protect yourself, then come back and kick everyone's ass when you're dialed in."

Freya wavered. "I don't know. Maybe—"

A massive wave of flames tore through the sky, incinerating several Urvalin ships unfortunate enough to have been directly in its path. The others on the periphery of the blaze caught fire but managed to stay aloft, at least for the moment.

"What the hell?" Daisy blurted as a flaming ship crashed to the ground.

"It's magic," Freya said with glee. "Magical fire. They were so focused on defending against tech, they let their guard down."

"But you said you couldn't cast."

"*I* didn't," Freya said, shifting course and blasting the ever-loving hell out of the surviving Urvalin craft.

Dropping in from above, a violet-and-green dragon swooped into the fight, pinning the fleeing craft while the AI ship picked them off before they could make a break for orbit. In under a minute not a single Urvalin ship remained in the sky.

It was then the dragon turned her attention on the ground.

Korbin arrived on a floating conveyance, ushered along well beyond its normal speed capabilities, just in time to witness the aerial tag team finish off the last of the Urvalin that Daisy, Amazara, and their Ghalian friend hadn't already dealt with. The aftermath was astounding, and there were no survivors. When he stepped off, the three combatants were calmly waiting for him.

"What happened?" he asked, rushing to Amazara's side. "How did you—"

"They saved us," she replied, gesturing up to the sky.

"Most impressive," Pimbrak said calmly, but with eyes sparkling with curiosity. "Marvelous, indeed."

The dragon circled once, making sure the battlefield was

clear, then flapped its wings hard and settled down on the ground before them. It wasn't as large as Ara, but it did wear a similar harness. Clearly, it had come from the other galaxy.

"Hello, Korbin," Nixxus said. "I've been looking for you."

"How did you get here? The portal is unreachable."

"It was tricky, and the Urvalin were not terribly keen on my flying through the sun, but I managed."

"You did *what*?" he asked.

"It really wasn't as bad as it sounds," Nixxus replied.

Daisy shook her head in disbelief. "Not bad? It's the freaking *sun*."

"Well, yes. But this particular star emits a rather powerful magic that bolsters my kind's power, as you know. While it was incredibly draining flying through the burning plasma, I gained marginally more power than I expended."

"In the sun?" Daisy reiterated.

"Yes, in the sun. I thought I was clear on that. In any case, once I was free of the burning plasma and on this side of the portal, the burning sensation shifted to a restorative one. Of course, that was when I discovered the enemy has a foothold on this side of the portal as well. Imagine my surprise. Here I was, coming to bring magic users to help fight the Urvalin back home, only to discover an absolute infestation of them here as well."

It was mind-boggling, and Korbin might have required a few more minutes to process all of those details, but a pair of figures climbing down from atop the dragon captured his attention.

"Kara? Visanya?"

"Hey, Uncle Korbin," Kara said as she jumped down the last few feet. "Wasn't that amazing?"

Korbin rushed to her and pulled her into a tight embrace. "What were you thinking? You could have been killed. I'm supposed to protect you in your father's absence."

"And you are. But let's face it, I could have been killed any number of times already, and there's only so much you can do to protect me. The fight is here, and it affects all of us whether we want it to or not. And from what Nixxus says, we're going to need all the casters we can get."

The dragon nodded her head. "She is correct. The Urvalin have blockaded Earth with a technology-dampening field of some sort. No ships can pass into or out of the atmosphere. The same holds true for the moon as well as multiple pockets floating hidden in space. Only magic seems to cross it without issue."

"The adults can do the fighting," Korbin said. "No more flying like this, Kara. It's too dangerous in space."

"Nixxus protected us with her power."

"But what if it fails? You have no means to breathe in space, and you do not know the spells required to keep you alive."

Kara set her shoulders. "Then teach me."

"Out of the question. It takes years to master."

"Well, what if we had space suits? Like what they use in Daisy's realm?"

"We do not possess any such suits. And in any case, you are not flying a dragon, Karasalia, and that's final."

Kara crackled with frustrated energy.

"Kara, please, calm yourself," Amazara said. "We only want to keep you safe."

"*Nowhere* is safe, don't you get it? Our friends are in trouble. Arlo and Ripley? They need us, and Charlie and Ara aren't there to help."

This caught Daisy's attention faster than a slap. "Hang on. Where are they?"

Kara looked to the dragon. "Nixxus?"

"They were caught in an Urvalin trap," she replied. "A hidden portal that pulled them through to somewhere unknown. Thus far no one has managed to track them down."

"So, they could be *here*?" Daisy asked. "I mean, if the Urvalin are in both of our galaxies it makes sense, right?"

"No. Rika was nearly caught up in it as well, and she said when she was close she sensed that there was a complete lack of any of this galaxy's power. They are definitely not in this realm."

"Then maybe they'll make it back to Earth to help fight," Vee interjected.

"Or maybe they've been thrown so far out into space they may never get home," Korbin replied. "No, it is foolish to pin our hopes on *maybe*."

"So we should go help."

"Kara, I said no." He looked at Amazara. It was clear she felt the girl's frustration, and he understood why. "Look, even if we were to try to find some way to cross over, we must acquire intelligence first. A warrior does not fly into battle blind and without a proper plan."

"But how do we do that?" Kara asked.

"Actually, I may know a guy," Daisy said.

Korbin cocked an eyebrow. "A guy? You are not even from this galaxy. Who could you possibly know?"

Pimbrak, silently observing up until this point, cracked a little smile. "Oh, you would be surprised," he said. "Daisy has proven most resourceful, even in our realm."

"And while you do that, I have a few things I need to attend to," Nixxus said, stretching her wings.

"You're leaving?" Kara asked.

"Only for a brief while," she replied. "I would take you with, but as your uncle has pointed out, I do not have any space suits for you."

Kara couldn't be sure, but it looked an awful lot like the massive dragon just winked at her.

"How will you find us?" Korbin asked.

"I've got your scent now," Nixxus replied, lifting into the air. "I will return shortly."

She flapped her wings hard, streaking toward the edge of space, then in a flash, she was gone.

CHAPTER THIRTY-ONE

Charlie and the others stared at the images blown up large on Kip's display screens.

"Well, if this doesn't fit the bill, I don't know what does," Charlie said. "I mean, holy hell, right, guys?"

"I must admit, this is most impressive," Bawb agreed.

"Told ya so," Kip chirped, thrilled with the solar system he'd navigated them to. "Just like I promised."

Nakk's command ship had accompanied them on the quest, along with a pair of smaller attack ships as a security measure. The rest of their forces, however, were lying low in a safe system while the leaders searched for the possible key to their victory.

"Well done, Kip," Nakk transmitted from the bridge of his ship. "You never cease to amaze with your skill set."

"Aww, thanks, Nakk. I do my best."

"And your best is greatly appreciated, my friend. Now, which of these worlds might be our target?"

"Ah. Yeah. That. I haven't quite figured out that bit yet," Kip admitted.

It seemed that the reports of a highly volcanic world in this system had rather buried the lede. Yes, volcanoes were abundant here, but they were also spread across numerous planets, some hot, some cold, and only one of them in the Goldilocks Zone. Picking where to start their search seemed to be a no-brainer, but you never could say for certain.

Yes, in the millennia since the Vortaxis had been hidden from the world, it was entirely possible that other planets that had once been inhabitable had slid either closer or farther from the sun, rendering them anathema to life, but the odds were slim. And from what they could gather, only one of the planets had ever hosted any significant settlements, and that world was the one they were going to visit.

Lava flows crisscrossed the planet's surface, and the sky was a constant reddish-brown from frequent volcanic eruptions spewing ash and molten rock into the air. Other areas, however, were still lush pockets of verdant growth. It was in one such area that they would be making their touchdown.

"This is a strange world," Ara transmitted. "I feel a very limited flow of magic within the planet's core."

"What does that mean for us?" Dukaan asked. "Are we at risk?"

"No, you should be fine. But I am afraid I cannot risk entering the lava on this world. My power drains quickly in this galaxy, and I would use mine much faster than it would be replenished."

Charlie scanned the landing area, clocking the hot spots that now posed a new threat to his Zomoki friend. Their landing and search would be a little more dangerous for them all with this handicap.

"Ara, you should hang back, then," Charlie said. "Given what we're trying to do, it might even be for the best if they didn't see us arriving with you. This way we might be able to get information from the locals with only subterfuge instead of threats."

She thought it over a long moment then slowly nodded her

head. "I do not like leaving you without my support, but your logic is sound."

Charlie grinned. "Don't worry, Ara. I'll have Bob and Hunze right there with me, not to mention Nakk and Skohla."

"Hey, what about me?" Dukaan griped.

"We need you to stay with Kip, just in case," Charlie replied.

"I may be a pilot, but I can also fight, you know."

"We do. And that's why we want you helping cover our asses while we're out there. Anything goes wrong, it's all riding on you guys to come bail us out."

The pilot considered that a moment then slowly nodded his acceptance.

"We should consolidate our team aboard one ship. When we land, we shall then disembark, and have that ship pull back to a secondary landing site," Bawb said. "It will throw off locals who might see us exit the craft. The rest shall remain in orbit standing by."

"Good call," Charlie agreed. "Ara, you'll hang back as well, obviously. As for the rest of us, let's saddle up and get this show on the road."

It was one of Nakk's smaller ships that delivered the team to the surface. The craft was of this galaxy and far less likely to draw any attention. Even so, once its passengers had been discharged onto the landing site, the ship lifted off as planned and relocated to a location across the city.

Curious looks greeted the team as they walked the streets. Apparently, visitors were something of a novelty here. Given the nature of this planet and its system in general, they could see why.

The orange sun emitted nearly powerless rays that cast everything in a warm hue that Charlie felt was quite appropriate given their quest had taken them to a volcanic world. If only it possessed at least *some* magic, or Allpower, or whatever you wanted to call it, then it might be of use to them.

In any case, this imposing place, for all appearances, looked like the kind of spot someone would choose to hide a dangerous relic. Now they just had to find out where.

They hadn't determined what the Vortaxis actually looked like—that detail was lacking from the information they had pried from Lord Florin. But they had determined that, whatever it was, the Vortaxis was made of a great many pieces, yet was small enough to fit in a medium-sized chest. At least that's what they'd managed to glean from the translations.

That container had been referenced repeatedly across the legends, almost like the Ark of the Covenant. No one had looked inside, but they knew what the box contained. If things went according to plan, Charlie would be the first to lay eyes on it in thousands of years. Hopefully, minus the nasty face-melting bit.

"There," Bawb said, nodding casually to a tavern up ahead.

"There?"

"*There*," he affirmed, adopting a more wobbly, drunken gait.

"Aah," Charlie said. "I see Binsala the trader is making an appearance."

"All the better to loosen lips, my friend," the Wampeh replied with a slur. "Come."

He swerved off toward the tavern, Hunze in tow, suddenly giggling like a moron. A wonderfully distracting pair, they made. Nakk and Skohla looked at Charlie with more than a little confusion.

"It's a thing they do," he said. "Just go with it. We'll have all the info we need in no time."

Nakk and Skohla, rather than protesting or asking questions, went with the flow and relaxed their postures, remaining on guard but not overtly. They trusted Bawb implicitly by now. There would be no need for clarification. In fact, they almost seemed to enjoy sliding into a new character for a bit, and after all they'd been through, Charlie could understand why.

Binsala the trader entered the tavern with a flourish, ordering rounds of drinks for his thirsty companions as he flopped down into a seat. A seat with its back toward a wall and a view of the entire establishment, Charlie noted.

It only took a few minutes before the jovial man had made the acquaintance of the rough-and-ready-looking adventurers at the adjoining tables. Three of them had already been seated there when he stepped inside, which is why he had chosen his position in the first place. The others had entered a short time after, greeting their friends and taking seats on the other side of their table. There were nearly a dozen of them now, all of them men and women of action by the look of them.

All the better for Binsala. The more the merrier, he would say. Also, the more he could extract information from, playing them off one another as he did. Like a master musician, he would coax a tune from even the most reluctant of instruments, and this lot looked like the sort who would know something of lost treasures and legends on this world.

By the time night fell, Binsala had generously plied their new friends with ample food and drink and talk flowed like water. It seemed that their initial impressions were right. These rough people were indeed treasure hunters. Treasure and anything else they could make coin with. And, apparently, they'd long heard rumors of some valuable artifacts hidden on this world.

"Remarkable," Binsala said. "Were you successful in retrieving them?"

"No," a very hairy fellow called Borxx replied. "There're a buncha legends pointing to this place, but the main temples and catacombs're both confusing and dangerous."

"Dangerous?" Binsala asked, his slur thickened even further.

"Whatcha mean, dangerous? Seems worth it for riches, if thass what's really down there."

Borxx shrugged. "We've looked, but so far it's been a wash."

Bawb glanced at Charlie, staying in character. Charlie knew what Bawb was thinking.

"Hey," he said. "That sounds like a really good opportunity. I mean, we're not seasoned adventurers like you are, but maybe a fresh set of eyes could help."

"You want to see the catacombs?" Borxx asked.

"Yeah, what've you got to lose?"

"Coin, for one," a woman with thick scars knotting the red-brown skin of her arms said. Clearly, she'd been through some things in her day. What was anyone's guess.

"Igza has a point," Borxx said. "We've put in the work mapping things out already. Whadda you bring to the table?"

"Equipment," Charlie said, pulling a basic scanner from his pouch. "And strong backs to dig, if needed."

The scanner was like nothing Borxx or his people had ever seen, but this was a galaxy where technology was a normal thing, so while it got their attention, it didn't raise any sort of alarm. All it did was show them that this new group of arrivals might actually be able to be of use after all.

Charlie saw them considering the offer and smiled to himself.

"Tell ya what," he said. "How about we make a deal? Split whatever we find fifty-fifty?"

"Even split? But there are more of us."

"Yeah, but you said it yourself, you've tapped out. Let's work together for all our benefit."

Borxx shifted in his seat and looked to his friends for their opinions. From their posturing, it seemed they were interested in coin, but not work. Letting the newcomers sweat for it seemed a fair trade.

"Okay," he said. "It's a deal."

"Excellent!" Binsala exclaimed, flagging down the waiter. "Another round!"

The drinks arrived in short order, and Borxx raised his glass to the others. "To success."

"To success," they all replied.

"Drink up. We start in the morning."

CHAPTER THIRTY-TWO

The nights were long on this world, which, given the amount of alcohol imbibed the previous evening, was a good thing for Nakk and Skohla, not to mention Borxx and his team.

As for Bawb, Hunze, and Charlie, they had employed the handy little Ghalian spell that sent whatever passed their lips to another location, usually fifty or so meters away. In this galaxy, however, that spell had a few hiccups, forcing them to adjust on the fly.

By the end of the evening, the drunk passed out at the end of the bar would be most perplexed to find his travel bag soaked with alcohol and partially masticated food though no one was near him.

"You all ready?" Borxx asked as the group met at their designated location.

"We are, my friend!" Bawb replied in his almost-sober Binsala persona. "The breakfast at the little cafe around the corner was as excellent as you said."

It was also blatant price gouging, but that was to be expected. It was almost certain that Borxx got a kickback on any sucker he might send their way. But overpriced or not, Charlie had found the meal actually quite satisfying. And seeing how busy they were going to be today, he wanted to get all the sustenance he could before they began their undertaking.

"Good. I've had oneuh my friends lend me his mover. It'll make the approach a lot faster. And easier."

"Oh, is it rough terrain?" Hunze asked perkily, her utterly vapid tone kind of freaking Charlie out a little.

"Don't you worry yer pretty head," Borxx said. "You'll be fine."

Something about the way he barely contained his leer made Charlie want to smack the ever-loving hell out of him, but that wasn't the plan. And if Bawb was okay with letting it slide, he would be too.

"*This*?" Nakk asked when a rumbling heap of a vehicle lurched to a stop before them.

"A beaut, ain't she?" Borxx replied.

A beaut, she was not. In fact, looking at the cobbled-together bits holding the hover bus in one piece, Charlie was amazed it actually flew. Sure, it only got about a meter off the ground at its best, but even that was unexpected given its condition.

The team piled aboard, filling the empty seats. Of the dozen members of Borxx's team, only eight were present.

"Where are your friends?" Charlie asked.

"Ahh, sleeping it off," Borxx said. "They appreciate your generosity, Binsala, but mebbe overdid it."

Bawb laughed loudly and with good cheer. Underneath the external show of merriment Charlie and Bawb had little doubt those friends would be somewhere nearby.

"All right," Borxx said. "Hang on. We're gonna move!"

With a lurch, the vehicle got underway. Surprisingly, despite its appearance, the ride was relatively pleasant. Whether it was tech or Allpower providing the suspension, they moved along at a decent clip without too much jostling and bumping. It was, however, a longer ride than they'd initially expected.

After two hours they had traveled far into the wastelands they'd spotted from their reconnaissance flight. There were no settlements out here. No cities. Just the ruins of some old structures long abandoned to the shifting sands or jungle overgrowth. It was a shocking juxtaposition, but the wildly varying extremes of nature seemed fitting for such an unusual world.

Bawb had maintained his chatty trader routine for the first hour of the drive before seeming to nod off from the several drinks he'd had along the way. In reality, he was just observing and soaking up whatever information Borxx might let slip.

Their ride began to slow as they approached a transition point between the sand, rocky outcroppings, and a splash of jungle green pushing up from a patch of fecund volcanic soil.

"Whoa," Charlie gasped, pointing up ahead. "What is *that*?"

Borxx grinned. "*That*, mah friend, is where we're headin'."

Peeking up through both sand and vegetation was the shape of an elongated building with several pyramid-shaped protrusions along its length. Charlie had to admit, it certainly was impressive and on-par with the scale they would have expected of a massive hiding spot for a powerful artifact.

"It's so pretty!" Hunze cooed.

Charlie fought not to laugh. It was just so absurd hearing her speak like that. But she had learned from the best, and her disguise as a ditzy companion was utterly disarming.

"Just wait till you see the inside," Borxx replied with a wink. "Now *that*'ll be exciting."

"Ooh, I can't wait!"

"You won't have to. We'll be at the catacombs' entrance in just a minute."

"Where?" Charlie asked. "I don't see anything."

"Ya wouldn't. Like I said, we're not your ordinary crew of treasure seekers. But if ya look up there, just to the left where the vines meet the rock—"

Charlie had actually seen the hidden opening long before then, but they all had roles to play, and he was damn sure not going to let Bawb and Hunze have all the fun.

"Wait, I see it! That's amazing. How did you find it?"

"Easy, Charlie," Bawb said over their silent link. *"You're overdoing it a bit."*

"So says Binsala the trader," Charlie shot back. *"The drunk-by-breakfast trader, I might add."*

"All part of his charm, but a fair point. But do ease off a little. We do not wish to raise any suspicions."

Charlie suppressed a chuckle but did tone down his enthusiasm just a bit. A few minutes later they pulled to a stop.

"Everyone out!" Borxx called to the group. "Wake up, Binsala, we're here."

Bawb shook off his faux slumber and looked around with a groggy expression. "This is the place?"

"Yep. Now shake it off, break out that nifty tech of yours, and let's see if you can find anything of value."

Borxx gathered a sack of digging tools and led the way to the entrance. It was partly buried by the shifting sands, and vines had been pulled across the opening. It was that sloppy camouflage that had actually made it easier to spot, but Charlie wasn't about to mention that tidbit.

Nakk and Skohla shouldered their bags and followed the first group into the opening. Four of Borxx's people stayed above, waiting for the remainder of the group to head below.

"Ara, we're going to go underground. If our comms get blocked I'll need you to relay to Kip, okay?"

"Of course," she replied. *"Be safe."*

"We'll do our best."

"Good. I hope this goes smoothly. But should anyone threaten you, I am feeling a little peckish."

Charlie couldn't help but chuckle.

"What's so funny?" the scarred woman from the night before asked.

"Nothing. Just had an amusing thought is all," he replied as he pulled out the scanner from his bag. Her eyes locked on the device for a moment. "Shall we?"

She turned her attention to her associates then back to the entrance. "This way. Stay close. It is treacherous down below."

"Oh, please, allow me!" Bawb said with drunken bravado, pushing to the front of the group.

By the time they were all deep underground, he had become the defacto point man, and Charlie couldn't have been happier. Bawb, or Binsala if you preferred, was a master of his craft, and his keen eyes were already picking out the somewhat obvious traps and snares well before they reached them.

Of course, he was doing it under the guise of a moderately inebriated buffoon, but even the foolish have skills, and much to Borxx and his people's surprise, it seemed Binsala's gift was evading traps.

"Another one!" Binsala called out, deftly deactivating a tripwire trap. "Whoever built this place sure was paranoid."

"It's partly why we haven't made much progress in here," Borxx said. "You've got a real knack for this sort of thing."

"Thanks, but I'm just lucky."

"You are so not just lucky," Charlie said over their silent link.

"And these are not ancient traps," Bawb replied. *"Be sharp and ready."*

"I've already clocked three of his buddies up ahead in the shadows," Charlie noted.

"Four, actually, though I assume there may be even more farther in."

"So, this is all just a shakedown."

"It would look that way. There are faint traces of prior scuffles. My guess is Borxx and his people have been robbing treasure hunters

blind for some time. It only stands to reason that others have deciphered the legends and come to this very volcanic world."

"Yep. So now what?"

"Now we prepare for a fight."

Bawb had only just made that comment when several large stones fell from the wall, crashing down right in front of them, separating Nakk, Skohla, and Hunze from Bawb and Charlie. A clever ruse, in most instances, but today this little diversion would not have the results intended.

Borxx turned to Binsala and Charlie, a very small pistol in his hand. Despite its size, they both knew, a small gun could kill you just as easily as a large one.

"What's going on?" Bawb asked as he and Charlie did a quick count of their adversary.

"I'm afraid I'm gonna need you to give me that scanner," Borxx replied, his team encircling the two men. "And all the rest of your gear too."

Charlie and Bawb knew a similar discussion was taking place on the other side of the tumbled rocks. And the outcome would be the same.

"Sorry," Bawb said, his slur gone and his posture straightened. "That is not going to happen."

Borxx looked at the very outnumbered men and chuckled. "I don't want to hurt you, but if you make me—"

"Oh, dude," Charlie said with an amused grin. "You don't know what you just stepped in."

The bandit was a bit taken aback by the reaction, but only for a moment. "Take them," he ordered.

His people swarmed Charlie and Bawb. The two men hadn't even drawn a weapon. It would be an easy score. Or so they thought. The reality was they wanted the attackers to move in close, overconfident. And Borxx's men seemed happy to oblige.

Bawb moved in a flash to his left while Charlie spun to the right, the two working in tandem as they'd trained for so long.

Elbows and knees flew, landing devastating blows on the would-be robbers. Borxx managed to get a single shot off before Bawb disarmed him with a well-thrown dagger.

The bandit shrieked in surprise at the blade jutting out of his forearm, then paled at the sight of not one, but *all* of his team lying unconscious on the ground. The drunken trader and his fool friend hadn't even broken a sweat.

Borxx looked to the rubble for help, and a sense of relief washed over him as the stones shifted and fell aside. That quickly became shock and despair when the ditzy golden-haired woman and her companions scrambled over the debris.

"Any problems?" Bawb asked.

"None, love. There were a few of this one's people hiding nearby, but I know you already saw them."

"Of course. I do hope you were able to spare their lives."

"All but one," Hunze replied. "I am afraid Igza proved unwilling to accept defeat. A shame. She had some skill."

Bawb nodded then turned to Borxx. He walked to the cowering man and leaned close, then abruptly yanked his dagger from his arm. Borxx dropped to his knees, but Bawb then did something unexpected. He cast a healing spell on the man's arm. Borxx was a new race for the outsiders, but the magic worked nonetheless, and in a moment the bleeding stopped.

"Why would ya do that?" the healed man asked.

"Because, while I do not enjoy having my time wasted, I can appreciate the racket you have going on here. I assume you set up shop to take advantage of those seeking the Vortaxis?"

"Well, yeah. Most are just treasure hunters, though."

"As I thought. And I also assume there is no actual trace of the artifact, nor of those who possessed it?" he asked, leaning in closer with a terrifyingly calm stare. "And, Borxx, do not lie to me. I will know."

"N-no. Nothing about anything like that," he replied.

Bawb seemed satisfied with the answer. "Very well. We shall

leave your conveyance for you," he said. "And for future reference, you should disguise your traps with aged parts. The newness of them stands out to any with a modicum of skill."

"Kip, you copy? We need a pickup," Charlie transmitted.

"Gotcha," the ship replied. "I'll burn hard and be there in sixty seconds."

"Don't draw attention to yourself. Take your time. We're fine. Plus, it'll take a bit to get to the surface again."

"Copy that," Kip replied. "See y'all soon."

Charlie keyed off his comms. "Okay, good to go."

With that his team trudged back the way they had come, heading toward the surface. Only once they were safely aboard Kip and heading back into space did Nakk pose the question that had been on his mind.

"Why let them live?" he asked.

Bawb turned to Charlie.

"Yeah, I've got this," he said. "So, the thing is, sure, we could have taken them out, but if the Urvalin are searching for this thing too, we'll be better served having a diversion in place."

"Ah, I see," Nakk said.

"And Bob just gave them a few pointers on how to better run their scam. So, if we're lucky, Borxx and his gaggle will make the Urvalin's day a bit worse."

"Logical," Nakk agreed. "But how do we know they'll even go to that system?"

Charlie grinned wide. "Oh, that's easy. We're going to leak its location, as well as a juicy rumor that we plan to go there."

"And in the meantime?"

"For now, we continue our search elsewhere," Charlie replied. "Speaking of which, it's time to dig deeper into those star charts, Kip. Find us a better option."

CHAPTER THIRTY-THREE

Nixxus had taken her leave of Korbin and the others and flown to a particular sun Ara had shown her during her and Gazz's tour of the galaxy. It was one of Ara's little secret places of refuge —a solar system uninhabited by people yet possessing a sun of exceptional power.

A place to recharge one's battery, so to speak. And Nixxus would need every bit of power she could manage with what she had in mind.

It had been a wonderfully restorative break, and her scales shone bright and healthy for it, her power brimming over. But the time had finally come. She had a plan, and that plan required immediate action.

Nixxus was going to fly home.

Of course, first she would have to avoid the Urvalin ships posted at the edges of the plasma field spewing out from the portal. That little trick would require a bit more planning than she was used to. She needed to avoid a fight if at all possible, because, even as the sun's rays would strengthen her, a fight with the Urvalin fleet would very possibly siphon off enough of her power that she might not survive the flight home.

She'd nearly burned up accessing the portal once already. She did *not* want a repeat of that experience.

Plus, if she was successful in reaching the portal, there were still the Urvalin on the other side to deal with once through. But that was something she would just have to deal with when she arrived. Without any intelligence there was simply no other option.

"Time to go," she said to herself as she called up her magic and prepared to jump close to the portal.

The idea was to arrive close, but not right on top of the portal. If she was off by even a little bit she might accidentally exit her jump *within* the flaming plasma, and until she had the right spells locked in place protecting her from that, she would need to use all of her magic to defend from the Urvalin.

In any case, there was no reason to wait any longer.

Nixxus jumped, arriving a fair distance from the plume of the sun's fire shooting through the portal. As a living object and not a ship, she was less likely to be noticed so long as she kept her power use to a minimum as she flew closer to the edge of the enemy fleet. By the time the Urvalin noticed her, hopefully she would be past them and it would be too late to stop her.

Hopefully.

The floating field of shattered asteroids and ships that had been melted to slag drifted in the general vicinity of the portal. It was among those that Nixxus would fly, using them for cover, moving closer to her starting point. The point of no return.

It would be difficult—there were at least a dozen Urvalin craft spread out around the edge of the deadly plasma field. Not all, she noted, were facing outward. Apparently, her little crossover adventure had given them something new to think about. The possibility, no matter how slight, that someone might find a way to use the portal despite its being submerged into the sun.

It worried them, and that was a good thing. The Urvalin

were uneasy, and that meant they might slip up and make mistakes. But for the moment it was an inconvenience, and she had work to do.

It took a solid hour of drifting like debris and hiding among the rocks and ruins before Nixxus finally arrived close enough to cast her protective spells specifically for the sun's power and make a run for it. She'd have to keep her other defensive casting to a minimum, and that was disconcerting, to say the least. Hopefully, the harness's AI would give her the added protection she needed.

"Just don't get shot," she reminded herself as she gathered up her magic. "Through the portal then jump clear of the area and make a cautious return to Earth." Beyond that, she would just figure it out as whatever new obstacles there might be came up.

The dragon focused on a point just outside the sun's plasma for her arrival. Close enough to allow a quick entry into the portal but far enough to let her confirm her shielding spells were properly cast. As for the Urvalin, she would have to hope they were lax in their preparations and she could get through before they had a chance to react.

As ready as she would ever be, Nixxus jumped.

She arrived right where she intended, immediately casting the protective spells even as the sun's power began to feed her more of its powerful magic. She didn't hesitate, however, but pushed forward as fast as she was able, diving into the sun's flames before the startled Urvalin ships had the opportunity to fire a single shot.

The pain of the burning plasma was minimal this time as she flew into the sun. Having her magic topped off to the max had given her enough of a cushion to easily protect herself from damage. It was still hot—*very* hot—but she would be unscathed. If she was to take a passenger, however, she wasn't so sure she could protect them. At least, not without a space suit. And, she feared, they would need an additional source of power.

Fortunately, she had learned about the novel device called a konus. If she could just learn to draw power from one, then there shouldn't be an issue carrying Kara with her at all. And that was the ultimate plan. Find a way for the young caster to join her on the trip to Earth to bolster the magical caster presence in her own galaxy.

To help defeat the Urvalin.

But first things first. For now, she would have to make it to Earth.

The blazing dragon exited the portal and burst out from within the sun like a xenomorph offspring, plasma flying as she flew clear of the startled Urvalin ships floating quietly in the area. They were more prepared for a fight than the others had been and managed to fire multiple weapons systems at her, magical and otherwise, but Nixxus was already spinning clear of their targeting and lining up for her next jump.

A moment later, she was gone.

She arrived at the edge of the rings of Saturn, quickly tucking into them for cover. It was a safe space, at least according to the mapping data she'd had when she first crossed to the other side, and a good one to get her bearings before approaching Earth. So far as she could tell the path was clear.

At least, she hoped so.

If the Urvalin had laid more invisible minefields she'd just find out the hard way, blow out her harness, and have to survive without the technological goodies the AIs had provided her. But the flight to Earth's atmosphere was quick and uneventful. Almost anticlimactic after her ordeal through the sun.

Nixxus powered off the minor AI and all of the electronic gear they'd given her. Once it was fully off, she dove past the energy-dampening micro-sats and into the fresh air of planet Earth.

It was there the Urvalin were waiting for her.

Pulse blasts and waves of magic peppered the sky all around her, sending her into an abrupt tumble.

"Damnable pests!" she grumbled, spewing a stream of flame at the nearest ship while keying the power-on sequence for her harness AI.

It would take a minute for it to wake up and activate her tech shielding and weapons, but if the fight was still underway by then, she'd sure as hell need them.

Another flurry of spells rocked her, but her focus was on magical defenses at the moment, and she negated their power with ease. Had it been pulse blasts she might not have been so lucky.

Nixxus dove into a corkscrew, blasting magical fire as she went. One of the Urvalin ships succumbed to the counterattack, pulling away to a safe distance to deal with their damage. It seemed a logical plan, and one that would work quite well to let them regroup, when the craft abruptly exploded, sending a shower of burning debris toward the ground.

"Hey, Nixxus!" Marty called out over his external comms as he swooped past her, railguns and pulse cannons opened up wide on the Urvalin.

Three other ships were with him and engaged the suddenly outmatched welcome party with great violence. The Urvalin attempted to flee and regroup, the newcomers to the fight pursuing tenaciously.

"Uncle Cal says welcome home," Arlo's voice called out over comms. "Are your systems still working, or do I need to use the external speakers?"

"My communications devices appear to be functional," she replied.

"Sweet. Are the casters close behind? Did you find Korbin?"

"I did, but they are not able to cross over even if the portal was clear of the sun. The Urvalin have launched a full-scale invasion on the other side of the portal as well. *Both* of our galaxies are under attack."

Arlo and Marty relayed the information to Cal, all of them shocked at the news.

"Hey, he wants you to head to the fabrication lab," Marty said. "You know the one."

"I do," Nixxus replied. "I am glad to see you are well, my friends."

"As well as we can be, all things considered," Arlo replied. "Okay, we're gonna help chase down those Urvalin before they get reinforcements. Welcome home, Nixxus."

With that, the ship and its young pilot zipped off in pursuit of the others.

"Welcome home, indeed."

Nixxus shifted course, making a bee-line for the facility that had outfitted her with her current harness. She arrived a short time later, her flight unnoted so far as her harness scanners could discern.

"I am glad you are safe," Cal said once she was safely inside. ***"But what is this about the Urvalin having forces in the other galaxy?"***

"They've invaded. And more than that, they are taking out the Council of Twenty and any other powerful casters. It's a mess. Korbin and Daisy and the others are doing all they can to hinder them."

"Daisy's there?" Habby asked. "Oh, I'm glad she's safe."

"Safe is relative," Cal noted. ***"And we cannot reinforce them, nor can they help us."***

Nixxus shook her head. "About that. I have made two successful crossings and learned quite a lot. With enough magic, and possibly the additional power of a konus to ease the transit, I believe my kind can likely carry a caster through, though it will still be risky. They will be protected by our power, but the slightest mishap could result in harm."

"Unless they have a reinforced protective suit," Cal mused.

"I was thinking the same thing," she replied.

"Habby, how is the Artemis project coming along?"

"Great, actually. Almost all of the components have passed the final stress tests."

"It will be your finest work, my friend. And what's the status of the new harness configurations?"

"Ready to go. All we need is a dragon to fit them to."

"And it would seem you have one," Cal said with a low chuckle.

Nixxus felt a surge of hope. "A new harness?"

"Yeah. I actually made a few of them," Habby said with glee. "Once I get started fabricating, I sometimes get carried away."

The dragon mused over his words a long moment. "Then I will bring you another customer," she finally said. "Prepare to outfit *two* of us."

CHAPTER THIRTY-FOUR

"Target is locked," Sergeant Franklin silently transmitted. "Teams one and Three have reached their objectives. Team Two is standing by to provide cover fire if necessary."

"Excellent," Cal replied. ***"Join your people and update me when it is done."***

The cyborg commando keyed his internal comms. "Copy that." He then quickly unplugged from the secret hardline link Cal had him install around the region not so long ago for a just-in-case situation. This was definitely one such moment.

George signaled to his team and set out, the group quickly fanning wide to better cover a larger area as they moved toward the rendezvous point. Of course, these were hardened combat units, so meeting up with the others would entail far more than just heading out and arriving at the correct coordinates. George and his team would be kicking Urvalin ass along the way, and in large quantities if they had their druthers.

After getting Daisy's and Sarah's families settled into the reconstructed cavern at NORAD, George and his men had begun running sneak-and-peek ops with increasing frequency, gauging Urvalin numbers, noting their positions and strategy, and logging every last detail, from the armor they wore to every nut and bolt they could see on the ships they piloted.

With that data, Cal had quietly conferred with the other AIs still connected in his network and had come up with a plan. This was clearly an invasion of occupation, not eradication. The Urvalin wanted to conquer and rule this world, and that meant the invaders could not simply nuke the site from orbit to deal with their enemies.

They needed this world clean and intact, it seemed, and that left an opportunity.

"Triggers ready," Team One reported.

"Copy that. Stand by," Sergeant Franklin replied. "Three, status?"

"Unable to achieve close contact with their ship," the team leader replied.

"Alternate targets?"

"You know it, Sarge. Their supply depot security was a joke. We penetrated easily. They didn't see a thing. We hid charges in a whole variety of containers. I only saw one loaded onto a ship, but if we give it long enough, I'm confident others will drop in to resupply. Just a matter of time before we have more than the original targets in our kill zone."

George smiled. This was an instance of taking a negative and turning it into a positive, something he'd discussed with Charlie and Bawb on more than one occasion and had since relayed to his young friends. Fortunately, Arlo and Ripley seemed to have taken the lessons to heart, to his delight.

"Sometimes an enormous difficulty actually makes things easy," he had told them. "When things go to shit and your original plan is simply not an option, other avenues present themselves. A wise soldier knows when to pivot and make the most of it."

That was precisely what Team Three had just done, and it seemed likely it would be far more effective than the original plan of ambushing just a few Urvalin ships and blowing them to hell. If more of them loaded up with explosive-laden cargo, they could, in theory, take down even more ships in different locations without a direct engagement.

It was asymmetric warfare. The sort of thing that could confuse an enemy and force them into making mistakes. Costly mistakes that could then cascade into a catastrophic failure within their command system. And if that happened, Earth's resistance fighters would be ready to seize the opportunity and answer the call.

"It's not going to make too big a dent in the overall Urvalin forces, Sarge," Franklin's right hand said as the data came in. "Should make for a pretty fireworks show, though."

"You know I'm all about blowing shit up," George replied. "But more than that, if we pull this off it'll sure as hell get the Urvalin's attention. And if we're lucky it might force them to slow their roll and reassess their plans down here. We need a little breathing room. Rika and the dragon can only do so much to help our people fight them off."

"What we really need is more people with a better grasp of magic."

"Cal's working on that," George replied. "Let's hope he can pull it off sooner than later. Now, come on. We've got mayhem to wreak."

Sergeant George Franklin was the only cyborg in Cal's very, very small circle of AI confidants. The information that wasn't shared with pretty much anyone, not for lack of trust, but because you couldn't be forced to leak information you simply did not have.

He was aware of something potentially game-changing in the works, but as was so often the case with leaders, he was not at liberty to reveal what he knew to his men. But if all went as planned, they'd find out for themselves firsthand soon enough.

In the meantime, Orgalius was working with Rika, throwing a wrench in Urvalin operations across the globe, the pair popping up unannounced and laying waste to the enemy forces before quickly pulling back, leaving the invaders without an enemy to fight back against. But they were not alone.

More dragons had come to help the cause since the engagement began, and among them was Gazz, the ochre-brown male who had traveled to the other galaxy with Ara and Nixxus not long ago at all.

It was Gazz whom Nixxus sought out upon her return.

The dragon was flying circles around an Urvalin transport ship, peppering it and its support craft with blasts of magical flame while a handful of Earth ships swarmed the larger alien vessels.

It was a surprisingly even fight, now that the dragon's magic was involved. Forced to defend against both magic as well as tech, the Urvalin had lost their advantage even if they were able to use their triumvirate of casters. Or, at least it *seemed* like an even fight.

A blast of powerful magic rained down from above as a large Urvalin battle craft joined the fray, its casters targeting the unsuspecting resistance fighters below. It was a classic tactical slipup, focusing on the ships around them and not the new arrival coming in quietly from above.

Had they been flying with an AI in their midst, perhaps it would have been able to multi-task mid-battle and notice the incoming craft. But AIs were in short supply, and most had been either neutralized or forced into hiding. It was a weakness the Urvalin had noted and were adapting to exploit.

"More from above!" one of the ships transmitted as its shields were pummeled by the strange Allpower spells. "It's too powerful! We're not going to be able to hold this one off."

"Stick with your target," another ship replied. "We've got them on the ropes. Land some damage before peeling off."

Another blast shook the craft. "I don't think we can withstand another direct hit."

Gazz saw what was happening and shifted his flight path, putting himself between the newcomer and his friends. Being a magical creature, his casting was able to block the non-tech assault. He was still thrown violently from the impact, but his shielding spells held. He was, however, unable to provide cover to the ships farther below while engaged with the one above.

It was a quandary. Which direction to fly and whom to fight?

Out of nowhere a flash of magical flame blasted out in tandem with a shower of railgun sabots, tearing into the Urvalin craft, the flames weakening the defenses enough for a few rounds to make it through. The supersonic projectiles smashed holes in the Urvalin battleship, sending it spiraling off course.

"Nixxus!" Gazz exclaimed as his friend swooped in from above.

The Urvalin, overconfident in their ambush, had just fallen victim to the same ploy they had employed themselves. The hunter was now the hunted, and they were outmatched.

The other Urvalin ships immediately disengaged, turning sharply and running away at maximum speed. The lead craft had read the writing on the wall, and the message was, "*We're going to kick all of your asses*."

Gazz flew to his friend, thankful she'd arrived when she did.

"Look at you! You are radiant."

"This sun's energy does wonders, you know," she replied.

Her friend's gaze shifted to the brand-new harness she wore. The design was elegant, and the weapons melded into its sleek lines were impressive in their power. "Where did you get this new toy?" he asked.

Nixxus grinned. "Our friend Cal. He has some very unusual associates, one of whom fabricated this for me."

"Nice. *Very* nice."

"I thought you would approve," she said with a chuckle. "Would you like one?"

"One what? A device like that?"

"That was the gist of the question."

Gazz sized her up. Nixxus seemed a little different than when they'd last seen one another. Engaged. Confident. Full of energy, and not just the magical variety.

"What's going on, Nixxus?" he asked. "What's the catch?"

"No catch, my friend. Just a fantastic mission, should you choose to accept it."

"A mission?"

She nodded. "You said you couldn't wait to return to the magical galaxy."

"That I did. It's an amazing place, and our visit with Ara was too short for my taste."

"Well, then. This is your lucky day," Nixxus replied. "But first, let's get you to see Habby."

"What's a *Habby*?"

"You'll see," she said. "And you'll love it."

CHAPTER THIRTY-FIVE

The trio of Urvalin fast raiders whipped through the skies above the planet Horga, the trading outpost's lush forests a deep green far below. Compared to the last world they'd been forced to fight their enemy at, this was a picnic.

"Readings?" Tamara asked as she angled the commandeered ship down into the atmosphere.

"It's here, all right," Shelley replied. "Only some trace drive residue, but now that we know what we're looking for, I'm pretty damn sure they're down there."

Tamara looked over the displays of the ground below. The stolen craft had taken a little bit of work to achieve a degree of comfort with its systems, but once the basics of Urvalin tech and Allpower had been figured out, the rest had been a matter of simple trial and error.

Fortunately, no one had been harmed during the weapons systems tests, and the other functions of the ship were far less dangerous. Within a few days Tamara and Shelley were operating as a highly functional team aboard the alien craft.

Naturally, they'd repainted it to their liking. This was a beat-up and patched Urvalin raider, after all. There would be no sneaking in under the guise of being part of the enemy fleet. They decided instead to opt for the in-your-face option.

Part of that was the paint job. The other part was the more literal take on the saying. Namely, the trying to shoot them in the face bit.

The other two ships were flown by crack pilots from Nakk's team of rebels, each of them itching for a fight and perfectly happy to take out their years of pent-up aggression on any Urvalin whose path they might cross.

Lucky for them, this was a chase, disable, and capture—if possible—mission. With the Urvalin proclivity for death before capture antics, this more often than not led to only achieving the first two goals before things took a fatal turn.

Of the fleeing ships they were pursuing, the more damaged of the two had been caught orbiting a small moon several systems ago. The Urvalin captain had set down inside a lunar cavern just below the surface to make repairs. It had almost worked as a hiding spot, but Shelley proved something of a whiz at cutting through white noise and honing in on a tangible signal.

The Urvalin lifted off at once, hurtling into a ferocious dogfight at a moment's notice. But as aggressive as they were, and in spite of their powerful casters and weapons, this ship wasn't operating at full capacity. The battle and pursuit had taken them across two moons and one planet before they finally cornered the damaged ship.

"I have a shot," Marxin transmitted. "Hit them with an Allpower attack in five. We'll fire directly after."

"Watch for it," their friends in the accompanying ship replied. "Casting."

The magic flew true, forcing the Urvalin to shift defenses to largely magical ones.

"Firing," Marxin said, letting loose with his ship's pulse cannons.

A blast of power slammed into the reduced shielding of the enemy ship, ripping their defenses to pieces along with the vessel contained within.

"Damn, no survivors in that mess," Marxin grumbled as they swooped through the wreckage.

"Gee, ya think?" Tamara replied. "Maybe turn down the cannons a little next time, huh? We could have used those parts."

"And intel from the crew."

"Sure, that too," she said, though she really had no interest in any more Urvalin loyalists.

They had proven themselves fanatical in their devotion to their cause, and as a result, getting anyone to talk had thus far been impossible. Tamara and Shelley had come to the conclusion that it actually made things easier that way. Less uncooperative mouths to feed and less time wasted talking to someone who clearly wouldn't break.

But there was still another ship out there, and after a fair bit of searching, it looked like they'd just tracked it down on the unlikely world.

"There!" Shelley called out, pointing to the small dot on the display. "They tried to tuck under those trees."

"I see 'em," Tamara said, banking the ship hard. "Marxin, you hear that?"

"We see them. Activating targeting."

"Wait," Shelley interrupted. "Don't shoot them."

"They're Urvalin."

"Yeah, I know. But they're clearly hurt if they set down for repairs. If they could have jumped or warped they would have."

"Your point being?"

"My point is there's a lot of gear and parts we could salvage from that ship. Hell, we might even be able to fly it with a little TLC."

"*TLC*?"

"She means if we fix it, Marxin," Tamara clarified. "Shelley wants to add their ship to our little attack wing."

"We need all the ships we can get," Shelley added.

"And the Urvalin crewing it? We cannot let them flee."

Marxin, for all of his aggressive bravado, was right, and the two women from Earth knew it.

"We'll handle them," Tamara said after a long pause. "Shel, you up for a little stroll?"

Shelley flexed her cybernetic arms, spinning the hands at the wrists as she assessed her combat readiness. "Oh, yeah. I think we're good to go."

While Tamara's one replacement arm was bleeding-edge tech, Shelley's were a bit older, though equally impressive. With three ceramisteel arms between the two of them, the pair made an imposing team. And that wasn't even taking into account their years upon years of combat experience and additional neuro-stim training.

In short, the degree of sheer badassery between them could put most squads to shame. And they were about to go hunting.

"There," Shelley said. "The rocky outcropping. It'll provide a good spot to park and should keep our landing quiet."

"I see it. Taking us in," Tamara replied. "Marxin, you guys keep an eye from high above. Don't let them see you, but if they manage to get off the ground before we can stop them, feel free to take them out."

"With pleasure," he said with an almost audible grin.

In Marxin's eyes, the only good Urvalin was a dead one, and in as painful a way as possible if he had any say in it. After so many years stranded away from his family, the two newcomers couldn't really blame him.

"Okay, we're going in. Keep an eye out," Tamara transmitted, then shifted her attention to the landing.

The craft had only come to a stop and powered down for a few seconds when the two women leapt from the open hatch, armed to the teeth and ready to bear. They quickly slid into formation, covering each other with the ease of constant training as they moved out into the overgrowth.

Tamara took point, her pulse rifle snug against her shoulder, the konus on her opposite wrist already providing a low-level magical defense. She'd taken to using magic quite well, all things considered, and it was now a standard part of her combat kit. Shelley was the same in that regard, adapting to the novel power with curiosity and eventual glee once she saw just what it could do.

Magic? The soldiers were using magic now? Why the hell not, she mused.

Tamara put up her hand. Both women dropped to a crouch. There were sounds up ahead, and given the proximity of the Urvalin ship, it was highly likely it was its crew who were making noise. Apparently, they'd successfully landed unseen. That meant if they were lucky most, if not all, of the Urvalin would be outside their ship helping effect repairs.

The two hunters split up, moving to opposite flanking positions as they approached their targets.

A blur flashed out of the trees, a bright blade swinging straight at Shelley's head. She spun and raised her arm, the metal catching the massive knife mid-swing with a loud clang. Her hand rotated a quick one hundred eighty degrees, reversing its position on her arm as it grabbed the attacker's wrist and squeezed.

The Urvalin, to his credit, did not scream when his wrist broke, but merely shuddered slightly even as he cast a killing spell. Shelley's other arm flashed into position in front of her, the konus blunting the impact and the arm absorbing the remainder of the spell.

The minor AI processor that helped the arm function glitched from the power, falling silent before entering a forced reboot mode, but Shelley didn't need it to deal with this attacker. She kicked hard, landing a boot square in his groin. No amount of training could shrug off a blow like that, and the man crumpled to the ground.

"Sonofa—" she grumbled just as all hell broke loose around her. "Shit, we're compromised!"

"Ya think?" Tamara shouted back, her words punctuating the roar of her pulse rifle as she unloaded on the enemy. Judging by the sound of the blasts, she'd turned it up to maximum.

They were no longer on the offensive, and if the Urvalin were trying to turn the tables then there was no reason to pull any punches.

The two women moved fast, making sure they positioned themselves in such a way as to not accidentally catch each other with their own fire. Then they opened up with everything they had.

The trees and bushes around them burst apart from the barrage even as defensive Allpower spells flew back at them, hoping to blunt the attack. But the Urvalin were casting out of desperation. They were ready to pivot into an aggressive stance in an instant, but they had not been prepared for an adversary as well armed and aggressive as this.

Tamara moved forward, pressing the attack. There were seven Urvalin, it seemed. The entire crew of their ship, at least if they were crewed like other fast raiders. That meant the likelihood of unwanted surprise guests was low. It also meant she could get dirty.

The nearest Urvalin trooper fired his pulse pistol at her, but the minor shielding in her cybernetic arm flashed to life, the little upgrade from Cal fanning out and providing a dampening field. The shots still hurt, but they were nowhere near lethal.

The metal fist that punched the man square in the throat, however, was. He dropped in a gagging heap, multiple vital bits irreparably crushed, but she had already moved on, ready for the next adversary, rifle firing and fist swinging.

Shelley moved in parallel, closing the gap between them, creating a kill box for the remaining Urvalin. This was a fast raider crew, not a team of shock troops, and while they may have been trained in combat, as were all Urvalin, wielding death from above was their style. Ground fighting, and especially hand-to-hand, was not their strong suit.

That would be their demise.

Pulse fire raged through the trees, shattering them and sending wooden shrapnel flying as the area quickly morphed from a botanical wonderland to a smoldering clearing. A clearing strewn with the dead and dying. Tamara and Shelley stopped firing as they reached one another and surveyed the area.

The Urvalin had lost, and horribly at that.

"Well, that didn't go exactly as planned," Tamara said.

"Yeah. Some sonofabitch came at me with a knife. Look, he even scratched my arm!"

Tamara looked at the minuscule scuff on the ceramisteel limb and chuckled. "Yeah, he really got you good, Shel."

"Shut up. He could have killed me."

"But he didn't."

"No. I gave him a good shot to the nuts for his troubles."

Tamara burst out in laughter. "Of course you did." Movement nearby caught her eye. Clearly, this was the man Shelley had spoken of judging by the way he slowly rose, clutching his groin. Ironically, with all of the fighting, being prone on the ground was the only thing that had saved him.

"Hey, you! Yeah, you. Put your hands up!" she called out.

The man rose to his feet defiantly and uttered a single word. It wasn't a powerful spell, but it was enough. He collapsed to the ground, dead, taking whatever secrets he may have possessed with him.

"Aww, man. Dammit!" Shelley blurted.

Tamara patted her on the shoulder. "Sorry. I guess we won't be getting any intel from him."

"It's not that. I just wanted to kill the little shit myself," Shelly grumbled.

Tamara's laughs echoed through the smoke-filled air. "You crack me up, you know that?"

Shelley shrugged and tried to maintain her poker face, but a little grin tugged at the corners of her lips.

"Come on," Tamara said. "At least we've still got a ship to salvage."

CHAPTER THIRTY-SIX

Charlie was not a big fan of water planets. Not that he couldn't swim, or had an aversion to large bodies of water, but because the magic required to maneuver under the sea was tricky, even for casters as powerful as himself and his friends.

And here in a new galaxy where not all of their spells worked exactly as planned? It made for a disconcerting bit of uncertainty. Especially when the crushing weight of thousands of tons of sea water was ready to smash down on their heads at the slightest misstep.

But a water planet was their destination, and there was no way around it.

They had visited several interesting systems already, driven to them by various interpretations of the cryptic words that allegedly would lead them to the Vortaxis. Volcanic was a key. The description of '*the flow, the flame, sleeping secure. The Vortaxis among the source most pure*' was a bit of a jumble, and the language not exactly standard. However, flowing flame could only mean one thing. An eruption or lava flow.

But in the days since they'd begun their search, other aspects of the trove of information began to also shape their quest. Most notably was the realization that the words *flow* and *flame* came from very ancient times and had likely been translated from a translation of a translation, and even then, that may very well have been a translation as well.

There *could* be a flow without a literal flame, Ara had noted. She had experienced them a few times in her youth, though she had not sought out an ocean with thermal jets in quite some time. But what if the volcano they had been looking for was actually another flow altogether? What if it was an underwater thermal geyser?

It made sense, especially after what Ara had experienced with a far different planet's lava core not too long ago. There was Allpower deep within some worlds, and if that power was superheating water, a great deal of that potential could transfer to the liquid.

In short, the "source most pure" could be water-based, not lava.

"We will have to be careful," Ara noted as they approached the largely liquid-covered world. "I can smell the magic of this planet. The Allpower."

"So?" Charlie said. "That's great. It means this could be the place."

"Yes, but it will also make a search dangerous. The core's power is definitely mixed with the water, and there is no telling what such a union might have done to the local sea life because of it."

"You're saying there are sea monsters?" Charlie joked with a groan. "Seriously? Guys? Am I the only one who thinks this is some serious bull—"

"The Wise One is correct," Bawb calmly stated. "I have experienced one such creature firsthand many years ago."

"Wait, seriously?"

"Yes. A non-terrestrial guardian of a target that was unfortunately not reported in any intelligence."

"And? What happened?"

Bawb cocked his head slightly at the memory. "Let us just say it was fortunate the beast contained enough magic for me to heal myself when I had finally bested it." A sour look flashed across his face. "I would note, the taste was *not* pleasant."

"Okay, so nasty-tasting monsters of the deep. That's just great."

"I do not possess the Allpower skills for my ship to travel underwater at any significant depth," Nakk transmitted to the others. "None of us do. As Charlie pointed out when we undertook this leg of our quest, it is a very particular bit of casting skill that we simply do not have. But we will ensure it is safe for you upon the surface when you return."

Charlie wasn't terribly thrilled about being shorthanded when they submerged, but it was looking like he and Ara would be doing the heavy lifting for the team. A little support would have been nice.

Kip could manage to dive maybe a few hundred feet, but that was only because of the retrofitting he received back on Earth. Most spacefaring ships were designed to withstand the pressure difference of a vacuum, keeping the interior habitable against the pulling forces trying to suck the air out. Underwater, however, the pressures were the opposite, with the water attempting to force its way inside the craft at any weak point.

Thirty-three feet wasn't a big deal. One atmosphere of depth. But each subsequent increment added to that amount. One hundred feet was a little over three atmospheres of pressure. And to visit the deep volcanic regions where the Vortaxis would likely be hidden required the ability to withstand incredible forces. Something that no spaceship could endure.

Ara, on the other hand, along with Charlie's help, could handle it, but not for long even with their power. And the magical cost would be high. But if they were to ever get home, the risk would have to be taken. Nothing short of the Vortaxis could do the trick, so there simply wasn't a feasible alternative.

"I believe it would be fair to say the more power-steeped geysers will be the most likely hiding places," Hunze said. "If the keepers of the Vortaxis were seeking the most protected and difficult-to-reach location, that would be my first choice."

Bawb nodded his agreement. "Hunze makes a valid observation. An artifact of its alleged potential would have to be not only well hidden, but also masked from easy detection by the Allpower around it. The underwater geysers and thermal jets would seem to fit precisely that requirement."

Charlie sighed. "Then it looks like Ara and I are going for a swim. Nakk, have the scout ships detected any hostiles?"

"The planet *is* inhabited," he replied, "but there is no Urvalin presence that we can find. Additionally, while there are a few traces of civilization on the small landmasses, it would seem the vast majority of this world's denizens reside in caverns beneath the surface."

"Magically sealed? I mean, Allpower?"

"Some, yes, but a good many are naturally formed caverns that have been occupied and developed. Small tunnels to the surface feed a constant supply of fresh air to supplement what their spells pull from the water."

"Clever system," Charlie admired. "But are they friendly, or hostile, or..."

"We have seen no signs of militarization on this world. Likely they are peaceful, but one should never judge by first impressions."

Bawb nodded his agreement. "Nakk is correct. I would also posit that a peaceful and unremarkable society would make for perfect cover if one was hiding something that others would expect to be robustly defended."

"Valid point," Charlie said. "Nakk, let's have the fleet fan out and scan for the hottest pockets of Allpower activity. Where they coincide with powerful geysers will give us a short list of places to search."

"I will send them at once," he replied.

"Cool," Charlie said. "And as for us, Ara and I have more than a little spell-prep to do. This could get interesting."

"Seventeen large geothermal locations," Nakk said some time later. "But only four of them possess a significant amount of Allpower."

Charlie was astride his Zomoki friend, both fully recharged with magic and as prepared as they could be to undertake this dangerous task.

"Then those are the ones we shall focus on," Ara said. "And it is a good thing."

"Yeah," Charlie agreed. "From what our trials with the diving spells showed us, we probably won't have too much juice left by the last location. It's a good thing there weren't any more."

"Will you be safe, Wise One?" Bawb asked.

"I will. And thank you. Your concern is appreciated."

Charlie rolled his shoulders and patted his friend's back. "What do you say, Ara? You ready?"

"As I will ever be. Let us begin."

The pair started casting in unison, forming a protective shell around themselves. So long as their magic held, it would protect them from the weight of the water around them while also providing a small bubble of air that would not reduce in volume as they went deeper.

Ara could survive for a long time on a single breath—she was a space dragon, after all—but Charlie was human, and his lungs still required air, though the magic he possessed had greatly reduced the amount.

The two dove deep to the first location. It was a thermal jet only a few hundred feet deep. It was the easiest dive, and therefore the best choice for their initial attempt. They sped to the bottom, swimming in the superheated current. Charlie hadn't been exaggerating when he said this would take a lot of power. Even with Ara absorbing trace amounts from their environment, they were both burning through far more than was coming in.

"Ara, I'm not seeing anything," Charlie said. *"No signs of anything man-made. No ruins. Nothing."*

"And I am not smelling any power here beyond that of the geyser. Even with this power blocking it, as close as we are, I would detect at least a minute trace if this Vortaxis artifact was here. We should conserve our energy and surface and move to the next location."

"Agreed," Charlie said. "Hey, y'all, we're coming up. This one's a bust. All clear up there?"

"You are safe to surface," Nakk affirmed.

"Okay then," Charlie replied. "We're moving on to number two."

The same search pattern was repeated two more times, each of the dives deeper than the last, and each time, while there was substantial Allpower present, there was no trace of anything hidden.

Even knowing the Vortaxis would have had its power disguised by the planet's naturally occurring Allpower, with Ara's incredibly sensitive sense of smell, even with this galaxy interfering with her power she would have noted its presence had it been there.

"One to go," Charlie said as they flew low over the water, closing in quickly on the final location. "How you holding up, Ara? I know I'm feeling it."

Ara was flying steady and appeared in fine shape to any observing, but Charlie could tell the drain on her magic was taking a toll, even on a being as powerful as she was.

"As you said. One to go," she replied.

"You need a rest?"

Ara flew silently a moment, circling the target site. "Let us proceed. Time is of the essence."

Charlie knew better than to argue. Her mind had been made up. She would not stop until they had done whatever it might take to cross back over and help their friends. Nothing less. As Leila was in danger on the other side, he was very much of the same mindset.

"Okay, guys," Charlie transmitted to the others. "We're going in. Keep an eye out up here. We'll be back as soon as we can, hopefully with the Vortaxis."

They cast in unison and dove for the surface. The magic parted the water around them, providing an effortless descent into the depths. This time, however, it was far deeper than they had ever gone before.

"We won't have much time," Ara said. *"The strain is far greater here."*

"I know. We'll be fast."

Charlie pulled deep, drawing all of the power he could from not only himself but also the twin konuses he had slipped onto his arms. Few could manage such a feat without risk of catastrophic results, but Charlie happened to be one of them. Even so, the magic was being drained at an alarming rate.

"Anything?" he asked as they approached the bottom, Ara's illumination spell lighting the area around them.

"Not yet," she replied, circling the multiple jets of hot water flooding the area with Allpower. *"So much power here,"* she marveled. *"Much more than the other locations."*

"The perfect hiding spot, then," he replied.

"Perhaps," she said, completing her first loop of the area. *"But I still do not sense it. There is no—wait."*

"What is it?" he asked, feeling Ara tense beneath him.

"Something is off," she replied. *"I am not sure what—"*

Ara abruptly spun left, pushing so hard with her power that Charlie actually felt her drawing from *his* reserves rather than the other way around. The massive snapping jaws that narrowly missed them made clear the reason before he even thought to ask her why.

"Run!" he urged, though Ara was already in motion, his comment utterly unneeded.

They were deep. Too deep for the ships on the surface to be of any help. And as weak as she was becoming, there was no way Ara could use her magical flames for defense. Likewise, the railgun and pulse cannon mounted to her harness could only be operated through their usual shielding spells in space. If they fired them underwater, there was a very, very real likelihood their thin layer of protection would collapse.

Ara reached out with a tenuous message. *"I cannot outrun it."*

"You have to," Charlie replied, his mind flashing to his unborn child who might never meet its father if they failed.

He looked over his shoulder as they sped for the surface as fast as they were able. Even in the dark, the massive form of a true apex predator was clear. At least, its gaping jaws were, illuminated by the natural phosphorescence in the water as it raced after them.

Ara was right, there was no way they could outrun it. Unless...

"Jump for the surface!" Charlie called out.

"I cannot jump underwater."

"You can!" he replied, his hands fast at work pulling apart the safety releases to her smaller pulse cannon.

Ara knew her choice was to either risk her spell failing and being devoured or withholding the last of her power and being likewise devoured. Given the options, she decided to at least go out with a fight.

"Hold tight," she said.

"Go in five seconds," Charlie replied. *"Four. Three."* He released the cannon, the pulse weapon falling away, passing their protective spell without disrupting it.

It was a crapshoot, but his gamble had paid off. The beast swallowed it a moment later as it closed in on them.

"Two. One."

Ara pulled the last of her power and jumped just as the creature's jaws snapped shut around the space she had just occupied. Above the surface a splash of water a hundred feet above the surface caught Kip's attention as Ara popped into existence.

"She jumped from *underwater*?" Dukaan marveled. "I thought she couldn't do that."

"Ara needs our help!" Kip replied, immediately rushing beneath her. "Come on, everyone help out!"

The two other ships in the immediate vicinity hurried into place, providing a stable platform for her to rest her exhausted body.

"Charlie, why did you jump? What happened?" Bawb called out.

"A fucking monster, that's what," he gasped.

"But where is—"

A blast of frothy blood and tissue exploded up from the deep in an enormous bubble of death.

Charlie let out an exhausted chuckle. "Overloaded the cannon," he replied. "Now *that*'s what I call indigestion."

With that, he passed out, as did Ara, the entirety of her mass going limp, supported solely by the three ships. They shifted course at once and hurried to the nearest bit of solid land as fast as they were able, setting down on the sandy soil.

Safely on solid ground, they then took turns standing watch over the pair as they slept and recovered. None had the slightest idea just how long that might take.

CHAPTER THIRTY-SEVEN

It was a full twelve hours before Charlie and Ara roused from their slumber. Theirs had been a sleep from an exhaustion so deep, stretching all the way to the core of their natural magic, that it threatened the very real possibility of permanent damage.

Charlie sat up slowly, groggily rubbing the sleep from his eyes with leaden hands. He felt different. Wrong, somehow. And oh-so weak. He reached for his magic and realized that was the new variable. Only the smallest spark was available to him. His internal reservoir, as well as the powerful link of magic he shared with Ara, had been nearly tapped out.

Knowing what he did now after years spent as a magic user, he breathed a little sigh of relief. They had gone well beyond what was safe, drawing far too much power in their desperate flight from the sea creature. But as he and Ara were still drawing breath, apparently it had worked.

He slowed his roll, paused, sitting quietly, breathing deep and assessing his body inside and out. He gently touched again on his own well of power.

Still there, and slowly replenishing. He then reached for his bond with Ara. That too was undamaged.

Amazingly, so far as he could tell, both of their power reservoirs had remained intact. They'd gotten lucky. *Very* lucky. Unfortunately, all of that risk and effort had been for nothing. The Vortaxis was not here.

"Charlie," Ara said weakly, "are you all right?"

He looked up into his friend's concerned eyes. She was exhausted.

"Yeah," he replied. "I feel like hell, though, and I was just a passenger. I can only imagine how you must feel."

She managed a tiny chuckle. "As you have said on several occasions, I feel like I have been hit by a truck."

"As big as you are, that'd have to have been one helluva truck."

"Which is precisely how it feels," she said with a tired grin.

Charlie laughed, but that quickly devolved into a coughing fit. "Oh, don't make me laugh. That hurts."

"At least we are alive to feel that pain."

"True that. That was way too close."

"Putting it lightly."

"Nicely done, though. Jumping from underwater? Impressive, Ara. Really."

"And exhausting," she replied. "I fear I am going to need more than just rest to replenish my power to any amount that will be of use to us."

Charlie knew what she was thinking even before she said it, and it was not a plan he was fond of. Not one bit.

"That system with the twin stars," he said. "I know their mix of power is the closest thing to what we had back home to recharge from, but there has to be another option."

"Believe me, I wish there was. But you are linked with me, Charlie. You feel just how close we came. We will be restored enough by this system's ambient power for flight soon enough, but this is otherwise going to be a lasting deficit of magic that only the most drastic of measures will rectify."

Charlie sat quietly a long moment mulling over what they would have to do. "I'll tell Nakk," he finally said. "Man, he's *not* going to like this."

"You want to go *where?*" Nakk said with utter disbelief.

Sitting across the table from Charlie, Bawb, Hunze, and Nakk were several of his most trusted captains, all gathered aboard Nakk's command ship to discuss their situation. Charlie shrugged and continued eating the spread Skohla had so graciously laid out for their guests.

"I don't like it either," he said as he chewed. "But this is what we're going to have to do. It's the only way to get Ara back to full strength that I know of. And if we want any chance of beating the Urvalin, we're going to need her."

"Yes, the failed attempt to acquire the Vortaxis was a blow to our plans," Nakk said.

"We will continue our study of the legends," Bawb noted calmly. "And with Kip's added resources processing the data, there is still a very real possibility of success."

Hunze nodded her agreement. "And regardless, Ara is our friend."

Nakk knew what she meant, and despite the relatively short time they had been working together, he agreed. "Aside from her power, Ara is not only a valued ally, but also a friend," he said. "But I have to reiterate, the system she wishes to fly to—"

"I know. It's frequented by Urvalin," Charlie said. "Not the best situation, clearly."

Skohla saw the look in Nakk's eyes as he bit his tongue, and shook her head. "It is not merely *frequented*, Charlie. That system is essentially an Urvalin base of operations for this part of the galaxy. It will be *full* of the enemy, and not only in space. They will have a strong presence on the ground as well, and on each and every inhabitable planet and moon."

Charlie shrugged. "I know. But it is what it is. And those twin suns are vital for Ara to recharge. It's the only place remotely nearby that we've found so far that comes close to what she needs."

Nakk and the others were clearly unhappy about even the suggestion, but they were also realists when it came to their plight. Without the Vortaxis, Ara was the most powerful weapon in their arsenal. Without her operating at full strength they would be at a severe disadvantage.

"Very well. We will do it," Nakk said at long last. "However, even getting her into that system will pose a significant challenge."

"But it *can* be done. It'll just take a lot of careful planning," Charlie said.

Skohla flashed a sarcastic grin. "And a lot of luck," she added. "Anyone coming into that system is going to come under immediate scrutiny, not to mention targeting."

"So, basically, we're screwed," Charlie sighed.

Hunze sat up a little taller, her head slightly cocked to one side.

"Love?" Bawb asked.

"I was just thinking," she replied. "What if we do not try to avoid their attention?"

"What are you talking about, Hunze?" Charlie asked. "I don't know what you're thinking, but I'm sure as hell curious."

She smiled at her friend. "This system is flush with Urvalin ships, correct?"

"That is the case," Nakk replied.

"And Ara will need to fly fairly deep into enemy territory to reap the fullest benefit of the two suns at the center."

"Clearly."

"And she will require a distraction. But one that will draw the Urvalin's attention from her position but not trigger defensive measures or put them on alert."

"Again, yes, that is the situation," Nakk said, his curiosity now piqued as well.

Hunze sat back and smiled a Cheshire grin. "Well," she said, "I believe I have just the thing."

CHAPTER THIRTY-EIGHT

"Oh, that's devious," Nakk said. "I love it."

Hunze grinned as Nakk began the final preparations to put the Ootaki's plan into motion. "I thought you might. Mind you, it will require some very careful casting to provide a safe flight compartment while maintaining the illusion."

"Don't you worry about that," Nakk replied. "We've got Allpower to spare as far as drive systems are concerned. Skohla, I think Orwin's ship would make the best decoy, don't you? And she does have a penchant for the dramatic."

She nodded her agreement. "That she does. And her ship still *appears* to be damaged despite the repairs done to its internal componentry over the years. From the outside they will not be able to discern the true status of its systems."

"And then we move in for phase two," Charlie said. "I really think this could work."

"Given our options," Bawb said, "I do believe this novel plan is the most likely to succeed. Well done, Hunze."

"I am pleased you approve," she said, casually leaning closer to her love. "Though I do also feel we cannot use any of the captured Urvalin craft for the second part of the plan. Without intelligence from any of their crew, we would be unable to respond to any challenge calls from the Urvalin fleet already in the system."

"Agreed," Bawb said. "And Kip is clearly not the craft for the job, nor are any of Nakk's main body of vessels. But one of the others captured in the recent weeks should suffice. A cargo ship would do nicely, I think. Slow-moving, not heavily armed. It would not raise suspicions or be perceived as a threat."

Nakk and Skohla approved of the idea.

"We'll make it happen," Nakk said. "Just leave it to us. Once all eyes are on the mess unfolding, Ara should be clear to jump to the narrow asteroid belt between the two suns. No one in their right mind would venture there."

"No one but a Zomoki who happens to be pretty much immune to the heat and will absorb all of that energy," Charlie added. "I really think this could work. Ara, how's your power?" he asked, though more for the others' benefit, as he could feel their link slowly strengthening from the suns' rays even on the outskirts of the system. "You good for that short jump?"

"It will require some effort, but yes, I am prepared," she replied.

"Well, all right then. Let's get to it."

"We need help!" the damaged ship transmitted across all frequencies, both tech and Allpower. "Please, if anyone can hear this, we require assistance."

The ship, battered and patched back together with a motley assortment of salvaged parts, had warped deep into the system only a few minutes prior to sending its distress call. From the looks of it, their warp core was suffering a breach, and not even their Allpower backup containment was able to hold it all back.

Whether it was the warp or some other system failure aboard their craft that had caused the issue, what the mid-sized ship was now facing was a very real possibility of a catastrophic warp core failure.

That, in and of itself, would be a tragedy but not one that would generally concern the Urvalin. One more lost ship, while a temporary inconvenience from the debris field it would scatter about the system, could be cleaned up easily enough and would not interfere with normal shipping operations.

This vessel, however, seemed to be leaking not only warp energy, but also Allpower jump energy. It seemed some fool had tried to squeeze a little extra life out of the ship's drive systems with a very risky bit of creative engineering, melding the Allpower to the warp itself. And it was going horribly wrong.

This would not be the biggest of issues normally, and the Urvalin would just ignore the derelict, but with both drive systems feeding one another and amplifying their power, it looked like if this ship went critical the mix of power could contaminate a wide swath of space with volatile debris, rendering it utterly impassable, not to mention the blast wave reaching far beyond the immediate area and potentially taking out any ships in the general vicinity.

"Damaged ship, stay back," the nearest Urvalin warship replied. "Do not come any closer. Turn around and exit the system."

"We *can't,*" the terrified voice replied. "If we engage any drive systems we will go critical. Please, help us! We need to land!"

"Do not approach any planetary landing site," the Urvalin replied. "Remain where you are."

More Urvalin ships were taking note, both moving a safer distance away from the damaged ship while also turning all of their attention to it.

Just as planned.

Charlie and his friends were listening to the impressive acting being put on display by Orwin. It was quite the show.

"Damn, she's *good,*" Charlie said.

"A talented captain as well as a skilled actress," Bawb agreed. "Her performance is selling the illusion."

Charlie looked at Kip's long-range scans of all the ships in the system. "It looks like she's got most of their attention. Now it's time to ramp it up a notch. Any minute now..."

"Distressed ship, this is Captain Norbitt of the cargo ship *Gezall*. What is your situation?"

"We're drifting. Our warp, jump, and drive systems are leaking. Only the bridge has containment spells, but I don't know how much longer they will hold!"

"I'm carrying a load of bandas," the ersatz captain replied. "I will try to help contain the breach."

The Urvalin now went into a full and proper freak out, as they had hoped they would. They couldn't fire upon either ship lest they risk a massive catastrophe, but bringing fully charged bandas near an already failing cascade of warp and Allpower would be like throwing rocket fuel on a fire. If things went wrong, they would go *horribly* wrong.

"Negative, *Gezall*. Do not approach the derelict," the Urvalin transmitted. Charlie could have sworn he heard a little falter in the man's voice.

"We have to help," Captain Norbitt replied. "It is our duty. Our trade stop can wait. We are coming. Prepare to dock."

"You're mad. The ship could blow at any time. Stay back, that's a command."

"You know we cannot. I suggest you stay back in case things do not go as we hope," Norbitt replied, then redirected his ship.

The Urvalin watched impotently as the cargo ship made its way to the damaged craft. Things had just gone from bad to incredibly worse. And like any good disaster, all eyes were now firmly locked on it.

"Ara, it's time," Charlie sent, their link holding strong thanks to the system's dual suns.

"Jumping," was all she replied, saving every drop of her strength for the pinpoint attempt.

She flashed out of existence at the far edge of the system and appeared in the blistering heat that buffeted the asteroids held between the two suns. The initial sensation was one of a most painful burning, but it was quickly replaced with a wonderful flow of power.

"Oh, this is fantastic," she sent to Charlie, but he already sensed it, his own magic strengthening almost instantly as he shared the experience through their blood bond.

Even Bawb felt the surge, his link with Charlie and Ara suddenly flaring to life. It had faded to the finest thread, barely there, but now, with her strength returning, the assassin felt his connection to them both rebound and recover as well.

"Nakk, it's working," Charlie transmitted over their encrypted comms, courtesy of Kip. "Ara is building power faster than we expected."

"This is excellent news. And the timing is good. The Urvalin are *very* agitated. I do not think we will be able to maintain the charade much longer. We will need to have the two ships limp out of the system to a safe distance sooner than later. Once they are clear of the Urvalin territory, they will be left to live or die without further concern. They should rejoin the fleet straightaway."

"I have the rendezvous coordinates set," Dukaan noted. "We should run on conventional drive power until we're clear of the system, but after that, whenever you want, we're ready to warp out of here to the rendezvous point."

"Let's start pulling back," Charlie said. "I'll let you know when Ara's ready to jump."

"And you're sure they won't notice her?" the pilot asked.

"Not a chance. At full power, and jumping from between two powerful suns, no less, even the strongest Urvalin triumvirate wouldn't be able to detect her," Charlie replied. "Nakk, Ara should be ready to go pretty soon. She's gonna top off her tank, so to speak, but then we can head to meet the others. You have those captured Urvalin ships waiting to escort our actors out of here if need be?"

"They are standing by at the edge of the system, as planned."

"Awesome. Finally, it looks like we caught a break."

Though he didn't want to tempt Murphy to make a visit, Charlie really did think things were looking up for them. And with Ara back to full strength, they could continue their search for the Vortaxis. They simply had no choice but to succeed.

Leila was pregnant and billions of light years away. Failure was not an option.

CHAPTER THIRTY-NINE

"Stand back."

"I'm not standing back, Grundsch," Sarah growled, her Mama Bear instincts flashing to life hard. "She's in *labor*."

"I understand your concern," the hulking alien said, "but you have seen the Magus stone and what it can do."

"Yeah, it's protecting her and the baby."

"Yes, it is. But you are forgetting, in her current state, no one, not you, not me, not even Charlie, is safe from its power. And in the throes of labor it is highly likely it will become even more reactive due to her vulnerable state."

Sarah didn't like it, but Sarah had to admit, Grundsch was right. Much as she wanted to help, she could very well become a victim in the process, and even with her nanite-enhanced body, there was no telling how much damage the stone might do to her.

"Dammit, all right," she relented, stepping back. "Leila, I'm right here, okay. Just breathe. Deep breaths, one after another."

Leila's brow was beaded with sweat as she reclined uncomfortably on the bedroll Sarah had hastily set up for her. They had been moving constantly, with Sarah making runs for supplies while she also sniped Urvalin troops who may have strayed into her range. Grundsch would stay behind to watch over the soon-to-be mother, though as she had demonstrated, thanks to the Magus stone, she didn't really need any protecting.

Walking, however, was another thing entirely, and more than once Grundsch had hoisted her up in his massive arms and carried her to their next hidey-hole. Normally, they would take up temporary residence in one of the countless homes left empty by the Great War. With a fraction of a fraction of a fraction of Earth's population having survived, there was no shortage of vacant homes.

But sometimes the Urvalin would increase their operations in the area, whether reacting to Sarah's guerrilla tactics or the aerial attacks the resistance fighters were engaging in was anyone's guess. What mattered was that in those instances they would get out of the open as quickly as possible, whatever that entailed.

And that was what had led to their current predicament. Taking shelter in the ruins of an old house. It provided cover from aerial observation, but with its windows and doors long gone, the elements had reduced the furnishings to moldy debris.

It was not the ideal place to give birth.

"Breathe, Leila," Sarah said as soothingly as she could. "You're doing great."

Leila did just that, relaxing as she exhaled a long sigh of relief.

"It's stopped," she said, relishing the absence of pain.

Sarah noted the glow to the stone around her neck was also fading. Her labor had ceased, and her water had not broken. The contractions had been real, but this was not her time.

Baloo, having been sitting quietly, watching from across the room, padded over and licked his mama's face. As her other baby, the Magus stone seemed to accept him without hesitation. Bahnjoh, however, knew better than to approach. Much as Leila liked him, the stone had already given him one warning jolt, and that had been more than enough.

"I want to make a run for the nearest hardline," Sarah said. "We haven't had an update from Cal in days. Will you be okay?"

"Go," Leila said. "I'll be fine."

Sarah paused, assessing her friend. She indeed seemed to be fine. One thing she had learned about Leila recently, she was tougher than she looked.

"Okay. I'll be as quick as I can."

Sarah hoisted her pack and rifle onto her back and took off at a quick jog. There were only a few hardline locations in the area, and they were careful not to patch in to the same one twice in a short period. Patterns were risky, and they couldn't afford to lose their one connection to Cal and the other hiding AIs.

"Grundsch?" Leila said.

"Yes, Leila?"

"I'm feeling awfully hungry. What do we have to eat?"

"I am afraid we are limited to nutrient bar rations and freeze-dried vegetables."

She crinkled her nose at the thought. "I need some *real* food."

He knew what she meant. Meat. Protein. Iron and Fat. Just a few of the things a pregnant woman often craved.

"I will hunt," he said. "Bahnjoh, stay with Baloo and watch over her."

Even without the use of the konus collar, the animals knew his meaning by now. He only had a few basic commands for them to begin with, and protect was one of the key ones. They were hungry too, but he knew full well they would have no problem capturing their own dinner once he had acquired sustenance for Leila.

"Rest. I will return shortly."

He headed out for the hills where wildlife had thrived in the centuries since the Great War had eradicated mankind. There was plenty of game, and for a hunter of both his size and skill, there was little Grundsch could not handle on his own, and without the use of any loud weapons.

He moved surprisingly fast for so large a being, and in a relatively short time returned to the derelict building, a deer slung over his shoulder and a pair of rabbits dangling from his belt.

"Oh, yes!" Leila exclaimed, her mouth watering at the thought of real, hearty food.

"I will make a stew."

"Just cut off a chunk and roast it."

"Your digestive tract will fare much better with a stewed version to break down the fibers and ease digestion. But here," he said, handing her a small bag of figs he'd claimed from a nearby tree. "These should help in the meantime."

She accepted the treat and devoured them in a flash. "Thank you," she said through her full mouth.

"It is my pleasure to be of help. Now, I will prepare a proper meal."

It never ceased to amaze her how different Grundsch had become since his days as a bloodthirsty Ra'az invader. At this point he was downright domestic, and she was reaping the benefits.

While Grundsch played chef, Sarah had reached the subterranean hardline hidden in the restroom of an old vehicular repair shop. As with his other access points, it was not the type of place you'd expect the most powerful AI on the planet to use as a base of operations, and that was precisely why he had chosen it.

"Cal, what's the news?" Sarah asked, jacked in to the hidden plug. "We've seen an uptick in sorties lately."

"Our people are getting better at combating the Urvalin," Cal replied. ***"Having Rika causing problems for them is also helping disrupt their operations."***

"She'd be able to go toe-to-toe?"

"Yes, for the most part. But when she is partnered with conventional forces it is becoming even more efficient. Also, you will be glad to hear that your family is doing well."

"Put them on."

"I cannot at the moment."

"Why not? What aren't you telling me?"

"Nothing, do not worry. They are with George and his men. With Marty flying support, the sergeant has been running guerrilla operations in a wide range of environments. Finnegan and Vincent have been very helpful in strategizing and coordinating with Sergeant Franklin."

"My kid had better be safe."

"I am sure she is. But what of Leila? How is her pregnancy coming along?"

"She's doing okay. She had contractions and I thought she was going into labor, but it passed."

"You left her with Grundsch and the canines?"

"Yeah, but I'm not worried about Leila. Hell, with her Magus stone she's probably safer than anyone else on the planet right about now. That thing's gone a bit crazy keeping her protected from anything remotely perceived as a threat."

"Interesting. Can she direct its power, or is it still out of her control?"

"Unfortunately, the farther along her pregnancy gets, the more singular its mission seems to be. Now that she's just about full term, it's a *very* touchy bit of magical potential she's got there."

"At least that is one less worry for you," Cal said. ***"She will be safe. You can focus on yourself without fear."***

"Yeah, I suppose," Sarah said. "But to be honest, I'm a little worried what might happen when she pops."

"Time will tell," Cal replied.

"That it will."

CHAPTER FORTY

"I'm sorry, I must have heard you wrong. Where the hell did you say they are?" Tamara asked, a vein throbbing slowly on her neck.

The poor man she'd cornered at the staging area for the now-reduced rebel fleet was at a loss for words. Makkus was his name, and he had never met a woman quite like either of the metal-armed commandos now grilling him for information.

"As I told you, they departed to seek the Vortaxis," he said.

Tamara shot him an annoyed look. "Again with the gibberish. Shelley, what the hell is this guy talking about?"

"Hell if I know," her partner replied with a shrug.

"The Vortaxis," the man repeated. "Surely you know. It's the *Vortaxis*. It is *legendary*."

Tamara shrugged. "Yeah, we're not from this galaxy, kid, so you're gonna have to enlighten us, here."

Makkus didn't know where to begin, so he started with the old tales his grandfather had told him as a boy. To his surprise, the intimidating women actually seemed interested. At least, until he got to the point where Charlie and company had gone off in search of it.

"It's a goddamn wild goose chase," Shelley grumbled. "We were out there busting our humps, fighting off all kinds of Urvalin, and Charlie decided to go tra-la-laing off across the galaxy looking for some make-believe pot of gold."

"Oh, they are not seeking gold," Makkus said. "They are—"

"We know what they're doing," Tamara interrupted. "The point is, this is a snipe hunt. An exercise in desperation."

She cut herself off. The poor fellow was just the messenger, and she had no reason or right to berate him for simply passing along information, no matter how infuriating it was. Tamara forced herself to take a deep breath, then another.

"So, they left the bulk of the fleet here," she finally said, having noted the number of ships they'd counted upon arrival. "Are they planning on coming back here? Or is this some one-way, do-or-die kind of thing?"

"They did not say. But I do know they now have some very difficult-to-acquire information. No one will say exactly what it is or how they came by it, but it appears as if Nakk and your friends are in possession of what is arguably the most complete set of clues as to the Vortaxis's whereabouts anyone has ever seen."

"For a mythological item no one can even describe," Shelley snorted.

"Yes, for a rare and powerful item that may save us all," Makkus shot back, his annoyance seeping through his fear of the pair.

The newcomers were to be treated deferentially, but that didn't mean he had to let them disparage his people's beliefs.

"And why are you so quick to dismiss the Vortaxis?" he asked. "What if it *is* real? What if this effort provides not only the means to defeat the Urvalin but also a way for you to return home? That is what you are seeking, is it not?"

Tamara and Shelley actually felt chided, which was no small

feat. They shared a knowing look and knew they owed an apology to the recipient of their ire.

"Look, man. We're tired and on-edge is all," Tamara said. "We just got back from flying all over the galaxy, chasing down bad guys and trying to keep the Urvalin who got away from reaching their superiors and reporting in. And now, after all that, we come back to find this mess."

Makkus nodded. "I understand your distress, truly. But we should have a little faith in our colleagues. They would not have undertaken this quest lightly, I assure you. And your large, winged friend seemed to believe there was merit to the endeavor."

Tamara was surprised. "Ara was for this plan?"

"She was."

"Well, hell. I guess if it's good enough for her it has to be good enough for us, right, Shell?"

"I suppose so."

"And we *do* have the coordinates of the secondary and tertiary rendezvous points."

"That we do."

"So, I guess that's that."

"Yeah, but now what?" Shelley asked.

Tamara began to smile, a wicked gleam in her eye.

"I know that look," Shelley said. "What are you thinking?"

"Nothing. Just that we *could* sit around here and wait for them to come back, but where's the fun in that?"

"There isn't any."

"Precisely. And we do happen to have the coordinates of some Urvalin supply chain stations and goods depots."

A wide grin spread across Shelley's face. "So, raiding party?"

Tamara let loose a little laugh. "You know it."

CHAPTER FORTY-ONE

Her name was Reeza, and she did not look like a spy. In fact, the ditzy barmaid seemed to be anything but. She was relatively short in stature, with long, wavy, deep red hair the color of brick. It contrasted nicely with her charcoal-gray skin and ice-blue eyes, and cascaded down to the low-cut top she wore to highlight her other attributes.

Of course, as a master of subterfuge, she was all too familiar with the art of diversion and distraction, and a great many men and women would spill information carelessly at the sight of something so silly as cleavage.

Reeza was not a Ghalian, though making themselves look the way she did would not require too much magic from the masters of disguise.

This woman, however, was simply a loyal ally, gladly repaying her family's debt to the order of killers who had freed them all from servitude. She had originally taken on the role as an obligation. A means of showing gratitude for the unlikely group who had resettled her entire clan after the Council of Twenty began taking their children for their kind's innate ability with metalworking magic.

It was a rarity among them, but enough possessed the skill that the Council had decided enslaving all of them to weed out the children with potential was a small price to pay. The Ghalian, however, had other thoughts on that matter.

Say what you will about the assassins for hire, they did have a code, and slavery was abhorrent to them, especially of children.

Interestingly, in her time learning the tricks of the trade, Reeza had discovered something quite unexpected. She actually enjoyed spycraft. And what's more, she was good at it. *Really* good. So much so that the Ghalian masters made her an offer not typically presented to any outside of their order.

Reeza accepted, and a long and mutually beneficial relationship began.

When the buxom woman arrived at Korbin's secret getaway's doorstep asking for the master of the house, Amazara looked at her man with amused curiosity.

"Korbin? A friend?" she asked, showing the visitor in.

Theirs was a rock-solid relationship. Any teasing or faux jealousy was merely a bit of diversion for the couple. But one thing confused the visla. He had no idea who this woman was.

"I am Korbin," he said to their guest. "But I'm afraid we haven't met."

"I'm Reeza. I've come with information for you and your friends."

"My friends?"

"Yes. Daisy, for one. I recognize the red hair. And her ship, of course."

"What do you know about my ship?" Daisy asked, her hand resting on her sword's hilt.

"No need to let your friend out to play," Reeza said with a laugh. "I'm not a threat. I've come with intelligence."

"Hang on," Daisy said, not moving her hand from Stabby's

comforting warmth. "Not so fast. How did you even know where to find us?"

"She is with me," Master Pimbrak said, entering the room.

"Master Pimbrak," Reeza said, bowing her head slightly. "A pleasure to see you."

"And you. You are well, I am glad to note," he said.

"Work has been steady, and with the Urvalin in town, the other sort of work has grown as well."

"She's with the Ghalian?" Daisy said, her hand falling away from her sword. "Well, that explains it."

Reeza chuckled. "You are just as I've heard you described, you know. Marvelous. Anyway, I have news for you, and it's a lot."

"We've become accustomed to surprises these days," Korbin said.

"Not like this, believe me."

Korbin didn't like the sound of that. "What are you getting at?"

"I'm to inform you that the Urvalin are not what you think. At least, not entirely. Yes, they're an invading force, but not from here. And they're not from your realm either, Daisy."

"*What's she talking about, Daze?*" Sarah wondered.

No idea, Daisy silently replied, an uncomfortable knot forming in her gut. "What exactly do you mean?"

Reeza didn't beat around the bush. "The Urvalin are from a *third* galaxy. And they are now attempting to link the three together to achieve control over them all."

"Wait a second," Daisy said. "You mean they're not only in my galaxy?"

"No. They are there, of course, but they are also in their own realm."

Korbin did not like where this was going. "How did you come by this knowledge? I have not heard any of this, nor has anyone I know, including your Ghalian friends."

"It's very recent intel," she replied, glancing at Master Pimbrak. He gave a slight nod. "We have a person on the inside," she continued. "It took them some time to be able to relay what they've learned, but it seems the Urvalin are trying to bring casters over to their side, offering them considerable power once the takeover is complete. Of course, they already have a lot of power themselves."

"We've noticed," Daisy said. "A real pain to fight, those casters."

"That's because they link their power in threes, overlapping for uninterrupted casting. A triumvirate, designed to make overcoming them nearly impossible. More disquieting is the commanding trio each utilizes an extremely powerful pendant in conjunction with what they call a casting platform to amplify their strengths and actually tie into each other's power across all three galaxies. Really, it's amazing power. Unfortunately, it is wielded by the wrong hands."

Daisy felt her head spin. If this was true, then her friends and family were in even more danger than she'd originally realized. "I need to get back. To get a message to our people. We have casters too, and we can fight back with them."

"You would be referring to the one called Charlie, if I'm not mistaken."

The knot in Daisy's stomach doubled in size. "Shit. What happened?" she asked.

"He was not pulled through a portal trap to a distant part of your own galaxy as originally thought," Reeza said. "From what our insider has learned, he, along with his Zomoki, the Ghalian known as Bawb, and his Ootaki partner, were all pulled through a portal and trapped in the Urvalin realm. The idea was to remove magical resistance from your galaxy entirely. But from what I've heard, they are raising hell in Urvalin space and have even formed a rebel fleet and are causing the Urvalin no small amount of trouble."

"Yep. That would be Charlie," Daisy said. "But your spies are on this side of the portal. My people have no way of knowing any of this. Cal and the others need to be informed."

"*Like you said, they're on the other side,*" Sarah noted, the ever-present voice in her head already knowing what she was thinking. "*Nothing can survive the sun's plasma and make that crossing. But you already know that. You're thinking of using a dragon.*"

If Nixxus is up to try, Daisy silently replied.

Little did she know, the dragon had already crossed back to her own galaxy.

"What are you thinking, Daisy?" Korbin asked. "You fell silent."

"Just had an idea. Lemme mull it over a bit and figure if it can work."

Pimbrak paced slowly as he considered the new intelligence. It was the most agitated they'd ever seen the assassin, and that in itself was cause for concern.

"To combat a power-sharing trio of casters we will need to utilize a similar magic," he finally said.

"The Bakana rods?" Korbin asked, recalling the battle that ended Malalia Maktan's quest for power.

"Yes," Pimbrak replied. "There are four remaining, but if we are to properly counter this new enemy, I believe we must use three, matching their combative style while holding the fourth in reserve. And if Charlie is indeed in the Urvalin galaxy, we need to get him one above all else. His power is considerable, and being in their domain could be a great boon for our cause. Master Farmatta is our strongest caster, so she will wield the rod that remains here. While we had thought to have Rika wield one of the rods, this new information changes everything. The third rod will go to Master Leif. Another strong caster."

"Great," Daisy said. "So let's send it to him and get on with it."

"That will not be as easy as you think," Pimbrak replied. "Master Leif is in your galaxy."

"Wait, you've got Ghalian on my turf?"

"His presence has been kept a secret until now."

"But why?"

"After what transpired with Visla Dominus—"

"That bitch Malalia Maktan, you mean," Daisy interjected.

"One and the same. After what happened, we felt it would be wise to have one of our own keeping tabs on her for the time being."

"She's stranded on a magic-less planet and drained of power," Daisy noted.

"Indeed. But we wanted to ensure she stayed that way."

Daisy couldn't blame them. Malalia had been a thorn in a lot of people's sides and had very nearly taken over her planet. Hell, her entire galaxy, along with this one. Keeping an eye on her sounded like a very prudent course of action.

"It is going to be difficult getting Master Leif a Bakana rod," Amazara said. "And to get one to Charlie it would have to pass both the portal in the sun as well as the one utilized as a trap. And once through, we don't even know how to find him."

Pimbrak nodded slowly, mulling over the finer points of the plan. "If we first get Leif the rod, he will link power with us from there. An advantage. We will consider Charlie's situation in the meantime. We may have no means to cross over yet, but I am hopeful we will find a way sooner than later."

CHAPTER FORTY-TWO

The Urvalin battleships stationed at the plasma-spewing portal had shifted their positions since the unlikely attempt by a dragon with more guts than sense had caught them unaware. Their captains were both furious and ashamed that they had allowed anyone to slip past them, even a space dragon of considerable power.

"Yours is not to apologize, but to fulfill your duties," Commander Prin had said, her displeasure clear not only in her voice but also the deadly Allpower that had already struck down one of the captains.

The most frightening part had not been the act itself, but that she had not even come to the portal in person, let alone boarded the ship. She had killed from afar.

That degree of power was why she and the other two commanders were in charge. There had been plenty of aspiring casters who wished to fill those shoes when a vacancy became available, but to truly rule the Urvalin, a commander needed not only the will to use power, but the potential within.

As a result, the surviving captains, as well as their newly promoted comrade in arms, had quickly scurried to devise a new formation to better guard the portal, while also summoning additional craft to help them avoid a repeat of their failure. The result was a three-ringed flotilla expanding out from the blazing geyser of molten plasma.

The Urvalin ships moved as close as they could safely approach, maintaining just enough cushion in case of solar flare. They had already lost one ship when an unexpected surge engulfed it, melting it to slag despite their casters' best efforts.

With the range dialed in, more or less, the vessels formed a dome of sorts, all angled in different directions like a deadly disco ball, each of them scanning the sky of the system around them, watching, waiting for anyone foolish enough to make another attempt to cross over.

Little did they know.

"No movement," Captain Durgin communicated to the rest of the ships. "Do not let the lack of activity lull you into a sense of complacency. The enemy is crafty, as we have already seen."

The other ships did not clog the airwaves with replies. Durgin had taken charge of the flotilla, which was a big step up from commanding a single ship. But with the added responsibility also came the potential repercussions for failure. Needless to say, he was taking the role *very* seriously.

What Durgin didn't know was the Ghalian already had several shimmer craft quietly hidden in the asteroid field not far from their location. Even with scans, the minimally powered craft would be nearly impossible to detect.

There weren't enough present for any sort of military action, but that wasn't their purpose. The Ghalian were collecting information. And they were about to get a very interesting addition to their observations.

The sun's pulsing energy moved in its own rhythm, surging and receding like a stellar lava lamp. But something had shifted within. Captain Durgin had only just noticed and was adjusting scanners to better read the anomaly when a pair of blazing streaks of flame burst from the plasma, trailing streamers of quickly cooling molten sun in their wake.

"Behind us!" Durgin shouted over his comms. "Fire!"

They hadn't been expecting visitors from the other side of the portal—their comrades on the other side should have put a stop to any attempts from that end—but he was far too seasoned a soldier to not have a plan for such an occurrence, just in case.

His ships swung their weapons as fast as they could and began firing at the two forms. Whatever they were, they were impervious to the flames. It seemed impossible, but he'd just seen it with his own eyes.

The Ghalian noticed too, and they realized what had crossed over long before the Urvalin had.

"Zomoki," Knoxx transmitted over the Ghalian-encrypted skree. "We must draw the Urvalin fire away from them."

He didn't need any further explanation than that. Five of the other hidden ships lurched into space, de-cloaked, and opened up with everything they had. The Ghalian spells slammed into the shields of the Urvalin ships, creating a crossfire, albeit a weak one they would easily survive.

The two dragons, *not* Zomoki, blasted their magical flames, clearing a path in front of them while the Urvalin scrambled to adjust to the ambush. Durgin was beside himself. His carefully laid plans were crumbling.

"Stay focused on the original targets!" he shouted, but it was already too late.

The dragons seized ahold of the gap in the attack and jumped away to safety, the Urvalin's spells and pulse fire meeting nothing but empty space. The Ghalian ships turned and did the same, first flying a brief attack pattern before jumping out of the system. If their maneuver worked as intended, the Urvalin would think they had only just arrived to meet the incoming dragons, and the remaining shimmer ships lurking in the area would be able to remain unnoted.

The Ghalian craft jumped away, leaving the confused Urvalin fleet to try to figure out what had just gone so wrong. The cloaked ships that remained set to work pulling loose stones and holding them against their hulls as an additional bit of camouflage, like outer space hermit crabs.

The debris was massive, but in the near-weightless environment of the asteroids they were utterly harmless.

With the intruders long gone by now, the Urvalin flew about like an angry swarm of bees whose nest had just been kicked, but they found nothing. And the dragons carried on, safe and unharmed.

CHAPTER FORTY-THREE

Kara and Vee were out back behind Korbin's home, enjoying the clear weather and casting attack spells at one another, responding with blocks and counters, as Korbin had taught.

Vee was still on training wheels when it came to using magic, and the konus she sported was her primary source of power. Even so, it was clear to anyone with even a modicum of sensitivity that the potential was there. And the thought of a self-powering Ootaki was enough to make the imagination run wild with possibilities.

"Good," Kara said, dusting herself off from a spell that surprisingly managed to upend her.

"You let me," Vee shot back. "Don't go easy on me."

"I'm not."

"Are too. There's no way I—"

Kara's sneak attack spell swept her off her feet, sending her tumbling ass over teakettle. Vee hit the ground with a thud.

"Hey!" she said, climbing back to her feet.

"You said not to go easy," Kara replied with a laugh. "And seriously, Vee, that really was you. I mean, I wasn't casting defenses at full strength, sure, but you managed to cast way above what you'd been doing up until now."

"Really?"

"You're my best friend. You know I'm not going to lie to you, especially not about something like that."

"Well, okay. You ready for another go?"

"You know I am."

The two young women were prepping for their next series of combatives when a pair of shadows streaked overhead. They looked up, momentarily blinded by the sun before seeing the familiar shape of a dragon. *Two* dragons, to be exact.

"Nixxus, you're back," Kara said. "Hang on, that's a new harness."

"It is," the dragon replied with a chuckle.

Vee rushed over to their winged friends. "And Gazz is with you? Oh my God, you crossed over again, didn't you?"

"I would think that much was readily apparent," Nixxus replied. "Besides, it's better for us to travel together. You know, safety in numbers."

"Not to mention some very interesting new armaments to play with," Gazz added with a low, rumbling laugh, spinning his cannons and railguns through a quick targeting cycle before retracting them into their housing. "I think Habby may have gotten a little carried away, but I'm glad for the additional shielding. We had a bit of a run-in upon our arrival."

"Urvalin?" Kara asked.

"Who else?"

Korbin and the others stepped out the back door and hurried to join the new arrivals. Fortunately, Freya had spotted them coming and had alerted them, lest they otherwise rush out ready for a fight.

"Nixxus, you're back," Korbin said. "You found us."

"As I said, I know the smell of your ship, not to mention you all have a unique magical signature."

Daisy was staring at Gazz and the new harnesses both dragons were sporting. "You crossed over again? And you didn't tell us?"

"Nixxus asked me to join her," the dragon said. "Who was I to turn her down?"

"And there are two of them now, Daisy," Kara said. "And look at the new harnesses."

"Oh, Freya already told me all about them," she replied. "New shielding, mini railguns, pulse cannons, and all of it EMP hardened, like in the old days."

"Yeah, it's pretty neat," Freya chimed in. "It's clearly intended to survive the energy-dampening tech the Urvalin are using. Really cool idea, actually, and totally retro. Not one hundred percent guaranteed, though."

"Stop fangirling, Freya," Daisy said. "We're going to need more than just two dragons if we hope to beat the Urvalin."

Master Pimbrak had joined them so silently they almost missed the assassin's arrival. He stood quietly assessing the dragons, listening to the discussion underway, nodding along as more details unfolded.

"What's in the crates?" Daisy asked of the flat containers mounted to the belly portion of the harnesses.

"A little present for the girls, courtesy of Cal, Zed, and Habby, of course."

"Oof. He's a weird one," Daisy noted.

"*Understatement of the year*," Sarah agreed.

"Indeed, he is. But also very talented," Nixxus replied.

"Those are for us?" Kara asked. "Really?"

"Open them up," Nixxus said. "One for you, one for Vee."

The girls popped the lids of the containers and pulled out the contents.

"This is amazing!" Vee exclaimed, holding up the sleek space suit made of the thinnest material imaginable for the harshness of the void. "I've never seen anything like it. It's fantastic."

Kara couldn't have agreed more. "These are ours? For real?"

"They are. And what's more, they are designed to conform to the wearer, once you put it on. There's a memory setting so it relaxes at key points and goes loose to make it easier to take off. It's also designed to snug up and be more fitted once it's on. Habby said it's also got a minor AI mounted in the power pack that adjusts all sorts of things I don't really understand. But I'm sure you youngsters will have no problem with that."

"What about the Urvalin back home?" Daisy interrupted. "What the hell's going on?"

"Cal said Freya could better parse that information. There's a firewalled uplink file I have instructions how to unlock. He stored it in my harne—"

"Got it," Freya chirped, blowing through the encryption. "Oh, crap. This is not good, Daisy."

"Talk to me, Kiddo."

"Joshua and Sid are blockaded by a dampening array. Their forces are stuck on the moon's surface. Joshua's been upgrading everyone like mad, but they can't fly up into the fight."

"But they're safe, right? They can defend themselves."

"Oh, that they can. They've been taking out anyone dropping into their airspace. But that's not all. Apparently, Zed has mapped out the hidden minefield of dampening zones. Unfortunately, it cost a lot of ships in the process."

"Dammit, we need to get back."

"Nixxus and Gazz might be able to, but the readings their harnesses took when they crossed over, well, we'd burn up, Daisy."

"*Let's not burn up,*" Sarah suggested.

"Yeah, I'm all for not burning up," Daisy agreed. "What else?"

"Sarah's good," Freya noted. "She's been running guerrilla ops. Really putting a cramp in their operations from the sound of it."

"Of course she is. That's my sister. What about Arlo? Is he okay? And Vince?"

"Hmm, interesting."

"What?"

"They've used NORAD as a hiding place of late, and Marty's been out on occasional recon runs. But now Sergeant Franklin and his team have been leading raiding parties to harass the Urvalin on the ground. And it looks like Rika has been teaming up with pilots to do the same in the air. From what I can tell, the Urvalin seem to have bitten off more than they can chew."

Daisy mulled over the new information. Of course, Freya had scads more data to share, but that was the important stuff. Her family was safe, at least for the most part, and Earth hadn't fallen. Not yet, at least.

"Okay," Daisy said. "We need a plan."

CHAPTER FORTY-FOUR

"No. Not a chance."

"But, Uncle Korbin—"

"I said no. With these two coming through the portal, the Urvalin blockade will be on high alert. There is no telling what sorts of spells and weapons systems they have in place now."

"But I want to go. I can help. You heard what's going on there. Arlo and Ripley are facing off against people they're not properly equipped to fight. They need casters there, and you've been training me for this."

"I can help too," Vee chimed in.

"We need casters here as well," he replied. "Nixxus and Drazz have power, and they are more than capable of engaging the Urvalin threat. And as we've already seen, they can fly back perfectly well without you."

"But we have plenty of casters here," his niece retorted. "Magic is the one thing we are not short of in our galaxy. But over there it's still not common. Even with konuses they're still horribly outmatched. You heard Nixxus's report."

"Which is why you will not be going."

"But Uncle Korbin!"

"No," Korbin reiterated. "Karasalia, I have not been training you for this. It is far too dangerous."

He'd used her proper name, she noted. Korbin almost never used her proper name. He'd taken it upon himself to keep her safe in the absence of her father, and he'd done a good job so far, considering the circumstances. But as much as she wanted to help find and rescue him from the Urvalin, she also knew that sometimes responsibilities meant *not* putting your own blood first.

"Uncle Korbin, I know you're trying to protect me, and I appreciate it, really, I do. But what good is having power if you don't use it when your help is needed? I know you wouldn't hesitate to act."

"What about your father? We are still searching for him."

"And I know you'll never stop until you find him. But people need help. Help only our kind can provide. I wouldn't stay back and ignore their call, and neither would my father."

He winced. They'd failed thus far to rescue or even locate the visla, and it was weighing on him. His lifelong friend was essentially family, and knowing he was enduring lord knew what at the hands of the Urvalin made him feel rather helpless. It was not a sensation he was terribly familiar with, and one he was certainly not fond of.

And now his niece wanted to leave the proverbial nest and fly out not just to another system, but another galaxy without him. And not for a mere vacation like other girls her age might, but to put herself squarely in harm's way fighting a seemingly unbeatable foe.

He hated to admit it, but once he put aside his concern for her, he was proud as hell of the woman she was becoming. Korbin felt Amazara staring at him before he even turned to her, just as he already knew what the look in her eyes would convey.

She loved Kara as much as he did and thought of her almost as a daughter. Amazara would do anything to protect her, even if that meant it cost her own life. That said, she also knew the young woman needed to be allowed to take charge of her destiny eventually. Much as neither of them liked it, it seemed this was that moment.

"Korb," she said.

"Zara, she's just a girl."

"I know. But we weren't much older when—"

"That was different."

"Was it, though?"

He hesitated. Amazara always knew what to say, but her empathic abilities as a reader didn't have anything to do with this particular instance. Kara needed to leave the nest, and they had to let her go.

"Uncle Korbin, I appreciate you wanting to keep an eye on me, believe me, and I'm so grateful for all you've taught me. But I need to do this. My friends are there, and I can make a difference."

"You make a difference here," he said quietly, knowing he'd already lost the battle.

"Maybe. But over here we've seen that technology messes with the Urvalin more than magic does. So I'm not really providing an advantage to speak of. But over there where they're shorthanded on magic? I can really help them."

"But you—"

"She's right, ya know," Daisy said. "Not to stick my nose in—"

"*Which is precisely what you're doing,*" Sarah noted inside her head.

"—but as the parent of a kid her age, and aunt of another, both of whom have proven themselves far more capable than I'd ever have imagined, I gotta say, Kara's right. You saw her fight Malalia. That crazy bitch is *strong*, but Kara held her own. And that was without training."

"She's right, Korb," Amazara agreed.

He took a deep breath. He had to let her go, but it wasn't

going to be easy. He hoped the two beasts from across the stars were up for the job.

Korbin glanced at the two dragons. Both were magnificent creatures, large and fit, with technological wonders and powerful weapons and shield systems seamlessly integrated into their harnesses. Harnesses designed to safely carry a rider. And with the impressive space suits they'd brought with them, that rider would essentially be as protected as they'd be aboard a ship.

Then there was the other quality to them as well. One that put him more at ease than any technology could.

Their magic.

It was stronger than he'd remembered. In fact, it seemed almost overflowing, they were so charged up. It was then that Korbin realized the pair must have stopped off at one of the suns their kind found so powerful to absorb its rays. He had to admit, the two dragons were as ready as they could ever be to make the attempt to cross back, and they'd do all they could to keep his niece safe.

He still wasn't quite satisfied, though.

"You will need additional power," he said after a very long pause.

"You mean I can go?" Kara blurted.

"Not before I provide you and your winged friends here with some of the most powerful konuses I possibly can. I will not have you flying into harm's way with anything less than the best I can give you. I'm not taking any chances."

"Oh, that's wonderful," Nixxus said. "The AIs actually crafted the harnesses to function as a casting platform for konuses, much the way they integrated them into the airframes of some of the AI ships."

"They are fast learners," Korbin said approvingly.

"They're AIs, Uncle Korbin," Kara said with an exaggerated eye roll. "Come on, Vee. Let's go try on our new space suits."

"*Armored* space suits," her friend corrected. "A very big and very *cool* difference."

"*Cool*?" Korbin said with a chuckle and a sigh. "I worry you both have already spent too much time across the portal."

Amazara stepped beside him and leaned in close. "Girls will be girls," she said with a grin. "And these two are destined for great things."

"I agree. But, much as I like them, I just can't help but wonder if their friends are on a similar path."

CHAPTER FORTY-FIVE

Arlo and Ripley had always enjoyed playing hide-and-seek in the hills around their homes. Since a very young age, the cousins had taken particular pride in their ability to blend into their surroundings and win the game.

Now, in the midst of an alien invasion, those same skills were coming into play but in a far different way than originally developed.

The two had been dropped off outside of Denver, the latest destination on their whirlwind tour of Urvalin-occupied cities. The aliens had made landfall and quickly secured the area, taking key positions and setting up a secured landing site.

Of course, the fact that Denver was sparsely populated made their victory that much easier. Had they tried to take one of the larger hubs of humanity, they would have undoubtedly met a far more intense fight.

With victory—even a moderate one such as this—came a sense of security. A *false* sense, to be exact. For the same reasons that made this city easy to conquer also made the Urvalin now stationed there vulnerable. And Sergeant George Franklin and his team of crack cyborg commandos were about to wreak merry havoc on them.

Marty was flying so low he actually broke a few treetops while delivering his cargo to their locations. He hoped the Urvalin were too busy to notice. The teens were dropped off on one side of town, the soldiers deposited shortly after on the other.

He'd dropped off Arlo and Ripley first for a reason, the additional time allowing them a bit of wiggle room to make the slow and stealthy trek toward the parked wing of Urvalin ships. Once George and his team began their engagement on the other side of town there would only be so much time to get in, get the job done, and get out, and all undetected.

Fortunately, the cyborgs had become somewhat notorious for their disruptive antics all across the continent. That meant that when the Urvalin realized who they were dealing with they would call in reinforcements at once. More importantly, it meant they would be tunnel vision-focused on one spot on the map. The spot where the kids were not.

"Ten minutes," Sergeant Franklin transmitted on their encrypted comm channel.

"We'll be ready," Ripley replied.

She and Arlo were close to the Urvalin landing site, a dozen ships of different size and configuration all resting quietly on the ground, just as they'd scouted in their recon, most of them still in the same place they'd originally been noted.

The Urvalin, it seemed, were habitually using the same ships to fly the bulk of their sorties, attacking pockets of resistance while the other craft were held back as a reserve. It was those ships they would be targeting for trackers. The other ships were simply too unpredictable in their movements to be able to approach with any reasonable promise of stealth.

The plan was to tag the ships with tracking devices, allowing the AIs in whichever region they were operating in to see them coming long before they got close enough to do any real damage. Unfortunately, they would have to get to the ships first, and that was looking like a more and more difficult prospect by the moment.

"You see those?" Arlo said, pointing to a trio of Urvalin guards patrolling the street. "They weren't supposed to be there."

"Yeah, I know. We just have to press on and make the best of it," Ripley replied.

"I don't think getting shot up or captured would really count as the best of it," Arlo grumbled. "The whole point is *not* to be seen. We'll only have a few minutes once George starts his operation. When the shooting starts it's gonna be a serious ticking clock, Rip."

"I know, I know," she said, scanning for an alternate route. There wasn't one. "If we stay low, we should be able to skate around them."

"And if they see us?"

"Then if the fight's already underway, we shoot them."

Arlo, who had zero compunctions about blasting the ever-loving hell out of the invaders, still wasn't thrilled about getting into an outnumbered firefight with an alien force, but they had a mission to complete one way or another. Cal and the other AIs were counting on them.

"All right," he said. "We can do it."

"Damn right we can," she agreed. "Any minute now George should start the show. Let's try to get a little closer in the meantime."

The two quietly left their hiding spot and crept closer to both the parked ships and the three guards. They were nearly there when the first sounds of gunfire and small explosions reached their ears from across town. It seemed the AIs, who never, ever made a mistake about time, had been forced to begin their firefight a bit early. Whatever the issue was, they'd find out soon enough, but for now they had to move, and fast.

"Come on," Ripley hissed, taking off running in a low crouch.

Arlo was right behind her when a series of pulse blasts forced them to dive for cover behind a low wall next to a decorative shrub. It wasn't much in the way of protection, but at least it was something.

"Shit, they saw us!" Arlo blurted.

"Yeah, I noticed," she replied, popping her head around the wall and firing off a quick shot.

A trio of spells pummeled the ground where they'd just been standing, the troopers zeroing in on the two youths. Ripley and Arlo both leaned out and fired at the Urvalin, quickly ducking back behind cover.

"This is bad, Rip. How are we supposed to get to the ships now?"

"We can't abort. There's no way they don't launch after this."

"I know. But we can't get around—"

A powerful spell shook the wall, knocking part of it free just above their heads, sending it tumbling to the ground, only narrowly missing the pair. A pulse rifle blast followed close after, forcing them to scurry back as a section of the weakened wall threatened to crumble.

"Eat me!" Ripley shouted, swinging her weapon around the wall and blindly firing in the general direction of the Urvalin.

A blistering reply shook the wall, forcing another section to tumble free.

"Rip, we've gotta do something," Arlo said, pulling a konus from his pack.

Ripley reached for the magic-charged device. "Give me that. My casting's better than yours."

"Like hell it is," he said, slipping it over his hand and calling up what he hoped was the right spell.

Arlo spun around the wall and uttered the words he'd memorized, letting loose a blast of magic, falling to the side as he did. The shot went wide as he fell, impacting harmlessly into the side of a building.

Ripley grabbed his leg and hauled him back behind cover with an exasperated grunt. "What are you doing? You missed. Give it to me!"

"No, you don't understand."

"Understand what? That you're a crap shot?"

"I had to miss."

"What do you—"

"Ripley, Arlo, it's safe to come out now," a voice called out. A voice they both knew quite well.

"Dad?" Ripley said, rising to her feet. "What the hell?"

Finn waved a bloody-handed hello to his daughter then pulled his knife from the dead trooper at his feet. Vince nodded a greeting when his son popped his head over the ruined wall, drawing one of his favorite short swords out of the chest of another Urvalin. The third lay in pieces, clearly the work of both men in tandem.

"Hey, Dad,"

"Heya, kiddo," he called back. "Thanks for not blasting us. You good?"

"Yeah, all good."

Ripley, however, was not so casual about their parents' intervention. "Daaaaad," she whined. "I told you we had this."

"I know, sweetheart, and I swear, me and Uncle Vince were only watching. But when you got pinned down—which you were totally going to get out of without us—we just thought it would be smart to speed up the process. George and the fellas are taking a lot of fire, and we didn't want them to spend any more time out there than necessary."

"But why were you following us in the first place?"

"Go on, tell her," Vince said, elbowing his friend.

"Well, I kinda had a little something special I wanted to try out."

Ripley crossed her arms petulantly, but her posture was one of curiosity. "Try out? Like what?"

"Oh, Rip, you're gonna dig this," Vince said. "Show 'em, Finn."

Finnegan unslung his pack and pulled out several small, dark-gray matte discs four inches thick and the size of a small dinner plate.

"Uh, Dad?" Ripley said.

"Giant hockey pucks?" Arlo asked.

Finn chuckled, handing them each one of the devices. "So much more fun than that," he said. "Your uncle Finn cooked up something extra special for these Urvalin pricks."

Vince shook his head. "What he's trying to say is these are massive bombs. Don't worry though, they won't go off if you drop 'em."

Ripley cast a curious gaze on her father. "Dad? Did you go digging in Mom's rainy-day locker?"

"Hey," he protested. "Just because the sun is shining doesn't mean it's not a rainy day. And if you can get these on the hulls of their ships, it's gonna be a very rainy day indeed."

"But if we blow them they'll know we were here and change their patterns and tactics. Not to mention the AIs won't be able to track flight patterns."

"Ah, but that's the beauty," Finn replied. "They're remote activated, so we can sit back and wait until they're in the right position to do the most damage and cause the most confusion. And then, *boom*."

"Tell them the other cool part," Vince nudged.

"I'm getting to it."

"All right, just saying."

"What cool part, Uncle Finn?"

"There's a default setting just in case we can't get a signal set up. If no link to the AI network is received twenty-four hours after installation, the fail-safe kicks in."

"It blows up?" Arlo asked.

"Well, yes and no. It'll blow, but only after they drop below five hundred feet, and only if they have ascended above that height first. Given the way the Urvalin have been hammering pockets of resistance, it's only a matter of time before these ships are moved at altitude to participate in the attacks."

Arlo nodded his appreciation. "And when they drop down below that level to attack..."

"*Boom*," Ripley said. "I have to admit, Dad, it's a pretty cool plan."

"Glad you approve. Now, what do you say you help your old man mount these on the ones parked here and get the hell out of here? There are a lot of other fights going on besides ours, and every one of these stuck on their ships could help."

CHAPTER FORTY-SIX

Far, far away from home, Charlie and Ara had been pushing hard, driving ahead on their search for the Vortaxis. The clues were being refined with every false lead, their understanding of the cryptic, ancient texts clarifying by the minute as their AI friend churned away at the central question of their quest.

Where did the tales point to?

It appeared from all of the stories and folklore to be very much a real item. Or, at least it had been at one time, though no one could describe it. Only a select few had ever actually laid eyes on it, and those who had, had kept mum.

It was Ara who put a few disparate pieces of the puzzle together, her knack for magic, or Allpower, as this case happened to be, giving her an edge their AI friend simply didn't possess. It was something one could not see on the page, nor read in words or pictograms. And it was incredibly faint.

The smell of magic. A very, very specific smell. The tiniest of whiffs, actually, watered down over millennia. She had detected minute traces of it on several relics, tablets, and scrolls. A power that had managed to still cling tenaciously to those items from mere exposure even thousands of years later.

"A power that could do this? It is almost unfathomable," she had said. "I know of no magic that would leave a residue that could remain upon an item for more than perhaps a few hundred years, and even then, that is incredibly rare."

"So, what you're saying is this Vortaxis is not only real, but maybe even more powerful than we thought."

"Oh, it most certainly is," she replied, a very curious gleam in her eye. "And I, for one, am very interested in learning more."

They had decided to shrink their footprint down to the smallest size possible while still maintaining enough firepower to handle the Urvalin should they have a run-in. That meant that all of their ships were dispatched to join the others to wait in their rendezvous system, out of sight and off the enemy's radar.

The less waves they caused at the moment, the better. While they had been enjoying raiding the Urvalin and taking their toys, in this particular quest they wanted blissful anonymity.

Charlie flew astride Ara, both of their power fully restored, while Bawb and Hunze traveled with Dukaan aboard Kip. Nakk and Skohla each commanded one additional ship, the former opting to leave his larger command craft behind in favor of a less attention-grabbing vessel.

"We have visited many systems," Bawb said as they went over the star maps and correlating volcanic worlds marked on them. "If the Wise One's observations are correct, we can now negate these options from our list."

He crossed out over a dozen previously marked systems.

"Of those remaining, it seems there is a pattern," Hunze noted. "See, here? The Lixxans had a presence in a great many of these places."

She was right. The Lixxans were essentially a cult, and they worshiped volcanoes. Unfortunately, often in unsavory ways, throwing sacrifices—typically alive—into the burning pools of lava. The group had come across several of their ruined temples along the way, each of them razed to the ground, but the foundations laid out in a fantastical design.

In their heyday they must have been quite the sight to see, the massive structures constructed in the shape of a variety of wild beasts. But now, all these years later, all that remained were piles of rocks lining the ground, leaving no more than a faint outline of what had once stood there. From the air, they looked almost like the Nazca lines of earth. Enormous designs clearly meant to be seen from above, made by a people long dead.

"This planet is our best option of those remaining," Nakk said when they looked over the possible target systems. "It is an odd place with a large amount of ambient magic from its sun."

"Why odd?" Charlie asked.

"Because this planet was *not* a planet only a few thousand years ago."

"Uh..."

"Allpower," Skohla interjected. "Massive amounts of Allpower, channeled and focused, pulling from the space dust and debris that had been soaking up the sun's power for millions of years. Someone, though no one knows who, found a way to channel that impossible energy and harness it, bending it to their will."

"So they forced it to coalesce into a planet?" Charlie asked. "But what about air and water? Vegetation and wildlife? All the things you need to actually survive."

Skohla was already anticipating that question. "Water was created over time, along with the atmosphere. From what we know of the animals and plants, they were then brought to the world and seeded across it later."

"It's not really much of a planet," Nakk noted. "Barely the size of a small moon."

Charlie was still extremely impressed. "But you're saying it's magic that made it all bond together into a planet. That's amazing."

"Amazing, and dangerous," Bawb added. "An entire world comprised of dust and debris brimming with magical potential? We will have to be very careful there."

"What are you thinking, Bob?" Charlie asked.

"That our magic does not always play nicely with Allpower in this galaxy, and it would be wise for us to avoid casting if at all possible. There is no telling how a spell might interact."

Charlie hadn't considered that but realized Bawb had a point. A very good, very scary point. If they cast, their spells might go horribly awry. It would make their reconnaissance of the world a bit more difficult to say the least.

Their arrival to the system was uneventful, Ara's jump magic and Kip's warp drive not causing a stir of any sort. But when Ara flew close to the atmosphere, however, an uncomfortable tingle spread across her body. Moments later sparks began pinging off her shielding. She quickly withdrew to the safety of space.

"It seems my magic is reacting with the planet's Allpower," she informed the team over her comms link.

"But you aren't even on it," Dukaan said.

"No, but I utilize magic to fly in space. It is an integral part of my physiology I cannot shut off."

"Which you wouldn't want to do anyway since it would kill you," Charlie noted.

"Yes, that too. But the point is, this world was created from its dirt to its atmosphere with manipulation of Allpower. I am afraid I cannot get anywhere near it without risking a dangerous reaction."

"Well, that sucks," Charlie said, unfastening from the harness. "Hey, Dukaan. Can you and Kip swing close? I'm gonna need a ride down, it seems."

"Comin' to ya, Charlie," Kip chirped.

Charlie pushed away from Ara, floating in space between her and the ship a moment before being swallowed up by the open airlock.

"I'm in. Hang tight, Ara. We'll be back up as soon as we can."

"I am sure you will," she replied. "Just be careful down below. We now have tangible proof that our magic and this world do not mix."

"No casting. Got it. See ya shortly. And keep your vid link open. We'll stream any relevant stuff up to you as we go."

"Thank you, I appreciate the inclusion," she replied.

Charlie buckled into his seat, and the remaining ships descended through the atmosphere to the odd little world, eventually settling down in a small landing area a little way off from the nearest town but close to the remains of what looked like an old temple.

"You think that's it?" Charlie asked as the airlock cycled open.

"There is only one way to tell," Bawb replied.

"After you, then. Assassins first."

Bawb chuckled and hopped out to the reddish soil. "I do not see any threats," he said. "Just locals curious at our arrival."

"As they would be," Charlie noted as he jumped out to join him. "What the hell?" he blurted as his feet hit the ground.

Bawb and the others looked and saw what he was finding so disconcerting. Everyone else was walking atop the soil as if it was normal dirt, but Charlie's feet were sinking down into it like a spongy sort of dry mud.

"Fascinating," Bawb mused. "You must stop casting, Charlie."

"I'm not casting, dude."

"You are, and it is reacting with the Allpower that holds this very world together."

"I'm telling you, I'm not—" Charlie realized he was using one very small spell. A shield spell just in case of ambush. It was something he'd done on instinct for so long that he hadn't even consciously realized he was doing it. He stopped at once, and the ground settled back to a solid as he pulled his feet free.

"Better," Bawb said.

"What about you?"

"My magic is not the same as yours, though I do not wish to tempt fate by experimenting with it here. Suffice to say, none of our other galaxy contingent should cast so long as we are in this place. Not even in the event of conflict. The results could be catastrophic."

Motion caught Charlie's eye, and it was moving closer. A group of unfriendly looking locals were walking their way with ill intent on their faces.

"Aww, hell," he grumbled, his fingers resting on his sword's hilt. "It looks like we're going to have to put that to the test sooner than later."

CHAPTER FORTY-SEVEN

"Your valuables. Place them on the ground."

The words sounded like they were formed by the rubbing together of a jostled bag of rocks, the grinding rumble somehow articulating speech. The command was spoken by a hulking brown-and-green-speckled man with shoulders that looked like bowling balls under the leathery skin. At least they thought he was a man—one couldn't always tell with alien races. Regardless, the threat of violence implied in those words was perfectly clear.

His companions were equally brutal in appearance, all large, rough, and ready for a fight. There was an interesting mix of species Charlie hadn't seen before, though all of them were bipedal, if not humanoid.

The bendy one appeared to have a skeleton made of cartilage rather than bone judging by the way it moved, making its fighting style a variable they would have to look out for. Charlie would leave that one to Bawb and Hunze. There were fourteen other hostiles to deal with, and only five of them.

Little did the bandits realize, this group was far more dangerous than they chose to appear.

"Hey, we're not looking for trouble," Charlie said, his hands up in the air. "We're just passing through."

"You have found trouble if you don't do as you're told," the bandit replied, pulling a pistol of some sort from the holster on his hip.

Charlie glanced at Bawb. The assassin was calm and unflappable, as always, his eyes quickly taking in the enemy and assigning each of them a priority ranking. Hunze was doing the same. The poor bastards didn't realize they were not being sized up out of concern, but rather to make their slaughter more efficient.

"Ara, there are some unfriendlies down here. We may need—"

Charlie stopped sending to his friend abruptly. The alien thugs were all staring at him with great curiosity, and he couldn't blame them. His feet had begun sinking into what appeared to be solid ground for no apparent reason.

"Shit," Charlie said in English. "I can't even talk to Ara. Any magic at all and there's gonna be a serious problem."

"I noticed," Bawb replied. "Now pull yourself free. I have the suspicion this will turn bloody sooner than later."

Charlie was thinking the same thing. At least it seemed not all of the bandits were sporting pulse weapons. Most, in fact, were wielding blades and clubs. Whether they were using those out of preference and confidence in their superior numbers, or because they were lacking power or ammunition for them was anyone's guess. At least it made picking the first targets easier.

"What's wrong with your feet?" the leader of the bandits asked, pointing his pistol at Charlie. "What sort of Allpower trickery is this?"

"No trickery," Charlie said as he pulled his feet free. "I guess your planet doesn't like me."

"Neither do I. Now give over your valuables. I won't tell you again."

Charlie could almost hear the imperceptible sigh from his

deadly friend. The fools were going to force the issue, and as a result there was only one way this could end.

The dagger that slammed into the man's hand pierced the vital bits normally used to contract one's fingers. Even had he been able to pull the trigger, the force of the impact flung his hand far to the side.

The thuggish brute would have yelled for his comrades to attack, but they were already reacting. It was a good thing for him as the next dagger sank deep in his neck. The last thing he saw was the newcomers move with frightening speed, his normally undefeatable group being ripped to shreds with unbelievable efficiency.

Bawb and Hunze fought at each other's side, their initial salvo of hidden daggers taking out the pulse weapon-wielding assailants. She was moving a little off from her usual style, protecting her midsection from the possibility of a lucky strike, but Bawb adjusted accordingly, and it barely caused a hiccup in their attack. From then it was a simple melee battle. Despite having the numbers, the bandits quickly realized the horrible error of their miscalculation.

Nakk and Skohla were casting with Allpower, their own flavor of magic operating just fine in this place. Nakk in particular was laying protective spells around their foreign friends, helping defend from Allpower attacks where they couldn't use their own version of power to protect themselves.

Skohla, in the meantime, lay into the ruffians with brutal efficiency. She'd learned a few tricks having trained with Leila and Bawb, and they were pleased to see her blending her attacks with smooth grace, negating her enemy's defenses and finding workaround attacks without losing momentum.

Charlie had slipped back into full gladiator mode, with a bit of pirate thrown in for good measure. The muscle memory of all those years of fighting had him moving without thought, and it was a good thing. The bendy alien had shifted its attention to him and was lashing out with a disconcertingly unconventional fighting style.

Had Charlie been thinking about his next move he would have surely been struck, the lack of magic leaving him vulnerable even with Nakk's Allpower assistance. Instead, his instincts kicked in, the conscious mind retreating and letting his peripheral vision and gut instincts react for him.

Charlie bent awkwardly to the side, narrowly avoiding a swerving stroke of the alien's blade. Rather than lunge forward as an overeager combatant would be expected to do, he dove the opposite direction, rolling to his feet then spinning back toward the alien.

The creature was clearly a very skilled fighter and had swung hard in the direction it had expected him to move, its attack meeting empty air. More than that, it left its flank exposed. It was only for a moment, but that was all the opportunity Charlie needed.

He flung his sword hard, drawing matching daggers from hidden sheaths as he did, flying into battle with the next adversary without missing a beat. He'd hoped to let Bawb handle this one, but it seemed his training had kicked into high gear and he'd managed it himself even without magic, and quite efficiently at that.

The bendy alien fell to the ground in a bloody heap as Charlie took on the next foolish enough to come at him.

"Skohla, on your left!" Hunze called out.

Skohla dropped low and swung hard as she turned, the unusual movement taking the attacker by surprise as well as separating him from his legs. She followed with an immediate blow to the neck, her blade driving up into the fallen man's head.

Bawb was moving slower than usual, enjoying the visceral exercise of an outnumbered fight. He was taking on three attackers at once, but rather than end them immediately, he allowed himself the rare luxury of taking his time with them. Of course, that meant they fell at his feet in twenty seconds rather than two, but that short bit of time allowed Nakk and Skohla to watch the master at work.

Even Hunze stepped aside to admire his skill, though she was still fighting off her own pair of bandits. But once Bawb had put an end to his opponents, she stopped playing nice and did the same. There was no point in keeping them alive for questioning. They were not Urvalin and would have talked, but it was clear these brutish goons had nothing of use to offer them.

The five of them stood over the fallen, reclaiming their own weapons from the corpses, wiping the blood and gore on their clothing. Amazingly, no one appeared to have noted the fight, both due to their distance from town as well as the skillful avoidance of pulse fire.

"Take their weapons," Charlie said. "The bandas too. Might as well add them to the arsenal."

They quickly stripped the dead of anything of use and loaded the booty into the ship, then returned to drag the dead into one pile of corpses.

"What if someone comes and sees this?" Skohla asked. "We still have our task to complete."

Charlie rolled his shoulders and climbed up atop the bloody heap like a conquering mountaineer. "Don't worry," he said. "I've got this."

With that he began to cast. Nothing big, just playing with his power, feeling it react with the world around him. The result was immediate, the ground quivering and loosening its Allpower bonds.

"What is he—" Skohla began.

"Shh. Let him work," Bawb cut her off.

They stood clear of the area and watched as the deceased beneath his feet quickly sank down into the destabilized soil. It was eerie. Almost like watching a planet eating the dead. After less than a minute he stopped casting and pulled his boots free. All of the bodies were submerged, and not a trace remained.

"There. Easier than a shovel, right?" he said, walking into the looming footprint of the ruins. "So, back to the task at hand. Kip, you see anything?"

The AI ship had been running scans since they first arrived at the planet, but it wasn't until they got close to the surface that he was able to get any sort of data that was worth a damn. Being a planet made from Allpower-charged dust made it incredibly difficult to get a read on things.

"Looks like there's a network of underground chambers. Nothing impressive. Sewage, storage, but not much else."

"Perhaps another location will be more fruitful," Nakk suggested.

"But this is the biggest temple on the planet. Or, it *was*, anyway."

Charlie began walking around the area, looking closer at the caved-in portions that led, as Kip had noted, to defunct sewers and aqueducts. He climbed down into one and peered through the long tunnel that had carried water, or something far nastier, so many centuries ago.

He repeated the process, descending into one after another, each time coming up empty.

"Nothing down here," he said as he climbed out of yet another hole in the ground. "And there are no volcanoes on this planet. I don't know, I think this is a bust."

He was about to walk back to the ship when he decided to try just one more. This one was a tighter fit, and he had to lie down and slide between fallen foundation rocks to get inside. Once in, he powered on his portable light, not about to call up even the smallest illumination spell.

"Holy shit! You guys, get down here!"

The others hurried to the opening and clamored down.

"You have found what appears to be the remains of an old temple of some sort," Bawb noted.

"Look, there is an altar," Nakk added.

"Guys, I'm not talking about that. *Look.*"

He shifted the light's beam, brightening the fresco on the wall. Much of it was cracked and fallen away with time, but a sizable portion still remained.

"What is that?" Skohla asked. "There is the symbol associated with the Vortaxis, but what else? Is that a solar scene?"

"Yep," Charlie replied.

"But it looks to have been damaged. The sun, it is running off to the side."

"No, it hasn't. That's the point. Hey, Kip, I'm sending you a feed. Tell me what you make of this."

He aimed his portable cam and transmitted the images back to the AI.

"Fascinating," Kip said. "Ya know, it looks like these folks had no real history of having artifacts, but this right here? It's a religious painting."

"But damaged," Skohla said. "So what good is it to us?"

"No, Charlie's right. It's not damaged," he replied. "That isn't running pigment. I did a spectral analysis, that's how it was painted."

Charlie was beaming wide. "Don't you see? It's not a messed-up painting of a normal sun, it's a normal painting of a messed-up one. It's dying. Spewing its core."

Hunze ran her fingers over the painting, feeling the ages passing beneath them. "It is pointing to the system where they hid the Vortaxis," she said. "It makes sense. If it was once housed here, a map would be left behind."

"And a map only those versed in astral anomalies could understand," Bawb noted. "Thousands of years ago the star charts available would have been far less comprehensive than those today. This system could remain hidden with little to no effort. Only those in the know would possess the means to find it."

Nakk and Skohla shared an uneasy look.

"What is it?" Charlie asked.

Nakk hesitated a moment. "There is rumor of such a system," he finally said. "We know of it. All captains do. A forbidden zone to be avoided at all costs."

"Some sort of religious ban?"

"No, Charlie. It is forbidden because it is not only a difficult journey to get there, but also because it is deadly to those who attempt it. In that system, Allpower fails. The foolish ships who ignore the warnings are lost."

Charlie did not like that reply one bit. But he also knew something about mythological impossibilities. He wasn't afraid. More than that, he also had a ship that was primarily tech-based. And the magic they had was *not* Allpower.

"So," he said, "you're essentially saying it'll kill us if we try to go there."

"Likely. But in all honesty, no one knows."

Charlie glanced at his two friends from home. The curious looks in their eyes told him all he needed to know. "Well, then. It looks like that's where we're going."

Bawb nodded his agreement. "The Vortaxis will be somewhere near that system, I would wager. The question is, where?"

"Let's hope we find out quickly and make it back to our friends back home," Charlie replied. "Leila's gotta be ready to pop, and I hate to think what they're all facing without us around to help them."

CHAPTER FORTY-EIGHT

The towering, heavily modified and upgraded mech that glowed at the joints where its pilot's powerful magic seeped out had become something of a boogeyman among the Urvalin captains. A giant machine running their troops ragged, destroying craft and encampments with its huge feet, fists, and weapons, not to mention the terrifying native Allpower the woman inside wielded.

Rika had spent so much time in her mech of late that its technology and her magic were now melding effortlessly into an incredible amalgam of destructive power, and the Urvalin were at a loss for what to do to contain this unusual threat. That was usually how people reacted to their tactics, not the other way around.

It was obviously a technology-based device, which they normally had an answer for, but with the addition of magic to power it, their thoughts of attempting to deploy an energy-dampening field in a limited area on the surface was pointless. If the mech's normal power went out, the magical force driving it would simply take over.

While the rest of his forces were beside themselves trying to figure out a solution, Commander Torgus kept his cool in the face of a seemingly insurmountable obstacle. He had a few tricks of his own up his sleeve, and one in particular just might work against this foe. A beast he held back as something of a fail-safe. A creature that sensed active technology. Sensed it, and sought to destroy it in a rage.

It was largely for that reason he hadn't wanted to unleash the Djinabb—they were more than a little unpredictable and therefore a weapon of last resort—but this troublesome Rika character had forced his hand. Morale was dropping among his troops deployed on Earth, and he simply could not have that.

So it was with a bit of uncharacteristic trepidation that he ordered the beasts sent to the surface.

"Where are you, Marxin?" Rika boomed over her comms. "I'm knee-deep in alien monsters, and the ground troops are getting away!"

"Coming in hot," the pilot replied. "Had to shake a boogie from my six."

"*Bogie*. You had to shake a *Bogie*."

"Whatever you call it, they were holding me up. Sorry for the delay. I'm targeting the ground forces now."

With that Marxin flashed past her on a strafing run, lighting up the troopers trying to open fire into the sky before they had the chance, then turning his guns on their ships before they could lift off.

Rika, meanwhile, was actually not quite knee-deep in alien monsters, but only because she hadn't been able to kick her mech's leg hard enough into the enormous creature's rear. Worse, every time she got the drop on one, the other would jump into the fray, forcing her to constantly adjust and shift her attacks and defenses between adversaries.

"Gah! Sonofabitch!" she growled as one of the Godzilla-like alien beasts landed a punch, sending her staggering backward.

Her shielding had diminished the blow, and the mech's

additional reinforcements—courtesy of Cal and his kin—had further spread the load. Even so, it had required a lot of effort just to stay upright.

The Djinabb had thick scales that were like armor, but while that shielded them from many of Rika's attacks, it also slowed their movements and hindered their arms and legs. They were protected to a degree, but Rika was much more agile.

She rebounded from the impact, digging her feet in hard and sending her mech lunging into the air, driving its massive knee right into the jaw of the nearest monster. The beast toppled over backwards, dazed, but before she could land a finishing blow its partner again crashed into her, pushing her aside.

It seemed the creatures were drawn to the mech more than just a normal adversary, focusing their attacks solely on Rika, ignoring the smaller craft buzzing around them. They did, however, seem to be trampling Urvalin and resistance fighters alike. These were not beasts of discretion. They were weapons of mass destruction.

Rika flexed her jaw and drew from her well of power, her tattoos glowing bright inside the mech's cockpit. "Okay, you shits," she said. "Let's see how you like *this*."

A blast of violent magic ripped through the air, sending the towering monsters tumbling. It was a large expenditure of magic to cast against a foe so big, but Rika had managed to do so without draining herself too badly.

"Sonofa—" she blurted as pulse blasts peppered her mech's back.

Six Urvalin attack ships flashed past, letting loose with everything they had. Only the combination of her mech's automated shield array and her own ambient magical protection kept them from any serious damage. The enemy, it seemed, had added a new player to the battlefield.

Two beasts and six fighters. It had just become a very uneven fight.

"Marxin, what are you doing out there?" Rika commed.

"Trying to not get shot down," the overwhelmed pilot replied.

Rika didn't bother with him another moment. He wasn't going to be coming to her aid, and there was no bandwidth to deal with him otherwise. Six in the air and two on land. If she was going to go out, she would sure as hell go out fighting.

Her pulse cannon slammed into place, loosing a flurry of shots before retreating into its protective housing just as she crashed her fist into the jaw of one of the creatures. Her mech shuddered, its shields blocking the return fire raining down on it from behind. But Rika was focused on one thing. Kill the monsters, *then* worry about the ships.

The other Djinabb raced to its friend's aid, closing the gap far too fast for a creature that size. But Rika wasn't giving up. No way, no how. She activated her smaller forearm railgun, the device locking in place just as the creature arrived to meet the metal fist at the end of that arm.

"Eat death, fucker!" Rika said with glee as she unloaded a dozen of the railgun's supersonic rounds at point-blank range.

The first several deflected off its scales with ease, but then one managed to find a weaker gap where the scales overlapped, the subsequent three rounds following close behind, breaking through with a sickening crack. The final round sealed the deal, punching into the Djinabb's body.

Rather than simply exiting the other side as it would have with any other creature, the Djinabb's own physiology led to its demise as its scales prevented the sabot from blasting free, instead causing it to ricochet destructively inside the beast's body. With a supersonic piece of high-density metal doing its worst, the creature didn't stand a chance.

The Djinabb toppled over, dead, and leaking a green ichor from the hole in its hide. Its partner saw it fall and let out an enraged roar.

"Oh, great," Rika grumbled, steeling herself for an even bigger fight.

Explosions rocked the air around her, but amazingly none hit her mech. In fact, three of the Urvalin ships had been blown to pieces, their remains dropping from the sky like so much debris. A moment later the *Coratta* flashed by, all weapons a-blazing.

"I thought you could use a hand," Marban's amused voice said over her comms. "Do not worry, I will leave the large one for you."

"Gee, thanks," Rika replied with a relieved chuckle, then set her sights on the Djinabb. "Okay, big guy, let's get it on."

The two rushed one another and locked arms, tumbling in a ball of meat and metal, battling for survival.

As they fought, Marban ripped into the shocked Urvalin ships. They hadn't expected a magically driven craft to drop through their blockade with ease and were slow in switching tactics. For several of them it would be their last mistake.

"Where have you been?" Marban transmitted. "You were not responding to my skree."

"Been occupied," she replied.

"I can see. But I have news," he said, blasting another enemy craft with a magical barrage.

"I'm still kinda busy here, Marban, in case you hadn't noticed."

"Yes, but there has been news. I spoke with Sarah. She has talked to our electronic friend. They think they now know where Charlie is."

"He's alive?"

"They believe so. But they won't discuss over wireless. Why, they don't even want me talking on a skree."

"Urvalin ears?"

"They feel it is possible, but definitely no wireless," Marban reiterated.

Rika knew what that meant. She had to make it to one of Cal's backup hardlines, and Marban was wisely not stating as much over open airwaves. There was no telling just how compromised their comms were, given the traitors in their midst.

"Okay, fuck this," she growled, then drew deep, pushing as much magic as she could concentrate into a tiny point at the end of the mech's fist. As she did so, the Urvalin troops dropped to their knees, falling over unconscious or dead as their Allpower was forcefully torn from their bodies to fuel Rika's attack.

Over and over she drove the massive fist into the Djinabb's gut, the punches actually lifting the creature off the ground. On its own, the mech would not have caused terribly much damage, but the pinpoint magic had penetrated its hardened scales, driving into its vital parts like a prison yard shiv.

When she stopped, the Djinabb was dead on its feet. She released her grip, letting it fall to the ground while Marban wiped out the last of the enemy ships. The aerial threat nullified, he then circled around the battlefield, taking in the sheer number of Urvalin dead at her hands, though without actually touching them.

Rika actually felt good. Better than good, in fact. Her power, despite the pitched battle, was strong. What's more, there was a new flavor of magic mixed in. Something she'd never felt before.

"What did you do?" Marban asked. "How did you take their power? I've never seen anyone but a Ghalian do that, and even they require physical contact."

Rika suddenly realized what he was talking about, snapping out of her Allpower-fueled high in an instant.

"Oh, crap," she said, her crackling magic lowering back to normal levels. "I don't know. It just happened. I mean, I felt frustrated, and I knew the fight needed to end."

"You *were* rather worked up," he noted. "But to claim their power like that?"

"I don't know, Marban," she said. "But there's no time to worry about that now. I can dwell on it later. Right now, we need to find out what happened to Charlie."

CHAPTER FORTY-NINE

Rika and Marban made a quick flight at extremely low altitude, using the terrain to cover themselves as they moved. Rika also cast her variant of a shimmer spell for not only her mech but also to help block Marban's ship as best she could.

The *Coratta* was a rather large pirate ship, and while it was equipped with powerful drookonuses, its shimmer cloaking was rudimentary at best. That was a Ghalian specialty, and the pirates, while on friendly terms with their unlikely allies, were not capable of making their ship disappear.

Marban had pondered the issue at length and had come to the decision that while the Ghalian *could* help him hide his ship better, they chose not to. Not that they didn't trust him—he'd earned that trust in combat many times over—but because they knew that eventually the ship would pass on to other hands, and that new captain might abuse the power.

Rika's own shimmer-like spell was an amalgam of magic from two galaxies, the spell crafted in her own way, unlike anything anyone had ever seen, just like her power. It wasn't perfect by any stretch of the imagination, but for a woman who had not even grown up using magic it was an amazing feat of ingenuity.

Standing still, she could make the mech blend into most environments. It wouldn't become invisible, as with a shimmer spell, but rather would make whoever viewed the craft see it with altered perception. A trick of the eye and mind rather than the manipulation of the air and space around the mech itself.

With that strange spell blocking the uppermost portions of their craft, Rika and Marban were able to evade Urvalin detection from above. So long as they didn't fly directly over the enemy, they would make their trip unnoted.

"Almost there," she transmitted to the pirate ship. "There should be a clear spot for you to set down on your right."

"I see it," Marban replied. "And no signs of Urvalin presence."

Rika had also scanned the area and found nothing. Fortunately, this particular hardline link to Cal was tucked away in what was once a wastewater treatment plant. It was industrial infrastructure, but not something any invader would view as a key strategic target like food, shelter, or medical supplies. As such, it was the perfect place to have a secret connection.

Marban set down in the open area between structures. It wasn't exactly what he'd call ideal, but it would require a bit of searching to pick his ship out among the buildings and processing equipment. Rika settled her mech next to him and climbed down to the ground.

"Come on," she said. "This way."

She led him into a cracked concrete building with a thick steel door. It was closed but unlocked, the entryway leading to a short staircase descending beneath the reinforced cement floors. The place was a dump, unused for decades. Or, at least it looked like it, and that was the entire point.

"Cal, you copy?" Rika asked after jacking her comms into the disguised hardline.

"I am," he replied. ***"I am glad to hear you are well."***

"She's better than well," Marban said with a laugh. "She just sucked a whole bunch of Urvalin troopers dry of their magic. It was remarkable."

"Am I understanding you correctly? You're saying she pulled the power from her enemy? Rika?"

"Yeah, I kinda did," she said, still a bit uneasy at what she'd unwittingly done. "But it was only the Urvalin. I didn't hurt anyone else."

"I would think not. For one, no one on the planet has internal magic. Konuses, yes, but our caster friends are not here. On top of that, the Urvalin's Allpower is an entirely new form in and of itself. And yet somehow you found a way to take it from them."

"Well, it wasn't exactly intentional. But things got heated, and it just sort of happened," she said. "It's weird, but at the time it was almost effortless."

"Hmm," Marban said, stroking the stubble on his chin. "Seems like a pretty impressive weapon, should you learn to do it on command."

"That's a *big* if."

"Still, it is worth considering."

"We do need magic," Cal said. ***"Really, we need more than we have available if we hope to properly engage the enemy. And I mean more than just a konus and a caster to use it. While the dragons are a great help, what we really need are native magic users, and that means our options are incredibly limited. Charlie, Ara, Bawb, and Hunze are gone, and without them we really have only two options."***

"*Two* options?" Rika said. "I thought you said I was the only one around."

"On Earth, yes. But there is one ***other caster of significant power out there in our galaxy. And much as I do not like even considering the option, I'm afraid we don't have much choice."***

Rika realized at once who he was talking about and felt a flare of anger surge through her body.

"No. No fucking way."

"We need her, Rika. This threat is dire. You know I wouldn't suggest it otherwise."

"There's always another option. I'm not signing off on this."

Marban shrugged. "If Cal thinks it's a good idea, we should listen to what he has to say."

"He wants us to release *Malalia*, Marban. Fucking *Malalia*!"

Marban froze in his tracks. This was different. "Wait. That evil bitch? On second thought, Cal, I agree with Rika in her initial assessment of no fucking way."

"I understand your reluctance to rely on her for anything, believe me. But the facts are the facts. We need magic on our side if we hope to prevail, and she's our best option."

Rika shook her head in disbelief at what she was hearing. "Cal, she tried to take over the planet, and not all that long ago, in case you forgot. Friends died because of her."

"Which makes this all the more difficult, I know. But we now have intelligence from Nixxus that puts things in a different light. The Urvalin have been attacking the Council of Twenty in the other galaxy and taking their most powerful casters prisoner. Malalia used to run the Council in her Dominus days. She will realize the threat the Urvalin pose."

Marban cocked his head slightly as he considered what Cal had to say. Far more than a mere pirate, he took the time to step outside of his own biases to view a scenario as objectively as possible. And in this case, much as he hated to admit it, Cal had a point.

"The enemy of my enemy is my friend," he said. "A quote Charlie taught me once. And I have to say, she would be a powerful ally."

"It's Malalia," Rika shot back. "You can't seriously think you can trust her. We stranded her on a planet with no magic anywhere near it for a reason. It was the only way to neutralize her as a threat without straight-up executing her."

"Which I would not have been entirely opposed to," Marban added.

"Yes, she is unable to replenish her power where she is. We've kept eyes on her all this time and are certain there hasn't been a single magical being for her to feed on to regain her strength. She is, for all intents and purposes, living out her life as a normal person. What magic she generates on her own normally is now entirely dedicated to maintaining her life."

"That's what happens when you steal Ghalian blood and live hundreds of years longer than you're supposed to," Rika replied. "She should have died centuries ago otherwise."

"And now we need her," Cal replied.

"She cannot be trusted with power. You know that," Marban said.

"I agree."

"Wait, you *what*?"

"I agree. Malalia Maktan is a dangerous enemy, and we cannot let our guard down where she is concerned even for a minute."

Rika was confused. She looked at Marban, his expression relaying that he too had no idea what Cal was getting at.

"Uh, Cal? Weren't you just championing us making her a part of our team?" she asked.

"Oh, yes," he said. ***"We still need her, no doubt. But, you see, I have a fail-safe plan."***

"A fail-safe for that devious snake of a woman?" Marban spat. "I find it hard to believe."

"Believe it. It's quite creative, I feel, and I think you'll like it."

Rika, annoyed as she was, knew Cal wouldn't dream of suggesting a Malalia option unless there really was no other choice. And if he said he had a safety plan, then he did. The question was, what?

"Okay," Rika said. "Consider my interest piqued. Tell me more."

CHAPTER FIFTY

Marban and Rika were sitting in the galley of the *Coratta* following their discussion with Cal. There were things afoot, gears turning and plans underway. They were actually going to work with Malalia Maktan. It was madness. But in this instance, madness might be just what they needed.

With an anti-tech field blockading the entire planet, Marban's ship was clearly the best option for making a run for space.

He had modified the craft with plenty of technological goodies since arriving on Earth, thanks to his many AI friends, but at its heart it was still a magic-driven vessel. As such, he could enter and exit the atmosphere at will, more or less.

Yet when Rika finalized her plans to retrieve Malalia from her banishment, the former pirate found himself surprisingly not a part of it.

"What do you mean you are going to use one of the ships from Zed's fleet?" he asked, frankly astounded at the mere suggestion. "The *Coratta* is a fantastic ship."

"I know it is, Marban, but you're also the most heavily armed and capable magic-powered vessel fighting on our side," Rika replied. "If I'm going to leave Earth on this crazy mission to retrieve Malalia, *you* are going to need to be the one to pick up my slack fighting the Urvalin while I'm gone."

He was not thrilled with being left behind, but he also knew she was right. One of them would have to stay behind to help keep the Urvalin in check while the other dealt with Malalia. And much as he was confident in his abilities, Rika was clearly the only one around who stood a chance against her should things go wrong.

"Fine," he grumbled. "But what if she gets out of hand? She may be powerless *now*, but once she has magic in her, there's no telling what she may try."

"Fatima will be coming with," Rika said. "If anyone can help deal with the mental aspects of Malalia's issues, she's the one."

Fatima was hundreds of years old by now and had lived through a lot. In real time, no less, as the reconstruction of the damaged parts of her body had left her permanently unable to utilize a stasis pod. As a result, she had crafted her own unique stem cell therapies to help her body clock stop, for all intents and purposes.

Having spent centuries living mostly alone she had developed quite a skill for introspection and growth. It was something she was now teaching to the more rowdy of the survivors of the Great War, helping them ease past the unsavory memories of their past that haunted them in the present.

"Nothing against Fatima, but she is not equipped to deal with a rogue visla. Her talents are better suited for ordinary people. You know, the kind who won't try to burn you alive for looking at them wrong."

"Hey," Rika said, resting her hand on his forearm. "Don't worry, I'll be fine."

"Will you, though? It took so many to stop her before."

"And it's not going to come to that. We have a safety in place, and I really think Cal's plan is a good one."

Marban cracked a little grin. "Well, yes, I do approve of that part of the plan. But what about your flight there? You will need to transfer to Zed's warp-capable craft in orbit. Without me helping you cross—"

Rika's tattoos flashed a deep purple, the glow of the pulsing lines suddenly tracing all across her body. "Oh, I've got the power to get us out there," she said. "All I need is to keep the ship's life support intact until we can power up again once we're outside the dampening zone. It's not my mech—that baby's dialed in—but I can do it."

"But you will also need to fly. Have you considered that?"

"I have, and unlike my unpleasant first meeting with the dampening field, now I know for a fact I can fly the damn thing if I have to."

Marban noted the downturn in her spirits.

"Jo will be okay, Rika. Cal has his best people looking after her."

"I keep telling myself that, but there's just no way to know for sure. It was a hard shutdown the likes of which none of them have ever dealt with before. For all I know, Jo might be gone."

The grizzled pirate looked her in the eye with a tenderness that would have startled any who didn't know him. "I sincerely hope not. But if she should go down that path, I am confident you will carry on the fight in her honor."

"Thanks, Marban. For now, I need to focus on getting to Zed's warp ship in orbit."

"I do have concerns," he replied. "If you push too hard you'll be drawing deep from your own power. And you may very well need it to fight clear of the planet."

She squeezed his arm. "Stop worrying, big guy. That's why I won't be doing it alone. I'll have help. Very large, very scaly help."

. . .

Rika and Fatima sat strapped into their seats in the cockpit of the small ship Cal had selected for their hop into space. As it was just the two of them, and since Orgalius was going to be carrying the little craft, all Rika had to do once they reached altitude was maintain a sealed, secure environment for them.

The ship from Zed's fleet would be waiting for them in a predetermined location near one of the hidden dampening traps, floating dark to avoid suspicion.

It was fortunate that they had Orgalius to make the trip to space to connect with Zed. It was a tedious way to relay information, but in lieu of normal comms, it would suffice. And once they had Malalia in tow, hopefully they would be able to take down the whole dampening array. But despite Cal's confidence, in Rika's mind that was still a big if.

"Do you really think you can get through to her?" Rika asked Fatima as the dragon lifted them from the ground and began his ascent.

Fatima's almond eyes crinkled a little around the edges. It seemed she found amusement in just about anything. Maybe that was part of her secret to longevity.

"I'll assess her," she replied. "And if possible, help her deal with some of her more unsavory tendencies."

"So, like, *all* of them, you mean."

Fatima laughed. "Oh, Rika. Even the most damaged soul has the potential to evolve. Despite her past, I like to believe Malalia is no different."

"She's a destructive, power-hungry bitch," Rika replied. "No offense."

"You say that, but you are also friends now with Grundsch, a Ra'az Hok. He and his kind nearly ended humanity, but he has proven himself a changed being. I like to think that perhaps Malalia can follow his example. He was a servant in her household, after all, and was close with the entire family."

Rika had to admit, Fatima had a point. She didn't want to, but the woman made sense.

"So, what then? What do we do if she agrees?"

Fatima shrugged. "We work with her to become a contributing member of our little band of resistance fighters."

"Do you really think you can do that?"

"Honestly, Rika, I don't know. But one thing I'm certain of is we have to try."

"We are nearing the edge of space," Orgalius transmitted. "It is time to shut down your comms device and begin casting."

"Copy that," Rika said, quickly flipping the unit off and drawing her power into a bubble around them within the ship. "Here we go. Don't mind the glow. It's perfectly safe. Just part of the whole casting thing."

"Don't worry about me," Fatima replied, relaxing in her seat. "I always love a good light show."

CHAPTER FIFTY-ONE

The planet had no name, its unremarkable sun nothing more than a number on a star chart. There was no magic in this place. No power. The one habitable world, tranquilly orbiting, lay smack dab in the middle of the system's Goldilocks Zone.

Animal life was abundant, as was a wide variety of flora, but only a minute few of them had even a shred of magic within them, and that magic was toxic to those from the other galaxy.

There were predators, of course, as there were on nearly all worlds capable of supporting life, but nothing huge and aggressive, and certainly no beasts that were difficult to avoid or simply drive away.

In short, it was the perfect place to deposit someone you didn't want to kill, but also didn't want to rebuild their power, draining magic from whatever she could use to regain her potency. But soon visitors would arrive, and that would all change.

The ship carrying Rika and Fatima was a modest craft, sleek and fast, designed more for evasion than confrontation, though it was still well armed and shielded for that eventuality should it arise. It was operated by a minimal crew consisting of the captain, her navigator and co-pilot, an engineering team, and a small security detail.

If all went according to plan, there would be no need for the armed detail, but that didn't mean Rika wouldn't be bringing them along. Things, she had learned in her life, had a way of going sideways on you when you least expected it. More so where this particular person was involved.

"Okay, you lot, listen up," she said to the assembled crew as soon as they'd exited warp and settled into orbit. "There's only one person down below on that planet. One. Now, while that may sound like a cake walk, I can assure you, this is not someone you want to take lightly. Do *not* underestimate her. Malalia Maktan is dangerous, so keep your guard up."

One of the security team raised his hand. "I understand your concern, but if it's just this one unarmed Malalia person—"

"Yes, just one person," Rika said. "But you've all fought against her and her forces before, only back then she was leading the invading fleet under a different name. Malalia Maktan is Visla Dominus."

The man blanched at the name. Of course he knew who Visla Dominus was. They all knew the alien leader who had damn near conquered Earth.

"Shit," he said quietly.

"Exactly. Now, if there aren't any more questions, time is a-wasting and we've got a job to do."

The crew had known only the most basic details of their mission up until this point. It was a need-to-know situation. But now that they had settled into orbit, they all needed to be brought up to speed on what they were dealing with. Fortunately, upon learning the true nature of the package, everyone appeared to be taking this far more seriously.

Malalia was easy enough to find down below. They'd been keeping tabs on her for the last year, after all, monitoring her with a tiny implanted microdot placed in her ankle at the end of the war. It didn't relay anything more than location, there simply wasn't a need. All they needed to ensure was that she remained on that world. Beyond that, live or die was her business.

"There," Rika said as they dropped down into a quiet valley. "Set us down in that field."

The pilot did as she was told, softly landing the ship on the untouched grass and popping the airlock open. Rika was the first out, her tattoos faintly glowing, ready for anything, though she logically knew there was nothing to fear. Still, after her experiences with Malalia, she couldn't help it.

The air was crisp and sweet, lacking the smells of industry of any kind. This was a truly untouched world. If not for their reason for visiting, she might have almost enjoyed the moment.

Rika looked at the small tablet on her wrist. "This way," she said, walking slowly with deliberate steps. It was habit, and the odds of Malalia having set booby traps were slim to none, but better safe than sorry was her motto, and for good reason.

After only a few minutes of walking they reached a small clearing with a crude hut and a basic stone fire circle. Malalia Maktan was sitting on a stump, wearing a tank top and shorts, sipping a cup of water as she watched the first people she'd seen in a year approach. She did not look like the terrifying visla of legend. Even Rika found herself surprised at the formerly imposing woman's appearance.

For one, she had several visible scars on her body, healed slowly and naturally with no help from magic whatsoever. Malalia generated her own power and was normally a very strong caster, but that had been before she stole Ghalian blood and mixed it with her own. Now it was all she could do just to maintain her youth after so many hundreds of years, a constant cycle of draining her own power so as to not fall into decay.

She was still aging, but at a normal person's pace. Any extraneous use of her power would have a catastrophic effect. As unlikely as it sounded, Malalia Maktan was simply living out her days in exile.

Fatima was fascinated by the woman. Perhaps it was because she had lived hundreds of years longer than her normal lifespan, just like Malalia. Or maybe it was the calm air the former terror had about her. As they walked closer, it only confirmed her opinion of the visla. She was at peace.

With no power to use against anyone else, she was also not a threat to anyone. At least not unless she overpowered the guards or managed to drink from Rika to steal her power. Both eventualities Rika was not about to let happen.

"Rika, you look well," Malalia said. "May I offer you a drink? There is a flower that grows here that makes a most refreshing tea. You must be parched from your walk."

"It wasn't very far, Malalia," Rika said as politely as she could manage to the woman she'd so recently called an enemy.

Malalia smiled with genuine warmth and amusement, which Rika found to be very disquieting. "Of course," she said. "And, of course, you wouldn't want to drink anything I offered anyway, though I can assure you the tea is not poisoned in any way."

"I'll take you up on that offer," Fatima said, walking closer. "My name is Fatima. A friend of Rika's along for the ride. Your world is quite lovely, you know."

"That it is. Funny, not long ago I wouldn't have even noticed anything here but the lack of a society to conquer. Isolation and forced introspection can have an interesting effect like that."

"Oh, believe me, that is something I am *very* familiar with," Fatima replied.

Malalia rose to her feet and gestured to the two women. "Come, this way. Your soldiers are welcome to join us, but I'm afraid it will be a little cramped inside."

Fatima gave Rika a look, the meaning of which was quite clear.

"That won't be necessary," Rika said. "You all stay out here. We'll be back shortly."

The guards quietly fanned out and settled into a perimeter around the hut. Malalia nodded her appreciation of their tactics but that was all. She was clearly aware of the firepower they'd brought with but no trace of unease was to be found. She turned her back on the armed group—something she would never have done in her former glory—and headed into her hut. Fatima nodded to Rika then followed close behind.

"I'll be right there," Rika said, then turned to the head of the security team. "We shouldn't be too long."

"Ma'am, you shouldn't trust her."

"Oh, believe me, I don't. If we're not out in ten minutes or if you hear anything out of the ordinary, I want you to come in there ready for action. Clear?"

"Crystal."

"Good," Rika said, turning toward the hut. "Then wish me luck."

CHAPTER FIFTY-TWO

Malalia's home wasn't exactly what one would call crude, but it was a very basic, utilitarian shelter, designed and built for function rather than style. Luxurious, it was not, and for a woman who had been accustomed to living like a queen, a visla, no less, doted on and served hand and foot, a woman who had damn near ruled two galaxies, the contrast of her current circumstances was stark.

And yet she was being pleasant. Kind, even. Rika didn't know what to make of it.

"Well, isn't this nice?" Malalia said as she used the tiniest spark of magic to ignite a piece of kindling in the corner of her hut. "The water is still warm from my last cup, this will only take a moment," she said.

Fatima hadn't paid much notice to the little display of magic, or at least she was making a good show of it, but Rika most certainly noticed. Malalia saw her staring and smiled, but there was none of the familiar malice behind her eyes.

"Yes, I do still possess my power," she said with a chuckle, adding tea to the pot. "All of it, in fact. But every day, every bit of it goes to maintaining this glamorous visage." She gestured to her plain attire and scarred body, so far from her refined and perfect look as the conqueror of galaxies. "If I use anything more than that trifling amount for anything else, I will begin to fade. Needless to say, that would not be pleasant."

"Yet all flowers are still beautiful, even those in their decline," Fatima mused.

Malalia nodded to the older woman. "Well said. You know, I am glad you brought your friend, Rika. She truly is a delight. But while I am enjoying the visit, given our history, you would not have come here unless you had to. What is it? The Council of Twenty acting up in my absence? A rise from the ashes, so to speak?" Malalia asked with an amused chuckle. "I'm afraid I have no influence with the Council anymore, as you well know."

"The Council?" Rika scoffed. "We should be so lucky."

While she'd been rather blasé up until that point, *that* comment caught Malalia's attention. For the first time in quite a while, she was *curious*.

"What is going on, Rika? What aren't you telling me?"

Rika only hesitated a second. There was no sense in beating around the bush. Not with this woman. She was as smart as she was devious, and she was *very* devious. On top of that, like her or not, Malalia truly excelled at the art of war.

"Urvalin," Rika said. "They're called Urvalin. A magic and tech-wielding menace. You ever hear of them?"

"Urvalin? No, I cannot say that I have. A nuisance from this realm, clearly. With my reach back home, if they were from mine I would have come across them long ago."

"Ah, and here's where it gets interesting."

"Interesting?"

"Yeah. We really don't know what they're up to or where they're from."

"You've not taken prisoners? Really, Rika, I'd expect more from you."

"Oh, we've taken prisoners all right, but they all kill themselves before we can get anything out of them."

"Their officers must be truly dedicated to take such an action."

"These are regular troops."

Malalia paused, a look of genuine curiosity on her face. "*Fodder* did this?"

"Uh-huh."

"Fascinating."

"Yeah. And it gets worse. They've managed to surround Earth and the moon with a technology dampening field. Nothing gets in or out that runs on machinery. Only magical vessels can pass. On top of that, they've taken control of the portal between our galaxies and dropped it into the sun. There's no calling for help from the other side."

"But Charlie has power. Ara, and their friends."

"Yeah, but they were pulled through a different portal. A trap. We have no idea where they've been spat out, but there's been no sign of them."

"Charlie and the Zomoki are gone? And the Ghalian?"

"Yes."

"So, you are the strongest remaining caster and the only one truly equipped to fight them."

"That's pretty much the point. And that's why we're here. Much as I can't believe I'm saying this, we need your help, Malalia."

The former commander sipped her tea quietly.

"Malalia?"

"As I've told you, I have my power, but I cannot use it to fight. I would die in the very first engagement."

"Ah, but that's why we'd power you back up. Get you charged beyond your own magic."

Malalia gave Rika a strange look. "You would actually work to restore my full potential? After all I have done?"

"Like I said, I'm not thrilled about it, and I can't believe I'm even offering, but yes, we would."

A long silence hung in the air as the three women sat quietly, two of them sipping their tea, the third a ball of conflicting feelings. After a moment longer Malalia put her cup on the table.

"I'm sorry, but I will have to decline."

Rika did a double-take. "You *what*? We'll get you your power back. Take you off of this rock."

"And that is what concerns me," she replied. "This is not my fight, and we all know I've done a lot of fighting. And, while the cause is just, honestly, I do not know if I would trust myself if I was brimming with power again."

Rika felt Fatima's eyes on her and knew what she was thinking, and she actually agreed with her. *That* sentiment was what she needed to hear. The sign that perhaps this wasn't such a bad idea after all. Grundsch had made the shift. Grown a conscience. Perhaps Malalia finally had too.

"It's for the greater good," Fatima said. "Please, Malalia, consider this request."

Malalia locked eyes with the woman. "You don't know how it is. How the power corrupts. The temptation. I could hurt people again."

Rika perked up at that. "Oh, we've got something for that. Fatima, would you, please?"

Fatima reached into her pack and pulled out a collar-like device, but thick and clunky, clearly not meant to be worn for any length of time. "A means to keep you from turning on us."

Malalia hesitated, but a shift of interest flashed in her eyes. To have power again? To not have to worry about aging?

"You say this would prevent me from hurting people?"

"If you let me," Fatima said.

Malalia slowly nodded and exposed her neck.

"Don't you want to know how it—"

"No. Do what you must quickly, before I change my mind."

Fatima didn't hesitate, locking the unit around her neck and keying the activation sequence. The device warmed up, humming slightly as it contracted against her flesh.

"Ow!" she blurted when a shock crackled around her neck. An electrical sensation similar to a magical collar pulse, yet different, pushing against her skin with an uncomfortable heat and pressure. A moment later the device stopped and went dark. Two seconds later the unit released entirely, and Fatima pulled it free.

Rika looked at the tablet on her forearm. A new light illuminated on the display. "Okay. We're good to go."

"*Now* you can tell me how it works," Malalia said.

"Simple, really. When this clamped around your neck it implanted a tiny bomb. Nothing huge. No bigger than a grain of rice, in fact. But if you attack any of us, *boom*. Use magic to try to remove it, *boom*. If you run and abandon our people in the middle of battle, *boom*. If you in any way misbehave and go back to your old ways, we blow your head off. It's crude, I know, but it's effective."

Malalia actually smiled.

"Something funny?" Rika asked.

"No, not at all," she replied. "It's just strange."

"Having a bomb in your neck would tend to be."

"No, not that. The unusual part is that it is actually a relief to consider having power again, *true* power, and not having to worry about my slipping and doing something awful."

Strange as it was, Rika actually felt a modicum of hope that this plan might work. That coming to Malalia wasn't the terrible idea she'd thought it would be.

"So, with that out of the way, in all ways that matter for this little quest, I am still powerless. How exactly are we supposed to begin?"

Rika reached into her pocket and pulled out a konus. Even

from across the small room Malalia could feel its exceptional power. Rika had been holding its potential in check with her own power, hiding it. Malalia had to admit to herself, it was the prudent thing to do.

Rika looked at the konus a moment.

"You want your power back?" she asked, then tossed her the konus. "Start with this."

CHAPTER FIFTY-THREE

Malalia's presence aboard the Earth forces' ship was causing something of a stir among the crew, albeit a very quiet one. Picking up a passenger, even a former enemy, was not a big deal. They had the numbers, guns, and a powerful caster on their side.

But when they learned it was going to be the former Visla Dominus joining them for a ride, a feeling of uneasy disquiet had begun to permeate the ship's every corner.

The reality of the woman, however, proved to be something of a letdown. At least at first.

She had the air of confidence they expected, but none of the menace she was infamous for. In fact, their guest was downright pleasant, going so far as to make small talk with the guards and crew. Having been utterly alone for the last year, actual conversation with pretty much anyone was a simple indulgence she took the greatest of pleasure in.

Rika and Fatima watched her interact with the crew with great interest. The flight home wasn't just a rush back to conflict, it was also a litmus test of her newly discovered peaceful demeanor.

The konus on her wrist was extremely powerful, and now that she had something other than her own power to draw from, Malalia had allowed herself a few touches of vanity for the first time since her banishment.

Her scars were gone, for one—at least most of them. She did still sport a few visibly, though Fatima thought it might be a reminder to herself of her former plight as much as it was a sign to others that she was a different woman than the terror they'd known before. Rika still had her doubts, though.

"If Grundsch can change, I'd argue anyone can," Fatima said as the two discussed their new passenger from the comfort of their seats in command. "But I do understand your hesitance, given your history with her."

"You'd be smart to take it with a grain of salt too," she replied. "She may have only used a tiny bit of the power we gave her thus far, but she knows we need her. And she knows that for that reason there will be more coming her way soon."

"Once we return to Earth, yes, we will have to provide her with additional sources of power. But from what I understand, so long as she is drawing from a konus, there is a limit to what she can do."

It was true. Malalia was incredibly powerful on her own, but with every bit of that going to simply keeping her at status quo, it would be near impossible for her to truly act up. To tap into her own magic rather than what they provided could very well kill her.

The ship dropped out of warp at the next waypoint to confirm their course and adjust as needed. The world on which she had been imprisoned was not a well-traveled route, and when covering such vast distances in space it would be far too easy to make a fractional wrong turn that could throw them massively off course. For that reason, the trip there, as well as the trip back, would take longer than they wanted, but there was simply nothing they could do about that.

The stop was relatively brief, the next checkpoint being a shorter warp than the last.

"Warping in ten seconds," the captain announced.

Rika sank into her seat. "Here we go again."

The ship popped out of existence a few moments later, hurtling through space in a flash to its next destination. A blast shook the craft only a few seconds after it exited warp, tossing it violently.

"What the hell?" Rika blurted.

"We're under attack!" the captain shouted. "Shields on full! Evasive maneuvers!"

"I count three Urvalin ships, Captain. Two are moving to flank us."

"Weapons hot! Fire at will!"

The ship rolled and spun, the crew only feeling some of the effects as they were moving at a slow speed having just emerged from warp. It meant the gravity generators could compensate for the shift in direction for the most part, but it also meant they were moving far too slow for a fight, especially three on one.

Rika pulled up her power and cast, reinforcing the ship's konus to hold off the magical attack. So far, it seemed there was no dampening field deployed. This was a system sometimes used as a checkpoint for Earth ships, and the Urvalin's traitorous spies had apparently spilled that bit of information to the invaders. Rika wondered how little it had cost to convince them to sell out their own people.

"Warp us out of here," she said, straining to maintain her defense as a powerful spell pummeled the ship from multiple sides.

"Do it," the captain ordered.

The ship, however, remained where it was, and the attack only increased in intensity.

"Our path is blocked," the pilot replied. "We need to break free of the one closest if we want to be able to attempt a warp."

The railguns and pulse cannons were firing nonstop, but targeting three equally difficult targets with both tech as well as magical shielding was straining their systems to the max. The power and ammunition were there, but this ship was designed to either run or engage only a single enemy. Two tops.

Unfortunately, neither was currently an option.

A violent impact shook them again. This time, however, warning alarms and flashing lights told them some damage had been incurred.

"Shields absorbed most of it, Captain," the pilot said. "But not all."

Fatima watched warning lights illuminate one by one. "How much more of this can we take?"

"She's a strong ship, but this is an uneven fight with pulse fire as well as magic, and it's one we can't run from."

Rika didn't like the sound of that. "So, not much?"

"I can't say. We're taking a hell of a beating. At this rate? Unless we get clear something's gonna fail. All weapons on the forward craft. Fire three salvos then re-engage your original targets. On my mark. Fire!"

The weapons briefly disengaged the flanking ships and fired upon the one blocking their warp escape. The Urvalin, however, were casting continuously as a triumvirate and as a result they were able to shift their power to the targeted ship with ease.

"Ineffective," the engineer called out. "We're going to need to give the weapons a minute to cool off."

"We don't have a minute," she shot back. "Options?"

"Uh—"

The door to command slid open and their guest lurched into the compartment, catching herself as another blast shook the ship. Malalia saw the displays showing their adversary and immediately pulled up her magic out of pure instinct.

"You brought me to them when I'm not even remotely ready? Oh, this arrangement is *not* starting out well."

"We didn't intend it. We were ambushed and the lead ship is blocking our warp," Rika said. "I'm bolstering the shields, but we need to get out of here."

"You would run?"

"It's that or die. What did you once tell me? Even the strongest warrior has to know when to retreat."

Malalia had indeed said that once, though it was more a display of combat wisdom spouted out to her underlings than a belief she held personally. In fact, to run from a fight was pretty much anathema for her. But times change, and survival was priority number one.

She reached deep into her power, testing it gently, blending it with her konus's power. It had been so long since she'd truly cast, but they had little choice.

"Prepare to warp," she said.

The pilot looked at her with confusion. "But the enemy—"

"Let *me* worry about that."

The captain caught Rika's look. She had faith in this woman. Malalia just might be able to do it. She nodded to her pilot. "Be ready."

Malalia began casting, small spells at first, simple diversions to draw fire away from them for a moment and cause the enemy to focus on something else. The blocking ship was matching their movements still, locking itself in and mirroring every shift of position.

That simply would not do.

"*Nextaris ammano dicto*," she said, casting a powerful disruption spell.

The magic drained from her konus, blending with hers, bolstering it. The ship in front of them spun aside, battered by the unexpectedly strong and violent magical impact. It was unlike any they'd ever experienced before, and that was precisely what Malalia was counting on.

The Urvalin quickly regained position, shifting their power

to steadying the ship. Just as she wanted. It was a trap she'd set, luring them to act in a brash manner, shifting their power in a way that left them vulnerable without their realizing it.

"Warp in five seconds," she called out.

"But we can't! If we try it we'll hit the blockade and overload the drive system."

"You will have the opening," Malalia replied.

The captain looked at her pilot. "Do it."

"Five. Four." Malalia then cast the most powerful spell she'd used since the throes of battle in her quest to conquer Earth, her magic blasting out, but not directly at the enemy. Instead, it targeted the perimeter ships, their shields lessened as they fed into the central one.

The magic tore one open, purging its atmosphere and killing most of the crew outright. The other managed to refocus some defenses, but the damage had been done. With one of the three casters gone, their magic was far weaker. What's more, they were unable to cast non-stop.

The blocking spells failed, leaving a gap. But Malalia wasn't done. Not yet.

"Three. Two."

With a final surge of magic she threw the dead ship at its comrades, forcing them to either redirect their defenses or suffer the impact. Malalia's hair flashed from gray to near white as her magic drained from the effort, her skin sagging as age took hold.

"One," she said, then collapsed to the deck.

"Now!" the captain commanded.

The ship's warp drive engaged and they popped out of the system in a millisecond. Malalia had done it. She'd saved them all.

Fatima looked at the unconscious woman with morbid fascination. This is what her life would have been like without her drastic gene therapy. And Malalia had just saved them all, but at a terrible cost. Worse, there was no way she could help them back on Earth. Not like this.

As an alien species, there was no way to know if the same gene therapy could help her. Even if it could, the treatment was used to stop the aging clock, not roll it back.

"We cannot allow her to perish," Fatima said. "She gave all she had to save us."

Rika reached out with her power and tested Malalia's internal force. It was so weak. No simple konus would reverse this level of drainage. Only one thing could. But there was no way Rika would let Malalia drink from her. That was simply not an option. But she couldn't let her die. She made a snap decision.

"Pixxal," she said. "Set a course for Pixxal."

"But that's a power-filled system. And that planet's life is full of it as well," the captain replied.

"It is. But at least it's not *people* who are full of power," Rika pointed out. "Look, she needs to take power to live, and the only way to do that is to drink. So we do what we have to. We land there and let her feed enough to regain her strength. Once she's out of the woods we can plan our next move."

The captain didn't like the idea, but Rika was clearly right. They needed her, and this was the only option. And it seemed far more reasonable than it would have just hours prior. Amazingly, Malalia Maktan had just risked her life for them. It wasn't something she would have done. Not the old Malalia. A flash of hope warmed in Rika's gut.

Her former captor, incredible as it sounded, was actually a reformed woman, it seemed. Now it was time to forge her into a weapon for the good guys.

CHAPTER FIFTY-FOUR

The flight to the unnamed forbidden system had been fraught with more difficulties than Charlie had imagined when Nakk had casually mentioned the arduous journey. They had already avoided spatial anomalies, asteroid fields, and a great many hostile scavengers.

Unfortunately, that wasn't all that was out there.

"Sons of bitches!" Charlie growled as he and Ara spun into a tight dive, avoiding the incoming pulse cannon and utterly massive amount of Allpower fire from the Urvalin ships pursuing them. "These bastards are persistent, I'll give 'em that."

Kip and Dukaan were right behind them, flying a dizzying evasion pattern while Bawb and Hunze helped cast defensive spells, firing the weapons systems in a spray as they tried to drive the enemy back.

Nakk and Skohla were doing the same, following the same trajectory as their friends, all of them working together as they fled the enemy battleships that had been lurking in the stopover system they had used some time earlier as a safe haven.

Apparently, the Urvalin had taken note. That, or they'd managed to capture one of the rebel craft and gotten them to talk. The entire fleet was currently posted up in a secure location, so if they'd managed to pry this system's coordinates from someone's lips, it was a ship taken some time ago.

In any case, whatever the reason, the Urvalin were here, and they were proving to be a very difficult nuisance.

"We're out of here," Charlie called out over comms. "Kip, you have the next coordinates dialed in?"

"Ready when you are."

"Nakk, Skohla, you two good to go?"

"Just jump, already!" the alien captain replied.

"Okay. Hit it!"

Ara's magic was linked to Kip's drookonus, her jump matching his warp seamlessly. As for Nakk and Skohla, they had received the coordinates from Kip directly just before warping. Even if the enemy found a way to read their encrypted communications, by the time they did, they'd have made another jump to another system.

A crackling flash was the only announcement of their arrival at their destination. It was empty space between solar systems. A void that was safe to navigate to in a hurry with no risk of accidentally hitting an asteroid field or even a planet.

"Everyone make it through in one piece?" Charlie transmitted.

"All present and accounted for," Kip informed him. "That was too close, though. The Urvalin—"

A series of flashes illuminated the darkness close by. A moment later, pulse blasts rocked their shields.

"How the hell did they find us?" Charlie blurted as Ara again took off in evasive maneuvers.

"They're tracking us through warp," Dukaan replied. "They must be able to follow our warp residue."

It wasn't impossible by any stretch, just incredibly inconvenient. The enemy was using their own tricks against them, it seemed.

"Damn, we need to shake these guys off our tails," Charlie said.

"No shit," Kip replied. "Any suggestions?"

"Actually, yeah. Plot a course directly for the void system. I'm talking not to the edge but just inside it. If I'm right, Ara and my magic should still work there, but if not, you guys can push us out into normal space."

"You wish to jump in blind?" Nakk's worried voice asked over comms. "It is a dark spot on the star charts. We do not have the information we need for a safe warp."

A furious barrage of Allpower pummeled their shields, sending them scattering before pulling back together on a new heading.

"I hate to break it to ya, but we're kinda screwed already, and if these bastards are tracking our warps, there's not much we can do to outrun them."

"But if we warp into the void it will negate their Allpower advantage, which should give them reason to back off," Skohla said. "At least we hope. A ballsy but logical risk."

"You approve of this?" Nakk asked.

"I do, sir."

"Then let us waste no further time. Kip, we will follow your lead."

"Gotcha. Everyone hang on to your bootstraps. This is gonna be a weird one."

He transmitted the rather terrifyingly lacking coordinates to nowhere to the others and powered up his warp drive. The Urvalin ships noted their actions and started preparation for pursuit.

Charlie and his team knew they'd be followed. They just hoped the arrival on the other end would prove a most unpleasant surprise for their pursuers.

"When you're ready, punch it," Charlie said.

"Going in two."

"Not three?" Charlie asked.

"One."

Kip warped, Ara and the others riding his proverbial coattails across space. They popped out of warp, Ara's jump emerging with them. Her magic, Charlie was very glad to note, held up.

"We're good, guys. Move deeper."

They didn't hesitate, quickly using their regular drive systems to power ahead into the Allpower-sucking space. Nakk and Skohla's ships were already running entirely on tech and made the transition seamlessly. The Urvalin blindly following close behind, however, were not.

The lead ships spun and tumbled into one another as their mixed systems failed the moment they arrived. They righted the problem as quickly as they could, but the damage had already been done. With mechanical systems only they limped back clear of the dead zone while their quarry raced away from them deeper into the void.

"They've pulled back!" Dukaan exclaimed. "It worked!"

Charlie was more than a little pleased with himself. It was a ridiculously risky plan, but they'd pulled it off, and without suffering any damage in the process. Amazingly, the Urvalin had not only pulled back, but they were not switching to tech systems for pursuit.

"Hey, guys. You see this? They're not following us."

"I would suspect they wouldn't," Nakk replied. "They'll just wait us out from the safety of open space."

"But why? I mean, they have powerful ships with more than ample drive systems. Why let us go so easily?"

Nakk let out an uneasy laugh. "Well, that's the thing, Charlie. On top of the lack of Allpower in this place, there is another threat."

"Wait, what other threat?"

"The locals."

"There are locals here? I thought it was an empty system."

"I said Allpower did not work here. I never said it was uninhabited. And the locals have something of a reputation, though by rumor alone."

"Why's that?"

"Because no one has lived to tell the tales themselves."

Charlie was tempted to mention that if that was the case, who told those tales, but he didn't think this was the time for a smart-ass reply. Instead, he just rode quietly, taking in the sights as they flew deeper toward the dying star in the center of the system. As they did the sun grew larger, its details easier to discern. It was spewing its core in a steady stream, a stellar death that would take hundreds of thousands of years if not millions. But more than that, Charlie now clearly saw what the sun looked like.

It was suddenly abundantly clear why the cult had selected this system. They'd been reading the legends right, but also wrong. A quick scan showed the planets here were not volcanic in the slightest. It didn't fit.

But the sun? That was something else altogether, because as it sprayed out its deadly plasma it looked very much like something so often repeated in the legends.

It looked like a volcano.

CHAPTER FIFTY-FIVE

"There are too many. Pull back to elevation marker three," Joshua commanded.

The ships swarming the skies above Dark Side base immediately disengaged the enemy and dropped lower, the big guns on the surface opening up on the ships lingering above them the moment they were clear, driving the invaders back yet again.

The Urvalin had been trying to find another way past the minor armada Joshua and Sid had put into play above the base. It was not their first attempt, nor would it be their last, but at least they were now held to the uppermost reach of the Urvalin tech-sapping devices.

Once a hard ceiling for operations had been established, no further ships had been lost to the dampening array. All were now carrying an auto-descent relay, courtesy of Joshua and his fabrication hangar. If anyone flew too close, their controls would automatically be overridden, and the ship would dive back down to a safer level.

Of course, this could also be terribly dangerous while in combat, both because there were people actively trying to shoot them down as well as having swarms of their own ships simply buzzing around in the same airspace.

The first issue was easy to address. Joshua had taken his inspiration from the common fly, incorporating a totally randomized redirection protocol that made targeting the descending ship near impossible. The pilot might be a bit nauseous after it all, but at least they would be intact.

The second issue was a bit harder to compensate for. In the course of running away, it was always possible a ship might crash into another. Short of installing an AI aboard every vessel, there was simply no way to anticipate where the others might be. So Joshua decided to try something new.

Each craft had been outfitted with a tiny repulsor beacon. It was innocuous enough, just a minor magnetic array that presented a faint charge across the hull. But when two ships neared one another, the repulsing poles would then trigger the primary evasion protocol, essentially pinballing them off of one another but without requiring any actual contact.

Since coming up with that idea, Joshua had been busy upgrading every last trapped ship, outfitting them with modified weapons, shields, and even a few konuses they had stored for Freya to play with in her research as well.

As for himself, he had placed his core systems into his massively shielded and incredibly fast base vessel. It was tiny, just big enough to contain him, yet so robustly built that even several direct pulse cannon hits would likely fail to disable him. As for the dampening array, well, that he doubted even his spectacular shielding could overcome.

He had inserted his base ship into the large form-shifting vessel he was so fond of, locking himself in place in the central hub of the interlinked ships, all of the small craft providing layers of protection and arms, but also capable of separating to attack in a swarm. It was one of his favorite tricks.

Unfortunately, with their forces trapped on the surface,

there was little they could do short of sit idle. At least all of his myriad cannons were pointed up. That much he *could* do.

"Why don't we just push hard and open up on all of their microsats?" Eddie asked. "We should be able to target them easily."

The little attack ship was right, but with the quantity of the devices in orbit, any attempt to destroy them would just lead to more being deployed in their place. That, and they would undoubtedly suffer casualties in the process.

"I appreciate the enthusiasm," Joshua said. "But it's simply not tactically sound."

Even as worked up as he was, the smaller AI knew better than to question Joshua when it came to matters of tactics. Unfortunately, while Sid's telescope array was providing them with visual intel on both Earth and the fleet's status, with their comms still jammed, there was little they could do but wait.

Meanwhile, down on the planet below, Sarah, Leila, and Grundsch were running small raids on Urvalin forces when opportunity presented itself. As pregnant as Leila was, they didn't actively seek out the conflicts, but Baloo and Bahnjoh had noses for trouble, and they'd been regularly finding it in small pockets around the city.

For that reason they kept moving, though Sarah really wanted to find her friend a safe, quiet place to sit tight and have her baby. Of course, Leila was adamant that Charlie should be there for the big day, but not knowing how far the portal that trapped him might have spat him and the others out, Sarah wasn't exactly holding her breath. Not that she told Leila as much.

Marty, George, and the others were staying active as well, Finn's new explosive design having proven almost undetectable when stuck to the hull of Urvalin ships. The teams had managed to not only take down a few supply depots, capturing some interesting armaments in the process, but they'd also mounted more than a few of the bombs to the enemy craft.

George and his commandos in particular were wreaking a particularly effective bit of havoc on the alien invaders. Experts in asymmetrical warfare, they had pinpointed the enemy's vital footholds and supply lines and were disrupting them with great efficiency.

Cal was heartened by the progress they had made and wasted no time relaying the command for the rest of the planet to replicate their tactics and disrupt the Urvalin's plans further. It was working thus far, with surgical strikes targeting very specific objectives, maximizing damage while minimizing risk.

In the process, Cal had tasked a number of small teams with another mission. One that would not be savory under any other circumstances. These specialized hunters were to do one thing and one thing only.

They were to hunt and eliminate the traitors who had sold out their own people.

Once, perhaps, there would have been imprisonment and talk of rehabilitation. It had worked in the past, after all. But with their galaxy on the line yet again, and their numbers so few, there was simply no time or spare resources for such a civilized approach.

"With no mercy," Cal had told them. ***"Do not hesitate. These are traitors of the highest order. They have sold out our planet, and if given the opportunity, they*** will ***cause more harm. This list has been verified by multiple independent sources. If there was even the slightest doubt as to a target's guilt they were omitted from this list. Knowing that, you may carry out your task with that certainty."***

With that urging from the top AI minds on the planet, the small hunter teams across the planet set to work, weeding out the guilty, more often than not disappearing them without a trace.

It was easier that way. There was no need to make an example. That would not deter anyone and would only serve to warn the others. Put them on alert. Instead, the guilty were simply removed from the equation without anyone being the wiser.

Anyone but the man who had set them in motion.

Commander Torgus was monitoring the goings-on from the bridge of his battleship high above the planet. These pesky resistance fighters were causing no small amount of trouble, and as a result his plans were already falling farther and farther behind.

"You have to do something, Torgus," Prin said when the three commanders linked up across the galaxies. "Earth is the key to that galaxy, and you risk losing control."

"I am *not* losing control," he hissed, his anger clear even over the vast distance separating them. "It is merely an inconvenience. One that I am going to handle *personally.*"

It wasn't exactly unheard of, one of the leading Urvalin Triumvirate engaging the enemy's lesser forces directly. It just wasn't done terribly often. But with his plans in more jeopardy than he cared to admit, Torgus decided that this was most definitely the time to put a stop to these rebels himself.

"Take us down," he commanded.

His number one looked at him with confusion. "Down? Do you mean to the surface?"

"As I said. *Down.*"

The poor man swallowed hard. "Yes, sir. At once!"

The order was relayed, and the ship disengaged all technology, switching to an entirely Allpower run system. For most it would take time to accomplish that, and with great effort no less. For the Urvalin, however, it was second nature.

Torgus watched as the coastal city of Los Angeles grew larger as they descended. A central location of disruptive activity. Soon he would establish decisive dominance as only a commander's presence could achieve. And once that city had officially fallen, the conquest of the rest of the planet could proceed under his watchful eye.

CHAPTER FIFTY-SIX

The moon, along with its Dark Side Base, were still surrounded by a floating network of microsats, all of them knocking out the power of any craft foolish enough to attempt to either enter or exit the planet's thin atmosphere.

That much was no surprise at this point, and all of Zed's ships battling the Urvalin in orbit as well, as the fleet champing at the bit to properly get into the fight above were well aware of the flight restriction.

It was frustrating to say the least.

Proximity relays were at least allowing Zed's craft to establish a tenuous communications link with the base on the moon's surface. The system allowed sharing of information between Sid and Joshua from their terrestrial position with Zed's command ship in one of the clear spaces out by Mars, and that had shifted things but only a bit. Neither could really act on any information shared, but at least they were in communication once more, albeit delayed.

Earth and its AIs, however, were still essentially cut off. The network of microsats blocking the planet was just too robust, and given the size of the area it was encircling, only a few ships had been able to get close enough to align with a receiving array on the surface to attempt to transmit. Even then their orbit moved too fast for prolonged contact.

Some information had been relayed, but not much, and real communications were still a no-go. It was better than nothing, but not by much.

The Urvalin's plans to disrupt things were working in that regard. At least, they had been until an unexpected variable decided to go and charge through their carefully planned embargo like a bull in a china shop.

It was called the *Coratta*.

Marban and his band of merry pirates had stepped up their actions. It was vexing to say the least. This crew had been flying ships using magic alone for their entire lives. Yes, the *Coratta* had been upgraded recently, receiving a wide array of tech goodies from drive systems to weapons, but technology was still essentially a recent discovery for the crew. As a result, switching back to an entirely magic and drookonus-driven mode of travel and combat was as natural as breathing.

And as pirates, there was little they reveled in more than a good fight.

Marban had been leading his men on a joyous series of violent and rather creative raids, boarding Urvalin ships using both tech and magic depending on the circumstances, laying waste to their crews. The utterly unconventional tactics they employed were leaving the enemy at a loss. The Urvalin were so accustomed to being an overwhelming force that having their own picked off one by one was simply not something they could fathom. At least, not at first.

Once the pirates had begun truly interrupting their plans and commandeering ships and equipment, however, they finally took note. Unfortunately for them, it was too little too late.

"Hang on down there," Marban transmitted as the *Coratta* zipped into the tech-blocking array surrounding the moon.

"We're targeting those pesky Urvalin giving you such a hard time from above. Kindly ease off on the defensive fire a moment, we're getting close."

"Copy that," Sid replied. "Diminishing ground cannon fire to a minimum. We'll be sure those blasts go nowhere near you."

"Much appreciated, friend. We should be sending a few of their ships down to you momentarily. In pieces, I would wager," he added with a chuckle.

The *Coratta* banked hard then dropped on top of the larger of the enemy ships. It seemed, for all intents and purposes, to have just been an impact attack, using the pirate ship as a battering ram of sorts. The Urvalin craft quickly banked away to regroup while the attackers moved on to the next craft, opening up with a magical barrage.

What the captain of that first ship had not realized was that the attacker had left a little something behind in the exchange. Namely, a small team of seasoned space pirates clinging to its hull, safely ensconced in a magical bubble while their point caster worked to open an entry into the unwitting craft.

It was a ploy they had successfully used repeatedly at this point, and Marban had collected a respectable little fleet of stolen ships. They were currently parked on Mars, where Zed's teams were going over them with a fine-tooth comb, removing anything remotely looking like a kill switch as they mapped the ships' systems.

They hadn't yet cleared them to be used by their own pilots, but Zed felt that was just a matter of time. Admiral Harkaway had already selected a core group of pilots and crew to operate them and had arranged for simulations based on what they'd learned so far to be uploaded to them via a modified neuro-stim.

Normally, they would slow-drip the information over weeks or months, but time was of the essence, so a faster version was devised and rapidly put into play. Those receiving the data would likely have a bit of a headache from the information dump, but they'd be able to fly the alien ships, and that was certainly worth the discomfort.

"They've breached the hull," Marban's second-in-command reported. "Kixxin reports they made it inside undetected."

Marban grinned like a madman from his command chair. Though he hadn't always been a pirate, it was a lifestyle he had adapted to and excelled at. And fighting the Urvalin? This wasn't financial, this was personal. For that reason he was particularly enjoying every victory.

"They should be able to take the ship intact if they can make it to their command chamber before being noticed," he said. "But have a rescue ship deploy and stand by just in case the Urvalin scuttle it rather than lose. We don't want a repeat of that fiasco."

"Already loaded and ready to go, Captain."

"You're a mind reader, you know that?"

"Just served with you a long time, Marban."

He supposed that was true as well, and years of friendship could definitely make it seem like one could read minds. In any case, he trusted his people to do their jobs to the utmost of their ability. Beyond that it was up to the fates.

"How clear are we of the dampening field?" he asked.

"We have room to maneuver, but it's close."

Marban considered his options a moment. "Power up the pulse cannons. Those systems only; everything else stays magic-powered. Can't risk losing the ship after all."

"We're on it," the gunners replied. "Should have power restored in a few seconds."

"When you're hot, fire on the Urvalin farthest from us. That should send the ones closer into a bit of disarray."

It was a little trick he'd been employing of late. Switching up and using tech where it shouldn't be able to be utilized. But in that little gap before hitting the dampening field, he had found he could inflict serious damage on the unsuspecting enemy as their defenses would be entirely focused on magical attacks.

Of course, he and his team were *very* accustomed to fighting asymmetrically with magic. As pirates it was their stock in trade. Tech was really just a novelty for them. But just because they didn't rely on technology didn't mean they didn't know how to use it, and to their advantage at that.

Marban's plan was unfolding as he'd hoped. Soon, if all went well, they would have a new ship captured and added to their ranks and several other enemy craft destroyed or disabled. It was actually fun for the pirate. He just wished Rika was there to enjoy it with him.

Unfortunately, she had her own task at hand, and he did not envy her one bit.

CHAPTER FIFTY-SEVEN

Two dragons from a distant galaxy streaked through space, Bakana rods stowed safely in their harnesses, their destination, a flaming portal surrounded by a fleet of Urvalin warships growing nearer with every jump. It was risky, but accompanying them were some of the most dangerous fighters in the galaxy, all of them unified in their goal of protecting the two magical beasts.

It was in their best interest to help. These creatures were the only things capable of surviving the transit through the deadly plasma spewing from the portal. But more than that, there were two much smaller figures accompanying them, riding on their backs courtesy of the state-of-the-art harnesses they each wore.

It had taken some doing, but Korbin finally consented to Kara and Vee's brazen attempt. The dragons had recorded their passage, and Freya had reviewed the footage and supporting data taken on their magic use in great detail. With a full charge of power, these two were more than strong enough to survive the flight. And with the help of a few strong konuses he melded to their harnesses providing an additional boost, they would be able to make the flight with minimal risk. At least, from the flames.

The Urvalin fleet guarding the portal, however, was another thing altogether.

"Don't worry," Daisy said as the support group prepared for their next warp-jump toward the portal. "We're not gonna let anything happen to you."

"Not a chance," Korbin agreed from his own ship, its systems powered to maximum and his additional weapons ready to go at a moment's notice.

"We're not worried, Uncle Korbin," Kara replied, the comms unit in her helmet transmitting clearly to them all. "We've got this."

She sounded chipper and confident, but Korbin knew his niece better than that. Brave as she might appear on the surface, this was far outside her wheelhouse, and only a fool wouldn't be at least a little worried about their prospects.

"It is fear that more often than not keeps you alive," he had frequently told her.

It was a reality that everyone fighting in this resistance knew firsthand.

The two dragons flew in a tight formation, the supporting craft spread out and ready to distract the enemy when the time came. It would be a multi-tiered engagement with the rebel ships peeling off the Urvalin ships one by one until the main anchor craft blocking the portal as a last line of defense had no choice but to engage. It was then that the dragons would jump as close as possible before entering the portal.

It would have been far simpler if they could just jump into the portal itself, but given the plume of flaming plasma shooting forth they couldn't risk it. If their protective casting was just a little bit off, both the dragons and their riders could be engulfed in flames, possibly fatally.

It was not something Kara or Vee were terribly keen on.

"There is powerful magic here," Korbin noted as they gathered on the outskirts of the portal's location. "And overlapping. Like the Urvalin, but different."

"What does it mean, Korb?" Amazara wondered.

"It doesn't matter. Whatever they're up to, we have to get the girls across safely. Everyone, take your positions. We begin as soon as the final volunteers join us."

They had a significant number of craft already, but even with Freya's astounding technology and Korbin's powerful magic, for this to work they would need every bit of help they could get.

The Ghalian shimmer ships would be an ace in the hole, distracting the Urvalin craft by popping off attacks from areas not expected. Unfortunately, the Urvalin seemed to possibly possess some means of detecting shimmer magic. It wasn't a sure thing, but they were not about to risk flying right into a crossfire should their camouflage not be as secure as they hoped.

"Sorry we're late," Olo's chipper voice called over comms. "Tym and I were hung up on the way."

"He means we were pillaging an Urvalin transport ship," Tym interjected.

"Hey, you didn't need to go telling them that."

"Why not? It's one less of them out there. I'd think it was good news."

Korbin rubbed his forehead and took a deep breath. "Tym, have you been drinking?"

"No! Well, yes, but not much. Well, not *too* much. One has to be properly lubricated for a battle, after all."

"Tym, this is serious," Korbin grumbled.

"He actually *does* fly better a little tipsy," Olo noted. "In any case, we're ready when you are. And I see the rest of the troops are here. So, when do we begin?"

"Now," Korbin replied. "First wave, jump in and do your thing. Second wave, be ready to go on my mark."

The most heavily armed of their group shifted position and jumped toward the portal, opening fire with a magic barrage of great intensity the moment they arrived in position. Before the Urvalin could react, however, they executed a short jump and shifted to new positions nearby, creating a crossfire of sorts.

It was risky doing that short a jump in such close quarters, but as long as the Urvalin hadn't moved toward them yet it would still be relatively safe. At least, as safe as space battle could be.

A massive wave of magic flashed out into the space they had just occupied, the intensity registering all the way back at the other ships.

"What was *that*?" Daisy asked.

"That was *magic*," Korbin replied. "Not Allpower."

Daisy didn't like the sound of that. "Hang on, that's not right."

"No, it's not. They're not using Allpower. They're using casters from my own realm."

Korbin was right. As it turned out, several of the Urvalin craft spread among the fleet were now each home to a trio of linked casters, all of them doing the Urvalin's bidding on fear of torture or worse. All except one very stubborn young woman with galaxy eyes.

"Oh, you are so screwed when I get out of here," Nipsenni growled between shocks from her control collar.

Visla Palmarian and Visla Samanna were already on the ground, their linked collars shocking them too every time their connected prisoner mouthed off.

"Stop fighting," Samanna managed to say.

"Like hell," Nipsenni replied through gritted teeth.

Another shock hit her, causing a knee-jerk flash of power. Quite unexpected by everyone aboard her ship, the craft abruptly jumped. It didn't travel far—just to the other end of the system—but the strange woman with Zomoki-like power had just jumped an entire ship, and while wearing a control collar, no less.

A control collar that abruptly increased its intensity until she slumped to the ground, unconscious. This craft, it seemed, was temporarily out of the fight.

The other Urvalin ships were picking up the slack, so the one member of their fleet not casting was just an inconvenience more than anything else. The battle would continue regardless. Little did Kara know, her father was so close by. And had he actually participated in the casting, she and Korbin would have sensed his power easily.

But the visla was flat on his back and not casting anytime soon. And Kara and Vee had a job to do.

"We're ready when you are, Uncle Korbin."

It was time to let his niece fly free of the nest, figuratively and literally.

"Second wave, let's go!" he sent to the remaining ships. "Olo, Tym, flank them and keep them safe. When you see us break out, make your jumps."

"We'll keep them from harm, don't you worry," Olo said. "Now, go clear us a path. It's gonna be a bumpy ride."

Korbin's attack wing flew into the fray, jumping, and, in Freya's case, warping to their initiation point. This time, however, the Urvalin were ready for reinforcements and met them with a furious barrage of magic and pulse blasts the moment they arrived.

Freya's regular shielding meshed seamlessly with her magically charged nanites, working together to block everything the Urvalin threw at them. The others were having a bit more of a difficult time, but some ballsy flying, along with a serious counterattack, leveled the playing field. At least for the time being.

Korbin had spent a lot of time getting the feel for the new

weaponry his Earth friends had provided him, and those hours upon hours of practice were now paying off.

"Pull them away," he transmitted while letting loose a spray of magically charged railgun sabots. "We need to clear the path for the girls."

The other ships reacted at once, shifting their flight to a more offensive stance, unloading on the Urvalin before quickly moving to a defensive footing and falling back. The Urvalin, sensing a weakness to exploit, quickly pursued them, just as planned.

"Okay," Olo said. "Here we go."

Olo, Tym, and the two dragons bound their jumps together and flashed out of existence, popping back into regular space just outside of the blazing plasma field. The smuggler and the fighter pilot spun off immediately, engaging the remaining ship and drawing both its attention as well as its fire.

"Hold tight," Nixxus said over her harness comms. "This may be a little uncomfortable."

Without further ado, she and Gazz powered up their protective spells and dove headlong into the flames.

The transit was both exhilarating and terrifying all at once. Molten plasma from the heart of the sun swirled all around them as they flew, slowing what was normally a near-instantaneous trip to what seemed like a crawl. The lights and shapes were putting on a dazzling show, dancing around them like a pyromaniac's wet dream. It was almost enough to make them forget the incredible heat.

Almost.

Even with protective spells and space suits designed for the passage, the heat was still enough to take your breath away. But Nixxus and Gazz were passing through fully charged, and without the worry of draining their reserves, they found themselves awash in the sun's magnificent power. They weren't simply maintaining equilibrium, they were supercharging their magic with every second.

When they emerged on the other side of the portal, the two dragons burst from the sun like a pair of rising phoenix, a spray of plasma trailing them as they flew.

There were Urvalin nearby, and they had been ready in case something should fly out of the submerged portal, but the dragons had the jump on them, blasting the ships with immense excess power spilling over from the crossing. Kara and Vee also let loose, their own flavors of magic confusing the enemy crews who only saw the dragons on their scans.

The Urvalin, as strong as their casters were, found themselves forced to quickly adjust their defenses, focusing all of their efforts on strictly defensive spells. It was all the dragon riders needed.

"Jump us out of here," Kara urged.

Nixxus nodded, and a moment later she and Gazz jumped away, their destination far from the sun, and far from Earth.

They would have to avoid the Urvalin now, and while they had a map of the tech-dampening dead zones floating through the system, there was still no absolute guarantee their system shut down would spare their suits and tech harnesses. Judging by the sea of floating, inert craft, it was clear that the minefields were still active. Only a fool would tempt fate by flying right through them.

"We made it," Vee said, the relief clear in her voice. "We actually made it."

"Ye of little faith," Kara chuckled. "But that wasn't the hardest part. Now we've got to get down there unnoticed and deliver the news to Cal, and then get the Bakana rods in the right hands."

"And then?" Nixxus asked.

Kara shrugged. "And then, I really don't know. Whatever we do, it'll be messing with the Urvalin, and that works for me."

CHAPTER FIFTY-EIGHT

The ship streaking back toward Earth was flying hard, blowing right past any Urvalin combatants who might foolishly hope to stand in their way. A fight might have slowed them down, but their mission was far too important to allow that to happen. Time was of the essence, though they didn't know just how pressing matters were.

Having been on standby on a distant world while Malalia Maktan fed to her heart's content on magical creatures, draining them of every drop of power they contained, had put them out of the loop. That loop included the fact that Commander Torgus had taken his command ship to the surface and was personally engaging in the domination of Earth.

Had they known that little tidbit, Rika would have likely pressed the captain to fly faster, if that was even possible. They were damn near red-lining as it was, pushing the warp system and running hot as soon as Malalia had eaten her fill. And if there had been any question as to her having eaten enough when they first landed, her return to the ship, bloody from her kills, dispelled that immediately.

Malalia, worn, scarred, and old after their battle with the

Urvalin was a changed woman. Even before she bathed away the aftermath of her feast, it was clear. She was young. Strong. And absolutely bristling with magic.

"Feeling better?" Rika asked when she saw the uncharacteristically filthy woman she'd formerly served stride out of the woods.

"Immeasurably," Malalia said with a broad grin. "Thank you for this. I can't tell you how much I needed it."

"Oh, I know," Rika said. "You really put yourself on the line back there, Malalia. You could have died."

"Ah, but I didn't," she replied with a forced chuckle.

"Yeah, but it was close. And believe me, your sacrifice hasn't gone unnoted."

It was strange, feeling not only sympathy but also appreciation for the woman who had caused her so much grief across multiple worlds and even timelines. But Malalia had done more than just talk a good game, she had acted, and unprompted at that. And in doing so she'd saved them all, at her own peril, no less.

The universe was a strange place, it seemed, and it was getting stranger by the day. First Grundsch, a murderous Ra'az Hok, had converted to a peaceful and productive member of Earth society. And now Visla Dominus, aka Malalia Maktan, had put aside her evil ways and was actively fighting on the right side for once. It was enough to almost give Rika hope.

Almost.

They still had the real fight ahead of them, and even filled with fresh magic, there was a very real possibility their ace in the hole wouldn't be enough.

Malalia walked into the ship, blood streaking her face and clothing.

"You've got a little something," Rika joked, tapping her chin.

Malalia flashed an amused smile. "I'll have to work on my table manners next time."

With that, she headed off to bathe and prepare herself for the coming ordeal, leaving Rika to marvel at just how much their dynamic had shifted since they'd first met.

"Huh," she said to herself. "Now I've seen everything."

When they exited their final warp close to Earth some time later, Malalia and Rika were seated in command with the captain and her team. There would be a fight down below, no doubt, but exactly what it might look like was anyone's guess.

There was only one way to find out.

"Kill all power," Rika instructed the captain. "Just like we discussed."

"Everything off," the captain called to her team.

"Even life support?" her tech asked.

"*Everything*. Whatever stays on will get blown out when we hit the dampening field."

"But how will we fly?" the tech wondered.

Rika slowly rolled her shoulders and took a deep breath. "Don't worry. I've got this."

Her tattoos, normally barely visible with their white pigment, abruptly began to glow, their brightness spiking until the entire compartment was almost uncomfortably lit by their glow. The tech shut down all systems, the ship's forward momentum carrying them into the dampening field as they brushed the planet's exosphere.

Rika's magic held them tight, keeping the ship sealed and safe while also guiding it through the turbulence and heat, protecting it as it eased into the atmosphere. Despite the bumps and shakes, she held strong, her magic flying the ship lower and lower until it was clear of the Urvalin threat.

"You can power up," she said through clenched teeth.

"Re-engage," the captain ordered.

"Aye, Captain. It'll take a minute."

"Just get her systems up and online as quickly as you can," she replied.

Malalia watched the goings-on with great interest, as well as grudging respect. Not long ago she had faced off against Rika, pitting herself against her former servant. Rika had won the day, and Malalia had taken her loss personally. But now? Seeing the impressive display of magic her former underling was putting on, she couldn't help but be impressed.

Rika wasn't just a run-of-the-mill caster. She was *strong*. Impossibly strong for one not born with magic. To be able to power an entire craft with her power? And she wasn't even a Drook. It was, for lack of a better word, incredible. So much so, in fact, that Malalia almost didn't feel bad about having lost their fight.

Still, some things were harder to let go than others, and that had been a particularly visceral defeat. But her appreciation for Rika's power, as well as her skill in wielding it, had just grown immeasurably.

"Propulsion back online," the pilot called out as the ship lurched.

Rika released her hold on the ship and slumped in her chair, her tattoos fading to a faint pulsing glow as she took a few deep breaths.

"There!" the navigator called out. "On the surface. Two hundred clicks due west. Some sort of massive disruption in Los Angeles."

The monitors zoomed in, showing a huge Urvalin ship on the ground. All around it was fighting, as well as multiple downed and burning Earth ships. Rika was heartened to see Marban's was not among them, but she did recognize more than one. And there was Allpower in the air. A lot of it. The ground forces didn't stand a chance. This was going to be a slaughter.

"Get us down there, now!" she barked.

The pilot responded at once, knowing the captain would echo Rika's demand. The ship dropped and banked hard, pushing on at supersonic speeds, rushing into the fray.

"Touchdown in ten seconds!"

The ground team was already at the airlock, ready to move the moment they hit the ground. The door opened and they rushed out, Rika and Malalia leading the way.

"There's a caster here," Malalia said. "Strong. *Very* strong. And an unusual flavor of magic."

"Allpower," Rika corrected. "One of their top casters, I'd wager."

"I can't get a fix."

"Neither can I. But they're down here somewhere." She slapped a comms unit in Malalia's hand. "Split up. Call if you make contact, but don't engage until we can meet up."

"And likewise for you. Together, I feel we can take this person."

"I sure as hell hope so," Rika said, then turned and raced off into the mayhem.

Malalia watched as the rest of the team fanned out to look for the visla, or whatever these Urvalin called their top casters, standing still and feeling the air around her. She stood like that a long moment, calmly sniffing the air. She then turned to her left, a little smile on her lips.

"Gotcha."

Malalia rounded the corner of a ruined building a few minutes later just in time to witness Commander Torgus smiting an entire squad of resistance fighters with his Allpower. The poor men didn't even have a konus between them. It was an incredibly lopsided fight, and it ended in seconds.

"I have him," she sent on her comms. "Follow the signal to my location."

"Got it. I'm coming. Don't engage. I'll be there as fast as I can."

"Of course," Malalia replied, turning off her comms. She then strode out from cover, toward the enemy caster, tall and unafraid. "Not terribly sporting of you," she said in a loud, steady voice.

Commander Torgus turned, an amused look on his face. His fingers grazed across the glowing stone dangling around his neck, then he cast, *hard*.

Malalia threw up a defensive spell with an embedded counter. It was highly unusual, and incredibly powerful, and Torgus found himself actually forced to cast his own defensive maneuver to stop it. He grinned wide. Now *this* was interesting.

"Ah, Visla Dominus. I was wondering if you and I might cross paths in this realm."

"I do not go by that name any longer," Malalia shot back.

He shrugged. "A shame. Dominus was a worthy adversary."

Malalia flashed a malicious, confident smile. "Oh, I think you will find I am more than worthy, yet."

Their magic and Allpower flared and flashed, the reverberations of the fight shaking the very buildings around them, the sound carrying for blocks.

"Dammit, Malalia!" Rika hissed as the sky lit up, picking up her pace even faster.

She raced toward the sounds of battle, not even needing to look at the comms locator. It was only a few blocks away, and there was no mistaking its location. A momentary lull greeted Rika as she reached the final corner. It was almost deafening in its silence, but the wail of hard magic filled the air a second later.

Rika rounded the corner to see Malalia wielding her full power, magic crackling in the air around her as she launched an enormous attack at the man down the street. He blocked it, but only just. His eyes flicked to the new arrival with the glowing tattoos. Apparently, he knew who Rika was and wanted no part of her as he turned tail and ran without hesitation before she could join the assault.

Malalia dropped to her knees, exhausted but victorious.

"I told you to wait for me!" Rika said, rushing to her side.

"I tried. But he saw me, and there was nothing else I could do."

Malalia's hair was rapidly graying from the enormous expenditure and there was no way they could turn around and fly back to a feeding planet. She needed magic, and she needed it now. Rika saw several wounded but breathing Urvalin and made an unpleasant choice.

"Come on," she said, dragging the exhausted woman to the nearest of them. "Most of them have Allpower. Some more than others. I don't know how well it will work for you, but you need to—"

Malalia had already latched onto the dying man's throat, drinking his blood and power with almost palpable desperation. A moment later the man slumped down, dead.

"Different," Malalia said, the gray in her hair slowly receding, "but it will suffice."

Lurching to her feet, she followed Rika through the battlefield, stopping to feed and replenish her power as they went, looming over the fallen like one of the battlefield hags of old times. By the time they rejoined the others, Malalia was almost as good as new.

"The fight is over," Rika said. "Malalia drove their main caster off."

"By herself?" a trooper asked, amazed.

Rika patted Malalia on the shoulder. "Yep. All by herself. Now, we need to mop up and help the others. We have wounded needing attention."

"And the enemy?" the man asked.

Rika glanced at the woman beside her and winked. "I think we can let Malalia handle them."

CHAPTER FIFTY-NINE

Marty and Arlo were flying close support from the air, providing cover for their friends on the ground. They'd dropped them off several miles from the Urvalin barracks and launched skyward, engaging the fighters who frequented the area.

They were providing one hell of a diversion while the real assault took place below.

Finn and the others were sneaking into the landing area, affixing the stealthy bombs to as many of the parked ships as they could. Unfortunately, this time they were spotted before they could finish.

A firefight had ensued, and a rather brutal one at that. There were a lot of Urvalin inside those barracks, and, unfortunately, that meant the stealthy team was outnumbered.

"Fall back," Sergeant Franklin called out over comms. "We'll try to draw their fire and buy you some time."

The commando squad opened up on the Urvalin from their hiding spots across the encampment, the ferocity of their attack startling the troops that had been pursuing their human friends.

"Let 'em have it, Rip," Finn called to his daughter.

Ripley responded immediately, using the konus she had

been saving for the right time to cast the strongest spells she could summon. The Urvalin were expecting a tech attack at this point, but Ripley was not a skilled caster, and her attempt was nevertheless blocked quickly enough, having only inconvenienced the Urvalin.

"Dad, that didn't work. We need to go!" she called out.

Finn and the others were already moving. "Don't have to tell me twice," he replied. "Hurry, Rip, this is too exposed! We need to get to cover!"

As if they heard them, a barrage of pulse fire and magic from the Urvalin forced the saboteurs to dive behind whatever could protect them. It was far too close for comfort.

"We're pinned down here," Vince transmitted. "Arlo, Marty, a little help, please."

"We're trying," Arlo replied as they managed to spray the advancing troops with some very sporadic pulse fire. "There's too many of them up here for us to get free."

Marty was diving and spinning through the skies as Arlo helped target the enemy ships. They were firing off pulse rounds aplenty along with occasional railgun sabots, but in this type of maneuvering dogfight, it was too risky just letting loose. An errant shot as they banked could accidentally travel into an unintended target.

"Arlo, just lay down whatever cover fire you can," Ripley replied. "We'll try to find a way out of this mess on this end."

"Looks like you guys need a hand," a new voice chimed in over their comms.

"Kara?" Arlo blurted. "How did you get here? And where are you?"

A blast of magical flames incinerated the Urvalin troops closing the gap on the ground forces as Gazz dove low. Simultaneously, a matching burst of fire from Nixxus took out two of the ships that were proving so problematic for Marty and

Arlo. Three of the grounded ships went up in flames while the rest took to the skies and fled as fast as they were able.

"Hey, guys," she replied. "We're up here."

"I see that," Marty said with glee as he leveled his flight and took proper aim at the now-fleeing enemy and let off a few parting shots.

"You're riding a *dragon*?" Arlo marveled.

"Yeah. Cool, right? Nixxus and Gazz brought me and Vee back across the portal."

"Holy crap, that's amazeballs!" Ripley practically squealed as the two dragons landed on the now-quiet battlefield.

Kara and Vee climbed down from their mounts and took off their helmets.

"Oh my God! You guys got armored space suits too?" she gushed.

"I know, right?" Vee said, hugging their friend.

Kara joined them in an impromptu group hug. "Cal and his friends really hooked us up. You should see all the goodies they put in those harnesses."

Finn and Vince jogged toward them, surveying the perimeter as they did. But George and his commandos were already streaming in from their positions.

"Did you say Cal made those for you?" Finn asked.

"Yep," Kara replied. "Well, his friend Habby, mostly."

"Oh, we know Habby," Vince said with a chuckle. "But how did you get through the portal?"

"Nixxus and Gazz were able to protect us. Plus, they have konuses mounted to their harnesses for extra power, so that helped. It was kinda scary, but it was also really cool."

"But the risk—"

"We had to. We came to help fight the Urvalin, but also to relay a message," Kara said. "Oh, and Daisy said to say hi and tell to tell you, you'd better be taking good care of Arlo."

"I'm not a baby," Arlo said, hopping out of Marty's airlock as the AI ship quietly set down nearby.

"Yeah, but moms are gonna mom," Ripley chuckled. "Hell, you know how mine can be."

"True, that."

"Lay off your mother," Finn said. "You know she means well."

George trotted up to them, waving a greeting. "You said you had a message?"

"You heard that all the way over there?"

He tapped his head. "Cyborg ears."

"We've got a message all right," Vee interjected. "The Urvalin are from another galaxy."

"We figured as much," Finn said.

"No, you don't get it," Kara said. "Not yours, and not ours. A *third* galaxy. One they are able to link power with, though I'm not entirely clear on that bit. Something about amulets their top casters wear."

"For real? This is *not* good," Arlo said. "Really not good."

"You don't know the half of it," she agreed. "More than that, apparently, that's where Charlie's been taken."

All of the assembled resistance fighters felt their stomachs sink.

"Did you say Charlie's in another *galaxy*?" Vince asked.

"Yep. And cut off from all of us. Him, Ara, Bawb and Hunze. They wanted to catch Rika too, but from what we heard, she somehow avoided the trap."

"How did you find this out?" Finn wondered.

"The Ghalian have a spy."

"Don't they always?" he mused. "But if Charlie's gone, and I mean *gone*, gone, we're going to have a really hard time against these bastards."

Kara reached up and opened the storage container on Nixxus's harness and took out a Bakana rod.

"They gave us this," she said. "One of the Bakana rods."

Everyone knew what it was. Without those rods sapping her power, Malalia would have been successful in her attempt to conquer the galaxy.

"Where did you get that?" Vince asked.

"The Ghalian gave it to me to carry over. They think if we can get this to Charlie it might be able to help him connect, even from another galaxy. It might even help him somehow get home."

She looked at Vee. Both silently agreed they would keep the other Bakana rod a secret, at least for now. These were their friends, but the less people who knew, the less likely it was the Urvalin could somehow find out about it. They trusted them all, but they also knew capture and torture were not impossibilities in this war.

"I hate to rain on your parade," George interrupted. "But we really should get the hell out of here. I don't think the Urvalin are going to let this go without a response, and there's no telling when they'll be back with their heavy hitters."

Vince quickly assessed their ranks. "George is right. We need to load up and boogie."

"Anywhere in particular?" Nixxus asked.

"Oh, we've got a place," Marty replied. "Just follow me."

CHAPTER SIXTY

"They don't look here?" Vee marveled. "But this place, it's so—"

"Impressive? I know," Ripley said. "NORAD was blown out a long time ago, but a lot of very quiet work went into rebuilding this part of it."

"Not just the cavern," Vee said. "Also this outside area. The doors are massive."

"Yeah, but we generally stay inside, just in case of a flyover. But the whole planet knows this place was destroyed, so not even the traitors can steer the Urvalin this way."

It was something Kara and Vee were unfortunately familiar with from their own galaxy and the machinations of the Council of Twenty. Some families would sell one another out for the right amount of coin. That it could happen here was no surprise.

"You say Griggalt was also lost with Charlie and Ara?" Nixxus asked.

"From what we know, yeah, it seems that way. All of them were pulled into the portal trap."

"But Orgalius is still alive?" Gazz asked.

"He's fine," George said. "Actually, he's been helping Rika a lot these days. They've become something of a fearsome team, taking down Urvalin all over the place. The Urvalin don't seem to do well with magic in this galaxy, and having our own fighters using it against them really messes them up. It's kinda funny. I mean, it was a classic overconfidence blunder. They were so sure they would neutralize any magical defense here that they didn't account for the dragons. Or Rika, for that matter."

"And let's not forget the dampening field," Finn chimed in. "We found out about it early on, and rather than everyone rushing into it and dying, our forces held back."

"Finn's right," Vince said. "It's ironic that the very thing they expected to separate and diminish our forces has actually served to concentrate them in smaller, more potent pockets of resistance."

George and his soldiers looked at one another and shared a little laugh. "Nice to see Murphy visiting someone else for a change," he said. "It's funny how war never seems to go quite the way you expect it to."

"Funnier when it happens to someone else, Sarge," one of his men said.

"Truer words have never been spoken."

Vince, ever the mechanic, had wandered over to better examine the new harnesses the AIs had whipped up for their dragon friends. They were impressive, to say the least, and he couldn't help but geek out a little as they walked him through all of the bells and whistles.

"Dad, you're fanboying," Arlo said.

"Can you blame me?" he replied. "I mean, look at this rig. And the girls' armor? It's pretty amazing, you've gotta admit."

Arlo was actually just as jazzed as his father, but he was playing it cool in front of the girls. It was pointless, of course. This was Arlo, after all. They all knew full well what was running through his mind.

"Hey, Arlo," Kara said. "I know it's been a while, and we haven't really talked about stuff—"

"All good," he said a little too quickly.

Ripley flashed him an annoyed look. "Let her finish, dork."

Arlo, for once, bit his tongue. Kara approved.

"As I was saying. I know it's been a while, and things maybe got a little weird, but there's a lot at stake here, and we could really use your help."

Arlo relaxed his shoulders a hair. "Oh. Sure, we'll help. I mean, we've already been going after the Urvalin as it is."

Kara looked up at Nixxus, and the dragon and her rider sharing an amused little grin.

"Oh, I was thinking of something a little more out of your comfort zone."

Two shadows flashed across the opening of the cavern, growing larger until a pair of large dragons touched down just outside. Drombus and Duzza were close cousins they knew fairly well. The both of them were a deep orange that glowed faintly in the full sunlight.

"How did they find us?" Finn asked.

"We signaled them as soon as we entered the atmosphere," Gazz replied. "Encrypted, of course, just as Cal showed us."

Arlo took a few steps closer. "Those are harnesses. They've got harnesses, just like yours."

"Courtesy of Cal and Habby," Drombus said. "We've spent the last few days learning their ins and outs. Wonderful things, though I never would have thought I would say that about a technology contraption strapped to my body."

"I rather like it," Duzza said. "Though, admittedly, it did take some getting used to, I do quite enjoy the added power of the embedded konus."

Ripley walked closer, running her hand over the metal. "Hey, what's this?" she asked as the container on Duzza's harness slid open.

"Something you might like," the dragon replied.

Ripley pulled out the contents. An armored space suit, just

like Kara and Vee were wearing. Arlo rushed over to Drombus and saw there was a suit for him as well.

"Oh. My. God!" he exclaimed. "Is this what I think it is?"

"If you think you are being asked to be a dragon rider with us, then yes, it is," Kara replied with a happy laugh.

Arlo looked at her with unguarded affection, his heart on his sleeve for a change. She played it cool, allowing him to keep his pride, merely smiling warmly and giving a welcoming nod in return. There would be plenty of time to talk later. For now they needed to get this show on the road.

Arlo's mood darkened abruptly. "But Marty," he said.

"You know I can't fly through the dampening field," Marty replied. "And like this you'll be able to operate both in and out of the atmosphere."

"But—"

"It's okay, Arlo. You go ahead. It's not personal, I know."

"Marty, we've been through *everything* together."

"Yeah, but maybe it's time to experience things solo. For *both* of us."

Arlo looked at his father. Vince was absolutely beaming. His son was going to be a dragon rider. If pride were flammable, he'd have combusted brighter than the sun. Ripley hadn't wasted a second and was already slipping into her armored space suit.

"Go ahead. Try it on," Vince urged.

Arlo didn't need to be told twice.

Just a few short minutes later the cousins were suited up and dialed in, their armor fitting as though it had been custom-made for them. And in a way, it had.

"Oh man, this is too cool," he said, squatting down then jumping up into the air. "It's so light and maneuverable."

"To allow freedom of movement," Nixxus said. "Though it will fit somewhat looser when we fly through the Urvalin dead zones. While we can protect you with our magic, we don't want to encounter a dampening field while the suits and harnesses are powered on."

"So, if we shut things down it shouldn't be damaged?" he asked.

"It's a reasonable assumption. It worked for us on the way to the surface. Now, why don't you mount up and get yourselves dialed in? We really should depart soon. We have a Bakana rod to deliver."

Arlo and Ripley took just one glance at each other then raced to their dragons, quickly scrambling up and settling into their seats.

"Hang on a sec," Finn called out, pulling a vid cam from his pocket. "Strike a pose for us!"

"Daaaad," Ripley groaned.

"Come on. Suck it up and give your parents a picture, okay? Neither of your moms are here, and it's not every day your kid becomes a dragon rider."

"Ugh. Fine," she grumbled.

"You can give us a better pose than that," Vince called up to them.

Arlo raised his arms wide in a victorious spread. Ripley, a bit more reserved, nevertheless sat upright and put her hands on her hips, her shoulders squared.

"Perfect!" Finn said as he snapped off a stream of images. He turned to his friend, a little tear in his eye. "Man, our babies are all grown up."

"Dad, enough!" Ripley groaned. "You're so cheesy."

"A dad's allowed to be proud. It's in the job description."

"Speaking of jobs," Gazz said as the girls settled back into their seats as well. "My apologies, I know this is abrupt, but we really must be going."

The cousins and their friends from another realm all took the cue and sealed their helmets to their suits and prepared for flight.

"Peace out!" Arlo abruptly hollered with a happy laugh over his harness's external speaker.

A moment later the dragons were aloft, and with a few powerful flaps of their wings, they were gone.

Vince put his arm around his friend's shoulder. "I don't think they'll ever be grown up," he said with a laugh. "But yeah, they sure have come a long way."

CHAPTER SIXTY-ONE

Charlie and Ara felt surprisingly fine as they flew deeper into the strange region of space where Allpower simply didn't exist. Their own magic, for whatever reason, remained perfectly intact, which was a good thing as they'd have been in pretty deep trouble if it hadn't. When your own life support relied on magic and not an enclosed ship, the loss of that power could be catastrophic, and immediately at that.

Nakk, Skohla, and the other Allpower users, however, were not so at ease. They were used to having both tech and Allpower at their disposal, and losing one of them so abruptly, so completely, well, it was unsettling to say the least. Even so, they pushed forward. With the Urvalin lurking just outside the system, they had little choice.

The volcano-looking sun was growing ever larger as they moved deeper into the system. It was dying, yes, but the time that would take to actually occur would be something in the hundreds of millions of years. Everyone alive today, along with their ancestors and possibly even species, would be long gone by then. Charlie and his friends were no more than a speck of sand on the beach of time.

That didn't mean it was not still dangerous, however. The radiation and erratic energy spewing out of the star could snuff out life with no effort whatsoever. Fortunately, and rather amazingly, there was one planet locked into just the right orbit so as to avoid the deadly effects of the dying sun.

Radiation, while bathing the sky around it, somehow missed the planet entirely, leaving it the one safe harbor in its own Goldilocks Zone of both temperature as well as radiation levels.

"That's where we're heading," Charlie transmitted. "There don't seem to be any Urvalin anywhere near. In fact, nothing is guarding it so far as Ara and I can tell. Kip, Dukaan, you guys see anything?"

"Just clear skies," Dukaan replied.

Nakk keyed his comms. "That is because even they are too scared to enter this system. The lack of Allpower is anathema for the Urvalin even more than the rest of us."

"Which makes it the perfect place to hide an artifact of extreme power," Bawb noted. "Though at the time it was hidden, the Urvalin were not the threat in mind."

"Yeah, they weren't even twinkles in their grandpa's eye," Charlie said.

Bawb glossed over the comment, more serious things on his mind. "Whoever they were hiding it from, the records do not name them. But if we are to assume they were powerful, then this planet would have been as ideal a location as they could hope to find."

Charlie thought about what it must have been like hiding the Vortaxis all of those thousands of years ago, and a distressing question reared its head.

"Nakk?"

"Yes, Charlie?"

"How long have your people had technology? I mean, you obviously had ships for thousands of years."

"Allpower has been in use longer than most societies have

existed, and with it, space travel was perfected. Technology as advanced as we know it is only a relatively recent development."

"So, a bare minimum back then is what you're saying?"

"More or less. Why?"

"Just thinking is all," Charlie replied. "Whoever flew to this system to hide the Vortaxis? They sacrificed themselves to do it. Without Allpower, they'd have been stuck on this world for the rest of their lives with no hope for escape."

It was the ultimate display of just how serious the power in question was. Not an abstract ideal, not some act of faith, but willingly giving up one's own future to protect the galaxy. The weight of it was not lost on the others.

"For an Allpower wielder of the caliber we are discussing to give all of that up, they must have perceived the artifact as even more dangerous than we do," Nakk said. "But look at your scans."

"What?" Charlie asked.

"The planet. It is not barren and lifeless. I actually see cities, and sprawling ones at that."

Kip dialed in his scans to a tighter beam and probed the surface. "There's no Allpower, but damn, these guys have some seriously advanced tech down there."

"The rumors are true, then," Skohla marveled. "A society built without Allpower."

"You knew about this?" Hunze asked.

"No specifics. Only that there were rumors from some extremely tech-heavy ships about trading the latest in technology in this place. Items that were fantastical in their description. Of course, no one believed them. Everyone knows that no one leaves this system."

"But now you're doubting them?" Charlie asked.

"It seemed so unlikely. But we are here now, intact and alive. And seeing this place, and observing how our ships still fly even without Allpower, I am forced to think that, perhaps, they were not stretching the truth as I'd believed."

"A tech planet?" Charlie mused. "Sounds like I'll fit right in. So, what do you all say? Hows-about we go and meet the locals? It'll be a learning experience at the very least, and, if we're right, this will be the final hiding spot of the Vortaxis."

The others agreed, though aside from Kip they were not nearly as enthused as Charlie was. Charlie transferred aboard Kip, then they dropped down into the atmosphere, moving slowly and deliberately, clearly not a threat to the society below. Even so, a strange scanning system locked onto them as they descended. No weapons were targeting them, so at least they had that going for them.

The ships settled down in a small landing area in what seemed to be the largest city on the planet. If there was going to be someone with knowledge of the Vortaxis, this would be the most likely spot, they reasoned.

Ara remained in space, her magical defenses primed but otherwise keeping her power hidden. If no one here had dealt with any form of Allpower in perhaps thousands of years, there was no telling what a display of it might trigger. And they had almost certainly not seen a Zomoki before, so that was a can of worms they would rather not open if they could at all avoid it.

There were a few other ships in the landing area, mostly small ones clearly intended for planetary use, as well as one large craft that appeared to be outfitted with significantly powerful weapons. Interestingly, their scans also revealed that it seemed to possess a drive system powered by a novel form of warp technology.

"Some elements of these ships are familiar," Skohla said. "Our tech incorporated into their craft."

"So, the traders really were telling the truth," Hunze replied.

"It seems that way."

Charlie was glued to his small readout, poring over the data Kip and Dukaan had gathered during their approach.

"What is it, Charlie?" Bawb asked as he stepped out of the ship to find his friend looking at the forearm tablet's display with rapt attention.

"Dude, there are temples here. Kip logged 'em while we were coming down."

"Most cultures have religious institutions," Nakk noted, exiting his own craft.

"You don't get it, these are familiar. And they're intact and fully functional, not just some ruins. The design, they're clearly from the same order that guarded the Vortaxis."

Nakk's eyes widened slightly. "You mean the legends were right?"

"I think so. It looks like we actually may have found the right place."

Charlie had the location of the temples pinpointed on his small tablet. He gauged the area around them and turned to face the direction of the largest of them.

"Plans?" Bawb asked.

"I think we go in quietly and with the utmost respect. If the Vortaxis is hidden in an active holy site, we really don't want to go pissing off the faithful by tearing the place up."

"Not to mention, a society such as this did not attain its reputation for no reason," the assassin noted. "I have little doubt we are being observed and targeted at this very moment, so I suggest no sudden movements, and only small arms. We do not wish to appear to be looking for an altercation."

"Good point, Bob," Charlie agreed. "Okay, then. Kip, you and Dukaan take off fly out of sight and engage your active camouflage before returning. I want you to monitor from above, and stay close. Ara will keep an ear open from orbit. As for the rest of us, let's go meet the locals. I hope for all our sakes they're friendly."

CHAPTER SIXTY-TWO

The general feel of the hidden planet was surprisingly normal for Charlie. Of course, being from a world with no magic—at least until he and his band of power users returned from another galaxy—meant that the absence of floating vehicles and impossible feats that defied science was an almost comforting sensation, and one he hadn't felt in a very long time.

The others, however, felt uneasy. Bawb and Hunze were more or less all right with it, as their magic was intact, but Nakk and Skohla and their people were almost going through withdrawal symptoms from the visceral absence of Allpower.

"Keep it together," Charlie said quietly as they walked from the landing zone into the city proper.

There were people out and about, and an interesting mix of them at that. Charlie posited that the planet had likely been populated by the various stranded craft over the years, leading to a true melting pot society. Odds were most of those who wound up on this world originally had come to it unintentionally.

Except for the truly devout, of course.

Those who came to hide the Vortaxis knew what they were

getting into, and those of their order who came later were undoubtedly equally aware. It was those they would need to seek out.

"Kip, you listening?" Charlie asked.

"Ears wide open," the AI replied. "I know what you're going to ask, and the answer is, I'll translate as fast as I can. But we'll need to hear their language first."

"More of the usual," Charlie noted. "We'll do what we can. And it looks like we'll have our first chance in just a moment."

A pair of short quadrupedal beings wearing a rather dapper ensemble made of a sheer fabric with what seemed to be fine filaments of metal trailing through them walked up to the visitors with curious looks on their six-eyed faces. They were unarmed, from what Charlie could tell, but the lack of overt weaponry didn't necessarily mean they were harmless.

He raised his open palm in greeting. "Hello. I am Charlie. These are my friends. We're new here, but if you would speak, maybe we can learn to communicate."

The two creatures looked at one another then let out what could only be a laugh.

"What is so funny?" Nakk wondered.

A stream of gibberish flowed out of the closer one's mouth parts.

"Ooookay," Charlie said. "Well, that didn't much—"

The other alien fiddled with something on its clothing.

"Is that better?" it asked in only slightly accented English.

"How do you speak our tongue?" Nakk asked.

"What do you mean, yours? That was my language," Charlie said.

"I heard another entirely," Bawb marveled. "Fascinating."

The locals chittered with amusement. "I see the pale one is clever. He understands."

"I get it too," Charlie said. "Some sort of universal translator.

But how do you make it transmit each of our languages independently and simultaneously?"

The creature shrugged as if speaking to a rural hick. "Science, of course."

It was a novel sensation for the spaceship engineer from Earth. Being talked to like a clueless neophyte was something he maybe expected in a magical setting, but a tech one? This was supposed to be his wheelhouse.

Then again, this was an entirely new galaxy, and this tiny pocket of it had developed its own form of technology independently of the rest of the millions of systems around it. Given that, it was akin to Madagascar or Galapagos back home. Some things were just not found anywhere else, and Charlie figured that could hold true for tech as well.

The realization was both humbling and exciting. If they played their cards right, this could be a wealth of new science at their fingertips the likes of which none of them had ever dreamed of.

But first things first. The Vortaxis took priority.

"It's new to me," Charlie said, still marveling at the translation tech. "But we're not from around here."

"Obviously," the unimpressed alien replied.

"Kip, you getting all of this?" Charlie quietly asked.

"Yep. Fascinating tech," he replied over the bone-conduction comm patch. "My scans are having a hard time with it, though."

The sarcastic aliens both abruptly looked up, tapping the fabric of their sleeves. Sirens blared to life, and what looked like no more than decorative sculptures flipped aside, massive cannons of a design Charlie had never seen before slamming into place, fully charged and ready to fire.

They were aimed at the sky. They were aimed at the camouflaged AI ship hovering above them.

"I'm target locked!" Kip said, the alarm in his voice clear.

"Don't do anything," Charlie hissed. He turned his attention to the locals. "We mean you no harm."

"You couldn't harm us if you wanted to, fleshy man-thing."

"Man-thing? Seriously?"

"Unless your species has gender physiology we are unfamiliar with, yes. Tell your craft to uncloak and land at once or we will remove it from our skies."

A small rabble of locals were rushing down the streets, all of them armed. *This* would be the danger of the locals that Skohla had spoken of. It was time for damage control, and fast, while there was still time.

"Kip, camouflage off. Do as they ask."

The ship didn't hesitate, his active camouflage shutting down at once. He slowly moved back to the landing site just behind them and settled to the ground. The two formerly harmless-looking aliens moved closer, waving their hands at the ship.

"You have tech built into your clothes," Charlie realized. "You're scanning our ship."

"Ah, he's not as ignorant as we thought," one of the aliens said. "Now, tell us, what sort of machine is this? We've never seen a craft like it before, nor the tech powering it. Most unusual."

"He is not from this—" Nakk began.

"Not from this *system*," Charlie interjected. If these people really were traders of tech, then Kip could be a very tasty prize for them, and he wasn't about to give them any reason to even consider prying him open for his secrets.

"You have come to trade?" a tall, gray-green-skinned being wearing a long, flowing robe asked.

Charlie recognized the symbols woven into the material at once, as did Bawb and Nakk. This person was affiliated with the religious order they were following. But having seen what the other locals were able to do with the simple touch of a sleeve, they had to tread lightly. There was no telling what someone of their stature and rank might be able to do with the systems at their fingertips.

Unfortunately, not everyone on Nakk's crew was as quick on the uptake.

"We're not here to trade, we've just come for the Vortaxis," a crewman named Gorkin blurted before Nakk could bitch-slap the ever-loving hell out of him.

There was a gasp from the locals and a shocked and stern look from what they now realized was a high priest of some sort.

"Oh, hell," Charlie quietly moaned. "He didn't mean it like that, I swear," he said.

"You may *not* defile the holy site," the tall priest said.

"We are simply learning about the power of the artifact," Bawb interjected, putting himself physically between his friends and the growing mob as subtly as possible.

The Ghalian, while master killers, were not the best assassins in the galaxy for nothing. They could blend in, manipulate, and steer events to further their goals. In this case, that talent would hopefully defuse a potentially dangerous situation.

"You are not believers," the priest said with disdain.

"We are not, but we mean no disrespect," he replied. "We are, however, seeking knowledge that may help us in our fight against the Urvalin threat."

The crowd began to murmur, and even the priest reacted, their posture shifting to a slightly less rigid footing.

"The Urvalin?"

"What are you doing?" Charlie asked with their silent bond.

"Look at the large red-skinned one," Bawb replied in his head.

Charlie saw it a moment later. Urvalin tech on his belt. They'd encountered them before.

"Yes. We have been battling them, trying to stop their spread," Bawb said calmly. "The Urvalin are a threat to all, regardless of belief."

The priest stared a long moment then gave a slight nod. "We are sympathetic to your cause. The Urvalin have learned not to intrude upon our realm, but not before demonstrating their true nature. If you fight the Urvalin, you are on the side of the just. But the Vortaxis—"

"We only seek knowledge," Bawb said. "Your order understands the legendary power, and we posit that may be able to turn the tide in the conflict."

The priest stared hard a long moment then nodded, waving off the crowd. The motley group of aliens seemed satisfied and returned to whatever they were doing before the alarm sounded, though a few of the rougher-looking ones lingered a moment longer before departing.

The priest clearly held sway in this place, and with a few well-placed words an alliance of sorts had been forged. Or, at least, a bit of grace that would prevent their ships from being stripped for parts.

"Come," the priest said. "We will dine and discuss the goings-on of which you speak. It has been some time since we have had such interesting news reach us."

"Your hospitality is greatly appreciated," Bawb replied, gesturing for the others to follow. But the look in his eye told Charlie to stay alert. This system didn't have such a frightening reputation for no reason, and a friendly repast could very easily become a deadly trap.

The meal turned out to be a welcome treat after so much time jumping from system to system engaging the Urvalin. More than just that, it was hosted within the walls of the temple itself. And that proved to be a most fascinating experience indeed.

CHAPTER SIXTY-THREE

A great deal of history was imparted over dinner.

It seemed the order that had essentially been the defacto founding influence on this hidden world had also played a pivotal role in forming the very fabric of its society over the millennia. The temples spread across the planet served as touchstones for those who found themselves stranded here, and over time became communal gathering points as much as they were religious hubs.

Slowly, over many thousands of years, the castaways learned to rely solely on the cobbled-together technology from their disparate craft, not only using what they already had, but teaching themselves the skills they had forgotten with the advent of machinery and use of Allpower.

Mining raw materials and smelting their own metal was a primitive but necessary start, but having already been from developed worlds, they knew it could be done. Only this time, it was entirely without Allpower, and that meant a long and arduous process.

But time was a funny thing, and after a few centuries struggling to achieve a level of indigenous industry that would support their operations, the growing population found they had a knack for life devoid of any sort of magical tricks.

Charlie was fascinated by what they had accomplished, and it turned out their hosts were happy to discuss their achievements. The newcomers were not a threat, and with Bawb playing diplomat to the hilt, it seemed an actual alliance might yet be formed.

Of course, the real goal was still to find and take the Vortaxis, new friendships be damned, but that was something they were keeping to themselves. The Urvalin threat across galaxies was simply too great to allow anything, even religious devotees, to derail.

One problem did hang heavy, though. As they didn't even know what the relic looked like or how big or small it was, they had no idea if they could manage to take it even if they did find its location. What if it was the size of a small house?

Fortunately, from what they'd managed to decipher of the legends, it seemed to have been carried by Allpower casters in the past. Unless they were seriously huge individuals, that pointed to a much more reasonably sized item.

The dinner concluded with a tour of the temple, something it seemed was reserved for special guests, as this was the largest and first built of the structures on the planet. They entered an ornately painted room, designs and runes covering the large, octagonal space across every inch. Charlie spun slowly, making sure his video stream was catching it all.

He couldn't transmit from so deep in the building, and there was a good possibility they would have noticed if he had tried, but at least he could upload the data to Kip when they were clear.

It was strange, he thought, how the pictoglyphs and designs seemed to show the symbol for the artifact crushed beneath something large. Yet in the middle of the room, surrounded by what was clearly a motion-sensing array of deadly countermeasures that would likely level an entire army if they stepped too close, sat a large ornate chest.

"The Vortaxis," their host said with pride.

The visitors moved closer—but not too close.

"Amazing," Nakk said in awe. "I never thought I would actually see it."

"A legend from my childhood," Skohla added.

The priest seemed pleased with their reverence. Charlie, however, felt nothing. No tickle of Allpower, not a hint of any containment spells. Nowhere in the legends did it say that the Vortaxis was robbed of its power when it was hidden on this world, and yet there was not a trace.

He strained his senses, reaching out with his magic, confident knowing that he and his close friends were the only ones even capable of wielding it on this world. *Something* tickled the periphery of his power. It was close, but it wasn't here.

"That really is incredible," he said, quickly gazing around the room once again. "This chamber is also an amazing feat of design."

"Built to protect the holiest of holys."

"I can see that. It is a very secure location. But I was wondering, what's through there?" he asked, pointing to a nondescript door at the far end of the room.

"One of the original restroom facilities," the priest replied. "The natural water flow here is why the temple was constructed atop it, though modern, cleaner options are available upstairs if you require."

"Oh, this will be fine," Charlie said, trotting off toward the strengthening hint of power. "I'll only be a minute."

He stepped through the door, and a blast of noxious effluent gasses assailed his senses. It seemed likely that *all* of the temple's bathrooms flowed through this chamber given the intensity. He cast a small blocking spell and took a breath of clean air.

"Better," he said, then walked all the way in.

There was a series of what were essentially toilets circling the room, though not designed for human use it seemed, at least, not with any modicum of comfort. All of them had a channel that fed to a slow-trickling flow of water leading to a central pool. It was there that the effluent collected.

Smack-dab in the middle rested an enormous boulder, as if it had splashed down and created the indentation thousands of years prior. Charlie's eyes widened slightly.

"Oh, hell," he gasped. "No way."

He reached out with his power, probing the foul, murky depths. The faint hint of power teased his senses. The Vortaxis, it seemed, could very well be hidden in the most disgusting part of the structure.

It made perfect sense, actually. For one, no one would ever be able to move that boulder without deconstructing the entire building to get to it from above with a crane or a ship's lift apparatus. For another, the repulsive location was the least likely place one would ever expect a group of the devout to place their most holy of relics.

That is, unless none of them knew it was actually there.

Charlie felt a surge of adrenaline as the realization hit him. The very first member of the order had hidden it there, rolling a boulder atop it long before the building was ever constructed. They then placed what was likely an ordinary chest atop an altar and simply told everyone who came after that it was *that* which held their most precious of relics.

The beauty was, without Allpower of their own to sense it in this place, none of them would ever know it was a lie.

Charlie had to act fast. He was only supposed to be using the facilities after all. He pulled deep and cast a lifting spell. Magic from his realm was still incredibly unpredictable here, so he cast very slowly, using the least power possible, gradually ramping up the intensity.

Like raising a sunken ship from a swamp, the boulder slowly

rose, muck and filth dripping from it with a sickening plop. But Charlie was focused. In the zone. With another tendril of power he cast a retrieval spell, pulling whatever was buried down there to the surface. A bubble formed in the sludge, then a small box broke the surface.

Charlie shifted his casting, lowering the boulder without a splash as he reeled in the true Vortaxis.

"Well, shit," he said as he wrapped his hands around the box.

It was thick metal and of some variety that seemed to block his magic from penetrating. A novelty to this galaxy, it seemed, and something they would need to investigate further. But not now. Now he had to rejoin the others and play it cool until they were back at their ships.

He rinsed the box and his hands in the clean water flow then wrapped it up in a tiny spell, sealing it from detection and tucking it within his clothes. He then washed his hands and walked back out to the others.

"You are ripe," Bawb noted.

"Yeah, it's a bit strong in there," Charlie replied. "I should wash up better. What do you say we get back to the ships? It's been a productive day," Charlie said. *"I found it, Bob. It's under my shirt,"* he silently cast over their magical link.

Bawb didn't show any surprise, as expected. "Yes, it has been a long day. I think that would be best," he replied, turning to their host. "If you do not mind, we will return to our ships for the evening. But first, I want to thank you from all of us for your exceptional hospitality. I feel this will be the beginning of a very productive friendship."

The priest smiled and nodded, pleased at the visitors' appropriate levels of awe at what he'd dedicated his life to. "Of course. I will escort you myself."

The walk was slower than Charlie would have liked, but there was no avoiding the leisurely pace of their guide. Bawb, it seemed, had been quite successful in charming them, and the scenic route back to the landing area was in the cards as a result.

Finally, they said their goodbyes and boarded the ships. Once the doors were sealed, Charlie pulled the box from under his shirt.

"That is it?" Bawb asked.

"It does not seem very—" Hunze's words fell short as Charlie's blocking spell dropped. "Oh, the smell!"

"What have you brought aboard?" Dukaan called from command. "I can smell it from here!"

"Gimme ten," Charlie said, hurrying off to the showers.

He returned soon after wearing fresh clothes and with a well-scrubbed metal box. He handed it to Bawb.

"Hmm, sealed, I see. It will require some force to open."

"Yeah, I saw that," Charlie said. "But can you feel it?"

"I can," Bawb replied. "There is power within. And in this place, none can exist."

"None but the Vortaxis," Charlie replied, giddy with success. "It's gotta be massive."

"I concur."

Charlie felt a surge of joy building. "We got it, guys. We actually got it."

"Great," Kip chimed in. "So what now?"

"Now? Now we gather the troops, kick some Urvalin ass, and get our butts home."

CHAPTER SIXTY-FOUR

Bawb brought some novel techie bits and bobs from Kip's storage bins and presented them to the priesthood as a thank-you gift for their generosity to strangers, telling them they needed to be on their way, but that they would return with more of this unusual technology to share with their new allies.

The gesture was taken well, as was the temptation of more interesting trade, and Kip and the others were allowed to depart with warm wishes and the beginnings of a new friendship rather than being stripped for parts. It was the ideal outcome.

Bawb had deftly utilized his diplomatic skills on this outing, and all of his friends, Charlie and Hunze included, were impressed. Better yet, as none of the devout had been aware of the true location of the Vortaxis, they had not only achieved an alliance, but had retrieved the relic without souring that new friendship.

Charlie was tempted to comment that things were looking up, but with Murphy always lurking around the corner, he thought better of it.

They departed with a warm send off, and the trip up into orbit was uneventful. They held off transferring Charlie back to his seat atop Ara's harness until they'd flown a fair distance away, however, just for safety's sake. Even with the delay, Charlie was amped up the entire time.

"I'm actually gonna make it back home, dude," he said, his voice cracking with emotion as warm hope filled his chest. "I'm going to be there when my kid's born."

"And we are all very happy for you, Charlie," his friend replied. "It is as it should be."

"Leila will be thrilled," Hunze added.

Charlie had kept his churning feelings locked up tight ever since they learned they were cut off from their own galaxy. He had to, it was the only way he could function and do what had to be done. But now, with the Vortaxis in hand, their return was not just a distant dream. It was a very real possibility.

Of course, they would still have to manage to get the sealed box open to access the relic, but that could be accomplished when they made their cautious return to the portal hidden between the black holes. All they had to do now was adjust course and make their way back.

"I am sorry to break up the festivities," Skohla said over their comms, "but we still have the Urvalin waiting for us just outside the system. And I would remind you, they are ready for us."

"Aww, hell. I'd almost forgotten about them," Charlie replied as he stepped out of Kip's airlock into the void. "It's gonna be a serious mess getting past them."

Ara flew close to Kip as Charlie drifted to his upgraded ride. "We know they are waiting," she said.

"And knowing is half the battle," Charlie replied. "But we're a little limited here. We'll only have our tech shields and weapons while they'll have stayed far enough back to have their Allpower still fully operational. We're gonna be coming out short-handed."

"I may have a solution for that," Nakk chimed in with a mischievous laugh.

Charlie's curiosity was certainly piqued. "Oh? Do tell."

The Urvalin fleet had grown in size since their targets had plunged into the system they didn't dare enter. Commander Fraxxis himself had even come to join in the hunt, his massive command ship sitting front and center. He was not about to miss the opportunity to take out these meddling interlopers once and for all.

While Prin and Torgus had suggested linking their power for any possible engagement, however, Fraxxis had nixed the idea with a laugh.

"It is but one Zomoki and a few ships. Their entire fleet is elsewhere," he said. "And once we crush their foolish leaders out of existence, the rest of them will lose the will to fight."

"Which is why we should pool our Allpower," Prin said. "Do not leave anything to chance."

"Nonsense. You have your own problems," he reminded her. "And Torgus knows full well he needs as much Allpower as he can summon after his recent run-in."

It was true, Torgus was still recovering from his fight with Malalia. The descent to the surface had seemed perhaps a bit impulsive at the time, but the need to hurry things along had inspired him to act. And what was the worst that could happen? He would have to expend a bit more Allpower fighting the few casters who were still there? The invasion needed a good kickstart, and his presence was going to be the tinder that lit that flame.

Unfortunately, he hadn't counted on Malalia's return, nor her absolutely staggering powers.

Ultimately, he agreed with Fraxxis and focused on restoring his own potency.

"I still think it is a bad idea," Prin said.

"They are massively outnumbered, dear Prin," Fraxxis

replied. "And more than that, if they emerge, they will be entirely without Allpower. By the time they manage to regain use of it we will have won the day."

He had a very good point, but nevertheless, she wasn't entirely comfortable with the idea.

"Very well," she finally said. "But do not fail."

"I have no intention of it."

"No one ever does."

From then it had been a waiting game. Allpower would not penetrate the system, and scans were likewise garbled by the anomaly, but far sooner than they expected, an unusual reading flashed across their monitors.

"We have something," the technician announced. "The signal is distorted by the anomaly, but I think they are coming out."

Fraxxis had to hand it to them. Going into the dead zone had been a ballsy move, but one that had saved their skins, at least for a short while. But now they had proven themselves even more resourceful. No one exited that he knew of. At least, not until now.

"Weapons ready," he said with a curious grin. "But standby. Do not fire until my command. Let us see if we might capture these meddlesome pests to better make an example of them."

Fraxxis pulled upon his significant Allpower, preparing to stun the defenseless rebels as soon as they came into range. Their non-Allpower shields would be powerless to stop his spell.

"They're coming," the tech announced.

Fraxxis felt the excitement of battle surge in his veins as he watched the images grow on the monitors. Incredibly, they were flying out of the dead zone at top speed. More than that, they weren't even trying to run away. They were actually going to engage the far superior force. Oh, yes, this would be most satisfying.

He summoned the stun spell but waited. He wanted them closer to ensure the full effect. Finally, he was satisfied at the range and let loose.

The spell blasted out toward the rebels, a massive surge of stunning Allpower. Abruptly, it ceased its progress and sprayed outward, countered and dispersed by an even larger wave of strange power. A magic that was somehow not affected by the dead zone.

"Wha-what was that?" he gasped just as Ara and Charlie came into view. The realization hit him like a slap at the end of a very bad date. "Switch to Allpower shielding, quickly!" he shouted over his comms. "Everyone, they are casting!"

The Zomoki and her rider had taken point, casting the most powerful shielding spells they could while the others fell in behind them. On this occasion being a small group had been to their advantage. There was no way they could have effectively protected a larger group of vessels.

"Allpower is active," Nakk announced a moment later as the other ships cleared back into normal space. "Get clear!"

Ara and the ships all fanned out in a flash, looping backward before returning to their original flight path. Only this time they were behind something else. They cast as one, Allpower and magic alike driving a massive pulse forward.

The Urvalin fleet had already shifted to an Allpower footing, ready for the change in tactics. They could stop the magic and Allpower attack with ease. But something was wrong. Something was *very* wrong.

"What *is* that?" Fraxxis wondered, squinting at the readout a moment before the realization hit him. "Tech shields up!" he shrieked as the first wave of space junk from wrecked ships along with bits of asteroids and debris slammed into his fleet.

The smaller ships were tossed violently from the impacts, their Allpower shields blocking the magic with relative ease, but not the completely inert junk it was pushing. Like a tidal wave running through a city, it wasn't just the water that was a threat, it was the wreckage mixed in.

The command ship took the impacts without too much damage, but it was enough to force them to shift their focus to compensate for the unconventional attack. Others in their group were not so lucky, breaking apart or simply voiding their atmospheres before the crew could react, their hulls punctured by utterly Allpower-free improvised projectiles.

The greatly outnumbered rebels seized the opportunity and broke for the gap that had formed, warping and jumping away in a flash before the enemy could react, leaving Fraxxis and his fleet reeling.

They exited the warp a good distance away, immediately prepping the next one. There was no way the Urvalin would give up, and once they recovered, Charlie knew they'd be back on their tails. But it would take them time to recover from the damage inflicted. In the meantime, congratulations were in order.

"Nakk, you're a genius!" he transmitted. "That was one hell of a plan."

"Indeed," Bawb agreed. "A very clever use of non-conventional means to engage a superior adversary. Well done."

"Thanks," Nakk replied. "I've always enjoyed a good surprise. But I have to admit, I've been in the rebellion business so long I worry what I would do if we actually win."

"Have you ever considered piracy?" Charlie asked. "You'd make a wonderful pirate, Nakk."

"Hmm," the rebel commander said, musing the idea. "First, let's win. *Then* we can discuss these more colorful options."

CHAPTER SIXTY-FIVE

Earth had undergone a shift in the tide of invasion. One that had put the Urvalin on their heels more than they would want to admit. Especially outside the atmosphere where their main forces lurked.

Space battles were one thing the newly indoctrinated dragon riders were quite familiar with. It was a rather unusual skill set for a bunch of teenagers to possess, but these were no run-of-the-mill youths.

Arlo and Ripley had grown up training in not only combat and tactics, but also survival and evasion. Their parents were not about to let their kids miss out on those vital skills.

Kara and Vee, on the other hand, came from relatively normal lives but had been given a crash course in the ways of war when the Visla Dominus threat reared its head. It was new to them then, but in ridiculously short time, they had taken to it like ducks to water, proving their skills in combat of the deadliest kind.

And now they were taking those lessons on the road, along with Rika and her flying mech, with whom they'd met up along the way. Though while they were currently operating in the planet's atmospheric bubble, where they were going they didn't need roads.

"Are you sure this is where he is?" Arlo asked over their new suit comms.

"Again, *yes*, this is where he is," Kara said. "The Ghalian were very specific."

"I know, it's just, this seems kinda, well, *odd* for a grandmaster space assassin, is all."

Ripley and Vee kept their mouths shut, and Rika took the hint. Arlo and Kara had much more than Master Leif's current location going on in that discussion, and neither was foolish enough to go wading into it. Also, Arlo did have a point. That is, if Vee hadn't heard Master Pimbrak relay the location with her own ears.

They were flying to an underground fight club's medical facilities, of all places. They knew that these sorts of establishments had been popular right after the Great War as the humans and Chithiid blew off steam and learned to truly trust one another. But in the many years since then they had pretty much all disappeared. At least, they were no longer easy to find.

"Down there," Rika said as they flew over the Scottish countryside. "This has to be it."

The directions had led them to Ayrshire, just outside of Glasgow. The big city was still a ghost town, as was most of the world since almost all of humanity was wiped out, but the nearby area had seen a boom in settlements in recent years. Humans and Chithiid alike had found the region beautiful, quiet, and far from the worries of the hubs of society.

Of course, those who were drawn to that sort of place also tended to be a bit more self-sufficient than most. And these were indeed that. A fight club seemed perfectly fitting, given the region's history.

"I smell something that is not human and not Chithiid," Nixxus said.

Gazz took a deep whiff. "Similar to Pimbrak, but only just. I believe we have found our Ghalian."

The four dragons and the mech set down beside what was formerly an artists' commune. The riders dismounted but kept their armored space suits on. One never could tell when a simple greeting could turn into a brawl, especially in places like this.

"There," Vee said, pointing. "The marking."

A doorway, unremarkable in every way, had the smallest of symbols carved into it. A symbol Kara and Vee had been told to look for.

"Yeah, that's the one," Kara said, walking to it.

"Uh, should we knock? I mean, you don't want to go startling assassins," Arlo noted.

"He's a Ghalian master. He undoubtedly already knows we're here," Rika said, pushing the door open. "You all going to stand there gawking? Come on, we've got stuff to do."

The dragon riders looked at one another, shrugged, and followed her inside.

Master Leif, it seemed, wasn't the only one with a secret in this place. The unimpressive building wasn't just some quiet little run-down commune at all.

"Holy crap, look at all this stuff!" Arlo gasped.

His cousin elbowed him. "Don't geek out, Arlo."

"But, Rip, look at it!"

"I can see, but we're supposed to be here on an important mission. Act the part."

Arlo reeled in the outward display, but inside he was still a kid in a candy shop. That is, if the candy shop was a med lab and weapons facility the likes of which few had ever seen.

A hunched man hobbled over to them from the back office, his knotted staff supporting him as he moved.

"Anyone else here?" Rika asked.

"We are quite alone," the cripple replied.

"Good. Then you can drop the gimp routine. Pimbrak sent us."

"Who? I'm afraid I don't know any Pimbrak."

Kara stepped forward. "Master Leif, I'm Karasalia Palmarian. We have been sent to bring you a message about the Urvalin and what they're really doing." She reached into the tall duffel slung over her shoulder. "And to give you this."

She had just begun to pull the Bakana rod out when the man waved his hand, his staff flashing a moment with power as the doors and windows locked and a powerful force spell enclosed the room. It wasn't a totally impervious fortress, but it would take a bit of doing if anyone wanted to get in.

"So, you *are* Master Leif," Kara said.

"Apologies," he said, shedding his disguise and standing tall and strong. "One cannot be too careful."

"Understood. This is for you. Master Pimbrak wanted you to be the possessor of it in this galaxy," she said, handing him the rod.

He held it but a moment before putting it down. The danger of the rods linking power was a very real one, and it was not to be wielded lightly.

"Why?"

"The Urvalin."

"Yes, I am unfortunately quite familiar with them."

"Then you should know they've been trying to take over not just this galaxy, and not just my own, but they also control a third galaxy, linked by at least one portal we know of," the teen said.

He seemed surprised by this. A Ghalian did not like to be surprised.

"How is it no one in my network here has heard of this?"

"Because we just flew back through the portal to my galaxy with the information one of your spies managed to acquire."

"And you brought the rod. Impressive."

"We're not done yet," Kara said. "Charlie and Ara have been trapped in that third galaxy, along with Bawb and Hunze."

Leif hid his emotions, but that was very disturbing news. "The Urvalin are attempting to separate the magic users, aren't they?"

Rika stepped forward. "You've got that right. They tried to get me too, but I was delayed, otherwise I'd have been pulled through as well."

"A good thing. I've heard about you and Orgalius disrupting the Urvalin," he said, his face growing more serious. "I have also heard that Malalia Maktan has been brought back to Earth. And you have allowed her to possess power."

He was a little scary when he said that, and for him to let that slip showed just how upset he was.

"We didn't have a choice," Rika said. "We needed a big gun to fight back. And she actually did it. She drove their top caster away."

"At what price? She is a menace."

"Not so much. We implanted a bomb in her neck. If she steps out of line, *boom*."

Leif pondered that a moment. He wasn't thrilled with it, but at least Malalia was not running around unleashed.

"Hey," Arlo said. "I was wondering. Why are you even here? I mean, Scotland?"

Leif flashed a little grin. "I am the medical tech for the fight club here. I patch up the combatants, and in the process, I gather quite a lot of interesting intelligence."

Rika smiled knowingly. "Of course. Only a certain type still frequents fight clubs, am I right? And they're the ones who run dirty ops on the side."

"Indeed. And several would appear to have betrayed their own planet, for which I have reported them to Cal."

"You have access to one of his hardlines?" Rika asked, surprised.

"Oh, child. Of course I do. It is not often I utilize it, but there is a location not too far from where we stand. But that is not my purpose here. At least, not my main one. I am in this galaxy to monitor Malalia Maktan and ensure she does not ever become a threat again. You seem to have just made that job a bit more difficult."

"I can't believe I'm saying this, but I think she's the least of our worries at the moment," Kara said. "We still have one more Bakana rod. And we're supposed to get it to Charlie somehow."

Rika cocked her head in thought a moment. "Don't worry, kid. I've got an idea," she said. "But we're gonna need a little backup."

CHAPTER SIXTY-SIX

"Are you joking?" Marban said, staring at Rika with a look of concern and resolve. "Tell me you're joking."

"It has to be done. You know that."

"That much we agree on, but not by you."

"Marban—"

"You haven't thought this through, Rika."

"I have, big guy, and believe me, if there was another way, I'd gladly take it. But the long and short is, we have to get this rod to Charlie. Period."

Marban knew she was right about that. From the moment she'd boarded his ship out near the moon where he was preparing for his next assault on the Urvalin he was certain someone would have to take what would very possibly be a one-way trip through a portal to a realm unknown.

Much as he cared for his dear friend, however, they didn't even know for certain that Charlie was still alive.

The dragon riders had landed in the *Coratta's* hangar bay and were standing quietly while Marban and Rika argued. Only, it wasn't really an argument as much as an uncomfortable discussion about the fate of not only their friend, but multiple galaxies as well.

Orgalius was lurking nearby, providing them a moment of respite to talk while he kept an eye out for any Urvalin trickery. They had been wreaking havoc on the enemy with their magic, of late. Marban was a fly in their ointment they just couldn't shake. He wasn't nearly as powerful as Rika in that regard, but his merry band of semi-reformed pirates were certainly making a good showing of it.

Orgalius had been engaged in another bit of subterfuge while they were at it. Namely, he was picking off the disguised microsats of the dampening array orbiting Dark Side base one by one. No destruction so massive that the Urvalin would take note, but a gradual thinning of their numbers. It would take time, and a lot of it at that, but he was confident he could eventually provide a narrow escape route for the ships trapped on the moon's surface.

In the meantime, it was skirmishes with the Urvalin, diving in and out of the dampening field with ease, pushing the enemy down into Joshua and his team's line of fire or up into Marban's. But now there was something even more pressing on the table, and Marban and Rika were not seeing eye to eye on it.

"Flying through the portal trap is out of the question. You'd be going in blind," the pirate said.

"We have to get the third Bakana rod to Charlie. That's more important than anything else."

Marban took a sip from his dented metal mug and looked quietly at Rika a long while then let out a deep sigh. "You do realize that if you go, you're giving the Urvalin exactly what they want, don't you? Getting you out of this galaxy was their original plan, and if you go through with this you'll be doing exactly what they have been so upset about failing to achieve."

Rika hesitated. "Well, yeah. But I'm the only one who has the ability to fly out there and avoid any dampening fields they may have on the other side."

"Or me. Or Orgalius," he replied. "You're not the only one with a magically powered ship, you know. And your magic is needed here, especially with Malalia back in action. We need you, and I mean you specifically, to keep her in check. With Charlie gone, I don't know if anyone else could handle it."

"But the rod has to go through."

"I know."

"So, do you have any better ideas?"

Marban took a bigger drink from his mug. It was something he didn't normally do in battle.

"*I* will carry it through. My ship runs on a drookonus normally, and any dampening field there won't affect me."

"But you could be stuck on the other side."

"As could you. And let's face it, Rika. I am more expendable than you are in this instance."

"You're *not* expendable."

Marban chuckled and wrapped his arms around her in a warm hug. "I know," he said softly. "But I have to do this, and you have to let me."

The dragon riders had stayed very quiet throughout the exchange, but this was as good a time as any to speak up.

"We'll go with you to the portal," Arlo said. "Me and Rip. We've got magic and weapons too, along with Drombus and Duzza's firepower. We can help clear the way and cover you when you cross over if needed."

Marban nodded his thanks.

"And we'll help Rika and Orgalius push back the Urvalin here, keeping them occupied," Kara volunteered.

Rika looked at them, then at Marban, and knew she was not going to change any of their minds. She rested her hand on Marban's cheek, her tattoos faintly glowing as she did.

"Be careful. And come back home."

"You know I will," he replied.

"We'll ride aboard the *Coratta* on the way, if you don't mind," Ripley said. "It'll save the dragons' energy.

Marban nodded. "Of course. I would be glad to have you with us for the journey."

Rika looked at Marban a long moment, locking his gaze, then turned and walked to board her mech.

"Come on, Kara," Vee said.

"In a sec," she replied, her eyes fixed on Arlo.

He saw the look and walked over to her, his heart in his throat. "Listen, I'm really sorry I've been so—"

She silenced him with a kiss, pulling him close a moment then stepping back.

"Just get back safely. We'll talk then."

With that she turned and joined Vee.

"Well, how's that for a twist?" Ripley said, elbowing her cousin. "Man, you live a charmed life, you know that? Screw up royally and she *still* digs you."

Marban rested his hand on the boy's shoulder. "You will work things out," he said. "Trust Uncle Marban, I have seen a lot of doomed relationships over the years, and this does not strike me as one of them. Now, come, enough delays. We have the portal coordinates. It is time to find Charlie."

Marban departed, heading to the bridge. Rika and the girls had just jumped away, and at any moment the *Coratta* would jump to the coordinates of the portal trap. Now that they had properly mapped out where it was located, a much more direct route had been established. One that would not fly into a sun or other obstacle. No matter how vast space was, there was still the very real risk of jumping into a planet if you weren't careful.

Arlo walked to Drombus and opened the storage compartment on his harness.

"What are you doing?" the dragon asked.

"Just checking out this Bakana rod," he replied. "I'm not a magic user, so it's not gonna do anything to me if I handle it."

He swung it in a slow arc, feeling the weight of the rod. It wasn't really designed to be a melee weapon, though. It was merely the shape the power linking device had been given.

"Hey, Rip. Check out the—"

The ship rocked and shook as a violent barrage of Allpower slammed into its shields.

"Urvalin have warped in!" Marban bellowed over internal comms. "Everyone, battle stations!"

Arlo didn't hesitate, quickly scrambling up into his harness and locking in. Ripley did the same, and in moments they were aloft, ready to fight. But when they launched, they realized there were too many Urvalin for them to stand a chance. And the path for Marban's ship to warp away was blocked. The *Coratta* was simply too big to squeeze past the Urvalin.

"We need to get Rika back here," Ripley transmitted as Duzza spun away from a wave of Allpower, spraying magical flames at the attackers as she did.

Arlo did the math. There was no time. "Marban, get out of here! There are too many."

"But the portal—" he replied. "And you are in danger."

"You won't make it. Go, hurry! We'll be fine. We're smaller and have a clear shot out of here."

Marban read the writing on the wall and made the tough call. A moment later his ship jumped away, heading in the opposite direction.

"You've still got the Bakana rod in your hand," Ripley said.

"Shit." Arlo stared at the device as long as he dared then made a choice. "Go meet up with the others. I'm gonna get this to Charlie," he said, tucking the rod snugly between the harness and Drombus's scaly back, making sure he wouldn't drop it.

"Oh, like hell you are."

"Rip, you can't stop me."

"I'm not trying to, dumb ass. I'm coming with."

There was no time to argue. The Urvalin had turned their full attention on the two dragons. It was now or never.

"Drombus, Duzza, get us to the portal!" Arlo called out.

The dragons had the coordinates and didn't hesitate, jumping seconds later, leaving the Urvalin attacking empty space. It was a long jump, but both were fully charged from their trip through the sun, and both had full konuses mounted to their harnesses. Even so, when they arrived at the portal, they couldn't help but feel a little winded.

"I can sense it, but where—" Drombus said, then was gone in a flash. Duzza and Ripley followed right behind, sucked through the hidden portal in an instant.

The two dragons emerged on the far side in a strange place devoid of magic. They felt weak, barely able to sustain themselves. Amazingly, Drombus had more power than Duzza, though it felt different somehow. Sensing Duzza's weakness, he pulled upon this odd magic to help her. If it failed, they would freeze and suffocate in the darkness of space.

Arlo looked at the horror surrounding them.

"Holy shit! Black holes! We have to get out of here! There's a planet!"

Somehow, the dragons sensed the danger lurking that direction and resisted the urge to make an emergency landing on the nearby world.

"I smell something," Drombus said. "A scent. A *Zomoki* was here."

"Ara?" Ripley asked.

"It must be. I am following it."

Without a moment to lose, the two dragons pushed ahead as fast as they could, the magic flowing through Drombus somehow maintaining even in this void of any power. But he felt it weakening. If they didn't get clear soon they would perish.

The flight was fast and panicked, and their magic almost gave out, but the two dragons and their riders finally burst free of the deadly black holes and into regular space, where a new kind of magic flowed into them, restoring their power, but only somewhat.

They didn't have a moment to gather their thoughts, though. That would have been too easy.

"Urvalin ships!" Ripley called out as the display on Duzza's harness flashed a warning. "Jump us out of here!"

"I do not know if I have the strength," she replied.

"I will help, Cousin," Drombus said, flying close and wrapping his wings around her. "If you can, jump now!"

The two dragons flashed out of existence in a panicked run to anywhere but there, popping back into space a relatively short distance away. It was close to a solar system, though they didn't know if the worlds there would possess any power.

It didn't matter. They needed to land, and now. Finding Charlie would have to wait. For now, they needed to survive.

Back in the galaxy they had just left, Rika, Kara, Vee, and Marban had finally managed to reconnect. As soon as he relayed what had happened, they all jumped to the portal in a more circuitous route to avoid the Urvalin, making sure to arrive a healthy distance away from the portal itself.

Rika sensed the dragons' magic immediately.

"They went through," she said with a gasp.

"They did?" Kara said, a tremor in her voice. "They crossed over?"

"I will go after them," Marban announced. "I may yet catch up to them."

"No," Rika insisted. "Wait. There's something else."

Marban waited, knowing better than to ignore Rika's senses. "There is magic here. *Powerful* magic, but not from a dragon.

How weird. I think I've felt it—" Her eyes widened as she recognized it. "Oh no. We have to get to Earth!"

"But—"

"No time. Come on!"

She jumped at once, leaving Marban and the girls little choice but to follow.

They flew hard, arriving in Scotland in record time. Rika leapt from her mech and rushed into Master Leif's facility, the others close behind. The master assassin was on the ground, the Bakana rod in his hand.

"Is he dead?" Vee quietly asked.

Rika knelt down and checked for a pulse. There wasn't one.

"He's gone," she said, kicking the rod from his hand. There were faint scorch marks from where the last of his power had been sucked through the rod.

"What happened?" Marban asked.

Rika sat down hard on the nearest chair. "What happened? I'll tell you what happened. It looks like whatever's on the other side of that portal is deadly, and somehow Arlo and Ripley used their Bakana rod to survive, not realizing Leif was connected."

"But they aren't magical beings," Kara said. "It wouldn't work that way."

"No, but the dragons are," Vee realized. "And they're very powerful. Powerful enough that they might overwhelm whoever was holding the other rod, draining them dry."

Rika looked at the dead man and had a horrible realization. She was now the strongest caster in this galaxy. At least, the strongest one they could fully trust. Reformed as she was, there was no way anyone would put a Bakana rod in Malalia's hands.

And that left just one option. Rika was now the wielder of the power-sharing device. The question was, had the kids survived the journey, and if so, would they be able to find Charlie in that distant galaxy?

CHAPTER SIXTY-SEVEN

"Jesus, Tamara, did you knock over an entire storage depot?" Charlie marveled as he looked at the enormous stockpile of guns and Bandas taken from the Urvalin. "How did you get all of this?"

Tamara and Shelley shared an amused little grin. "Well, Chuckles, while you were out on your whole Ark-of-the-Covenant-quest thing, Shelley and me, we were putting the hurt on the Urvalin."

"Yeah," Shelley agreed. "We hit 'em where it hurt."

Nakk and Skohla surveyed the stolen goods the women and their little band of raiders had brought to the rendezvous site with appreciation. The women had been busy, it seemed. And more than that, they had claimed some ship-sized armaments as well as smaller weapons.

"Nicely done," Nakk said. "*Very* nicely done."

It had been a pleasant surprise, finding their friends had not only met up with the rest of the rebel fleet but had been busy in the interim. But then Tamara wasn't exactly one to sit around and wait for things to happen. Not by a long shot.

"So, can you get these working?" she asked, tossing one of the locked pulse rifles to Charlie.

"I can get them working all right, but it'll take time. I think we should focus on getting the big guns working and then mounting them on our ships. We're ready to cross back over."

"Hang on. You mean you actually found it?" Tamara asked.

"Yep. Locked up safe and sound in a damn near impenetrable box, but we'll get it open, don't you worry. And when we do? *Blammo*, the Urvalin lose and we force the portal to do our bidding."

"Even in the middle of those black holes?"

"If the Vortaxis is just half as powerful as they say it is, that shouldn't be a problem."

"We will escort you to the edge of the black hole dead zone," Nakk said.

"I really wish you could come with us, man, but I understand. You've gotta keep up the good fight in your own galaxy."

"That we do, and with all of us freed at once thanks to you and your friends, we actually have a sizable fighting force at our disposal. Not to mention all of the ships and equipment we have been capturing bolstering our forces."

Bawb nodded his approval. "I would posit that you will give the Urvalin quite a run for their money, Nakk."

"And we'll be back," Charlie added. "Once my baby is born, you can bet your ass we'll be coming to kick ass and take names. With the Vortaxis, I'd think we should be able to travel back and forth without a problem. And lemme tell you, we've got some seriously kickass firepower on our side." He turned to Bawb. "Dude, just imagine what Joshua has up his sleeve. Those poor bastards won't know what hit them."

Dukaan walked over to join the others, his arms loaded with fresh food from the makeshift mess tent the rebels had set up.

Being a Chithiid, he had a fondness for plant-based food, and after some experimenting with the planet's local ingredients, he and his new friends had whipped up a healthy assortment of dishes.

While they were served to the hungry crews waiting for action, he had the foresight to pack some treats for his crewmates and himself. A going-away meal of sorts.

"I will stow these in the galley," he said. "Kip and I are ready to depart when you are."

"Thanks, Dukaan. We'll be there in a minute," Charlie replied. "Ara, you good to go?"

"Indeed," she said, spreading her wings wide. "I have absorbed as much power as I can in a reasonable time. It should be more than sufficient for the journey."

"Excellent. Then I guess this is it." He headed off to board the ship and settle in for their flight home.

Charlie, Ara, Bawb, and Hunze said their in-person farewells, confident they would be back soon enough, then boarded their rides, the Ghalian and his partner aboard Kip, and Charlie atop the Zomoki's back.

The transit to the portal trap world was quick enough, though it did require a few detours along the way to ensure the Urvalin didn't backtrack their flight to the bulk of the fleet.

Of course, they had a backup location selected, as well as a backup to the backup, but that was never a plan they wanted to put into action if they could avoid it.

"One more jump," Charlie said. "Then we're at the edge of the black hole cluster. You guys ready?"

"Good to go," Kip said.

"We are prepared," Bawb chimed in.

"Ready," Nakk added.

Charlie took a deep breath. This was it. "Okay, y'all. Let's go home."

They all jumped and warped, the Zomoki and the handful of

ships traveling as one, emerging as planned at their desired coordinates.

"Urvalin!" Nakk shouted over comms, peeling wide and firing off his newly stolen cannons. The other rebel ships accompanying them did the same, engaging the enemy with their own Urvalin weapons.

Charlie and Ara avoided the attacks, allowing the harnesses' tech shielding to do the bulk of the work. They didn't have the magic to spare to get in a full-on battle. Kip knew that, of course, and positioned himself between them and the largest of the enemy ships.

The attacks were coming fast and steady, the triumvirates of Urvalin casters keeping the pressure on non-stop. But the massive command ship and its top-tier caster was not there, and that meant they still had a chance.

"Go on!" Nakk transmitted. "We have their guns now. We will hold them back."

His ship let off another burst of cannonfire, but suddenly the weapons fell silent. In fact, all of the stolen cannons went dark.

"Oh, shit," Charlie gasped.

"I thought you made them work," Hunze said.

"I did. But there must be something I missed. It's an alien system, I've never—"

A magical blast shook the ship and the Zomoki it was shielding.

"We gotta get out of here," Kip said. "There's no time to argue."

"I agree," Bawb said, reaching for his hip.

Hunze's eyes widened. "Are you going to—"

"We have no choice," he replied, drawing his wand free from its case.

Here, outside of the magic-sucking trap, it still held all of its magical potential, and while in other situations he had to use it with the greatest of caution, against this foe, he could let loose.

"Nakk, pull your people back," Bawb transmitted.

The commander knew better than to question him and ordered the immediate retreat of his forces, leaving the Ghalian a clear shot at the much larger Urvalin fleet.

"When I cast, *move*," Bawb said.

Dukaan didn't need to be told twice. "The course is plotted. Ready when you are."

Bawb took a deep breath, connecting viscerally with the dangerous wand, holding its power in check as best he could, steering it away from his friends and directing it only toward the enemy. Satisfied he had walled in the destruction as much as possible, he let loose with a shockwave spell, the magic flowing harmlessly out of Kip's hull but building into a tidal wave of power as it flew toward the Urvalin.

They sensed something coming, though this form of Allpower was unfamiliar to them. All of their shields switched to Allpower, and at maximum potential. Despite the defenses, the spell slammed into them, tossing the ships about like toy boats in the open sea.

"Go now!" Bawb shouted.

Kip was already in motion, Ara close behind. The recovering Urvalin had to make a choice, and given the immediate chase they engaged in, following them down the narrow path of safe space toward the portal, it seemed that Charlie and his friends were far more important a target than the rebel ships they'd left behind.

It was a huge power suck, and Ara felt her magic being pulled hard by the black holes. She wouldn't last long in this environment, but the Urvalin were also draining their magic at an alarming rate. It was essentially a game of chicken, the two sides waiting to see whose power would give out first.

Of course, tech still worked here. So long as they didn't stumble into the planet's dampening array, both sides were still fully able to maneuver with non-magical means. Unfortunately, that didn't much help Ara and Charlie. Fortunately, they had a secret weapon.

"We're almost at the portal," Kip transmitted. "If you're gonna do something, this is the time."

Charlie pulled the box from the storage bin on Ara's harness and held it tight. *"You ready to show these assholes they messed with the wrong people?"*

"Indeed, I am," Ara replied.

"Be ready," Charlie told his friends. "Once we get this thing open, we're gonna pop off a spell at the Urvalin then cross the portal."

"We're right behind you," Dukaan said.

The mighty Zomoki and her bonded human joined their magic, directing it at the Allpower latch holding the container closed. It was incredibly powerful, designed to withstand a brute force attack. But it hadn't encountered the flavor of magic these two wielded, and after a moment, the latch began to give.

"Almost there," Charlie grunted, sweating inside his space suit from the strain.

The latch abruptly gave and the box sprang open.

There, resting in resplendent glory, lay the Vortaxis. It was simple in design, almost looking like a dumbbell with a handle in the middle and two large balls on the ends, but it was no mere piece of exercise equipment. The sheer volume of Allpower contained within it was almost blinding in its intensity.

Charlie reached into the container, his hand wrapping around the handle of the Vortaxis, its mass warm even in the void of space.

"Showtime!"

He pulled the weapon free and felt his and Ara's power latch onto the ancient relic. Then he felt something else.

"No!" he shouted, but it was too late.

The Vortaxis vibrated, then broke apart into dust, the magic scattering into space. The Vortaxis was gone.

He realized at once what had happened. He'd felt that before. The Vortaxis must have been formed out of the Allpower charged particles of dust and debris so many centuries ago, just like the planet they'd stepped upon. And just like that world, the magic they carried inside of themselves was anathema to it.

In a flash the last particles swirled off into space, gone forever, leaving Charlie and his friends very much on their own.

CHAPTER SIXTY-EIGHT

"Make for the gap!" Charlie shouted.

Of course, with the tech of their comms link working just fine, he really didn't *need* to shout, but the sheer panic that ensued after the Vortaxis dissolved into oblivion was enough to make even the most stoic of warriors falter.

Or, in this case, *run*.

"*Charlie, I am weakening,*" Ara said, her voice only faint in his head.

Their link was becoming tenuous, and he felt his own power faltering as well.

"*Hang on, Ara. We'll get out of this.*"

Charlie shifted his focus to the weapons on her harness. They were still functional, and with manual targeting he could use them to create at least a little room for them to operate. Unfortunately, with the black holes looming so close, the Urvalin were also crammed into the narrow pathway of passable space with them.

"Guys, Ara's fading. We need to get her out of here, and I mean now!"

Bawb cautiously tested his wand while Hunze tried to pull magic from her hair. No go.

"Charlie, we are too far in to utilize magic," he said.

Kip's railguns suddenly went hot, firing off a blistering stream of sabots, spraying across all of the enemy ships. Charlie hadn't expected the AI ship to panic, but it seemed that was exactly what was happening.

"Kip, what are you doing? Stand down!"

"Nope," the AI replied. Charlie noted he sounded as calm as could be, given the circumstances.

"What do you mean, nope?"

"I mean, I have an idea." Charlie marveled as his own weapons systems flashed to life as the AI reached out and hacked into them.

"Kip? What the hell?"

"I'm tying your cannons into my systems for synchronized firing. Hold tight and be ready to move."

Ara's harness weapons fired all at once, as did Kip's array of cannons, a flurry of pulse cannon blasts raining down on the Urvalin just as they began to fire their counterattack. The synchronized blasts got there first and stopped them cold in their tracks, the smaller ship's bombardment intercepting them before they even had a chance to get clear of the much larger fleet.

The disruption in the space around the larger ships pushed them, transferring force as normally happens in a battle, only this time, unlike a regular space battle, there wasn't much wiggle room to compensate and resume the attack.

Four of the Urvalin ships abruptly shifted all of their efforts to drive systems, desperately fighting the pull of the black holes' gravity fields they'd been unexpectedly pushed into.

"Holy shit. Kip, you're a genius!"

"Super-smart AI," he replied. "It's kind of a given."

Another massive volley launched from the little ship and the Zomoki's harness in unison. The Urvalin, realizing their proximity, along with the power of their counterattacks, were playing right into the laughably smaller enemy's hands and frantically moved aside, opting to risk ramming into their own ships rather than be pushed past the narrow safe boundary into the black holes' grasp.

"Ara, grab on!" Kip transmitted, hoping she had enough energy left to cling to his hull.

The Zomoki did as he said, landing roughly atop the ship and using what little strength she had left to cling to the craft. Kip adjusted his shielding to surround her as best he could and prevent her from being bucked off, then raced ahead, weaving through the distressed enemy ships as they pushed hard for the safety of open space.

The Urvalin were at a disadvantage, unable to simply turn around like their smaller prey had done. Most of their ships would need to exit the narrow pathway to the small, clear area near the trap planet, using the wider space to properly reverse their course.

A few of the lesser craft were able to spin, albeit carefully, and set off in pursuit as best they could.

Kip rocketed free of the Allpower-draining trap and into open space. Allpower flooded across them, restoring at least some of Ara's power. Bawb and Hunze were more restored, having been unable to even touch their power to drain it while in the void and thus retaining most of their power.

"There are more out here," Dukaan warned. "And a group on our tail."

Nakk had jumped away to rejoin the rebel fleet once his friends had made their run for the portal. It was a simple calculus, either they would make it through the portal, or they would die trying. Either way, he hadn't anticipated their return to open space.

Unfortunately, that meant Charlie and his friends were on their own.

The smaller Urvalin support craft that hadn't pursued them were still fighting at a significant advantage even without the larger ships at their disposal. The triumvirates of lesser casters were having no problem assailing their target with a variety of attacks.

Bawb and Hunze cast hard, blasting the Allpower aside. They had strength on their side, but the question was, for how long?

"We need to make a hole," Bawb called out.

Charlie couldn't agree more. "Use your wand!"

"They are too spread out, but I will try."

Bawb drew and cast, but as expected, only the ships directly in the line of fire took the brunt. The rest, however, continued to swarm.

"We must join power," Ara said.

"We're already linked."

"No, Charlie. All *three* of us. The Geist is bonded to us as well. If we pool our magic, the sum will be far greater than the individual parts."

"Like the Urvalin," he realized.

"More or less. Now, focus. We must link our magic."

"You heard that, right, Bob?"

"Less talking and more focusing, Charlie," the assassin replied.

"Okay, then," he said, shifting his mindset and channeling his power to meld with the others.

It was a funny thing, the way Bawb had come to be linked with Charlie and Ara. A blood bond that would have killed him had he not taken it from Charlie rather than their Zomoki friend. And now, countless billions of light years from home, they were going to put that union to the ultimate test.

A ball of magical potential began to form around them,

deflecting the lesser attacks of the Urvalin as Kip and Dukaan did their best to keep them at bay.

"That's it," Ara said. "Keep channeling."

The energy continued to grow, protecting them from the Allpower attempts with growing ease.

"It's actually working," Charlie marveled. "Now we just need to find a clear—"

A massive blast of Allpower tossed them aside. Ara barely maintained her grasp on Kip's hull. The magical shielding faltered.

Dukaan looked at the display with horror. "The larger ships, they're already coming out!"

The bulk of the fleet had apparently been more efficient than they'd assumed, and once the chaos of battle was moved out of their proximity, they'd managed to spin their ships and reverse course post-haste.

Another blast of magic, then another shook them.

"There are too many," Dukaan cried out. "We can't hold off against—"

Suddenly, Charlie, Ara, and Bawb felt an impossible surge of pure, powerful magic flow through them. It was so much more than what they should have been capable of, but it coursed through each of them, growing with every second. It took a moment, but Charlie and Ara realized what that power was. Bawb, however, was not surprised.

"Hunze? How?" Charlie marveled as the Ootaki's massive magical potency compounded their own powers.

"Bawb and I are bonded," she replied, a strange calm in her voice despite the heat of battle. "My power is his, just as his is mine."

"And that's how you linked with us," he realized.

"Precisely."

He could almost hear the serene smile in her voice. And to be honest, he was feeling pretty good himself. The Urvalin used a triumvirate to increase their casting power, but this group? They weren't merely three casters. They were four, interlinked in a way the likes of which this galaxy had never seen.

Had Commander Fraxxis been present, it was still possible his connection with Prin and Torgus could have overcome this foe, but he was not there, and his ships did not stand a chance.

Magic blasted out from the foursome, shattering the defensive spells of the Urvalin and breaking their fleet apart. Even the large craft were crippled by the sheer magnitude, though they did maintain enough structural integrity to turn and run. Or, more accurately, stagger away.

Charlie and his friends let them. The battle had taken quite a toll on them. Fortunately, the fleeing survivors of the Urvalin fleet didn't know just how weak they now were after the expenditure.

A long time they floated in the void, recovering as best they could from the ordeal. Ara finally let go of Kip's hull and drifted past his shielding back into open space, free of any outside protection. It was then, clear of the shell protecting her, that she smelled something. Something familiar. She was so very tired and couldn't quite place it, but with a little time, and a little rest, she was confident it would come to her.

In the meantime they would limp back to rejoin Nakk and the other rebels, having miraculously lived to fight another day. Exhausted and still stranded in a distant galaxy, but victorious.

EPILOGUE

"You did *what*?" Nakk asked again.

"I told you, the four of us joined power," Charlie said yet again.

Apparently, it was even more impossible than he'd already believed it to be, and Nakk, as well as everyone in the rebel fleet who heard, was astonished. Charlie, Ara, Bawb, and Hunze were celebrities of the outlaw world, it seemed.

"You have dealt the Urvalin a major blow," Skohla said, barely hiding the giddy awe in her voice. "Do you realize just how important this is?"

"We won, I get it."

"No, Charlie, this is more than winning. Word of what you four did will begin leaking out. There is no way the Urvalin can stop everyone from talking. And when the rest of the galaxy hears what you did, the Urvalin will lose some of their hold over us all."

"We only did what was needed to survive," Hunze said.

"And in so doing you just bolstered our cause while making the Urvalin look over their shoulder at every future turn," Nakk said with a jovial grin. "This is *marvelous*."

"My child is about to be born and I'm in the wrong galaxy," Charlie said.

"I know, and for that I am sincerely sorry. But we will find a way to get you back, of that I am now confident. If you can utilize your power together like you describe, there is no telling just what you four may be capable of."

Skohla was pacing excitedly. "We should head back as soon as possible. Together, they might be able to force the portal to do their bidding even without the Vortaxis."

Charlie's posture sagged slightly. "Yeah, sorry about destroying one of your holiest ancient relics. My bad."

"It was a myth until you proved it otherwise," Nakk replied. "And just knowing it was real is a marvelous revelation I never thought I would experience in my lifetime. But Skohla is right. The time is now if you are to attempt to cross back over. Before they reinforce the portal's hiding place with an even more substantial armada."

Charlie liked the sound of that, but he knew they couldn't. Much as he wanted to get home, there was now something even more pressing here.

"We can't," he said. "Believe me, I want to, but we can't."

Nakk was taken aback. "I-I don't understand."

Charlie glanced up at his Zomoki friend. "Ara?"

"What Charlie is getting at, though rather indirectly, I am afraid, is that we *cannot* leave. Not yet, at least."

The rebel commander looked at her with confusion. They had just risked it all to cross back, and now they might very well have the ability even without the Vortaxis, though admittedly no one knew for sure. But even so, to dismiss even attempting it so quickly? It made no sense.

"But your home."

"Will be there tomorrow," she replied. "But when we were at the portal I smelled something familiar. In my exhaustion it took a while to recognize what it was, I am embarrassed to admit. But once my strength returned, it was there, as clear as day."

"What are you talking about?" Nakk asked. "What did you sense?"

"Someone crossed over from Charlie's realm recently," she said. "Someone*s* to be precise. A very particular flavor of magic belonging to dragons of Charlie's galaxy, as well as two humans whose scents I know well. Arlo and Ripley are here now, though how and why they crossed is quite the mystery."

"So you see," Charlie said, "much as we want to give crossing the portal a try, we can't leave. Not yet. Because now we've got a new task on our plate."

"Oh?" Nakk said. "And what is that?"

"Simple. We're going to replenish Ara's power. And then? Then we go and find Arlo and Rip."

PREVIEW: END GAME CHARLIE

THE DRAGON MAGE 12

Charlie ducked aside, a meaty fist swinging through the air where his head had just been. He replied with a flurry of elbows, driving them into the thick-skulled attacker's jaw until he crumpled to the ground in a heap.

He flashed a look at the assassin at his side, likewise introducing an angry man to his new friend, Mister Ground.

"I'm sorry, I must have heard you wrong, Bob," Charlie blurted as he stepped over the unconscious attacker now lying at his feet. "You're kidding, right?" he asked, his jaw all but hanging open in shock.

"You did not hear me wrong," Bawb replied, slowly walking backward around the downed man, his hands still empty but ready to spring into action at a moment's notice. "I am positive the two of them and their dragon friends were most certainly here. And they have clearly made quite a mess of things."

Here was a dangerous planet in a deadly system. A system where Allpower could not function and technology was king. The forbidden planet upon which they had found the Vortaxis.

Of course, the massively powerful artifact had been inadvertently destroyed by Charlie and Ara as they attempted to fight off the Urvalin and force their way back across the trap portal that had dragged them into this galaxy. A fluke of their incompatible flavor of magic, apparently, and one that obliterated the oldest, most powerful relic this galaxy had ever known.

Fortunately, the more than slightly fanatical religious order protecting it hadn't even realized that they'd stolen the actual Vortaxis right out from under their noses. In fact, when Charlie and his friends had last departed this world, they'd taken their leave confident that a new alliance had been formed. One built on a mutual hatred of the Urvalin.

Now, however, it seemed Arlo and Ripley had gone and blundered into things in epic fashion and had stirred up one hell of a hornets' nest in the process.

Space beasts similar to dragons had been extinct here for millennia, so when the two dragons had landed on the planet, they'd made quite a stir in the system where magic should not have been able to function and their kind did not exist.

For the local inhabitants, going from confidently superior in firepower on their home turf to a state of doubt, unsure what destruction these magical beasts might be able to bring upon them, had put the entire world on edge.

It wasn't a lost cause at that point, but, unfortunately, Arlo and Ripley lacked the vital skill of tact and nuance that might have defused that situation. Diplomats, they were not. They were bulls, or more accurately, dragon riders, in a china shop.

Charlie batted aside a stun grenade of a rather novel design, knocking it from the air with a vicious slice from the long knife he wore on his hip before it could discharge. This was only getting worse, he realized. Any minute now it would turn into a free-for-all. He just couldn't believe how they'd wound up in this mess to begin with.

From what they had heard before being attacked, it seemed that upon entering this new galaxy, the dragons the teens were riding had not only managed to avoid the magic-sucking deathtrap of the black hole-ensconced portal, but they had gone on to do much along the lines of what Ara was doing now. Namely, backtracking the scent of a familiar friend.

And that scent had led them here, of all places.

It was a mess to be sure, but worse yet, in the middle of the locals' panic and confusion, the intruders had asked for Charlie and Bawb by name.

That was pretty much all that Bawb had managed to glean from the head priest he had gone to see upon their return to the planet before the angry locals took up arms, surrounding the newcomers. Some of the mob even foolishly engaged them. Fortunately, the priest had the wherewithal to restrain himself, at least for the time being. The common rabble? Not so much.

"These guys look *really* pissed, Bob," Charlie said, his fingers loosely resting on his pulse pistol's grip, a spell on the tip of his tongue, ready to fly if things escalated further.

"That is because they *are* pissed. And with good reason," Bawb said, quickly stepping aside and delivering a carefully placed incapacitating blow upon the man charging at him. He made sure he spoke clearly, remembering that these people possessed robust translation tech.

He, Charlie, Bob, and Ara could still communicate with one another through their silent bond, though the Zomoki was currently hiding out on a nearby moon. With the whole damn planet on full alert, Charlie and his friends were of the belief that these technologically advanced people might very well possess the means to even detect magic. And *that* could just make things much, much worse than a fistfight with an angry mob.

As it was, the head priest who had so recently been a welcoming host to them had given in to the will of the crowd and was now leading the substantial and well-armed group surrounding the visitors. Worse, not just a mere handful of guards. At least two dozen ships now hovered in the sky above them, armed to the teeth and ready to engage.

Whatever the kids and their dragon counterparts had done, it had made quite the impression, and it had not been a good one.

"What did they say to them, Bob? What the hell did they do? We're all friends, here. These guys know we don't mean them any harm. We're all on the same team fighting the Urvalin," Charlie said, hoping their translated discussion amongst themselves would perhaps sway the native from attacking.

"It sounded as if Arlo and Ripley flew to the surface in something of an overly ambitious rush, flaring magic and with weapons hot."

"Why the hell would they—" Charlie began to say when a stun blast hit his shielding. "Hey! Knock that shit out. We don't want to hurt anyone!"

Another shot flew, then another. Charlie clenched his jaw when a full-fledged volley threatened to drop his tech shields.

"Oh, the hell with this. Enough is enough!" he growled, flaring his magic into a protective bubble.

That certainly got the natives' attention, and not in a good way.

"Charlie, what have you done?" Bawb groaned just as three large warships dropped out of orbit, orange-hot from their scrambled descent, the sonic booms shaking the ground around them.

The priest at the head of the mob took his hand from the glowing symbol on his tech-thread-embedded sleeve, looking at the pair with distrust, scorn, and disapproval. Apparently, he had just called in the big guns, both figuratively and literally.

"So, you also wield *Allpower*?" he spat. "All this time, nothing but lies and subterfuge."

Charlie raised his hands "You don't understand. We're only trying to—"

A thundering crash the likes of which Charlie had never heard before rang out, then darkness surrounded him.

"Bob, what the hell?"

"I do not know," the assassin replied, quickly casting an illumination spell, the locals' distrust of magic be damned.

A slight rumble vibrated through their feet as their surroundings lit up. What he saw chilled his already frosty blood.

"What in the world..." Charlie trailed off, and with good reason.

Surrounding the two of them was a metal orb perhaps ten meters across at its widest. There was a seam at the top with bits of dirt and pavement still clinging to the edges. Not a sound penetrated from outside, nor any light. They had been sealed off.

Bawb increased the spell's brightness and studied the trap. He cast a force spell, attempting to open the orb, but rather than freedom, quite the opposite happened. The orb, it seemed, had contracted slightly, the ground at their feet buckling as it did.

"Interesting," he said, testing the orb's seal again with his magic, but this time using far less.

Again, their prison shrank around them.

"Bob?"

"Release your power, Charlie," he replied. "Do not attempt to cast."

"But we're strong casters. And you've got your wand."

"True. But these people have had a very long time to prepare to counter such powers, and it would appear we are now locked within a most ingenious of cages."

A memory of childhood flashed through Charlie's head. Finger cuffs he had played with in his youth. A simple toy, but effective. The more you pulled, the tighter they became. Resistance only worsened your situation, and that was exactly the predicament they were in now.

"What can we do, Bob? We need to get out of here."

Charlie's pale friend slid to the ground, sitting cross-legged and looking as relaxed as one could, given the situation.

"*Do*?" he replied with a somewhat amused grin. "We *do* nothing," he said as he began releasing the illumination spell, the slow rumble at their feet lessening as he did. "What we do now," he said as they settled into darkness, "is wait."

ALSO BY SCOTT BARON

Standalone Novels

Living the Good Death

The Clockwork Chimera Series

Daisy's Run

Pushing Daisy

Daisy's Gambit

Chasing Daisy

Daisy's War

The Dragon Mage Series

Bad Luck Charlie

Space Pirate Charlie

Dragon King Charlie

Magic Man Charlie

Star Fighter Charlie

Portal Thief Charlie

Rebel Mage Charlie

Warp Speed Charlie

Checkmate Charlie

Castaway Charlie

Wild Card Charlie

End Game Charlie

The Space Assassins Series

The Interstellar Slayer

The Vespus Blade

The Ghalian Code

Death From the Shadows

Hozark's Revenge

The Warp Riders Series

Deep Space Boogie

Belly of the Beast

Rise of the Forgotten

Pandora's Menagerie

Engines of Chaos

Seeds of Damocles

Odd and Unusual Short Stories:

The Best Laid Plans of Mice: An Anthology

Snow White's Walk of Shame

The Tin Foil Hat Club

Lawyers vs. Demons

The Queen of the Nutters

Lost & Found

ABOUT THE AUTHOR

A native Californian, Scott Baron was born in Hollywood, which he claims may be the reason for his rather off-kilter sense of humor.

Before taking up residence in Venice Beach, Scott first spent a few years abroad in Florence, Italy before returning home to Los Angeles and settling into the film and television industry, where he has worked as an on-set medic for many years.

Aside from mending boo-boos and owies, and penning books and screenplays, Scott is also involved in indie film and theater scene both in the U.S. and abroad.

Made in United States
North Haven, CT
28 December 2024

63626805R00264